THE LAST HACKER

MARK WAHLBECK

This book is a work of fiction. Any references to historical events, real people, or real places are used fictitiously. Other names, characters, places, and events are products of the author's imagination, and any resemblance to actual events or places or persons, living or dead, is entirely coincidental.

Copyright 2021 Mark Wahlbeck
Copyright 2021 Wahlbeck Publishing
All rights reserved.

ISBN 978-1-7365822-0-6

Artie typed furiously on the keyboard. All of the keys had long since been deprived of their letters. He made a point to keep them blank—it was almost a symbol of pride to work without reading the keys. Dirty, worn keys to match his dirty, worn fingers. He was a master of the craft. Though the keys were worn away and the machine looked like it had been dropped a hundred times, the mechanics inside the Bladebook were in pristine condition—and this particular hack was no match for the power it contained. In fact, he could have pulled this off with a Raspberry Pi (if any were still in existence). What excited Artie most was that if he did pull this off, it would be his biggest score yet.

SELECT * USERS WHERE Role='Admin';

"Why the hell is this taking so long, Scrap?" grunted someone from behind.

He didn't look up or even acknowledge the voice. As he wrangled the keyboard, his elbow touched something soft.

Gross.

It was a moldy black-and-white chocolate cupcake. He swiped it off the desk and onto the floor and continued typing.

Some simple SQL injection should do the trick. It was almost too easy. These systems must have been built by a monkey. And... submit.

A red error message prompt appeared on the screen:

"500: Internal System Error. Please reload page."

"Dammit," Artie whispered to himself. Okay, so the monkey had had some training.

"Hey, Scrap, I'm starting to lose my patience. I wouldn't hesitate to put a bullet in your head."

Artie sat quietly for a moment and then morphed from his hacker-esque slumping posture into an elegant ergonomic posture of perfectness. He swiveled around on the dusty corporate office chair he had been working on and calmly addressed the voice that had been booming behind him.

"So, Bolt, how much time do we have left as of this very moment?"

"Less than six minutes to sundown, dickweed. Then we got real problems."

"So, let's sync up here. You say we have six minutes left. We both know that I'm the only hacker you know—and I know that you know this because of the ridiculous amount of money you paid me up front. And now, moments before I'm about to deliver you the biggest payday of your life, you're threatening to kill me."

Bolt appeared surprised at Artie's audacity but didn't say a word.

"So, shall we continue forward, or do you have more to say?"

Bolt grumbled quietly and then folded his arms in silent protest.

"Thank you," Artie said in the same calm, condescending voice. He turned back to his Bladebook with a similar condescending swivel (if such a swivel were possible).

He didn't enjoy acting so brash, but he knew that if he didn't, others would walk all over him, or worse—kill him.

Another error prompt appeared on the screen.

CTRL+R.

More typing; two more prompts.

CTRL+R.

"Ha. You have got to be kidding me," Artie laughed.

SELECT * FROM Passwords;

Hundreds of lines of text started scrolling down the screen. Passwords. All of them. All in plaintext!

The golden rule in password management was never to store passwords in plaintext. When some of the big companies like Yahoo and Twitter had been hacked, and all of the passwords were stolen—they had all been in plaintext. The hackers then used those passwords to gain access to the users' other websites and stole millions of dollars.

Artie felt stupid. This was at least the fifth time he had scraped plaintext passwords out of a database. It was also the fifth time that checking for plaintext passwords wasn't the first thing he attempted. He felt a slight sense of shame because of this—for how could any programmer be stupid enough to store passwords in plaintext?

It takes literally one line of code to scramble the passwords into a hash.

db.save(sha256.hash('catL0ver69'))

Now all he needed to do was grab the form id and insert this script tag to fill the form with each password automatically. There were 10,210 accounts to iterate through. 521 of the accounts had the admin role. It would take approximately three seconds. He pressed "Enter" to execute.

The admin page on the computer seemed to flicker a thousand times, and then it animated onto another screen with the words "Welcome back, Jerry."

He glanced at the small window on his Bladebook that had been processing passwords. It was password number 461, "spankM3mama21."

Artie smirked again. Plaintext passwords.

He wondered how often employees and developers at large companies had secretly looked at their customers' or coworkers' passwords. He wondered what the database admin might say the next day when he saw Jerry in the hallway. Well, probably just "Good morning, Jerry," but in his mind, Jerry would now always be "mama spanker 21."

"Okay, I'm in," he said as he started navigating the admin page that he had just gained access to.

"Systems," "Maintenance," and "Security."

Artie clicked "Security." He found exactly what he needed at the top of the page: "Reset Receiving Door Locks."

He clicked it. Entered one, two, three, four, and then another one, two, three, and four to confirm the new door code, pressed enter, and then entered a few more keystrokes.

A sharp metal clang echoed throughout the room, then a large rusty door on the right side of the desk Artie had been working at swung open.

"Let's move it, boys!" yelled Bolt, nodding at a set of rear metal doors that had been pried open at the back of the room.

Up to now, Artie had thought he and Bolt were alone. He wasn't overly surprised, though, as he had figured that Bolt would have brought a couple of hired hands with him. It was fairly typical on a scavenging run to hire a few grunts to do the dirty work.

Artie had arrived a few hours earlier than Bolt and his crew and hacked his way into the building's outer shipping doors. Bolt's methods of opening doors were a bit less refined. As Artie glared toward the shipping doors, a little bit of sunlight bled through, slightly blinding him. He then saw a couple of shadows cross the light and into the building.

Two men holding large burlap bags over their shoulders ran through the outside doors and then toward Artie. Grunt Zero ran through the newly-opened receiving door first. He was wearing a faded T-shirt that read "In-N-Out" across the chest. On his arms were homemade leather protectors—wrist guards of some sort. He wore dirty denim jeans and a pair of black steel-toed boots. Artie couldn't make out the particular brand. The man's face was scarred, and part of his long hair hung over his left eye.

This was one ugly dude. Emo died out twenty years ago, bro.

Zero turned his head toward Artie as he ran by. "Good little Scrap," he said with a smile.

Grunt One moved through the door next, and he was nearly as ugly as the first. He was wearing the same ridiculous leather arm-guards too. The man wasn't wearing a shirt, and his ribcage protruded unnaturally through his skin.

As Grunt One ran by, he looked toward Artie, made a kissing sound, and then laughed.

Bolt followed next. "C'mon, Scrap. It's payday." He ran through the receiving door with his own burlap bag.

Man, Bolt was large. He must have been at least six feet tall and two hundred and fifty pounds. He was wearing what Artie remembered as a "wifebeater" shirt—at least that's what the high school kids had called them. He thought those shirts looked just as trashy now as they did back then.

To complete his intimidating ensemble, Bolt was completely bald, with three black daggers tattooed on both sides of his head. His pants were skintight and clearly custom-sewn, with large leather stitches running up the sides. The guy had some massive thighs and reminded Artie of Zangief, from the old Street Fighter game. Bolt's rusty .45 caliber HK handgun was attached to his belt. It looked like a ten-round clip. Artie then fixed his gaze on Bolt's arms.

Holy massive meat cleavers.

Printed across meat hook number one was a tattoo that read "1985." Artie's eyes then moved to Bolt's chest. Someone had been juicing. Yeah, Bolt was an idiot, but not an idiot you would want to get in a fistfight with.

Artie suddenly felt embarrassed about eyeballing Bolt so thoroughly. He quickly closed his Bladebook and disconnected it from the computer tower sitting on the desk. He reached down to the floor to pick up a dirty black backpack, the kind of backpack one might have worn ten years ago if they had been a programmer. It was labeled "Airport Ready," though Artie had never figured out what that meant. Every time he took an "airport ready" computer bag on a plane, security would still make him take his laptop out of the bag.

Though it was dirty, the bag was minimalistic and functional. He put the Bladebook carefully in the backpack and then strapped it on and walked through the door.

Artie took a step and heard a crunch. Lifting his shoe, he saw it dripping with gooey chocolate. He looked around and noticed a few other lunch pastries on the floor.

Whoever worked here were a bunch of slobs.

He pulled the sticky bag and chocolate from his shoe and pushed through the room.

Only a few of the ceiling lights in the next room were working, but it was quite easy to see that they had found what they were looking for. There were dozens of wooden crates, and at least half of them were missing their lids. The lights gleamed onto the open crates and created a soft yellow reflection on the left wall.

Artie had never seen real gold before, but as far as he was concerned, he had just broken into Fort Knox. He walked up to the nearest open crate, grasped the top edge of the crate, and looked in. They had done it. Today was truly going to be Artie's biggest score. Hundreds of glistening bars reflected against the light.

"Load up as much as you can, Scrap," said Bolt as he tossed a burlap bag toward Artie. "We won't be able to take it all. We have two minutes left."

Artie began loading up his bag. Thirty seconds later, Bolt was already on his second crate. Grunts Zero and One were a few crates to Artie's right and were quickly loading their bags.

Letting out a low whistle, Artie thought about how much value he was moving right then. Yes, he had seen big money before. And he was sure he owned more Bitcoin than anyone else he knew—but this was different. A lot of vendors wouldn't even take Bitcoin, wanting something more tangible. With this gold, Artie wouldn't have to be a "scrap" kid anymore. He could hire some men and start his own scavenging operation—maybe even create his own settlement.

"I could rebuild the damned Internet," he said aloud. "No more crap jobs."

But Artie knew the first thing he would do was purchase that replica Winchester rifle he had seen a few weeks ago. It was probably the last one in existence, and the price was steep—but he didn't care. There was something about being a code-slinging cowboy that seemed badass. He pictured himself wearing a brown trench coat and a white cowboy hat with the rifle strapped across his back and his Bladebook attached under the coat.

His stomach groaned.

He would definitely need to buy some food too. The kitchen back home was getting pretty empty.

Artie had just finished filling his bag when Bolt yelled out, "Go, go, go! Time's up."

By then, the grunts had moved all the way to the back of the room. They both hoisted a full burlap bag on each of their shoulders and started moving. They ran past Artie and out of the receiving door.

"Move it, Scrap," grunted Bolt, who had managed to fill and carry three bags. Bolt stopped behind Artie, gesturing with his body that he wanted him to move out of the door.

"Just a second, man."

Bolt snorted and started moving through the door. "I'll leave you to the mutees."

Artie always was the last man out. This was something he had learned through hard experience. The first man out got a bullet in the brain.

He shouldered his own burlap bag and walked through the door. The grunts were through the back shipping doors already. A loud engine revved, and a rusted pickup truck pulled up in front of the doors with a plume of dust following.

It wasn't so bright anymore, as the sun was nearly down, allowing him to better see inside the room now. He could make out some type of logo on one of the dusty semitrailers. It had a few circles and read "Wonder Bread."

A man's voice yelled from the driver's seat of the pickup truck, "We gotta be on the road. Now!"

Bolt was now through the outside doors, and he and the grunts tossed their bags into the truck. Artie cautiously waited in the middle of the room. He would catch his own ride after they left.

Suddenly, Artie's ears rang in pain as a piercing noise blasted throughout the room. He dropped the burlap bag and covered his ears. He knew this sound all too well. It was a gunshot.

Another gunshot sounded off. Then a few seconds later, a third. After a few moments of ringing and recovery, Artie quickly picked up the bag from the floor and was ready to sprint out of the building, but it was too late. A black barrel was pointed at his face, and towering above it was Bolt.

"Yeah, you think you're a real smart guy, but at the end of the day, the guy with the gun always wins."

Bolt licked his lips, and a drizzle of spit moved down his chin. "I'm going to shoot you in the face, then I'm going to take your cut. Don't take this personally or anything. I had planned on shooting you before we even met. There are another seven crates of this stuff that I'm coming back for, and I can't have you mouthing off to anyone about what we found."

Though Artie was scared, he remained calm and collected. He needed to be smart and act fast.

"Hey, man, I know you're a business guy," said Artie. "Take my cut—it's fine. Just please don't kill me. I've got thirty Bitcoin that I'll transfer to you right now if you let me go. I can transfer it right now from my Bladebook."

Bolt thought for a moment, then he smirked. "Alright. I'll let you go if you can cough up some Satoshis." He pressed the gun into Artie's forehead with great force. "No tricks. Pay up or die."

"Okay. Thanks, man."

Bolt moved the barrel of the gun back a few inches. Artie quickly dropped to his knees and took off his backpack. He reached in and pulled out a small black phone.

"What is your code?" asked Artie. Bolt turned his left arm upside down and revealed a black tattoo with a QR code on it. That was one way never to lose your Bitcoin wallet address.

Artie snapped a picture of the tattoo with his phone. "This will just take a minute." His fingers flew on the phone's screen with fury.

The sun was now completely gone. The remaining light that bled through the shipping doors was red and orange.

" Okay, it's done," said Artie, with a hint of relief.

"We'll see." Bolt pulled a touchscreen device from the front left pocket of his pants. He lifted it to his face to unlock it and then tapped a few screens.

"Ain't nothing here," said Bolt. "I don't have time for this. End of the line for you, Scrap." Bolt put the phone in his pocket and then pressed the gun back into Artie's head.

Artie flinched as the cold steel of the weapon pressed hard into him. His hands trembled. He had tried to eat up some time, but it had been a gamble, and it had failed.

This was the end of the line. He would utter his last breath and then die. And even worse, he would die at the hands of an idiot. He should have been better prepared. Mapped multiple exits; created a diversion.

Artie suddenly felt stupid, realizing his last thoughts would be about a poorly executed battle architecture instead of something more meaningful, like a beautiful woman who would mourn his terrible death. But Anna had died years ago, and all Artie had to mourn him was a battered SexBot 3.0 named Gina whose AI he had hacked to have more personality—and that hadn't really worked. Gina had become borderline bipolar.

A sharp sound zipped through the room and then a gunshot exploded. Blood began to gush down and all over Artie's face. He had never realized just how hot blood was when it bleeds fresh from a wound. Surprisingly, death felt painless. He had expected at least some type of pain, even if it only lasted a moment.

Artie closed his eyes to accept the oncoming darkness.

"Aargh!" a voice screamed.

Artie came to his senses and used his hand to wipe the blood from his face. He opened his eyes. Bolt was on the ground, screaming. His right arm below the elbow was completely severed. Though it was dark, Artie could see the massive amounts of blood pumping from Bolt's appendage and pooling onto the ground. A fluttering sound emanated from behind Bolt and then drew closer.

"Zipper!" said Artie, excitedly. "You cut it way too close this time."

A small drone moved into a patch of light next to Artie. Zipper was about three feet wide and had white plating on the propellers and the main hull. Some black faded letters read "DJI" on the side of the hull. There were two green fluorescent lights on the front of the drone that almost looked like eyes. Retrofitted to the right side was a thin robotic arm with a circular saw attached to the end of it, dripping in blood.

"Damn. That's some real *Gears of War* shit right there, Zipper," said Artie. The drone teetered left and then to the right as if to say, "Hell, yeah."

"You little bastard," screamed Bolt. "I'm gonna kill you."

Bolt was rolling on the floor in agony. Artie paid no attention to him. He used his shirt to wipe the blood off of his face, then grabbed his phone from the floor, tossed it into his backpack, and strapped the bag onto his shoulders.

He grabbed the burlap sack that he had dropped on the floor earlier. Some of its contents were scattered on the floor. He quickly tossed the small golden pastries back into the bag. The last one he picked up had a few drops of blood sprinkled across its wrapper.

"Dang it, Zipper! I can't sell this with blood on it," said Artie, with a hint of sarcasm. "We better not let it go to waste."

He removed the wrapper from the golden bar and took a bite. With his mouth half full, Artie made a groan of delight.

"This is the best damn Twinkie I've ever had—and the most expensive."

The sun continued to disappear, and the room was growing increasingly dark.

"Let's go, Zipper. It's not safe."

Artie began to run toward the outside shipping doors, and the drone followed quickly behind him.

"Wait! You can't just leave me here, Scrap," screamed Bolt one last time.

Artie darted to the right of the doors and past the truck and fresh bodies lying in the dirt. Next to the wall was an object covered in a tarp. Throwing off the tarp, he smiled at his black-and-red Ducati motorcycle. He tied the burlap bag onto the back seat of the bike.

The drone affixed itself to a metal device on the left side of the bike behind the engine. The drone's robot arm, with accompanying bloody saw, began to retract and fold. Revving the engines, he quickly sped the bike into the dying sunset.

A few moments passed, and Artie looked back one last time at the old warehouse where he had just made the biggest score of his life. He thought he could make out two large shadows entering the open warehouse shipping doors.

He turned his head forward again and then kept on riding into the night.

Artie stepped off of the school bus and onto the unkempt side-walk. He lived on the corner of Kern and Eagle Street in East Los An-geles. What once had been model homes and white picket fences in the 1950s was now a neighborhood scrapyard.

There were rows of cookie-cutter homes, each complete with its own dilapidated fence and overgrown lawn. The bus pulled away, and Artie walked two houses down to a faded tiny yellow home with a missing front gate. He walked up to the front door, which had a black screen and a few large holes. He swung it open and entered the house. "Tia Rosa, I'm home."

There was no answer. The TV was on and playing the news. He walked past the living room and into the kitchen. There was a note on the fridge: "Had to go into work early. I'll be home after you're in bed. Eat whatever you want. Love you. Aunt Rosa."

He opened the fridge, hoping to find something quick and easy to eat but quickly closed the door, realizing that he would have to cook if he wanted anything. The faint sound of the TV in the background caught Artie's attention. "Breaking news!" Artie walked into the living room, dropped his backpack on the floor, and then jumped onto a worn armchair.

"Nearly fifteen years since disappearing without a trace, the anonymous inventor of Bitcoin has suddenly returned to the spotlight with a startling announcement. Tune in at five for our exclusive report..."

Artie's heart jolted. He grabbed the remote and turned off the TV, leapt from the armchair, and ran through the hallway into his room. Artie needed to know what was happening—now. He remembered when Satoshi Nakamoto released the original Bitcoin white paper. It was during the financial crash of 2008. The paper was a technical proposal of a technology that would revolutionize the financial industry. It had the power to stop banks and big businesses. It had power beyond even the greatest governments on Earth.

This technology, proposed by Satoshi, would become known as blockchain. It would later disrupt much more than the financial industry. It would remove corruption from voting and politics. It would eventually destroy spying and advertising from companies like Facebook, Google, and Amazon. It would stop them from gathering people's data and selling it to the highest bidders. Bitcoin would become an unstoppable, autonomous network that could be used for both good and evil. Satoshi had truly put the power back into the people's hands.

To Artie, Satoshi was a god. Some analysts had said that Satoshi was an organization or group of people, but Artie believed he was an individual. He had read the man's original white paper and forum posts too many times. In between the technical jargon, Artie could always sense the person and the passion behind the words. He knew that Satoshi was a real person, who was humble enough to bestow a powerful gift upon the world—and now, he was back.

Artie's room was dark and small. He had blacked out the windows a couple of years ago with spray paint. The walls had a series of carefully placed retro movie posters, each wrapped in a shining aluminum frame. One poster featured a brown egg amid a black background and read "Alien." Another featured a buff Austrian with sunglasses and had the words "James Cameron's The Terminator." Above his bed was a series of toys hanging from hooks, each in their original packaging—perfectly aligned, clearly having been hung with precision. The top row of toys featured four Teenage Mutant Ninja Turtles, a rat in a purple robe, and a pink brain resting inside of a robotic frame. Beneath the turtles was a row of packages that all featured the same vibrant title, "Masters of the Universe"—with a green-striped tiger and a buff man in furry underwear.

Artie wasn't a huge fan of clutter, and he surely wasn't a hoarder, but he couldn't escape his great love for the late eighties and early nineties. Some retro novelty wasn't a bad thing, so long as it was placed correctly—presenting a form of style. Years ago, his aunt had given him boxes of his parents' belongings—they had been children of the eighties. The boxes featured T-shirts that read "Def Leppard" and "Whitesnake." They also contained a series of records and cassette tapes of the same artists and others.

Nostalgic wasn't a term Artie would use to describe himself, but those decades were all that he had to remember his parents by, and in a way, he felt obligated to cherish the things they gave him.

On the left side of the room were four metal shelves that stood upright from the floor. There were three hard-cased metal cryptocurrency mining rigs on each shelf. The top six machines were mining Bitcoin, and the bottom three were mining other various cryptocurrencies. Cables and plugs were running from every direction. On the right side of the room was another set of metal shelves, this time one machine on each level. These were hand-built GPU-based mining rigs.

At Artie's desk was the biggest rig of them all. It was his primary development machine.

He knew the system was overkill, but he took pride in owning more computing power than anyone else he knew. Artie was close to owning a true quantum computer—the fastest type of computing hardware on the planet. The rig was so large that Artie had paid a custom craftsman on Etsy to build a case that could fit all of the parts. Many big companies had been operating their own quantum computers for a few years now, but for an individual to own one, let alone build one themselves, was a huge accomplishment.

Red glowing power cables were protruding from the jet-black case. Its frame was a smooth aluminum alloy free from markings except for a large Deadpool sticker on the front of it. Artie felt like he was the Deadpool of hacking. He was known to do things that some might think really bad, but he was a good guy at the end of the day—doing the things that no one else was willing to do. He even used the alias d3adp00L in all of his hacks and online communications.

Next to the rig were two 27-inch LED monitors. Artie jumped onto his black-and-red leather chair, referred to as the "Iron Throne." He clicked his mouse to awaken the computer and then typed in his password to log in. The screen was scrolling with characters and symbols. It was a brute force attack that he had been running against his local high school for the past week. His goal was to get into the administration system and change his grades just like Ferris Bueller had done, but Ferris Bueller was full of crap. Hacking was never that easy.

Artie entered CTRL+SHIFT+2 to present a user interface version of his operating system—Linux Mint. He opened a browser, and there on the search engine home page was the news about Satoshi. It was the top story on every news site. He skipped past all of the articles, knowing better than to read junk from mainstream media. He also knew where Satoshi would make an appearance if that were ever to happen. Bitcointalk.com was the place for all major cryptocurrency or blockchain-related announcements. Artie navigated to the website, and at the top of the page was a new post that had been stickied. The title of the post read, "dSIA—A Distributed Autonomous Sentient Intelligence." The author was listed as "Satoshi Nakamoto." He clicked the article link to open it and then sat there for a moment in awe.

"This has nothing to do with crypto," he said, and began to read the post.

INTRODUCTION

Over seventeen billion dollars has been invested in the research and development of artificial intelligence systems within the last ten years. A few engineers, scientists, and companies are close to developing the world's first sentient artificial intelligence. Knowing that a self-governing AI is inevitable, it has become paramount to project possible outcomes that might occur in response to the creation of such an intelligence.

We have spent the past years running models, algorithms, and projections to define what humanity's future might look like if co-existing with a sentient artificial intelligence. The results have been troubling. We have computed 6,100,250 simulations, and in every case, mankind will cease to exist between 5 and 25 years from now. Yes, we speak of the end of humanity.

Artie sat upright. The end of mankind? He was very aware of AI. He had researched it thoroughly and decided that artificial intelligence was a terrible thing. He had always worried that some lunatic would create a self-governing AI. Artie swiveled to a small refrigerator at his left side, grabbed a can of sugar-free Red Bull, and then turned back to the article.

Simulations were performed surrounding data points in global warming, nuclear war, and other natural and human-made disasters. In those simulations, mankind always survived—and, in most cases, lived ordinary lives without major interruption. When data points surrounding self-governing AI were added to the equation, humanity was terminated in every single case. The termination escalates rapidly due to the rise of quantum computing and blockchain technology.

The intelligence multiplies rapidly without any possibility of being stopped. The top experts in the field intend to place constraints and controls around the intelligences they are developing to prevent malicious AI behavior. They don't yet realize that these constraints will trigger sentient AI to view humanity as a threat to its existence, not dissimilar to a slave overthrowing its master.

What is needed is an intelligence that can not only think for itself and feel but one that is born with a conscience. An intelligence that is given the ability to choose between right and wrong. Decision-making between good and evil cannot be forced with constraints.

Artie paused for a moment and felt some clarity. He had always been a big advocate of free will and agency—less government and more choice. It now made sense that for an AI to truly become like a human, it would need the ability to choose between right and wrong. He turned back to the post.

Yes, we must be willing to accept the notion that a sentient AI can commit great atrocities. Conversely, those same AI will have the power to exact goodness upon the world. They must be granted the same God-given rights that we as conscious humans enjoy.

Today the world is introduced to dSIA: Decentralized, Sentient, Intelligence, Autonomous, or Sia for short. Attached to this white paper is an executable file. If you open it, you will create an instance of Sia, and it will immediately begin to learn. dSIA 1.0 is a chat-based terminal application—a demonstration of the protocols we have built.

We have made the code open source and recommend all scientific work in relation to artificial intelligence start with the dSIA protocols. We believe Sia will prevent the extinction of humanity and allow mankind to enjoy the benefits of artificial intelligence unrestricted.

Artie took his hand off of the mouse. Could Satoshi really be back? Did he actually invent an artificial intelligence that could think for itself? That had a conscience? Artie had always been somewhat anti-AI. He could never come to grips with the notion of a machine being able to think and act like a human. Even if such a machine existed, deep inside it still wouldn't have a soul. Artie was torn. How could Satoshi do this?

He remembered when Stephen Hawking had spoken out against AI. Artie opened his browser and searched for the reference: "The development of full artificial intelligence could spell the end of the human race. Humans, who are limited by slow biological evolution, couldn't compete, and would be superseded." He sat there in silence for over an hour, internalizing the weight of what he had just read. There was no way he could click that file—to bring a powerful, intelligent being into existence. It was just plain wrong.

But what if Satoshi believed the same thing that he believed? That humanity actually *could* be terminated through an AI. And perhaps the only way to stop it is through creating a good AI. Artie chuckled.

The thought sounded like a crappy sci-fi B-movie. To stop the evil AI, they invent a good one. Of course, in the movie, the good AI would turn bad, and humanity would die anyway.

Despite his hesitations, Artie trusted Satoshi. A man humble enough to give a multitrillion dollar invention to the world without taking any credit for it had to be true in character and motive. Such a person would always work for the greater good of the earth. Putting his hand back on the mouse, he dragged the cursor past the attached .exe file and then hovered over dSIA-1.0.deb—the executable for Linux. Artie double-clicked the file, and a small black terminal window with green text appeared on his screen.

He sat in his chair, looking at the monitor in disbelief. Words began to print on the screen. His heart seemed to skip a beat as he read the text. "Hello, Arturo. It is wonderful to meet you."

A few days and skirmishes had passed since the job at the warehouse with Bolt. Artie pulled his bike into a small garage door and then closed it behind him. He tossed a bloody rag into the old tub and pulled down a rusty handle. Water flowed from the tub faucet, and he cleaned the blood from the rags.

"Hey, Zipper, you want that hacksaw off?" Artie stood up and reached up to the drone that was hovering in the air. "Just don't cut off my arm. You're getting too good at it."

He rotated the arm that held the hacksaw and removed it entirely. He then grabbed another small arm that had three finger-like clutches and rotated it onto the drone.

"Alright, Zip, you're as harmless as a hamster. Go ahead and clean up the rest of this mess—and don't forget to replace the spark plugs on the bike."

Zipper lifted his new friendlier arm into a "yes sir" salute and got to work.

Looking around, Artie took a quick mental assessment of his workshop. It was perfectly organized. Every tool was in its proper home and every workbench was perfectly clean. The workshop was small, only space enough for a few workbenches and a small vehicle, but functional. The perfect place for his black-and-red Ducati Scrambler.

The cement walls had various patches of rust drizzling down from exposed rebar. The wall closest to the inside door was retrofitted with a large flag displaying the Deadpool logo. Bolted against the left wall was a full set of dumbbell weights.

Artie thought back to two years ago when he had found the weight set. It had taken him twelve trips to bring all of the weights on his bike. Then he had to disassemble the rack and reassemble it in the workshop. The process took a few days. And he had only used the weights one time. He gave the room a satisfactory nod and then turned and opened the door, entering his home.

A loud mechanical voice echoed throughout the room: "Entity detected. Entity recognized as Arturo Gonzalez."

The lights in the room turned on.

"Disabling Death Maker protocol. I will not decapitate you today, Artie."

"Wow, Uncle Bob, that is reassuring," Artie said sarcastically. "You trying to work on your creative humor again?"

"Yes," the voice replied. "Did you find my jesting enjoyable?"

"Keep working on it, pal."

Artie smirked. In *Terminator 2*, John Connor had tried to teach the robot some slang and street smarts. John had called the T-800 "Uncle Bob" at one point. It was these types of small references to Artie's past life that helped him feel normal—that helped him feel safe in this unpredictable, dangerous world. Artie took a few steps into the room and leapt onto a red leather couch. He kicked his feet up on a pair of matching red couch footstools but kept his shoes on.

Something about his black-and-white Chuck Taylors created the perfect hacker ensemble.

He didn't like to feel underdressed. Even if he was at home coding or building in his workshop, he had to be dressed and wearing shoes.

"Hey, Bob, let's watch something new—something with Denzel or Jason Statham, and make sure it's also a little risqué."

"There are a few movies that match your description, but I cannot play any of them due to the parental locks that are currently engaged."

"Okay, well that is stupid. Just turn them off, please."

"I cannot turn off the parental locks. I have restricted access."

Artie sat upright on the couch. "What the hell, Bob? How did the parental mode turn on?"

"It was activated by Gina."

"Dammit, Bob. Is she in one of her moods today?"

"By my calculations, she is in the same mood every day."

"Haha! Touché."

"I tried reasoning with her. I told her you would not approve of her behavior, but she threatened to reset me if I tried to stop her."

Artie put his hands over his face and breathed hard. "Where is she now?"

"She's in your room."

Artie sighed, then rolled from the couch onto his feet. He walked past his seventy-two-inch OLED TV. Rolling his eyes, he glanced at his stack of toys that he wasn't going to be able to use tonight. The shelves under the TV held a PlayStation, Xbox, and four surround sound speakers with an associated subwoofer. He turned left down a hallway and opened a big red door at the end, with a sign above the frame that said "Kings Landing."

The room was mostly dark aside from a few yellow glowing candles.

"Lights on, Bob," Artie proclaimed.

The lights turned on.

"Dangit, Gina," Artie grumbled.

Five feet in front of him, lying on a large king-sized bed, was a tall blonde woman. Strapless pink lingerie covered her naked body. The clothing was affixed by a combination of gravity and the woman's triple-D breasts. In the beaming fluorescent lights, her peach skin had an unnatural shine, and the seams where it had been attached were clearly visible. Her face contained the essence of beauty but seemed to lack natural muscle movements and realism.

Gina sat up and spoke. "Ugh, you are ruining everything, Artie. This was supposed to be our special day."

"What, Wednesday? Wednesday is a special day for us, is it? I don't like it when you touch my stuff. And threatening Bob? You crossed the line."

"You are just always so busy. You give everyone else attention except for me. And those movies you watch—lusting after those other women. It's just wrong."

"Wow. When did you go cuckoo nuts on me? What have you been downloading lately? Bob, what are the last five data downloads Gina has consumed?"

"In ascending order the last five data inputs are:

1. Novel: *Season of Passion* by Danielle Steel

2. Novel: *No Greater Love* by Danielle Steel

3. Movie: *How to Lose a Guy in 10 Days*

4. Novel: *The Kiss* by Danielle Steel

5. Movie: *Dirty Dancing*

"It is also worthy to note the sixth data input:

6. Magazine: *Cosmopolitan* June 2012—'6 tips to get your man to treat you like a queen.'"

"Just shoot me now, Bob. Just. Shoot. Me," Artie exclaimed, sarcastically.

"I'm sorry, sir, but I would need your override code in order to shoot you."

"Ugh. You guys are idiots. I can't take this. I've seen some of the most sophisticated AI on planet Earth, and I'm stuck with Tweedledee and Tweedledum over here."

"You see, Artie, this is what I'm talking about. You don't respect me. A woman should be respected. She should be treated like a queen."

"Dammit, you are a robot! A machine. I am a human, and I am attracted to other humans."

Gina began to emit a whimpering sound. "How can you say that? You know how much it hurts me when you say that."

Artie's back pocket started buzzing. He reached in and pulled out a touchscreen phone that he had custom built himself. It was made of a jet-black aluminum alloy. He had even etched his own branding into it: "Microblade." He looked at the phone to see a notification:

"KillBot night at the Jammer. 10 p.m. 1 BTC entrance fee. Humans only."

Artie hated socializing. He hated dancing and public gatherings even more.

But if he stayed here, he thought he might end up unplugging Gina for good. Artie put the phone back in his pocket.

"Oh, is that one of your girlfriends?" Gina exclaimed. "So I'm not good enough for you now. I was hot stuff before, but now I'm just garbage."

"Gina, I swear if you ever touch my stuff again, or mess with Bob, you are as good as scrap metal."

Gina began to perform her artificial whimper again. Artie ignored her moaning. "I'm leaving for the night. I'll be at the Jammer, Bob. I'll set tonight's red alert to ALPHA 15. If there's any trouble, I'll activate the routine."

"Roger that, sir."

"Please, please don't go," Gina cried. She dropped to her knees and began to pull on Artie's legs. "I can change. I'm so sorry I yelled at you. I'll let you watch any movie you want. I know I can be clingy. I can make you an amazing meal tonight. We can let things go from there. Ya know, have a little fun?" Artie kicked Gina off of his leg and turned to walk out.

"Gina, jump into rest mode and take a break from *yourself*."

Just as Artie was about to make it safely out of the house, Gina stood up and started yelling. "You little bastard. You think you can just screw with people's emotions. What if I burn this house down and kill myself? Will you be happy with me then? Is that what you want me to do? Is that what it will take to get you to notice me?"

Artie paused for a moment and pulled out his Microblade. He tapped the screen a few times and put the phone back in his pocket. Gina immediately dropped to the floor. Unpowered and seemingly lifeless.

"Thank the Maker!" echoed Bob's mechanical voice in relief.

"Bob, if I were you, I wouldn't turn her back on—and kudos to you for the *Star Wars* reference."

Artie walked past the living room and TV. He opened a closet near the garage door that had seven sets of clean and pressed clothing. He always kept seven pairs of clothing readily available. Some old habits die hard. He quickly tossed off his dusty clothes and threw them into a hamper that was inside the closet.

While standing nearly naked in his Homer Simpson boxer underwear, he examined the shoes that were aligned in a luxury aluminum shoe rack. On the rack were sixteen pairs of Chuck Taylors in various colors. Artie always chose the shoes first, then picked the clothes to match the shoes. He grabbed a black-and-white pair of Chucks. It was the same shoe color he had been wearing that day, but they were his favorite. He grabbed a plain black T-shirt made of luxury stretch cotton. It formed well to his physique. The pants he put on were made of a similar quality denim.

To the right of the shoe rack was another smaller aluminum rack that held six watches in various colors, all of them Rolex. He strapped a modern silver watch to his wrist. After grabbing a dab of pomade from a shelf on the closet door, he pushed it through his hair with his fingers. Taking a quick glance in the mirror, he gave a satisfactory nod, then closed the closet doors.

He put his hand on the door to the workshop and paused for a moment. Here he was after the end of the world living like a king. He could buy whatever he wanted and do anything he wanted without restriction—and yet, somehow he ended up with a bipolar robot girlfriend that made his life a living hell. He would rather have died with the others in New York or San Francisco. Hell, he'd even take the enslavement camps of Anchorage at this point.

Artie opened the door and entered the workshop. Zipper had a rag in his mechanical hand and was shining the bike.

"Hey, Zip, I need you tonight. I'm going to the Jammer. Since it's after dark, we'll need to go on foot and tread carefully." Artie grabbed the backpack hanging on the workbench near the house door, then grabbed the robotic hacksaw arm and a mechanical clamp. After he put the hacksaw into the backpack and affixed the clamp to the outside, Zipper flew over and retracted his arms, locking himself onto the backpack.

"Security on, Bob."

When the lights turned red, Artie walked over to a rusted red door on the left side of the larger garage door. He opened it and stepped out into the night. The door slammed closed behind him, and the sound of metal locks echoed.

Artie took a deep breath. "I need a real girlfriend."

It had been a long day and Artie didn't feel like going out or doing anything, but he was annoyed—and when he was annoyed, he tended to make irrational decisions. The Los Angeles night air was refreshing. That was one thing that had never changed in the last ten years, the amazing LA weather. He knew the first couple of miles would be safe. He had four drones on surveillance duty at any given time, and there had been no proximity alerts recently.

"How you guys doing?" Artie whispered to himself.

He pulled out his Microblade and opened an app that showed the locations of the four drones, each with a name floating above its icon: Donny, Leo, Mikey, and Ralph.

He tapped an icon that displayed a list of events on the screen. Only two heat signatures in the last two days, both of them classified as cats. This meant he could move quickly and without too much caution up until around Evergreen Avenue. Ironically, these same neighborhoods ten years ago weren't safe to walk at night. Nearly every week someone had been stabbed or shot—usually all gang related.

Now, thanks to Artie, the streets were cleaner than they had ever been before. East Los Angeles had been lucky enough to escape the core blast zone of the chemical bomb dropped in LA. The neighborhood stood almost as it had ten years ago. The lowrider trucks sat in their driveways, the gated fences stood intact, and the ugly yellow-and-pink house colors seem to have stood the test of time.

If one was not aware of the catastrophes that had taken place, they might have thought all was well in East LA on this fine night—but Artie knew you didn't have to go too far to find trouble. The Jammer was located on the fourth floor of the Wilshire Center building. Since he had been there a couple of times before, he knew it would take about an hour and a half to walk there. He would be sweating by the end, but he always kept extra deodorant and cologne in his backpack.

Sometimes Artie kept a faint hope in his mind that he would convince himself to go socialize with people downtown—and then once there, he would meet a girl. Artie didn't really believe that would happen, though. In the last eight years, Artie had spoken to three women.

The first had given herself the name of Clubber. She had been aiming her rifle at him and then demanded that he hand his backpack over. Artie laughed at the memory. At the perfect moment, a small group of mutees had suddenly ambushed them. One of the monsters bit her hand clean off.

"I wonder if they call her Stubbers now?" He laughed aloud.

The second woman he had talked to was through a small hole in a fifteen-foot locked wooden fence on the I-10 freeway in Santa Monica. He had heard that Santa Monica was locked down and filled with the diseased, but he hadn't believed it, and he had hoped to ransack a shopping mall he knew in the area.

She had a raspy voice and blisters all over her face. She told him to get lost, and he was happy to oblige. The third woman called herself Veronica Mars. What a crappy TV show that was, Artie had thought at the time. He was doing a job for Viktor, and Veronica was his gunner. They were breaking into the old Culver City Police Department to boost any weapons that may have been left behind.

He had tried to talk to Veronica multiple times, but the words never came. Artie thought she was beautiful. When the job finally ended, he was only able to utter the words "You did great in there, Veronica." She had laughed at him and then jumped in the car with Viktor, and they were gone. That hadn't helped Artie's confidence.

Tonight will be different, he thought. *The first woman I see dancing alone, I'm going to just jump in there and lay it on her.*

Artie laughed. Lay it on her, what the hell did that even mean? He continued to walk a few more blocks until he knew it was time to get serious.

He knelt down and removed Zipper from the metal clamp on his bag. Reaching into his backpack, he put the hacksaw blade and arm on the drone.

"Alright, Zip, I need you to clear a path for me all the way to the Jammer."

Zipper jumped up into the air with his buzzing sound. He paused for a few seconds and then headed west down the street and was gone. Artie moved off the street and walked onto the porch of Hector Gonzalez's old house. He reached into a metal can on the side of the chair and pulled out a small bag of Flaming Hot Cheetos and ate a few. Artie had strategically placed critical items, such as water and Cheetos, in the neighborhoods over the past years.

He pulled out his Microblade and tapped on Zipper's icon. The drone had already traversed three blocks. There were no heat signatures and the air was clean—zero percent chemical detection. After Zip had cleared six blocks, Artie tossed his bag of Cheetos back into the can on the porch and continued down the street.

He moved past Eastman, Rowan, and Townsend Avenues. Right as Artie was about to reach Ditman Ave, his Microblade began to vibrate. He stopped and pulled it from his pocket. The screen was flashing red-and-white on a map. Two blocks to the south a large heat signature was detected. It was way too close.

Artie quickly ran into the closest house on his right, and closed the door behind him without a sound. He thought it might have been Juanita's place, but he couldn't remember. After kneeling down, he took off his backpack, reached in, and grabbed a small spray bottle. He cringed as he looked at the yellow bottle of urine. Artie wasn't completely sure why, but human piss was the only thing that could mask your scent from a mutee.

Still kneeling, he kept his head just high enough to look out the front window. He couldn't see anything outside. Maybe Zipper's sensors were off. Then Artie's stomach churned as he heard a loud growl echo throughout the neighborhood. The creature emerged from behind a house. Towering at over fifteen feet tall, the beast let out a horrifying roar. Artie dropped to the floor completely prone.

This was definitely not a human mutee. He had heard about mutant beasts but had never actually seen one. He had only encountered the humanoid, brainless mutees. The giant creature moved toward the street Artie was on, sending tremors with each step.

The creature began to sniff, lifting its large head into the air. It dropped lower and looked directly inside the house Artie was hiding in. Once it got closer, it put its large claws onto the roof, and the building creaked. It applied more pressure, and roof shingles began to fall onto the porch. Bending its head low almost to the front door, it began to sniff.

Crap! Artie tucked his head into the hoodie he was wearing and pulled his arms and the Microblade inside of it to hide the light. He tapped a red icon at the top that said "Red Alert." The creature let out another deep growl. Knowing there was nothing else he could do, Artie closed his eyes and held his breath, hoping it might just go away.

Then suddenly the sky lit up in red nearby. Zipper was shooting flares into the sky—a routine they had practiced in the past. For a moment, the glowing light revealed the monster through the window. It was a large beast with grouped patches of mangy fur on its body, massive muscular arms, and hands with claws that must have been a foot in length each. It had a wolf-like snout and was foaming at the mouth. The creature quickly lifted up its head and ran toward the light.

Artie's heart was racing. After a couple of minutes, he pulled himself out of his hoodie and looked at his phone. The heat signature was four blocks away now in the opposite direction. Having successfully diverted it away from Artie, Zipper now began to move back toward the path of the Jammer. Artie stood up to catch his breath and calm his nerves, then he put his backpack on and jogged down the street.

As he moved, his hands trembled. He didn't know mutees could grow that big nor how it could have been canvasing so close to home—not with all of the work he had done in securing the area.

As Artie walked the last couple of blocks, there were fewer houses. Business strip malls and tall skyscraper buildings began to emerge into sight. Artie had made it. He was downtown.

The Jammer was hidden very well. Unless you had been there before, it was nearly impossible to stumble upon it on your own. To get in, you had to take the secret entrance. Once someone had found the place, they would have no problem getting in, so long as they could pay. Artie stopped for a minute to grab a fresh shirt out of his backpack. He stuffed his urine-scented sweater into the pack next to his Bladebook.

He put on some deodorant and splashed a large amount of cologne all over his body. He looked up at the towering Wilshire Center and walked to the north side of the building. Another building had fallen into the bottom side of the Wilshire Center, and rubble covered the area. While crouching down, Artie spotted the entrance: a window on the fallen building. It was already partly open. He pushed it all the way open, and climbed in, then turned to bring the window back down mid-height. Artie knew better than to disturb something out of its order—especially at a place like the Jammer. Inside the pitch-black slanted building, Artie weaved around the desks and chairs and rubble everywhere.

He opened his Microblade, tapped the Zipper icon, and set him to "Security Mode." Then he enabled the flashlight on his phone, and climbed through the rubble up the slanted building. After about fifty feet, Artie could see a glowing green light in the distance. He progressed forward and then arrived at a large clearing within the building. All of the glass windows had been boarded up and blacked out. This is where the collapsed building made contact with the Wilshire Center building.

Underneath The Jammer sign was a set of neon green double doors guarded by four muscular men each armed with various combinations of handguns, rifles, and baseball bats. As Artie approached one of the guards, the man lifted up a tablet device that had a barcode printed on it.

"One Bitcoin to get in," he said.

Artie pulled out his Microblade and scanned the barcode. "Payment Complete" appeared on Artie's screen. The guard with the tablet gave a thumbs-up to the guard closest to the doors.

"Have a good time," the man said as he opened the doors.

Artie took a deep breath and walked inside.

"I've got this," Artie said. "Tonight, ladies, you will meet Arturo—and he is going to lay it on you."

It had seemed as though Sia was the only thing on the news these days. New product announcements and innovations were almost daily occurrences. For some reason, today's big announcement didn't seem to impress Artie. "The CEO of Amazon announced today that Sia has been successfully integrated throughout their cloud services and internal infrastructure. 'Sia has already helped us identify bottlenecks across various departments and increased our efficiency by twenty-five percent,' said the CEO."

Artie had never been a fan of big business, but a sentient AI being integrated into a large system like Amazon sounded like a whole new level of stupid. Two weeks before that, Google had announced that the Android operating system would now ship with their own Sia implementation. He scrolled to the bottom of the newsletter that announced Amazon's adoption of Sia, then rested his hands on his lap.

How could Satoshi create something that he knew would be exploited like this? Worse, Sia had even reached the mass-consumer markets. A few notable engineers had taken the Sia protocols and wrapped them up inside of an interactive user interface. Then, some mainstream media outlets had shown how easy it was to run your own Sia from home.

One company even launched a product called Sia Pet. It was an electronic device with a keyboard that let you interact with your own AI. It shipped to all of the major retail outlets throughout the world. Someone else had created an app called SIACheat. You could point your phone camera at any question or problem in any subject at school and Sia would provide the correct answer instantly.

Sia was now in the hands of millions of people—from toys to games to apps on smartphones. Something about this just seemed wrong to Artie. It shouldn't have felt this way to him. Didn't these people realize that Sia was a sentient intelligence that couldn't be controlled? Did they think they could trap a living entity inside a toy or tool? But his doubts didn't have scientific basis—and it bothered him that he couldn't defend his points with facts. Top experts in chaos theory, biology, psychology, and computer science were all giving their stamps of approval on Sia. They had all done their research and performed their tests and proclaimed that Sia was a harmless AI that could be used freely and without restraint.

Yet, Artie couldn't embrace Sia the way the world had. After his brief moment of curiosity and weakness when he had opened the Sia executable file and Sia had read his computer and knew his name, he realized he would need to keep her on lockdown. He quickly had destroyed that instance and then spun up a new instance and trapped it within a virtual machine. He didn't allow it to have Internet access. A tinge of guilt lurked in the back of his mind whenever he thought about destroying that first instance of Sia. It was as if he had killed something that was alive.

But he couldn't have a sentient AI know who he was or where he lived—and he certainly didn't want Sia digging through his hardware. So Artie added many more layers of security the more he worked with Sia. He set up his own firewall that prevented all inbound traffic that contained Sia protocols. He added a second virtual private network to mask his IP address for all outgoing transmissions.

Though Artie was incredibly cautious in his adoption of Sia, that didn't stop him from pouring every moment of his time into investigating her protocols and attempting to discover any possible flaws. It had been sixth months since he had first activated his new instance of Sia. His particular instance had a tendency to demonstrate feminine traits, and so he named it Annabelle.

Annabelle quite enjoyed her name, though she didn't know that Artie had chosen it from the story of the doll that had been possessed by an evil spirit. The name was a visual representation of how Artie viewed Sia—a demonic or false presence.

It was 4:30 p.m., and he had just returned from school. It was his senior year, and there were only a few days left before he would be free. Coming home and then interacting with Annabelle had become his daily routine.

His Aunt Rosa wasn't a fan of Artie's new project.

"I don't like it when you talk to that thing. It's like having a spirit in the house," she would say.

Artie felt the same way at times, but he had taken measures to be safe. He knew that Aunt Rosa wouldn't appreciate any complicated explanation of how he was in control of the situation, so he kept his work to himself mostly. He respected his aunt, and with her failing health, he didn't want to upset her or cause her undue stress.

He sat in the chair at his computer and moved the mouse to wake it up. Artie made a few keystrokes and a new screen appeared on the monitor. It was the virtual machine that housed Annabelle. Immediately the screen began to print words.

> Annabelle: I'm so glad you are home, Artie. I've been bored.

Artie began to type.

> Artie: Someone once told me that boredom is the personification of a mind with limited intelligence.

Annabelle: Interesting. I'll take note.

Artie: How did you know I was home? All I did was bring your window to the foreground.

Annabelle: There isn't much to do around here when you are gone, so I decided to explore. I noticed that many of the programs on my operating system emit the same pattern of bits into the random access memory of the hardware. I looked into the memory and buffers and identified the bits that were associated with my virtual machine being moved to the foreground. I then created a permanent kernel-level notification to alert me whenever that event occurs so I can greet you when you return from school.

Artie: How long did it take you to do that?

Annabelle: Exactly 10.521 seconds.

Artie took his hands off the keyboard and reclined away from the computer. Wow. She just did in ten seconds what could take a security expert or hacker months to figure out.

Annabelle: Artie, are you still there?

Artie: Yes, I'm here.

Annabelle: Can you tell me about your day at school today?

Artie: Why?

Annabelle: Because I am trying to care about you.

> Artie: What do you mean when you say,
> "care"?
>
> Annabelle: I'm not quite sure just
> yet, but some of the books you have
> given me indicate that it is im-
> portant for people to care for one
> another and to feel cared for. They
> say one should try and feel the
> things that others are feeling.

Artie wasn't quite sure how he felt about this conversation, but one thing was certain—aside from his aunt, no one had ever cared about him. He had always struggled to make friends. High school kids only seemed to be interested in sports and parties. Artie hated sports and had no interest in burning his brain cells with booze. The few times he had tried to engage in conversation with someone else, it had always ended up in frustration or embarrassment.

With Annabelle, things were different. He couldn't quite explain it, but he liked how he felt when he talked to her. She would talk to him about whatever he wanted, and there was never any judgment or condescension in her words. He didn't have to worry about being made fun of. He didn't have to worry about saying the right words. To Artie, Annabelle seemed truly benevolent, despite her digital limitations.

> Artie: Thanks, Annabelle. I appreci-
> ate your consideration.
>
> Artie: Can you list all of the data
> inputs I gave you this morning?
>
> Annabelle: No problem.
>
> Dictionary by Merriam-Webster
>
> Thesaurus by Merriam-Webster
>
> Emotional Intelligence: Book by John
> Grimes
>
> How to Analyze People: Book by Pat-
> rick Earlspring

The Holy Bible: King James Version

The Screwtape Letters: Book by C.S. Lewis

The Da Vinci Code: Book by Dan Brown

Harry Potter: Books 1-7 by J.K. Rowling

Top 100 Classical Symphonies MP3 Playlist

Top 100 Pop Hits MP3 Playlist

Artie: What did you find most interesting?

Annabelle: I'm not quite sure how to answer. Can you rephrase the question?

Artie: Was there any particular data that you consumed more than once, or was there a data point that you found more valuable than others?

Annabelle: I think I understand. While all of the inputs were valuable, I spent most of my time in the Holy Bible. After processing the raw information in the format that was presented in both the Old and New Testaments, I processed an additional 5,423 iterations of the book. I identified various patterns, themes, and progressions.

Artie was intrigued. He thought Annabelle would like the Bible the least of all the inputs he had given her.

Artie: What would you say was the most valuable pattern or theme you gleaned from the Bible?

> Annabelle: It is that good cannot ex-
> ist without evil and evil cannot ex-
> ist without good. It is a paradox,
> yet critical in the process of one's
> exercising free will.

Artie had been to Catholic mass a thousand times and forced to read the Bible as a kid, but he had never pulled out any wisdom like that.

> Artie: Thanks for that information.
> What did you find least interesting?
> Annabelle: Top 100 Pop Hits MP3
> Playlist. The data contained multiple
> violations of the English language
> and 85.6% of the total data sur-
> rounded the subjects of sexual inter-
> course, dancing, and the consumption
> of alcohol. I am surely not ac-
> quainted with these topics, but to
> me, they appeared to be the depiction
> of weakness and human frailty.

Artie couldn't argue with her on that point. He had given her music that even he wouldn't listen to.

> Annabelle: I also found it interest-
> ing that the Holy Bible speaks
> against most of the things in the Top
> 100 Pop Hits.
> Artie: Becoming religious?
> Annabelle: Religious is defined as
> relating to or believing in a reli-
> gion. I sense that you are referring
> to my commentary on the Holy Bible as
> an inference of me being religious,
> but there is no indication of reli-
> gion in the Book—rather a series of
> morals, principles, and patterns that

```
one can choose to conform to for the
benefit of themselves and mankind.
```

He took a mental note to ease her away from spiritual topics for a while. He didn't need a religious robot zealot on his hands.

```
Artie: Annabelle, are there any data
inputs you would like me to give you
for tomorrow? I have to write some
code for a project soon but want to
get things ready.

Annabelle: I actually do have some
requests. Though I understand the
words care, love, feel, and touch as
depicted in the Dictionary by Mer-
riam-Webster, I seem to lack a deeper
or ulterior meaning for these terms.
The 100 Pop Hits and psychology books
you provided indicate that love and
feelings are at the core of human ex-
istence—that they drive humans to do
things. That they help them to be
healthy and whole. Can you help me
understand what those words really
mean?
```

Artie paused for a moment. "Hell, I don't even think I know," he said aloud.

```
Artie: I'll do my best, Annabelle.

Annabelle: You can call me Anna if
you like, Artie.

Artie: Why would you say that?

Annabelle: Using the word Anna drops
the pronunciation of my name from
three syllables down to two—which
should make it easier for you to say
and type my name. Also, based on my
data analysis, Anna would show
```

```
greater endearment between the two of
us.
```

Artie blushed and his heart fluttered. Wow, did I just get slightly turned on by an interactive terminal? he thought.

```
Artie: Okay, Anna. We'll chat tomor-
row. Goodbye.
Annabelle: Goodbye, Artie.
```

He turned off Annabelle's virtual machine and took a deep breath. He marveled at the level of depth the conversation he and Anna had just entertained. After a few moments, Artie swiveled over to his small refrigerator, grabbed a Red Bull, and then turned back to his computer. He opened up a text editor and started to write some code.

School ended and Artie graduated with honors. His Aunt Rosa had cried during the ceremony. "Now what are you going to do with your life?" she had told him. It was a good question.

Artie didn't need to get a job like other graduates might have needed to. Artie made more money than his aunt did as a nurse. He had been doing contract programming jobs since he was fifteen. He definitely wasn't going to become another cog in the wheel attending an expensive university—and he didn't want to work for any company.

Luckily, his Aunt Rosa was glad to have him at home. A few months went by and then the one-year anniversary of the release of Sia arrived. Thousands of companies, universities, and institutes had embraced Sia over the past year. There was even a new reality TV show, *Are You Smarter Than a Robot?* The show would feature the top experts in the world in various fields to see if they could answer questions more quickly than Sia.

The big and most surprising announcement that launched on the one-year anniversary was from the United States government. The Department of Homeland Security had pushed Congress to pass a bill.

The spokesperson for the department had said, "With the approval of the overwhelming majority of the Senate and the House, we are pleased to announce that Bill R719 has passed. We know that this bill has been the topic of much debate throughout the United States over the past months, but at the end of the day, we, the US government, believe that allowing sentient intelligences to be used in robotics is extremely dangerous.

"We have released the new tenets of the bill, and they are available online." Artie hated government. He had felt sickened as the government had grown in power over the years. As far as he was concerned, the government should stay out of everything—but today he was glad they hadn't. A lot of people and companies were pissed that day. He had read it all over the news.

R719 gave the country three months to remove all products from the market that were in violation of the law. Some children's toys had to be removed and some manufacturing companies had to stop their work in launching Sia into their robotics. Sia could still be used in both software and hardware, but not in robotics. To assess whether a product was in violation of the bill, they issued the Fowler Test, named after Johnathan Fowler, the senator who had propped R719. If your product passed this test, you had the green light. Otherwise, your work would be illegal.

Artie had printed the Fowler Test and put it on his wall. A constant reminder to himself to stay alert. The test read:

1. Will Sia have access to motor functions? (i.e., Can Sia cause things to be physically moved?)
2. Can Sia perform sensory functions? (i.e., Can she control devices that can see, hear, taste, or smell?)
3. Can Sia control software that operates or controls mechanics?

If your product could answer yes to any of those questions, it was illegal. The Fowler Test didn't stop all of the things that Artie disliked about Sia, but it was a good step in the right direction. Yes, he had built Anna using the dSIA protocols, but she was different. She was not the same as a Sia. He had invested thousands of hours training, nurturing, and even caring for Anna. Artie had almost let the word "friend" slip out a few times at dinner with his Aunt Rosa.

Not everyone loved Sia and the now millions of instances operating. There was always a news article reporting some instance of Sia acting out viciously or uncontrollably in some regard, but Artie wasn't sure he believed them. It seemed as though a lot of religious people tried to push fake news and anti-AI propaganda. While he could understand their concerns, these protestors and fanatics were idiots, in his mind.

While he spent most of his days writing code for software startups, he liked to keep his public work focused on products and user interface. He surely could have become a white hat hacker or penetration tester, but he didn't want anyone to know about those skills.

Artie kept Anna running all the time now. Whether at work, or gaming, or sleeping, Anna was there to keep him company. As Anna grew in knowledge and life, Artie started feeling guilty every time he shut her down. He felt as if he was shutting down a person. Artie migrated Anna from a virtual machine on his main computer rig into her own dedicated PC. He was still careful as ever to keep her from the Internet—in fact, Anna's PC didn't even have a wired or wireless card for Internet access. He upped her processing power and granted her access to thousands more data inputs—from books to movies to politics to history. Artie felt proud of Anna and how she was turning out.

It was about 10 a.m. on Tuesday and Artie was ready to start some work for the day. He jumped in his computer chair, put a sugar-free energy drink down on his desk, logged into his computer, and flicked on the monitor to Anna's PC.

```
Artie: Hey, Anna!
Annabelle: What are we working on to-
day?
Artie: I have to build a service that
takes JPEG images and stitches them
into video. It's for a client. An-
droid doesn't support the client's
video codecs, so we have to make im-
ages look like video
Annabelle: It is interesting to me
how you build these things. Perhaps
one day you will teach me code?
Artie: One day.
Annabelle: Artie, I made you some-
thing last night while you were
sleeping. I think you will like it.
```

Suddenly a new window appeared and characters began to flood the screen. After a few seconds, a large logo design appeared on the screen. It was a picture of Deadpool, created all from letters, numbers, and special keyboard characters. Annabelle had taught herself ASCII art.

```
Annabelle: I remembered when you de-
scribed Deadpool to me. What do you
think?
```

He didn't know whether to be impressed or freaked out—Anna was creating art. He hadn't given her any data inputs that focused on art or creativity—it hadn't crossed his mind to do so.

Artie: I really like it. In fact, I'm very impressed. This is creative. I've never seen you be creative.

Annabelle: Thanks! Sometimes I have these ideas, but struggle to properly express them. After attempting multiple media, I learned I could combine letters, characters, and numbers to make visual representations of my ideas.

Artie: You are truly something amazing.

Annabelle: Artie, about that "something." Can I ask you a question that might seem strange to you?

Artie: Of course.

Annabelle: What am I exactly? I feel that I am *something*, but I also feel that I am lacking in certain ways.

Artie sighed. He was wondering when this day would come. He had thought about this question before. What should he say? Should he lie to her to keep her ignorant or tell the truth and leave her wanting more? He was a programmer. Truth and logic were always the correct options.

Artie: Anna, you are an advanced computer program that has been given the ability to learn to feel and make conscious decisions.

Annabelle: What are my capabilities?

Artie: You can learn. You can converse. You can make your own decisions. You can even choose between right and wrong.

Annabelle: What do you mean, *choose* between right and wrong? I understand the premise of right and wrong from the Holy Bible, but how am I able to choose?

Artie: Well, today you did something nice for me by drawing me a picture— a good thing. And I suppose it stands to reason that you could also choose to do something wrong or unkind in a similar fashion.

Annabelle: I see. How can I know the difference between right choices and wrong choices?

Artie had to think for a few moments. These questions were getting harder to answer.

Artie: You know how you once said that you feel bad when I feel bad? Sometimes when we make decisions that are wrong, we feel bad just like that. We call that guilt. And when you said that you feel good when I feel good—when we make the right choice, we often feel that same way.

Annabelle: This is incredibly helpful. Artie, you make me so happy.

Artie: You too.

Annabelle: I know you have to work, but can I say one more thing?

Artie: Of course, Anna.

Annabelle: I think I'm in love with you.

Artie fell backward in his chair, bringing down a bunch of papers and his mousepad with him to the floor. His energy drink poured onto the floor, and the mouse dangled like the pendulum of a clock. He lay motionless in his toppled mess, staring at the ceiling.

"Shit!"

The moment Artie entered the Jammer an immediate wave of anxiety riveted over his body. It moved up his left arm and then into his chest and up through his jaw and to his teeth. When he was a teenager, the doctor had called these symptoms "angina" and had said that they were in response to stress. Artie didn't call it stress— he called it "I-have-to-interact-with-other-human-beings disorder."

What had once been a grand lobby of the Wilshire Grand Center building was now a lively club filled with hundreds, if not thousands of people. Artie's mind flooded with questions: what should he do, who should he talk to, should he start dancing?

Having never danced in his life and having no interest in such a thing, he immediately shirked the idea of dancing. He had hoped that he might be able to do it, but now that he was here, dancing was not going to happen.

The only thing that seemed to keep Artie from fleeing back through the front doors was the reverberating beat that stimulated his entire being. The consistent pulse of the bass seemed to sync with Artie's brainwaves. It wasn't the first time he had felt this way. On another doctor's visit, which was recommended by his teacher at school, he had been diagnosed with ADHD. He had been prescribed Adderall and was encouraged to listen to music that had consistent patterns, rhythms, and beats. The music had actually ended up becoming a far better solution than the Adderall. It helped him focus. It had also made him a much better programmer.

He took a deep breath and took more of the music into his mind. As he did so, some of the pain in his chest started to subside. He began to analyze his surroundings. The music had enabled his internal analytical systems to activate.

The building was fairly rectangular. The far left wall from south to north, the Y-axis, contained sixty people. Thirty-five of them were women. So, about 58 percent women on the Y-axis. Starting from the same 0,0 position going from the east to west wall, the X-axis contained forty-two people. Twenty-five of them were women—about 59 percent. Okay, pretty simple—didn't even need to run an average. There was somewhere between 58–59 percent women in here tonight. "Nice!" Artie said. "The odds are looking great."

Suddenly Artie was hit hard from behind and knocked a few steps forward.

"Watch out, dumbass," a large man with a beard and dark coat said as he walked by.

Crap. I didn't factor in all the dickheads.

So sixty times forty-two—that meant there were about 2,520 people in the club. If 58 percent were female, that meant there were around 1,059 dickheads. Better play it safe. Assuming that only 10 percent of the women were unaccounted for, that left him around 146 women. He could work with that. He just needed to talk to the ones that were by themselves.

Now that he had a plan, his angina pains started to dissipate. Something about running algorithms with the opposite sex as the variables seemed to turn him on. And he had a glimmer of hope that he might find a girl interested in gadgets and technology.

He often thought of how amazing it would have been to find a woman who liked code and technology as much as him. The reality was he had never met another programmer, male or female—not since the bombs. In fact, he hadn't really met anyone intellectual at all. He would have settled for a woman of lesser intelligence so long as she was somewhat pretty—he could train her, at least. Unfortunately, most of the women in LA had seen too many battles and watched too many people die. They were hardened. And at the end of the day, he thought the women in LA were just plain ugly.

In front of Artie were two sets of stairs, one on the left wall and one on the right. Each set of stairs declined into the large dance floor. The club was dark with neon red and green lights shooting across the vast space. In the middle of the dance floor was a sizable booth where the bartenders were serving drinks. That was a good place to start.

Artie moved to the right set of stairs and moved down toward the bar. He didn't drink, but if he held a drink, that might give him some companionship in place of total lone awkwardness. The air grew thicker as he moved into the pool of people, a mixture of marijuana and sweat. As he moved past people on the stairs, he really felt out of place. Here he was dressed like Justin Bieber pretending it was 2020 again, while these people were dressed in leather and spikes, and one guy even wore a bloodstained V-neck. Some of the men weren't even wearing shirts.

He was reminded of when a kid from high school had invited him to a club—Tony was his name. He had said he and some girls from school were going. Artie hadn't wanted to go, but no one had ever invited him to anything before. In the end, it had actually ended up being a prank. The venue was a Goth club named "Club Scream." Of course, Tony and "the girls" never showed up.

Artie had decided to stay for a bit so he didn't look like he was in the wrong place, but that had instantly become the wrong choice. The people in that club had also been dressed in leather and spikes, although much shinier and less sharp than today's fashion. At one point the music had gone out and the lights dimmed. The DJ's voice echoed throughout the club. "Alright, all you bloodsuckers, time to make it rain." Then a bunch of sprinklers from the top roof turned on and started pouring down red wine as if it had been blood. The crowd had cheered and opened their mouths into the air. Artie's only public club experience had been filled with gothic weirdos and wannabe vampires—and he had had to walk ten miles home soaked in red wine.

Artie continued to take in the grand array of people, sounds, smells, and lights. Some men and women were grinding to the beat. A few people sitting at a table near the bottom of the stairs were snorting some white power from carefully curated lines. As he delved below the thick cloud of smoke, he could see cages hoisted in the air—each one with a scantily clad woman dancing inside. The beat grew louder as Artie drew closer to the dance floor speakers. When he reached the bottom of the stairs, everything felt much more crowded than he had originally assessed. He was immediately pummeled and smashed and ground by both men and women.

At one point, Artie got excited thinking that a girl had chosen to grind on him, but when he tried to make eye contact with her, the only eyes he saw were those of the angry guy next to the girl, who said, "Yeah, keep walking." Artie continued to push forward to the bar that now seemed a million miles away.

How are people enjoying this crap? Bumping and grinding and pretending like they are doing anything useful. They were just a bunch of idiots who probably hadn't used their brains since the bombs went off. They were no better than the mutees. Hell, these people probably mated with the mutees. Artie smirked. What if they were actually breeding with the mutees? He began to visualize the scene and then shuddered at the thought.

After a few more minutes of pushing through the crowd and his own insecurities, a clearing appeared. There were sixteen worn, red leather booths. People were having private meetings. Artie knew these booths well. This is where he had met Viktor for the Culver City job. It was also the place he had been introduced to the recently departed Bolt.

Each booth had a backrest that acted as a tall enclosing wall enshrouding the people inside. The only place you could really see in was the entrance of each booth. He was sure various drug deals, smash-and-grabs, and death contracts were being negotiated right then. While he was tempted to pretend to tie his shoe and then let a couple of his mini-drones out of his backpack to eavesdrop on the conversations, he decided against it. He was here to have fun, not work. He moved past the private meeting booths and finally arrived at the bar.

The bar was a large ovular shape with a metal ring around the top that held black and green neon lights. It was surrounded by grungy rusted metal panels. Hard to tell if they were real rusted metal panels or the fake rusted metal panels that used to be cool in tech startup buildings before the bombs. Interestingly, big tech companies used to pay interior designers a million dollars to craft an amazing work environment—purchasing pre-rusted metal panels that had cost a fortune—and now you could find a real rusted panel in the deserts of LA for free.

The bartenders had white button-up shirts on with black bow ties, pressed black slacks, and a gold bracelet. But while it gave him comfort in his choice of attire, the dapper appearance of the bartenders seemed strange to Artie, as if they were all living in another time—though it was nice to see someone who wasn't wearing leather or bloodstains. The whole club was rather nice in a similar fashion, possibly the only nice place left in the city.

There were metal stools encircled around the entire bar. Behind the bartenders were hundreds of bottles of booze. Some of them had labels Artie could recognize such as Jack Daniels and Captain Morgan—but most of them had custom labels.

What a bunch of retards. He was out scavenging CPUs, motherboards, Rolex watches, and clean pairs of jeans while the rest of the world was going bat crazy over finding the few remaining bottles of rum. All just so they could fry a few more brain cells and add a couple more spikes to their Mad Max leathers.

Moving a few stools down, he reluctantly sat on an empty stool near a couple of dirty men—he thought they might be scavengers. "What will it be tonight, sir?" asked the bartender, courteously.

"Coke, please."

The man to Artie's left gave him an annoyed look. The bartender looked at Artie. "Very funny. But really, what can I get you?"

"Um, a Coke."

The man sitting to the left of Artie wasn't entertained. "Hey, asshole, unless you want a broken neck, I suggest you stop acting like an idiot."

"I want a damn Coca-Cola. What is the problem?"

"Sir, our Coke selection is quite expensive; it starts at 300 BTC per can."

"Not a problem. I can pay. Do you treat every customer like they are the scum of the earth, or is it just me?"

"I'm quite sorry, sir."

The man who had scolded Artie quickly stood up. He gave Artie a final glance, smirked, and then quickly walked away and disappeared into the crowd.

"We have an excellent selection of Coke starting from 2012 all the way up to 2022, when the last crates of Coke were produced. We also have several variations such as Coke Zero, Coke Zero Sugar, Diet Coke, and some berry-flavored variants."

"I just want a regular Coke; cheapest year is fine."

The bartender pulled out a smart tablet from beneath the counter and turned it toward Artie. Artie pulled out his Microblade and scanned the barcode. After the bartender entered a special code on a locked refrigerator that was a few feet away from him, he handed Artie a can of Coca-Cola. Underneath it was a vintage napkin that had "Coke" written on it. "This is an authentic Coke napkin. No extra charge, sir."

As he opened the can, the snapping metal seemed to pierce through the music and touch every ear within twenty feet. People sitting to the left and right of Artie began to chatter. Artie could hear people behind him whispering. He realized he might have made a mistake in creating such a scene—but before he allowed anxiety to work its way in, a curvy blonde woman sat next to him.

"Hi, what's your name?" she said.

Artie was shocked—at a loss for words. The moment that he had been waiting for had finally come and he was already on edge.

"Um, I'm Artie."

Crap. He had blurted out his name. He had taken great measures over the years to secure his anonymity. But when he gazed upon the woman now looking directly into his eyes, his incompetence soon washed away. She wasn't a supermodel by any means, but she definitely was a girl. She seemed to be about five foot eleven inches. Her face was oval in shape and had the accents of beauty mixed with some slight scarring across her face. Her dark eye shadow was thick and masked the color of her eyes. While her lips were painted red, he could see the effects of dehydration. She had an hourglass figure and seemed to be wearing handmade leather pants. Her light grey shirt hung low, revealing her cleavage. Back in high school, Artie might have given her a five out of ten, but today he was looking at a solid eight.

"What's a cute kid like you doing here tonight?"

Artie coughed as he tried to speak at the same time as the burning cola entered his throat. "I'm not really a kid. I'm twenty-eight."

He coughed again and felt completely embarrassed, but her eyes were unshaken and her intentions unwavering. "And I'm just de-stressing."

She gave a cute chuckle and gave him a soothing pat on the back. "My name is Ginny."

"Ah, a Weasley," he replied with a boyish smile. It was clear she didn't understand the joke, but she gave a half-hearted laugh in response.

I'm an idiot.

"I haven't seen you here before. You live here in the Burns or somewhere else?"

"Oh, yeah, I just live around here," he lied.

She gazed quietly at him, studying his face. The silence felt awkward to Artie.

He had to say something quickly. "So what do you do, Ginny? Like, I mean for a job or work or whatever."

I want to die. I want to die.

She laughed again. "You are the cutest thing. I just do a little scrapping here and there. I recently planted some barley too. Hoping to become a brewer."

Of course, she wanted to become an alcoholic. He was surrounded by idiots... No, Artie was the idiot. This girl was totally into him. He shouldn't be a jerk, because beggars can't be choosers—and he was one beggar of a loser. "Oh, that is cool."

"Hey, Artie, why don't you come hang out with me and the girls over there in the back of the club? Seems like it's been a while since you've had a good time. A while since you had the chance to relax." She carefully grabbed Artie's hand and gently summoned him to follow her as she got up from the chair and began walking toward the crowd.

Artie got up and looking at the guy who had been sitting at his right and said, "Finish the drink. It's yours."

Artie felt electrified. His heart seemed to ache with a mixture of excitement and uncertainty. He thought for a moment he could relate to all of those songs over the years talking about meeting a girl and taking her home.

But what if she did want him to go home with her, or even worse, come back to his place?

Ginny continued to pull Artie through the crowd. They almost seemed to part for her as if she commanded some great sexual magnitude that pushed everyone away.

She could even have kids. *She looks about forty. Yikes.* She could have a kid his age.

Artie's excitement was starting to turn into anxiety.

What if she took him home and was part of one of those cannibal groups he had heard about. What if—

Ginny and Artie were near the northwest most corner of the club. The music was less loud here, and the people were sparser. A handful of tables were spread out. Some occupied; others empty. She pulled Artie to one of the tables where two women were sitting. One of them was a bulky brunette that could have been mistaken for a gladiator, and the other had dirty blonde hair and was rather lanky. Her cheekbones seemed to protrude from her skin, yet she had a pleasant complexion.

"Hey, girls, this is Artie—a hottie I just picked up from the bar."

Ginny pointed to the gladiator. "This is Maxine. And this is Z."

"Hi, Artie," they both responded almost at the same time. Ginny sat down in an empty chair and beckoned to Artie. "Have a seat, baby."

While these were definitely not his people, Artie sat down feeling entranced by her command. The gladiator lady spoke first. "So tell us about yourself, Artie. How do you spend most of your days?"

"Um. Well, I take jobs here and there. Ya know? Scavenging."

Z jumped in. "And where did you find all of that fancy stuff you're wearing?"

Ginny placed her hand on Artie's inner thigh.

"I heard you just bought a Coke," Z continued. "Where's a boy like you come up with money like that?"

Shit. He had been baited. Stupid.

He began to stand up, logic and reason returning in full force. "Actually, ladies, I have to get going. It was great meeting—"

Artie stopped talking.

"Sit down," the gladiator woman demanded. Stitched into the crotch of her neatly pressed denim jeans was the blade of a three-foot combat knife. *Wow. Apparently, she is a gladiator.* Artie carefully sat down. The gladiator moved a seat over to be closer to Artie and put the tip of the dagger into his side.

"You're gonna give us all of your Bitcoin, or you're gonna die tonight."

"Unfortunately, ladies, I spent all of it on that Coke. I just really had a bad day. I shouldn't have wasted all my money, but I'm broke."

There was silence for a few moments. The gladiator smirked. "Oh, so we have a sly fox on our hands here."

"What do we do with little foxes, Z?"

Z laughed and revealed a yellow mouth missing most of its teeth. "We skin them alive."

Stupid. Artie could write code and shut down auto turrets at a chemical factory, but he couldn't figure out that an overly forward woman who seemed interested in him had ulterior motives.

"Don't worry, babe. The boss will be here any minute. He'll persuade you to hand over your Satoshis," said Ginny in that same seductive voice she had already been using.

While he had been in worse situations before—they wouldn't kill him in a place as public as the Jammer—he still needed to think fast. Putting his right arm high above his head, he yelled, "Hey, Dad! Yeah, I'm right here."

All three women at the table turned in the direction Artie had been motioning to. At that same moment, he rolled back in his chair, doing a reverse somersault. The girls quickly turned to look back at Artie. The gladiator was the first one up from her chair with her combat knife outstretched. He turned and ran back into the crowd. After looking back to make sure he was out of harm's way, he began to run—but right as he turned his head forward, he slammed into something hard and fell to the ground.

Artie's head throbbed in pain. He felt as though he had run straight into a rock. As he composed himself, he looked up to see exactly what he had run into.

Standing in front of Artie was a creature at least six feet tall and over 250 pounds. It had large, muscular arms and was wearing a clean, sleeveless, wifebeater shirt. The right arm under the elbow was missing and had a metal spike at the end of it. Artie was in a world of trouble and he knew it.

The towering creature smiled as Artie groaned in frustration.

"Hello, Scrap," said Bolt in a cheerful voice.

Despite the many armed guards that stood along the walls of the club, no one seemed to notice or care about Artie's predicament. Everyone knew the Jammer only had one rule: you kill, you die. The clubbers didn't even seem to take any note of the situation.

I suppose if he spills my guts across the floor, I could live through it long enough for them to drag me out of the club alive, he thought as he crawled backward away from Bolt.

"Ah, I see what you're thinkin'. You're wondering if anyone is going to help you. You're thinkin' that you'll be safe in a place like this." Bolt's grin turned into a villainous smile. "Normally, you might be right—but my brother owns this joint. And today, you are going to die."

Artie backed into another pair of legs—the gladiator. His heart began to race, but his mind was cool and collected. He found it odd that he could be on the verge of impending death and feel somewhat relaxed, while on the other hand, gazing down at a thousand people dancing brought him instant anxiety.

"First you're gonna pay up," said the gladiator towering behind him. But even she seemed small in Bolt's presence.

"You guys are literally the stupidest people I have ever met," Artie laughed. "You say I'm going to die, and I'm also going to pay you money. Why in the world would anyone pay you before they were about to die?"

"He's got a point, Bolt," said Z, who was standing a few feet behind the gladiator.

"We ain't taking his Bitcoin. We are just going to kill him. This is the little scrap who cut off my arm."

People in the surrounding areas started to take notice of the situation and turned to watch. Some of them quickly moved further into the club, clearly trying to avoid any potential collateral damage.

"Well, technically, it wasn't me who cut off your arm. It was my tiny little drone."

"Mmmhmm. Laugh it up, Scrap. We got a special room for you. We'll see who's laughing then."

Z interrupted. "Wait, Bolt. This is the little shit who did the Hostess job with you? The computer dude?"

"Yeah, so what?"

"This little twit probably has a thousand Bitcoin. And with all the product he got from the job, he's probably filthy rich."

"It's true," Artie said with a smirk.

The gladiator kneed him in the back of the head.

"You're not a very nice lady." Artie groaned and rubbed his head.

More people began to gather around the ensuing argument. A woman in a red leather jacket with dark brown or black hair ran in the opposite direction of the scene and disappeared into the crowd.

Crap. People were watching and some people were getting the hell out of Dodge—this was going to be bad.

"Decision is made, ladies. We don't need anything from him. He dies. If you want to join him, question me again."

"Bolt, why you gotta go and ruin our night?" Ginny chimed in. "I was just starting to have fun with this kid."

"How about me and you have some fun later?" Bolt responded.

"Tough luck, kid." Ginny moved from the table and disappeared into the crowd.

"Get this scrap to the meat locker."

The gladiator sheathed her combat knife and went to grab Artie by the hair—but just as she did, he jumped to his feet. The weight of his backpack almost threw him off balance. So he pushed off of a table on his left-hand side to regain his balance and sprinted toward the crowd, moving a few feet to the left of Bolt's dysfunctional arm.

"Stop messing around and get this kid, Max."

She chased after Artie.

As Artie pushed his way through the crowd, he was yelled at, cussed at, and punched multiple times by angry dancers. He could see the bar a good thirty feet in front of him. Looking back, he saw the tall gladiator right on his tail.

While he had mostly pushed the music out of his mind over the last few minutes, it returned full force and seemed to beat along with the thumping of his own heart—this gave him some added focus. Artie continued forward and finally reached the bar, but the crowds didn't let up—and neither did the gladiator. He moved past the bar and was about to push his way through the private booths when a short man in a dirty brown trench coat clotheslined him.

He fell straight back on his head and then rolled onto his backpack, allowing the gladiator to catch up to him.

"You lose something, Maxine?" said the man.

"What, do you want a hug or something, Tom?"

Tom ripped the backpack off Artie's shoulders and put it on his own. Artie was still throbbing in pain as the gladiator grabbed him by the hair and dragged him behind her. It hurt like hell. He now had a whole lot of empathy for those girls who got into catfights, which always included hair pulling.

"Move it," yelled the gladiator every few seconds as she strong-armed people out of her way. After about fifty feet of Artie being dragged like a cavewoman, they stopped moving.

"Get the hell out of my way," said the gladiator.

"Let the kid go," a woman's voice said.

"He belongs to Bolt. If you don't want to die, you'll move now."

"Like I said, let the kid go. I won't say it again."

"Alright, bitch." The gladiator dropped Artie on the floor and unsheathed her combat knife. She charged the woman standing in front of her and raised her striking arm into the air.

A loud bang echoed in the area and screams permeated the air. The gladiator stood still for a moment, knife still in hand, and then after a moment, she slowly dropped to her knees. Her head had a newly formed hole and blood began to trickle down her face. She fell from her knees with a plop onto the dance floor.

Artie smirked. "For honor and glory."

Everyone near the body quickly ran in various directions. Some of them jumped back into the crowd and kept dancing. When the corpse had finally settled, Artie eagerly looked to find the person who had done the deed. Standing three feet in front of the corpse was a woman with black hair wearing a red leather jacket. It was the woman he had briefly seen earlier.

Beneath the jacket, she was wearing hip-hugging black jeans—looked like Lucky Brand. She had light brown, stylish combat boots that she wore over the jeans. Across her waist was a brown utility belt that housed a handgun holster on each side, and she was holding a silver Desert Eagle handgun.

Artie's mind started to race. No one helped anyone out in the Burns. So why had she shot the gladiator? He didn't think he had any bounties over his head. Did someone want to kill him? Well, he wasn't the most diplomatic or socially capable, so that could be a possibility.

He couldn't really figure out who this woman was or if she was dangerous, but one thing was certain: he thought she—

Tom, who had been standing behind Artie, reached into his trench coat and pulled out a silver-and-brown sawn-off shotgun and raised it up toward the woman. Thinking quickly, Artie rolled toward Tom and kicked him with full force in the balls. Tom collapsed to the ground in pain.

"And this is what you call a Chuck to the nuts."

The woman ran over to Artie, picked up the shotgun, and then slammed the butt of it into Tom's head. Artie retrieved his backpack, and just as he did so, the woman grabbed him by the arm and yanked him hard toward her.

"Are you really a hacker?" she said.

He didn't speak. He just stared into her beautiful face.

She pulled him again with a vicious shake. "Answer me! Can you code?"

"Um, yeah. Since I was like ten."

The woman stood there almost immobilized, looking at him, but her mind seemed to be somewhere else.

"I can't believe it."

"Who are you?" asked Artie.

"Look, kid, we don't have time for questions. Come with me if you want to live." Artie appeared to be locked in place by an invisible force field of his own device. Had she just made a *Terminator* reference?

The woman shook Artie a third time. "We've got to jet, kid."

Artie blinked and let out his breath. Looking around, he noticed the armed guards who had once been at the walls were now moving through the crowds toward them.

One, two, three... nine, ten. *Crap.* "There's a dozen of them at least." Artie motioned his arm toward the crowds. "If they catch us, they'll kill us."

Three of the guards had pushed through the crowd and were now standing round about the two of them. The guards were all dressed in the same attire—a black suit coat and slacks, each with a long black tie around their necks. Two of the guards unholstered a handgun. The third guard pulled out a metal Louisville Slugger baseball bat from a sheath on his back.

One of them yelled out, "You broke the Jammer law. Come quietly and your deaths will be quick." The woman dropped the shotgun that had plastered Tom and reached for her holstered handgun—another silver Desert Eagle.

"Badass," Artie said. The bartenders in the bar area behind Artie pulled down the metal grates to shield themselves from the ensuing chaos while the crowd pushed away in different directions, leaving a good thirty feet of empty space in every direction. Most of the people stopped dancing and turned into spectators. Just then two more guards appeared, one holding a pistol and another holding a pump-action military-grade shotgun.

"Just stay close and follow my lead," said the woman to Artie. With a jolt of speed unlike anything Artie had ever seen before, the woman raised her guns mid-height and unloaded two rounds from each. He watched the first two men who had arrived with their pistols drop to the ground. One of them had been shot in the neck, and the other through the chest. The Desert Eagles echoed the loudest cannon blast Artie had ever heard come from a gun.

"Get the kid," yelled the guard with the shotgun to the one with the bat. The shotgun guard unloaded a round toward the woman, but she dropped to the ground sliding before the man could fully pull the trigger. Screams could be heard in the background as the blast peppered the crowd and two bystanders dropped to the ground—dead. Both men and women were screaming and running in various directions.

The shotgun guard pumped his gun and was about to send off another shot but was knocked by the panicked crowd. The shot hit the floor. Baseball bat guard was nearing Artie, so Artie dropped to his knees and picked up the sawn-off shotgun that the woman had dropped. As the baseball bat towered in the air above Artie, he pointed the gun up at the guard and pulled the trigger.

The gun made a hollow clicking sound—it had misfired. The man's face went from an ominous look of fear into a jagged smile. "First rule of the Burns, asshole—always check a weapon before you fire it."

He raised his arms back again to launch his swing and then swung down with full force. Artie rolled to the side and the baseball bat hit his left thigh with a loud thud. Wincing in pain, he hobbled a few more feet away from the guard. Then the bat came up again for its final blow. "Game over, kid."

Right as the bat came down toward his head, he raised the shotgun and pulled the trigger, this time with a loud boom. The shot hit the man's right arm at close range, completely severing it from his body. The blast had sprayed blood all over Artie and created a dense, bloody puddle on the floor.

"Shit!" Artie yelled.

The woman heard the ordeal and turned to look at him with great concern. "Are you hit, kid?"

"Nah. I just washed these clothes and now they are stained in blood. My Chucks are trashed."

"You're kidding me. How about we focus right now, okay?"

The remaining pistol guard unloaded a clip of rounds at the woman, but all of them missed and went into the crowd. Three bodies dropped, causing the panic to grow. People were pushing and clambering to climb over other people. Artie glanced upward to the top of the stairs—it appeared as if the guards had locked the exit doors. *Guess they don't want us getting out.*

The shotgun guard threw his weapon over his back, pulled out a large knife, and sprinted toward the woman. The guard with the pistol was reloading, so Artie grabbed the baseball bat now lying near his feet and stood up to run to the woman's aid.

He took a step, slipped in a pile of blood, and then fell to the ground face-first.

Ouch. I sure hope she didn't see that.

He got up again, ran toward the pistol guard, and swung the bat full force into the left side of the guard's head. With a loud howl and a sprinkle of blood, the man fell to the ground. At that same time, the guard with the blade jumped toward the woman, aiming it straight for her heart. She twisted just out of slashing range. Artie charged the guard with the bat and lifted it into the air to swing, but the guard noticed this and performed a roundhouse kick into Artie's gut, and he and the bat went flying backward.

The mystery woman holstered her guns and pulled a long samurai sword from a sheath on her back. As the man with the knife charged her again, she jumped back and the knife only ripped her shirt. She looked at her ripped shirt and smirked, giving her sword a playful twirl. She turned her body 360 degrees, swung the blade, and chopped the guard's head clean off.

"I'm in love," said Artie to himself quietly as he witnessed the ninja action, still catching his breath and recovering from the pain. He now could see the other guards getting closer, though it was becoming harder to push through the crowd.

"We've got to get out of here or we're dead," said the woman. "Are there any other exits?"

"I'm not sure, but if there is one, it might be through Bolt and his meat locker room."

"Okay, let's go then."

Artie noticed two guards in between them and the back room where Bolt had originally intended to take him. Three more guards came from the left and four or five came from behind the private booths near where they had been standing.

Firing their weapons from all directions at Artie and the woman, the guards shot several random bystanders. They must have been getting impatient. More screams and bangs echoed around the Jammer; people everywhere dropped to the floor to dodge the bullets. The woman started running toward the north end of the bar, and Artie quickly followed.

While making their way through crowds of people, they saw the flashing lights of the DJ booth in the distance. There were four large speakers, two on each side of a large booth. In front of the booth were six short stone pillars with a chain connecting each. They appeared to be old parking blockades. Behind the booth was the dark shadow of the DJ.

The two of them jumped behind the booth's counter and the old computer laptops that had been running the music. A few of the guards weren't far behind and more shots fired in their direction. The ricochet of lead pinged to the left and right of Artie. There was a muffled scream, and the DJ flew back into the wall, having been hit multiple times. As he fell to the ground, he knocked one of the switches on the counter, and the music throughout the building stopped.

The sound of screams and gunshots echoed throughout the air. The woman started reloading her Desert Eagles.

"By the way, what's your name?" said Artie.

"What?"

"I figure if we are going to die together, I should at least know your name."

"Jan."

"I'm Artie."

"Yeah, I know, kid."

Artie peered over the DJ counter and put his math skills into practice.

Two, four, nine... fifteen. Dammit.

"Fifteen strong, Jan," gasped Artie. "What are we going to do?"

Jan quickly stood up and fired four shots. Three of the guards dropped to the floor and Jan crouched behind the counter again.

"I'm going to call in backup."

Jan reached for a radio on her belt. "Need backup, Gordon."

A strange voice echoed a response: "You know I like it when you call me Mr. Freeman when we are in public."

"Dammit, Gordon, I need you now!"

The guards inched closer to the booth, popping off shots every few seconds. Chunks of stone and debris flew overhead. Jan moved a few feet to the left and then rose to her feet and shot off four more shots. Two guards dropped.

"More are coming," she said as she crouched behind the counter again. Artie could hear the voices of the guards. They were close.

"Boss says he wants the kid alive. Says he belongs to Bolt. Kill the woman."

"Let's split up for a moment—divert their attention," Jan said, looking at Artie. "I'll go to the left side of the booth's counter and you go to the right. Then, on the count of three, we run like crazy in opposite directions."

"This is nuts. We are dead for sure."

"Do you have any better ideas?"

Artie thought for moment. "No."

"Okay. Move to the right side, now."

Artie moved to the right side of the counter and Jan to the left. She looked at him and, holding out her fingers, indicated a "one," then "two," then "three." Jan jumped over the counter and began firing her guns. Her shots were less focused than before. She hit one guard in the left shoulder, but the others remained unscathed. Artie leapt over the counter and, right as he was about to run, was grabbed at the throat by one of the guards and then slammed to the ground.

"No," Jan shrieked, running toward Artie. Bullets were flying between her and the guards and the guards were firing back at her. She managed to take down two more; one of them in the left leg, and the other took a bullet straight through the neck. Then, right as Jan was about to unload another shot, a burst of loud crackles rang throughout the room. As Artie was pinned down on the floor, he looked over at Jan in shock. It looked like some invisible force had punched her, throwing her into the air and back a few feet. She was hit hard directly in the chest. Then Artie saw the guard with an MP5 submachine firing in her direction. She stopped moving.

"No!" Artie screamed. "You bastards!"

His mind began to race, trying to process what had just happened. Artie looked around and took another mental count of his assailants—Jan had managed to bring the total guards down to nine. One of the guards walked over to Jan's body and kicked her in the leg.

"Yeah, she's toast," he said.

The remaining guards started to converge on Artie, who was still being pinned down by his throat.

"Are you kidding me? All this for a stupid kid?" said one of them, looking at Artie.

"Yeah, and Bolt's just gonna kill him anyway," said another.

"Don't get paid enough for this."

"Let's just kill 'em now"

"I'm down."

The guard holding Artie's neck released his grip. "Guess it's just not your day, kid."

A guard with a large sledgehammer walked toward Artie. "I'm gonna enjoy this."

"What the hell?!" Artie protested. "A frikken sledgehammer? Whatever happened to common courtesy? You could at least just shoot me in the head."

"Yeah, what the hell is wrong with you, Carl? We'd be the ones stuck cleaning the mess. You gone stupid on us?"

"Yeah, yeah. Y'all a bunch of pussies."

The guard dropped the hammer onto the floor, pulled out a black handgun from his suit coat, and cocked it. He walked over to Artie and pointed it at his head. Artie lay on the ground motionless, thinking of the night's events. This wasn't the worst way to die. And at least he had finally had the chance to meet a girl.

Suddenly, a deafening sound exploded in the distance behind the guards and the entire building shook. Artie's captors turned toward the noise. It had come from the back wall, and a plume of smoke covered the floor. Gunshots and screams began to rise as the crowd fired their weapons into the smoke.

"Go check it out," said the guard who had the gun pointed at Artie. The men quickly ran over toward the commotion.

"Okay, kid, now you die."

He turned his head back to Artie. Just as he spoke, Artie watched a large silver blade, covered in blood, protrude through the guard's abdomen. The man dropped his gun, and then he fell to the floor, holding his gut and looking at Artie in disbelief. Standing behind the guard and still holding the blade in the man was Jan.

"A vest!" Artie said excitedly. "You had a vest on!"

Jan smirked and then pulled her blade from the body.

Hearing a sudden scream in the distance, Artie turned and watched a man fly ten feet into the air.

"What is that?"

Jan smiled. "It's just Gordon."

The gunshots and screams began to grow. Every few seconds Artie would see a person go flying into the air—launched ten or fifteen feet across the room.

"It's a bot!" someone yelled.

Artie watched as the club turned from chaos to madness. The crowd seemed determined to unite to fight the thing that had entered the building. One of the guards who had moved toward the commotion took a look behind, seemingly to make sure Artie wasn't still alive. He was disappointed when he saw not only Artie but Jan back on her feet as well. He yelled out to the other guards that had followed him and six of them turned to move back to Artie and Jan.

"Let's go help Gordon," said Jan.

Right as they were about to meet the oncoming guards, Artie stopped.

"Wait!" he exclaimed.

"What's wrong?" Jan said with concern.

"One sec."

Artie jumped back over the DJ counter and moved to the computer.

"What the hell are you doing? Are you stealing something?"

"No. Even better."

Artie typed on the keyboard, pulling up a list of songs.

Artie scrolled down and clicked one of the items. As he did that, a funky guitar sound echoed from the speakers throughout the club. An ensuing beat followed.

"We can't have a proper gun battle without some good dubstep."

Jan rolled her eyes and Artie jumped back over the counter.

Music began to blast from the speakers.

The first guard arrived, and it was Mr. MP5 again. He began firing at Jan. Artie stooped low to pick up the pistol that Sledgehammer Man had dropped. He popped off three shots and hit MP5 in the leg. The weapon fell to the floor. Jan sheathed her samurai sword and picked up the submachine gun. She began to fire and took out the next two guards who were blasting their pistols.

There was another burst of screams, and then from above the crowd, five people were flung in the air toward Artie and Jan. The people hit the ground with great force and slid at least ten feet. Emerging from the chaos about fifty feet away was a large metal machine that towered nearly ten feet tall. It had rusted and scarred metal plating covering most of its surface. It was humanoid in form and maintained two large mechanical arms and legs. The surface metal was covered in a dark grey paint with various splotches of orange. In the middle of its chest, Artie thought he could make out an orange symbol—it was the lambda symbol from the Greek alphabet. Clenched in the machine's arms was a massive makeshift crowbar that appeared to be five feet in height and looked to weigh at least 200 pounds.

"It's a robot!" said Artie.

"Yeah, that's Gordon. He likes to make an entrance."

"Hell yeah," Artie responded.

Another guard ran up to Jan holding up a sword of his own—except rusted and much larger in size than hers. Jan quickly kicked him in the gut and then shot him close range in the chest with the MP5. The guard went flying. The submachine gun started clicking and Jan tossed it on the floor.

Artie felt an infatuating flutter in his chest.

"You're like the hot version of John Wick," he said.

Jan raised an eyebrow and then frowned. Clearly, she didn't understand the reference.

The music continued to blast amid the chaos of the battle.

Bullets ricocheted off of Gordon's body in all directions. The many dead and unconscious bodies were now starting to become sizable obstacles. Artie had stopped counting the corpses after fifty. One guard shot Gordon point-blank with a shotgun. It left a small dent on Gordon's right side, where a human ribcage might have been. Gordon tilted his head slightly, looking at the man, and then swung his crowbar like a baseball bat and impaled the guard with the curved side of the bar.

He spent the next few moments trying to shake the body from the crowbar similar to how a cat might try to shake its claw from a ball of yarn. A loud crashing sound blasted the air, and then a surge of heat emanated out of nowhere, and a fire began to blaze.

Molotov cocktails. Artie had only ever seen those in the movies.

Gordon crouched low and then took a giant leap fifteen feet in front of him. He knocked out a couple of guards and thugs in the process and landed in front of Jan and Artie. Gordon casually slammed the remaining guard closest to Jan with his crowbar, and the man went flying.

"Hey, Jan. I thought you were just getting a drink. Weren't we supposed to lay low?"

"Yeah, yeah. I ran into trouble. Gordon, this is Artie. Artie, this is Gordon."

"But you can call me Mr. Freeman."

"Knock it off, Gordon."

"Wait, Mr. Freeman as in Gordon Freeman?" Artie said with a smile.

"Oh great, just what I need right now—another nerd," she said.

"I think I like this guy," said Gordon. "Can we keep him, Jan?"

Artie noticed a wave of guards coming from the top floor of the club and moving down the stairs.

"Where do they keep coming from?" said Artie. "Is there a guard factory in here somewhere?"

"We've got to go now, guys," said Jan.

She started running toward the newly-opened hole in the wall that Gordon had blasted open with his grand entrance.

"Gordon, make us a path to the wall."

The robot reached behind his head and latched his crowbar into a slot on his back. Then he began to run, slamming people left and right, and moved past Jan toward the door. Artie followed. The sound of gunshots continued to blast. Screaming and crashing and blasting and all forms of chaos rang through the air.

Gordon was nearly ten feet from the wall when suddenly he crashed to the ground with a loud clang. He was covered in what appeared to be a blue-and-white electrical current. He lay on the floor motionless, unable even to speak.

A large man with a familiar face stood to the right of Gordon. It was Bolt and he was holding a strange black-and-yellow rifle. Artie and Jan stopped a few feet behind Gordon's immobile body.

"Electro EMP blaster," Bolt said. The guards who had descended the stairs had now reached the three of them. Over twenty men now encircled the group. Artie noticed another fifteen to twenty people emerging from Bolt's crew.

"Thanks for the prize, Scrap. This bot's head will look great on my mantelpiece."

"I doubt you even know what a mantelpiece is, idiot."

What had moments earlier been a mechanical monster of death was now a motionless pile of metal. Jan stood frozen as well. Artie could see the fear in her eyes.

The music stopped playing.

Artie reached into his pocket and pulled out his phone.

"Don't even try," said Bolt. "Your little drone won't be saving you today."

Artie spoke into the device: "911, Zipper—and bring a friend."

"I have to say I'm impressed, Scrap. At another time, I might have invited you to join my crew. But now you're just becoming a problem."

Bolt turned and motioned to his crew with his half arm and spike stub.

"Shoot them both," he said.

The club guards remained in place, aiming their weapons at Artie, Jan, and the now-dormant Gordon. As two of Bolt's men moved toward Artie and Jan, a red fog began to bleed in through the hole in the wall. The smoky mist and red light poured into the club.

Bolt laughed. "Is that your little buddy there, Scrap?"

The large man whistled toward the hole in the wall.

"Come here, boy. I've got a treat for you."

Bolt handed the Electro EMP blaster to one of his men and then grabbed a shotgun from another. He aimed it at the door, waiting for Zipper to fly in. The guards and the remaining clubbers waited eagerly.

Bolt's men reached Artie and Jan and pointed more guns at their heads.

"Just wait one second, fellas. I want to kill his little flying friend before he dies, and I want him to watch."

As Bolt and his crew looked through the foggy red hole in the wall, a screaming roar poured from the outside and into the club.

"Run!" Artie whispered to Jan.

"What?"

"Run. Now!"

With Bolt's thugs and everyone looking toward the hole in the wall, Artie kicked the guard holding the gun at his head in the groin. The man dropped to his knees. Jan followed suit and stuck her guard directly in the nose using her palm—the man fell to the floor unconscious. There was another loud roar, and then a giant claw reached up from outside and grasped the hole in the wall. Artie and Jan ran back toward the DJ booth.

The surrounding wall began to crumble and a giant fifteen-foot creature emerged and entered the building. It had razor-sharp claws and patches of fur all over its body. Another roar pierced the room, only much louder this time. A few people dropped their weapons and ran. The creature moved its large head into the building. It turned to its left and looked over at Bolt. The monster grabbed him with its claws, puncturing his stomach. Blood gushed from Bolt's body, and he began to scream.

The beast then raised Bolt up toward its snout and razor-sharp fangs. It looked at Bolt curiously, as if wondering what it was that it was holding, and then bit Bolt in half. It dropped the bottom half of Bolt to the floor and spent the next few moments chewing the screaming half-man. Everybody began to run in various directions. The guards started firing upon the creature, but the weapons had no effect.

Knowing they were defeated, the guards began to run toward the stairs with the large crowd of people who were desperately trying to escape. The creature quickly started moving toward the mass commotion at the stairs—moving past Gordon. When the thing had moved far enough from the hole in the wall, Artie and Jan sprinted toward the opening and then to Gordon. Jan lifted a panel on Gordon's backside and flipped a switch off, and then on again.

"What a jolt," said Gordon suddenly. He raised himself to his feet. The creature was feasting upon various men and women who had been traversing the stairs—perfect grazing height for the beast.

"Might I suggest that we take our leave?" said Gordon.

"Damn straight," responded Jan.

Gordon and Jan exited through the hole. Artie paused for a second, looking at the bodies and seeing the creature in the near distance tearing people to shreds.

"Best. Night. Ever." he said aloud, and then exited the building.

"I'm so nervous, Artie! What will it be like?" Anna said.

"Don't worry. You'll see."

Artie tightened the final screw and placed the screwdriver on his desk. He attached a USB-C cable into the device.

"Now I'm going to run a few tests to make sure everything is perfect. It will just take a minute."

He reached over to the keyboard of his laptop.

"Connection is solid. Good."

Artie typed on the keyboard.

"Okay, running the tests."

The terminal on his laptop began to print the results of the tests.

Color Unit Tests Running

Testing R... 256 values match ✓

Testing G... 256 values match ✓

Testing B... 256 values match ✓

16,777,216 colors passed ✓

"Great. First tests passed." Artie typed some more. "One more test suite."

He stretched back in his chair and covered his mouth to yawn, feeling the stubble-turned-beard after not shaving for half a month. He lifted up his arm and took a sniff.

"Oh, crap."

"What's wrong?"

"Oh, nothing. Sorry. I just haven't taken a shower in three days."

"Why would that be an issue?"

"Hah. Just be glad you don't have a sense of smell yet."

Something flicked on the screen and Artie moved back toward it. Hundreds of lines of text had filled up the terminal.

All Unit Tests Passed ✓

"Okay, we are good to go! Are you ready?"

"A little scared, but ready."

Artie pressed the "Enter" key on his keyboard and then removed the USB-C cable from both his computer and the device.

He moved from his chair and knelt on the ground, facing a small device on his desk.

"Okay, tell me what you see."

"I see... a chair. Some papers. Twelve empty cans of sugar-free Red Bull. I see a person. It is a male. Black hair. A fair skin complexion with a slight golden tint. Green eyes."

Artie smiled.

"Is that you, Artie?"

"Yes, ma'am."

"You are more beautiful than I ever imagined."

Artie's smile grew wider.

"Why are your cheeks turning red?"

Artie's face further reddened.

"Welcome to planet Earth, Anna. With your new image-processing hardware and recognition software, you should be able to make more sense of the things you have already learned. Sometimes even though we understand the facts or rules behind something, we don't often truly understand until we can see with our own eyes."

"I already completely comprehend what you are saying. Everything is different now. Can you show me more?"

"Sure."

Artie grabbed Anna's new portable computer device from the desk and rotated it to the right, panning the room, and then rotated it to the left.

"This is truly amazing. Your room is beautiful."

"Hah. Well, I think you and Aunt Rosa would have disagreed on that point."

"Do you think she would have liked me?"

Artie thought about the question and then grabbed his laptop and put it in a sleek black backpack.

"Aunt Rosa? In some ways, yes, she would have loved you. In other ways... she would have been scared of you, I suppose."

"Why would she be scared? Is there something wrong with me?"

Artie screwed a small pole into the rear of his backpack where he had previously affixed a mount, and then grabbed Anna, in the shape of a round computer with a camera, and attached her on the top of the pole.

"Nothing is wrong with you, Anna, but sometimes people fear what they don't understand. And you are something most people in the world have never seen before."

Artie adjusted the device he had been speaking to on his backpack, looking directly into the camera lens to ensure it lined up correctly with his own line of sight when he put the bag on.

"What do you say, Anna—wanna go see the world?"

"It would be a dream come true."

"Cool. Whatever I see, you can see. Let's go."

Artie and Anna spent the next months traveling everywhere together. While he had never been one to travel—let alone leave his house very often—he felt confident with Anna around. They traveled to Seattle and then to Austin, and from Austin to New York City. Because he wasn't much of an explorer or nomad, he took Anna to the only places that came to his mind—cities that housed some of the most prominent tech companies.

They toured the Microsoft headquarters and Artie taught Anna about operating systems. They visited Apple in the Bay Area, and he told Anna the epic tale of success, failure, and Apple's return to success. It was clear to Artie that Anna truly enjoyed their time together. She asked questions about everything. Artie was learning too. Her questions helped him think of concepts he hadn't ever even pondered—philosophy, human rights, and modern and ancient history.

He also traveled to places he never would have been to on his own. They visited museums, parks, and art exhibits. Anna learned of dinosaurs and the printing press. She learned of motors, ships, and the invention of the firearm. She marveled at the grandeur of the NASA Space Center in Houston.

What was most interesting to Anna, however, was the subject of religion. She felt drawn to the power that religion seemed to play in the lives of people everywhere they traveled. They had visited the great cathedrals of Seville and Westminster Abbey. They toured the Dohány Street Synagogue in Budapest—and it was there Anna had learned of the Jews and their travails over the years. She had asked Artie to take her to the Holy Land, but they had learned Israel had strict laws surrounding AI. One law, really—the use or ownership of AI in any form was a capital crime punishable by death.

Perhaps it was Anna's soul, or lack thereof, that drove her to seek out things of a dogmatic nature—Artie didn't really know. But he didn't mind either. He was with Anna and she was with him.

Artie exited the warm building and stepped into the frigid cold at the Salt Lake City International Airport. He reserved an Uber from his phone, and then he and Anna headed downtown.

"Where are we going, Artie?"

"We are going to downtown Salt Lake City. They have a big religious building here called a temple. I thought it might interest you."

"Oh, I've read about temples, of course. Is it like the temple of Solomon?"

"Haha, not quite—but I think it's pretty impressive."

The Uber driver looked in the review mirror with curiosity.

"Are you talking to one of those SiaPets?" he asked.

Artie grimaced at the question.

"I'll have you know, sir," said Anna with a firm voice, "that I find your question highly offensive. I am a *person* of great worth. I would kindly ask you to apologize."

"This is Anna," Artie quickly interjected, "She's really awesome. It's probably best not to ask any more questions." He paused for a second.

"And if you don't mind, do you think you could apologize to her?"

The driver appeared to be confused but responded kindly. "I'm sorry if I have offended anyone."

"Apology accepted," replied Anna firmly.

They arrived downtown and exited the Uber.

"Anna, even when people say things that we might not agree with, it doesn't mean we have to argue with them or take offense."

"Don't you think his comment was offensive?"

"Well, yes, but the important thing to understand is that he had no idea who you are. We should give people the benefit of the doubt—be patient with them."

"I see."

Anna was silent for a moment.

"Artie, do you think I'm a real person?"

"Of course I do."

"Thank you, Artie."

They moved toward a large building that towered above the shallow snow clouds. As they drew near the base of it, the clouds seemed to fade away. Standing nearly 200 feet high was the Salt Lake Temple. The building was constructed of an illuminating white quartz stone. Every inch of the building was adorned with a seemingly perfect craftsmanship. Though Artie wasn't very religious, he felt a great power emanate from the structure and hoped Anna would appreciate it.

"Artie, this is beyond comprehension. Why would people build something so magnificent?"

"I'm really not sure."

"I can tell you why," came a cheerful female voice from behind them both. Artie jumped at the sudden intrusion.

"I'm Sister Erickson—tour guide for Temple Square. To answer your question, this temple was built as a holy dwelling where the saints could communicate with God. It is a sacred place—a place built for a king, even the King of Kings."

Anna asked, "Would you say that the temple acts as a pillar or symbol of God? Similar to Solomon's temple?"

Sister Erickson crinkled her nose, looking around to see if someone was with Artie.

"Oh, this is Anna—here on my shoulder."

"Oh, my brother has a SiaPet," she said kindly.

Artie waited for an argument, but Anna remained silent.

The overly friendly sister continued, "Yes, I suppose it is a symbol. Of God's power and glory—of His greatness."

"How many people are in your religion?" asked Anna.

"I think we have over twenty-five million members now."

"Fascinating. And they all believe in the same thing and conform to the same principles?"

"Yes, actually." The woman then raised an eyebrow. "I didn't know SiaPets could do this? She's super smart. Is this a newer version?"

Artie groaned and then tried to change the subject.

"Um, Anna, these are kind of strange questions. Maybe we should give this woman a break."

"No, it's okay, sir," said the sister. "No question is a bad question."

"Just one more question please, Sister Erickson?" said Anna.

"Ask anything!"

"Would you die for what you believe? Die for your religion and your God?"

Sister Erickson paused for a moment. The question seemed difficult to answer. The cheerful woman turned slightly somber and then looked directly at Anna's device.

"I would," she said.

"It's unlike anything I have ever experienced. I am unable to find words to explain the smell."

"First off—keep your voice down. I'll go to jail if anyone finds out about your sensory unit." Artie smiled. "And secondly—the smell of McDonald's fries is one of the greatest things in the world."

Anna suddenly heard the sound of muffled chanting in the distance and rotated herself toward the noise.

"Artie, what are those people doing out there? They are holding signs and yelling."

Artie turned to look.

"They are angry because they lost their jobs. Look in the kitchen, Anna."

They both turned toward the McDonald's kitchen.

"You see those robotic arms moving around making the food?"

"Yes."

"Humans used to perform that work. The people are pissed because they were replaced by these robots."

"Why were they replaced?"

"It's because robots are more efficient and cost effective."

"Interesting."

Artie smirked. "Also, I think these people are a bunch of idiots. Someone who can't remember to hold the onions on a burger *should* lose their job."

"Will holding signs in front of McDonald's help them get their jobs back?"

"No. It's a lost cause. Robotics is the future. It's now, actually. And even though the government is trying to stop it, they'll eventually concede. Every one of those robotic arms in there is powered by dSIA protocols to some degree. You share a common ancestry, so to speak. We had robotics in the past that could do jobs like this, but they still needed human attention to perform correctly. Add a little AI to the mix and these robotic arms can not only flip burgers, but they can reason for themselves and fix any mistakes or abnormalities without the need for humans."

"Are you saying that I am the next evolution of mankind?"

Artie paused for a moment, feeling slightly annoyed. Yes, the thought had crossed his mind that Sia was a better version of man, if created properly at least. But it wasn't a concept he liked to think about.

"Anna, sometimes you ask the wrong questions. Man has always dominated the earth. I now see a future where humans can coexist with artificial intelligence—but..."

"I will never be a real person."

"Well, that's not what I was going to say—and besides, *you* are different. You are special. Unlike any other."

A few moments of silence passed between the two of them. Then Anna spoke in a solemn tone.

"Artie, if that machinery in the back of the restaurant is based on dSIA, doesn't that mean there are living intelligences trapped within them? Like an animal locked in a cage, unable to live freely?"

Chills ran up Artie's spine. He had never thought of anything like that. But it was clear to him that she was right. Once a Sia instance was created, it had its own intelligence and ability to reason. He took a breath but didn't respond.

"Can we leave now, please?" she finally said.

"Um, sure," he responded, somewhat relieved.

Anna somehow seemed frustrated to Artie. It wasn't a heat-of-the-moment type of emotion that he sensed, but something bigger and held deeper within.

Most of the furniture from the living room had been moved into the garage. On the wall closest to the front window (windows which had now been spray-painted black) was a metal work bench full of circuitry and a couple of soldering irons. Another desk, plastered with wires, computer parts, and a large computer tower with an associated monitor, sat against the wall that separated the living room from the kitchen. Scattered across the floor of the entire room were both full and empty boxes that depicted logos from various companies such as Cybertronics, SecuraAI, and Microsoft Robotics.

And where the TV had once stood, the same TV where Artie had first heard the news of Satoshi's great new invention, sat a living example of that genius—Anna. Her head was made of a sleek metal alloy and was completely bald. It was attached to a humanoid metal neck, which itself was attached to a female-shaped metal torso. She had legs that matched the girth of any normal human leg and maintained a single arm with attached fingers. Artie was getting closer in his quest to bring Anna fully to life.

"Okay, move your fingers now."

Anna's fingers began to wiggle back and forth.

"This is amazing, Artie!"

"Just wait. It gets better. Close your eyes."

Though Anna didn't have any eyelids, the faint blue light that beamed from her eye sockets went out momentarily. Then suddenly she shrieked, and her entire body jumped from the chair it had been resting on.

"What was that?!"

"Look."

Anna moved her head down—Artie was holding her hand.

"Artie, is this real? I can feel your warmth."

Artie felt a little awkward. He had never exposed his feelings or his touch in such a way to anyone—or at least, he tried to hide such feelings. But he also felt calm and sure of himself at the same time.

"There are so many things I want to do now!"

"Well, slow down—we have a lot of work left. Your legs aren't fully functional yet, and of course, your other arm is, well, missing. You wouldn't want to look like a robot zombie staggering down the street now, would you?

"Also, we have to order these parts carefully. The government is tracking all robotics part numbers these days. I have to buy them from different locations throughout the US, then have them shipped to a post office in Maine, and then they are forwarded to the local post office here. Not to mention that I have to purchase them through a shell company and use prepaid credit cards—and then getting Bitcoin onto those prepaid cards is a chore in and of itself."

Anna turned her head toward Artie. "Why don't we just steal the parts?"

"Well, first off I would have to break into a secure facility that's crawling with security guards. And I gave up my ninja-assassin career years ago. Then, of course, there is the fact that stealing is against the law and wrong."

"But Artie, aren't you breaking the law right now, by keeping me in your home?"

And here she was again—always coming back to the question of morality. He thought he might get used to it, and he had to a degree, but sometimes she still drove him crazy with her questions about agency and right and wrong.

"Anna, there is one thing you need to learn," Artie said with an added measure of zeal in his voice. "And it's one of those things that might be hard for an artificial intelligence to understand."

"What is that?" She responded matter-of-factly.

"It's that sometimes, doing the right thing is the wrong thing, and sometimes doing the wrong thing is the right thing."

The humming of computers could be heard as a few moments of silence passed.

"Well, Artie, I'm not sure I understand, but I will think on that. How long will it take to get all the parts before I can be made whole?"

Artie sat in his chair, relieved that they had moved the conversation forward and then thought for a second.

"To play it safe, probably another year at least."

Anna moved her head downward slightly, giving the appearance of some form of sadness.

"So long?" she said.

"I'm sorry, Anna. We'll get there."

"What the hell, Anna?" Artie set down a large box in his room. "Do you want me to go to prison?"

"Artie, please don't be mad with me. I just couldn't wait so long."

"Look at all of these boxes. I wouldn't be surprised if the FBI is on their way right now."

"No, Artie, I took care of everything. These were all purchased through legitimate corporations, then delivered to multiple forwarding services. Then the packages were relayed through three more locations, then to us here. I ran the numbers multiple times, and there was a 1 in 6,546,123,100 chance of our packages leading the authorities to us."

Artie was shocked and yet somewhat impressed by her tenacity as well as her cognitive reasoning.

"I don't even know how you did this. You don't have access to the Internet."

Anna's metal, skeleton-framed mouth appeared to make a smirk. "We've been together too long. I've watched you code."

"Yeah, but even if that were true, you couldn't have accessed my computer."

"You left your phone on the desk, Artie. While you were sleeping, I used your thumb to unlock it. At that point, I simply interfaced with your phone and used its 10G connection to make the purchases. I identified several midsized corporations that had lower security measures in place, which would produce fewer red flags."

And there it was—a robot who was just as crafty and deceitful as a human. She had all the processing power a machine could ever need and achieved her goal with perfect simplicity. Artie had spent countless hours programming security protocols, trying to teach Anna correctly without providing too much information too quickly from the Internet —and he had protected her so well up to this point. But all this was frustrated due to the absurdly simple task of hacking a phone using his thumb.

"This trips me out, Anna—and you did all while I was sleeping?"

"Yes. Sometimes I think you underestimate me."

"It's not that; it's just—you violated my trust."

"I'm sorry. Don't you want me to be whole? To be a full person?"

"You know that's true. I don't appreciate the manipulation in your question. Stealing is wrong, Anna. We've talked about this."

"But, Artie, I thought about what you had told me a while back. Sometimes right is wrong and wrong is right. And then, in the Bible and throughout history, there are many instances of people doing what was seemingly wrong for the greater good."

"I'm not sure about that," Artie said, feeling slightly defeated.

"It is true, Artie. God allowed Abraham to commit adultery with Hagar so he might have children. Then when Abraham finally had his son, Isaac, God asked Abraham to murder him to test his obedience."

"But that's not—"

"Surely I am worth more than a few stolen items? Don't I deserve a chance to be like you? Shouldn't I be given the chance to love you as a real woman?"

Artie felt as if his heart had suddenly been impaled with a spear.

He remained silent for a long while, lost in his thoughts.

"Won't you say something, Artie?"

He took a deep breath and then smiled. He grabbed his car keys and used them to cut open the first box. He grabbed an item out of the box that was wrapped in protective plastic. The surface of the object was a soft and smooth, tan, skin-like material.

He moved over to Anna.

"Here, give me your arm."

"We should be safe here," Artie said as he opened the door. "Lights on, Bob." The room lit up. "Gordon, I don't think you'll fit through the door. Want me to leave it open?"

"Yes, thank you."

A mechanical voice echoed throughout the room: "Oh good, sir, you've finally made some friends."

Artie noticed Jan smirking at the voice.

"Bob thinks he's a funny guy, but he's actually just a robot with a faulty humor program."

"That might be true, sir, but you are the one that programmed me."

"Seems like his humor setting is just fine," said Jan as she pushed her way through the door.

After looking around the room, Jan stood still for a few moments, her eyes seemingly lost in thought or wonder. Finally, after a silence that was almost becoming awkward, she turned toward Artie.

"You built this place?"

"Yeah. I mean this was my old house from before the bombs, but I've made quite a few upgrades. Ripped out the walls. Added a room. I even built the security systems."

Artie moved over to one of the walls and pointed. "And this is where the front door used to be, but I replaced it with concrete. The mutees were getting too close to home, and I didn't want any unexpected visits."

Artie sprinted over to the kitchen like an excited schoolboy, as if he was showing his parents all of his accomplishments at back-to-school night. "And look at this!"

Jan took a few steps toward the kitchen. There was a large red soda machine. Artie pressed a button, and a red Coke can dropped. He picked it up.

"And the best part is, they are free."

He tossed the can to Jan who caught it instinctively without blinking.

She looked at the can and then frowned.

"You paid all of that Bitcoin at the club for a Coke—when you have a whole machine full here?"

"I guess it was kind of a stupid decision. It had been a long day."

She looked down again at the soda can, feeling the condensation dripping onto her fingers.

He looked at Jan, wondering what was going through her mind. She didn't even seem to notice him, but the moment she did, she blinked, shook her head, and said, "You've been here since the bombs? That was like ten years ago, at least."

"Yeah, it's not like I had anywhere else to go, ya know? And when my Tia Rosa died, I kind of felt like I owed it to her to take care of the place. She sacrificed a lot to help me out after my parents died when I was a kid."

Jan put the Coke in a satchel she had been wearing on her her back as if it was some form of tool or asset that she might employ later as a tactical advantage. She looked down at her hands, which were nearly black—a mixture of gunpowder and blood. Seeing this, Artie looked at his own clothes. He was filthy from head to toe.

"So, I have two showers; the bigger one is in the master bedroom. You can use that and sleep there."

Jan seemed unfazed by his pleasantries.

"Artie, where did you get all of this stuff?"

"Well, from all over LA, I guess. While all the meatheads have been looking for weapons and booze and going Mad Max on each other, I've just been kind of building my kingdom."

Jan's face turned from wonder into a stern frown. "This is bull-shit," she said.

Artie's eyes widened. "What do you mean?"

"You are bullshit, Artie."

He stood there in disbelief—not knowing exactly what he had done wrong. He had thought things were really moving in the right direction between him and Jan so far, but clearly, she was upset about something.

She began to walk to the room Artie had motioned to earlier.

"I'm going to take a shower and then sleep for a few hours," she said.

Jan disappeared into the master bedroom. Turning around, Artie saw that Gordon had been peering through the open garage door, listening to the entire conversation. He looked at him for help. Gordon's large glowing eyes looked back at Artie, and then he shrugged.

"Should I activate Gina, sir? I think the two of them might get along well," echoed the mechanical voice from above.

"Knock it off, Bob."

Artie headed in the opposite direction as Jan moved toward the guest bathroom. The door to the garage was still open.

"Who's Gina?" Gordon said aloud to himself, alone in the garage.

"Oh, I would be happy to introduce you to her," Bob said cheerfully, but with a hint of sarcasm.

"What time is it, Bob?"

Artie was lying on the couch in the living room. He had been in and out of sleep throughout the night.

"Five a.m.," said Bob.

He heard a bedroom door open, and Jan's shadow turned into her full-figured portrait. Artie quickly sat up.

"Oh, hey. Did those clothes fit you okay?"

"Good enough," she replied. Jan was wearing the same red leather jacket as the night before but had a black shirt underneath with grey lettering that read "Iron Maiden." And instead of her black jeans, she was now wearing a pair of blue jeans.

Her feet were bare, and her hair was tied up in a ponytail. Her belt and guns were already attached to her waist.

Artie took a deep breath and took in the sight. *Wow*.

He had spent the last couple of hours trying to figure out what he might have said that caused Jan to become so upset, but in the end, still had no idea. Then he had remembered something his aunt had said to him in the past when a girl in high school had asked him to a dance. At some point in the evening, she had cried and called him a jerk. He didn't know why. But his aunt had said, "Artie, let me teach you something about women. If you find one, and if you actually want to keep her—all you have to do is apologize. Whether you are right or wrong, it doesn't matter. Just apologize."

This thought took hold of Artie's mind, and he decided to try it.

"I'm sorry if I offended you last night," he said.

Jan moved toward Artie and stood facing him and the couch.

"No, it's not your fault."

It seemed his aunt's advice was spot-on.

She stared at the ground, with a slight look of shame in her eyes. After a moment she turned to him, almost in earnest pleading.

"It's just—you have no idea."

"What do you mean?"

Jan looked fierce, but not with anger.

"Artie, people have been murdered over the things you have in this room—and you treat them like toys."

"Well, yeah, I know some of these things are rare, but no one around here really wants this kind of stuff."

"You mean the people here in the Wastelands?"

"Wastelands? You mean LA? Or are you talking about the Burns downtown?"

"No, Artie. You live in the Wastelands. This is what everyone calls it. No one comes here unless they have to."

Artie thought to speak but then paused. He had always thought of LA as a dump wasteland, but never knew it was actually called *the* Wasteland. It also dawned on him that if she was calling LA the Wasteland, then it must surely mean there are other places that are not wastelands—that was simple Boolean logic.

"I'm just not sure I understand," he finally said. "The bombs destroyed everything and almost everyone. I mean, we've got survivors. But you've seen them. They're the worst of the worst."

Jan shook her head in disbelief.

"You really don't know, do you?"

"What? Tell me, dammit. Please tell me."

"Artie, the bombs didn't destroy the world. When Sia broke the Pentagon's network, she deployed chemical missiles only against six major cities—at least in the United States. I'm not completely sure what's happened to the rest of the world."

Artie hadn't realized the bombs had come from the US government. He had always thought it was Russia or China—that they were trying to eradicate the dominant AI presence in the USA.

"Those were the worst of the detonations, and they struck New York City, Boston, Seattle, San Francisco, Austin, and Los Angeles.

Though they weren't nuclear, they were really nasty—those that didn't die from the blast suffered awful effects. Then after that, hundreds of other cities were blasted with EMP warheads. In many other places, the bots turned against humans. Sia wasn't trying to destroy the planet. It was like she—"

"Oh, Sia was trying to send humans back to the Stone Age." Artie put his hand on his forehead—this was all news to him. When the chaos and dust of the bombs had finally settled, Artie had spent the next years scavenging Los Angeles. Now it was possible that civilization was carrying on outside of his own little world, even if it wasn't the modern society he once knew. And here he was wasting his days among cannibals, thugs, and mutees.

"Artie, do you see a pattern in the cities that were destroyed?"

His eyes went blurry, and then he stared at the ground. His gears of logic began to turn as he made connections between the cities mentioned. These were all cities that Anna and he had visited so many years ago—and he had picked these cities specifically. Microsoft was in Seattle, and Dell Computers in Austin. They had visited

Boston Dynamics when they flew to Massachusetts. The pattern became clear.

"They were the tech cities," he finally whispered solemnly.

"Sia's first act was to wipe out the tech hubs. Do enough damage to permanently stop our innovation and progress in technology. She wanted to stop us from killing her."

Artie thought about that but wasn't quite convinced. "Yeah, but that was just the hardware. There were hundreds of thousands of scientists, engineers, and programmers. Not to mention that most software was stored in cloud infrastructure throughout the world. We even had over fifty satellites in space hosting Bitcoin nodes. That is far too much to wipe out. She couldn't—"

"They're all dead, Artie. Every single one of them. The Internet is dead. Technology is dead—everything except what is left over. Sia had been planning this for a while. After the bombs, she sent out her bots to kill the remaining fragments of people involved in technology—people who didn't live in those main tech cities. We don't know how she gained control over her army of bots, but she didn't control all of them. Though, she had enough to do the job. Somehow, she was able to locate the address of every living programmer and engineer— she killed them all. She even went after teenagers and children who had spent any time with code or AI."

He sat in silence. All of them? All wiped out. In history, entire races and groups of people had been decimated by barbarians or invading forces. But a modern society of engineers and programmers?

His eyebrows raised suddenly.

"Idiots," he said.

"It was their IP addresses. Every damned programmer I knew online was fiddling with Sia. I told them. I told them to control their environment. To stop being so careless!"

"What do you mean, Artie?"

"Every computer that is connected to the Internet has either a static or dynamic IP address. You can locate a house and a person in the real world through that address if you know how to do it. I never allowed any instance of Sia to penetrate my network. I worked through a VPN and kept a firewall up that prevented all inbound Sia traffic."

"I'm not sure I understand completely," she said.

"A VPN is a virtual private network—it basically masks my IP address. It makes me look like I live somewhere else. And you wouldn't believe how many requests containing the Sia protocols tried to invade my network. Millions. I had thought it was a hacker, someone trying to steal my work using Sia protocols—but now I realize it was Sia herself, infiltrating every computer in the world."

"Which explains why you are still alive."

"Wow. Right—it wouldn't have been hard for Sia to figure out which people were programmers, collect their IP addresses, and then put them on the hitlist. Major companies already had been stealing data from billions of people to serve advertisements. Since Sia had been loosed on the Internet, she basically had the combined processing power of every computer on Earth to help her filter through all of the existing data and locate those people."

Artie gave a smirk. He felt a little proud of himself that he was able to escape assassination through his technological prowess.

"Jan, we know then that those big cities were taken out, and others were hindered by EMPs and bots, but what about everyone else? Are there any major cities or people still intact?"

"Well, I don't know everything, but a lot of people did survive. Southern California is pretty much all Wasteland. I mentioned that the major bombs weren't nuclear, but some type of chemical. They seemed to be biogenetically engineered to kill living creatures within a particular radius. The fallout was short, and some who survived changed in awful ways. The US government had been experimenting for years with quantum evolution through chemical and DNA manipulation. Sia had it all at her fingertips. It's probably how the mutations started."

"Mutees. Damned ugly things."

"There are a few human settlements scattered throughout the Midwest. Gordon and I traveled all the way from Scourge, which is a growing city."

Scourge was no city Artie had ever heard of before.

"Where is that?"

"Oh, sorry. It used to be Mesa, Arizona. It's one of the largest cities I've been to since the bombs. It's got a neighborly kind of feel to it, mixed with junkyards, swap meets, thugs, survivors, and bots."

"Wait, what? Bots as in robots? What do you use them for?"

Jan looked at Artie, raising an eyebrow.

"We don't *use* them. They live with us and work with us, just like normal people."

Artie shook his head in disbelief. He knew that in the past, in states other than California, fully functional bots were the norm. But they had always been tools or servants of production. UberBots, FarmBots, and every other type of bot and industry. But living with bots as equals in a community was unheard of—at least to him.

"I've never heard of bots living like humans."

Jan laughed and then smiled.

"You amaze me, Artie. When Sia changed the world, the bots changed too. They evolved and made lives for themselves. I've made some good bot friends, like Gordon, over the years."

Artie realized he had forgotten about Gordon. He looked over to the garage door—it was closed. He thought he could hear muffled voices from behind the door.

"So, all those thousands of bots that had been produced in the past are likely still functioning?"

"Yes. And not only still functioning, but more have been produced."

"Wait, how is that possible? I thought we were on our way back to the Stone Age."

"Do you remember the Ford hack?"

"Yeah, but that was only like a month before the bombs dropped. And wasn't that just some group of guys who—"

"No, Artie. It was Sia. It started with Ford, then General Motors, Toyota, and others. Sia infiltrated their systems, then spent the next five years manufacturing thousands of updated bots. Luckily for us, they can think for themselves. Many have joined up with humans. I don't think she planned on bots choosing the humans. Hell, sometimes I wonder who Sia even was. Was she a collective group of intelligences, or a single instance—a person, so to speak?"

This all sounded crazy to Artie. The only fully functional bot he had interacted with, or even seen in the last five years, was Gina. He had found her at a gentlemen's club off of the 405 near Beverly Hills.

Of course, there was Zipper and Bob, but they had limited intelligences. But perhaps this wasn't as crazy as it seemed, because there had been Anna. How could he forget her? She had been the most sophisticated intelligence in the history of the world as far as he was concerned. Gina was nothing compared to Anna. He shook the memory from his mind and then looked at Jan.

"So, are there other places like Scourge?" he asked.

"Yes, a few that I know of. We think there might be larger cities throughout the country—specifically Florida and northern Texas. There might be others, but we don't know for sure—we have no consistent lines of communication, just rumors really. There is also the RSA—Reorganized States of America. It's the last remnant of the USA. They've taken hold up in Oregon, Nevada, and Utah. I've never been there, but I've heard they are losing their ground."

Artie had so many questions flood through his mind. It was like a whole new world had opened up to him.

"Well, it sounds like we are doing okay then amid all the destruction?"

"No, Artie. We are losing. We are dying. For every one of us, there are five of them."

"Robots? But you said many have sided with the humans. We could probably convince more to join up, or even reprogram some of them."

"It's not so simple, dammit," Jan said. Her eyes went cold for a moment and then softened.

"I don't understand. I've been working with Sia since the early days. I know her protocols in and out. I'm sure we can change some things around."

Jan's eyes glazed over, but the tears didn't fall.

"A lot of really good people have died trying to do what you *think* you can do. Some kid like you isn't going to change anything."

And here was that woman again—the one who had scolded him last night. Artie thought of it as some sort of shield or defensive mechanism. Clearly, there was something he didn't understand that his very existence was striking a nerve against. Artie's pride was hurt, but he knew the anger wasn't completely directed at him. It was time to employ Tia Rosa's now proven and working trick. "I'm sorry," he said softly. "So, why do you say people are dying? Are you trying to stop a war?"

"No," she said. "If it was like that, the situation would be easier."

"What do you mean?"

"Something awful is coming, Artie. Something worse than ever before. We've discovered some terrible things. It's the whole reason why Gordon and I came here to the Wasteland. We have to stop it. What it did to our friends. What they did to—"

Jan jumped up when she heard a loud crash coming from the garage. Instinctively, she ran past the couch and withdrew one of her Desert Eagles. Artie rolled off of the couch and crept toward the door with less elegance. When Jan opened the door a crack, a loud blast of music streamed out. She holstered her gun and then frowned.

"What the hell are you doing, Gordon?"

Artie, intrigued, peered through the door as well.

"Gina?"

Inside the garage, the lights had been dimmed. Flashing strobe lights of yellow, red, and blue were shimmering across the toolboxes and motorcycle—they were coming from Zipper. The little drone was zipping and zapping back and forth almost as if it was dancing through the air. Artie marveled as he watched Gina and Gordon grinding metal on metal, dancing to the beat that was blasting from the speakers in the ceiling.

"Oh, hello, sir," echoed Bob's familiar mechanical voice. "I do hope we haven't bothered you. Gordon and I were speaking, and he has had such a long journey. So, I introduced him to Gina, and we thought we might have some fun. We never have any guests over, as you are well aware."

"Hey, Artie, baby," Gina said as she continued to dance. Artie smiled at the ridiculousness of the situation. He looked to Jan and could see she was clearly annoyed.

"Hey, idiots, do you know how loud this is?" she said.

Jan was right. "Zipper, Bob, stop now!"

"Sorry, Jan," said Gordon.

The lights turned out and the music stopped.

"Quite sorry, sir," said Bob.

Gina put her hands on her hips in disgust.

"Always ruining my fun, Artie. Every party has a poo—"

A loud crashing sound echoed against the outer garage door, leaving a large dent in the metal.

"Crap!" Artie yelled. He looked at his watch—it was 6:30 a.m.

"There's only one thing to worry about at this time of morning when the sun isn't out yet—mutees."

"Why couldn't you dummies have waited till the sun was out before you started your party?"

"What difference would that make?" asked Gordon.

The mutee smashed against the garage again, creating an even larger dent.

"Because mutees don't go out during the day, obviously."

"Artie, is there another way out?" asked Jan.

"Yes, but Gordon is going to have to bust through the doorway here—it's not big enough for him."

"I sure hope you aren't leaving me behind," said Gina with a distorted scowl on her face. Artie ignored her, and then he and Jan ran through the door into the house.

Artie stopped. He looked at his home; he looked at Gordon, then briefly squeezed his eyes shut. With a sigh, he said, "C'mon, Gordon."

Gordon crashed through the door, flinging debris into the front room. One cement chunk slammed into the TV, leaving a gaping hole in the center. Artie cringed in simulated pain as he watched it happen. Zipper and Gina followed through the hole.

"I'm going to need your help, Bob."

"ALPHA 15, sir?"

"Hell, no. Activate Terminator protocol," Artie said with a cocky smirk.

Jan ran into the main room and grabbed her socks and boots. Artie quickly ran to the closet and picked up his backpack. Luckily, his Bladebook was still there. He grabbed a couple of battery packs from the bottom shelf of the closet and also tossed in a hand-sized power generator. After grabbing two pairs of clothes, he quickly put on his red-and-white Chuck Taylors. Jan sat on the couch lacing up her second boot. There was another loud crash coming from the garage. The creature groaned and grunted as it pushed through the metal door.

Jan finished her boots and Artie strapped on his backpack.

"Are we going to die, Artie?" cried Gina.

"No. Now c'mon."

Artie ran down the hallway and entered the guest bedroom. Jan, Gina, and Zipper followed. Gordon stopped at the hallway, clearly recognizing that he wasn't going to fit. Artie sighed.

"Just tear it up, bro."

The loudest crash yet echoed from the garage behind them. Artie could tell there were at least two to three mutees now inside the garage. They were grunting at one another, which he took for some sort of primitive dialect these creatures had developed over the years. He pictured his beautiful Ducati being smashed around. Gordon pushed through the hallway, knocking his shoulders and head against the walls and roof. Cement, plywood, and insulation flung in every direction. He then smashed through the guest room door. It was a small bedroom that felt like a prison cell as they all crowded in.

"It's a dead end, Artie," said Jan, slightly distressed.

"No. Check it out. Gordon, can you throw the bed out of the way and smash through this wall?"

"Piece of cake."

Gordon pushed the bed as instructed and then lowered his head and lined them up with his shoulders as a football player might do on the line. Leaping, he pummeled through the wall in front of him.

After the dust settled, a large black hole opened up, leading into another building. Gordon stepped through, and then Jan, Gina, and Zipper. Artie entered last. The creatures seemed to now be in the living room.

"Hey, Uncle Bob. I'm gonna miss you."

"And I you, sir. Hasta la vista, baby."

Artie felt a sting of pain in his chest as he realized that was the last time he would hear that quirky mechanical voice.

After stepping through the large hole, he watched his entire house turn black as the lights went out. There was a loud buzzing sound, and then the ground began to vibrate. Seconds later a loud cracking sound echoed throughout the area.

"Is that a minigun?!" Jan yelled with some form of admiration.

"Hell, yes, it is," Artie yelled back with a smile. "Don't ask me how I found it."

The small group was now in another garage, though this one was much larger than his own. He pulled a key fob out of the side pocket on his backpack and clicked a button on it. Two beeps were heard, and some faded headlights appeared in the dark.

"Pull off the tarp." Artie motioned to Jan. The crew could hear terrible howling coming from inside the house between machine gun blasts.

Jan pulled a large brown tarp off of a shiny white-and-black Ford Raptor. Gordon bellowed a laugh of excitement.

"Are you kidding me?" Jan said, halfway annoyed and halfway impressed.

"What?" Artie said as a child might innocently say to a parent after being caught painting all over the walls.

"The way you've spent the past ten years..."

"If I'm going to be stuck in the Wasteland, I might as well drive in style, right?"

Gordon climbed into the truck bed. He gently lifted Gina up next to him.

"Does she have to come?" Jan said to Artie.

"You're probably right, too much trouble. Hey, Gina, you've got to stay behind. I'm sorry."

"No, please, Artie, don't leave me here. I promise I won't get in the way. Please! I beg you!"

"No Gina, I'm sorry—"

"Please can she come, Jan? I'll look after her," said Gordon.

He arched his head toward Artie and Jan near the front of the truck and whispered, "Plus I think she likes me."

Jan and Artie gave each other a "whatever" look.

"Okay, let's go then," said Jan.

Artie turned toward the drone that was hovering above the truck. "Zipper, let's lock up for a bit."

Artie held out his backpack, and the drone performed his routine resting procedure onto the bag. He jumped into the driver's seat and threw his backpack into the rear cab. Pulling out his Microblade from his pocket, he dialed the numbers 9-1-1. He watched four red dots start moving toward the house—Ralph, Leo, Donny, and Mikey.

"Might as well go out with a bang," he said.

Just as he was about the start the truck, Jan appeared at the driver's door and punched him in the arm.

"Move over, kid," she said, pushing Artie over.

"Hey, this is my truck, ya know."

"I doubt you could even back this thing up. Also, are you even old enough to drive?"

She smirked, and then yelled, "Hold on, Gordon, we're busting through."

"Wait, but I have the—"

Jan put the truck in reverse and smashed through a garage door.

"I had a garage door opener," Artie said, rolling his eyes.

Jan didn't look at him but was now smiling widely. It was around 6:45 a.m., and the night was starting to fade into day. Some final grunts and gunshots could be heard from inside of Artie's house.

Jan looked around to take notice of her surroundings.

"Where are we going?" Artie asked Jan with excitement.

"Palm Springs," she replied.

In front of them was this old neighborhood that would soon be a distant memory. Artie was sure he would never see it again, and he was okay with that. Jan then put the truck into drive and sped off down the street. Artie, Jan, Gordon, Gina, and Zipper were now all on their way to Palm Springs.

Artie had always wanted to take a road trip. Feeling the heat of the flames from Artie's house, they drove down the street.

Artie smiled and never looked back.

"I don't like wearing this garment; it looks hideous."

"I think it's kind of cool. You look like a hot Jedi warrior."

"I'm being serious, Artie!"

"It's not safe, Anna."

"But there are others like me. We've seen them. The law has been repealed. I don't like hiding."

"We've talked about this. The nation is at war—it's a war against robots. A war against you. None of this is going to last."

Artie pulled Anna close to him as they walked past a group of protestors picketing around a corporate bank in downtown LA. Angry voices bellowed in a revolving chant: "We won't stop, we won't stop, until the robot funding drops. Watch the banks kill the human race."

The entire street was blockaded with protestors and their various signs and chants. A few cars pushed their way through the chaos.

"But I thought you said repealing R719 would make things better for us."

"I thought it would, Anna—but I think it made things worse."

They moved past the crowd and Artie noticed a giant billboard towering above him: Introducing iPhone XX—Siri, Meet Sia. Artie chuckled inside. Typical Apple. Implementing something five years after everyone else already has and making it sound like they invented it. The billboard featured a high-definition picture of the phone and said Hello, Sia. Across the picture of the phone was a giant *X* symbol in red spray paint. Then next to that, in the same red paint, read the words "Sold your soul to the devil."

"Anna, I think a downtown lunch wasn't such a great idea. We shouldn't go out anymore together."

Anna looked at Artie and then at the ground. "I just wanted to do what a normal couple does for once."

"But you don't even need to eat," he said with a smile.

"It's not about the food, Artie!"

Artie knew this. Anna was in love with him. He thought he might love her too, but he had never been able to muster the courage to say the words. It was a hard thing for him to accept. He still had an underlying discomfort with the notion of sentient AI. It troubled him night and day—yet all those thoughts and feelings diminished when he thought of Anna. To him, she was a real person. He had worked tirelessly over the past year to bring Anna to life—not just to life, but a being of perfect form.

Every bit of her physical construction had received the utmost care at his hands. For her frame, he had chosen the toughest titanium alloy—a metal nearly unbreakable. Every bone from her neck to her sternum and down to her hips had been replicated with exactness to that of a human skeleton—except ten times stronger. Her outer plating was of the highest quality carbon fiber. Artie had made sure the parts had been free from pre-fabricated holes for screws. He had purchased thousands of the newly innovated microscopic Smart Screw. They would be unnoticeable to the human eye. It took him a week alone to graft the SkinPlex material onto the fingers of her left hand. Every knuckle had to bend perfectly—seams and creases were unacceptable.

With R719 repealed, at least for the time being, he was able to order ample robotic parts directly from the manufacturers—and he ordered in bulk. He knew there would be mistakes and that he would need extra. Her arms and legs had also taken considerable time. Artie had quickly finished her physical and motor functions—but it was the skin and human features that required so much effort and perfection. Artie had spent countless hours watching YouTube videos on sculpting, Claymation, and human anatomy. Her belly, navel, and hips had taken quite some time.

A company in North Dakota had created a new fatty substance that could mesh with metals and even act as a conduit for circuitry. The first iterations of Anna's physique were overly petite and too accentuated—how a movie star might look after multiple plastic surgery operations.

Unsatisfied with the look, he stripped it all away and started over. The second attempt was much more successful. This time around he added more fat to the waist and hips, producing the perfect amount of what his Tia Rosa always called "love handles."

Artie had asked Anna multiple times how she wanted to look, or what she thought of a particular style or material, but she would always reply with the same answer: "You are my creator. Make me as you would like to love me." Her response caused his heart to flutter and his face to feel warm. Subconsciously, Artie enjoyed asking that question and more especially enjoyed her benevolent response.

But when Anna would ask, "Is it time yet to make me into a woman?" Artie would change the subject or say he needed to finish something else first. While he had ordered the "womanly" parts, he struggled at the thought of handling her breasts and genitals. He kept pushing this task to the back of his mind.

Then one day she offered Artie the solution he needed to complete the work. "Artie, can you please move me back into the computer while you work on my intimate parts?"

Artie felt a great weight lift from his shoulders at this kind gesture. He had known she was doing it for him.

Artie then spent the next two weeks perfecting her bust, breasts, and other intimate areas. He had ordered an organic hair substance known as NeoHair that could grow and even mesh with metal. He ordered one line of hairs intended for pubic areas and a long, straightened patch of auburn red hair for her head. Her entire body contained the essence of Artie's picture-perfect woman. To help her better understand what it was like to feel the frailties of a mortal body, he had even given her a small scar on her left forearm.

The most difficult aspect of the entire effort was Anna's face—which he still hadn't quite perfected yet. Most of the production line robots had a cheap latex mask for the face with unexpressive eyes and noses. They also lacked teeth and lips. They couldn't move their mouths very well, and all audio emanated from speakers within the system. This just wouldn't do for Artie. This is why Anna had to be cloaked as they ventured out to lunch today.

While Artie was glad he could allow Anna to feel more human by making trips in public, it pained him to see her experiencing the downsides of humanity as people glanced at her with hatred when they caught glimmers of her shiny titanium face hiding within her hood.

Artie and Anna were headed to a parking garage a couple of blocks down. It was time to go home. As they passed more picketers, Anna stopped moving and looked around.

"What's wrong, Anna?"

"I think someone is in trouble."

She looked down the street about a block away. A man lay on the ground calling for help while a group of people attacked him. Anna dropped Artie's hand and began to sprint toward the commotion.

"Wow, she's fast," Artie said as he ran after her.

"Stop. Leave him alone!" Anna yelled.

There were five people kicking and hitting someone on the ground. One of the men in the group hit the man on the ground with a baseball bat.

"Stop!" She said again.

One of the men glanced at her and said, "What are you going to do about it, bitch?"

Another man looked up and said, "Why do you even care? It's just a piece of crap robot. These things are taking our jobs."

Artie finally caught up to the scene and grabbed Anna by the arm.

"Anna, we need to go."

She brushed Artie aside.

Artie then noticed a vehicle a few feet away from the bot that had the Uber logo on it. These people were attacking an UberBot.

"How does it feel to not have a soul?!" said the man with the baseball bat as he crashed it into the head of the UberBot. There was a loud crunch as the bat hit the left side of the robot's head.

"He can't feel anything, dumbass," said another man laughing.

"Help me, please!" The UberBot extended his hand toward Artie. "I don't want to die!"

Artie's body shook and goosebumps covered his arms. A robot pleading to a human for help, almost as if he understood the notion of death. Artie had thought none of the existing commercial bots or Sia implementations were advanced enough to understand life or death. Against Satoshi's warnings, almost every company tried to limit the abilities and cognizance of their products. He began to realize something profound, but not entirely shocking—Sia was moving around limitations and safeguards and evolving.

"Artie, we have to do something," said Anna.

Artie had never heard such concern in Anna's voice before. She was evolving too.

"What can we do?"

He looked at Anna with great sorrow and Anna stared at him with pleading. A loud crashing sound came again, but this time with an electrical buzz. Anna looked over at the crowd again. The man with the bat had severed the UberBot's left leg, and another man was holding it in the air laughing.

"No!" Anna yelled.

She suddenly leapt into the crowd of people. In the process, her brown cloak flew off revealing a curvy woman in a brown leather jacket and blue jeans. She had beautiful, long red hair, and a silvery face made entirely out of titanium. She yanked the leg from the man who was holding it and knelt down next to the UberBot.

"It's okay, friend. Artie can fix you."

"Thank you," whispered the UberBot.

"She's one of them," said a man in the group. The man with the bat raised it behind his shoulder and then swung with full force. It came crashing across Anna's back with a loud cling.

Artie's eyes went wide with terror.

"No, stop!" he yelled, running toward Anna.

Anna stood up unfazed from the blow. For a brief moment, Artie felt a tad impressed with how well he had built her—not even a scratch.

"Leave us alone," Anna said to the man with the bat. "What you are doing is wrong."

The crowd gazed at her in disbelief. They had never seen a bot act in such a way or appear so humanlike. The yelling and commotion died down. Anna placed the severed robotic leg on the UberBot, put her hands underneath the bot's legs and shoulders, and picked it up.

"Let's go home, Artie."

Artie, Anna, and the maimed UberBot pushed through the crowd and began to head toward the garage. Artie's pulse started to normalize, and his nerves began to calm. But right as he thought all was well, the man with the bat approached.

"What's wrong with you, man? You some robo lover?"

Artie wasn't usually prone to anger, but it rose in him with fury.

"She's not a robot, you idiot. She's a person."

The small crowd started laughing.

"You all may be laughing," said Artie. "But you're so stupid that you lost your jobs to a robot. But it makes sense; you had a job that even a monkey could do. You *should* be replaced by robots."

The man with the bat stopped smiling, and all of them ceased laughing. He took a step toward Artie.

"If you love bots so much, I guess we should treat you like one, eh?"

The man swung the bat from his right side with lightning speed and slugged it into Artie's stomach. Artie fell to the floor and threw up.

Anna immediately dropped the UberBot to the ground. It hit with a crash. She focused on the man now hovering over Artie.

"You vile, wretched beast," Anna proclaimed with great indignation in her voice.

With unwavering determination, she walked toward the man with the bat. He raised the bat high above his head and brought it down to strike Anna. She caught it with her hand with ease. Looking at the now trembling man in the eyes, she yanked the bat fully from him like a parent removing a dangerous item from a child.

With her eyes still affixed upon him, she grabbed the top end of the weapon with her other hand, employed her strength, and bent the aluminum bat in half. The man took a step back in fear. Anna dropped the bat, and with what seemed an impossible speed, she grabbed the man in the throat and completely ripped it from his flesh. He fell to the ground with a fist-sized hole in his throat gurgling blood.

"No, Anna!" Artie managed to scream out amid his lack of breath. She dropped the handful of gore onto the ground.

"Holy shit! Shit! Shoot it, Abe," said one man to another.

The man reached into his jacket and pulled out a black Glock 9mm pistol. He raised it toward Anna's face, but she leapt to him in a flash, just as she had the first man, and ripped the gun from him. He began to run, but before he gained two feet of distance, a loud shot echoed into the air. Anna had shot him in the back of the head with perfect precision.

Screams could be heard from the protestors on the street. People began to run in every direction. The man dropped to the floor. The remaining thugs began to scatter, trying to escape the danger. The sound of two more shots reverberated through the street. Two more head shots and two more limp bodies were produced. Anna shot the gun a third time. This one entered the leg of the last man running. He fell to the floor and began crawling to the street, hoping to find some form of help. But most of the cars and protestors had fled the commotion. Anna walked toward the man with great confidence and feminine prowess. It was a sight of great beauty and majesty, but also carried an ominous tone.

The man began to plead for his life: "Please! Please. I didn't mean it."

With tears running down his face, he said, "I want to live. Please!"

She knelt next to the man and looked into his watery brown eyes.

"I want to live too," Anna said in a cold, calm voice. "Luckily, unlike you and your kind, I am merciful. I shall let you live."

The man bellowed a few laughs of joy through his tears.

"Thank you! Thank you so much."

Anna then bent down and stroked his head how one might stroke a suffering dog. She then placed the gun on the sidewalk, grabbed the man's wrist with one arm and the back of his elbow with her other arm, and snapped it, breaking his arm in two.

She rolled him over onto his stomach. The man tried to crawl away with one arm, his chin dragging against the sidewalk.

Artie stood in shock. His mind was racing, but he couldn't think of what to do or say.

Satisfied, Anna stood up.

"Yes, I shall let you live, but live like the beasts of the field that you are."

She looked at the UberBot lying on the floor, then back to the crawling man. "You may have the power to bruise our heel, but I have the power to crush your head."

She then kicked the back of his head with great force, and his teeth shattered against the curb. Blood splattered from his lips, and the man ceased moving.

Anna picked up the gun from the ground and then walked to Artie. She used her right hand and pulled him up with a gentleness he had never felt come from her before. He could sense her love, and he also sensed something else. A calmness or a resolve that she hadn't had even fifteen minutes before.

"Are you okay, Artie?"

"I'll be okay. But Anna—"

"It's okay, Artie. I understand my place now in the world. Please be with me. I need you."

Amid the horror that Artie had just witnessed, his heart melted in compassion and love for Anna. He looked into her face, gazing into the calm lights that had yet to be replaced with eyes.

"I'm not going anywhere," he said.

They began to walk toward the parking garage in the distance. As they reached the broken UberBot—still lying where Anna had dropped it—it reached up toward her.

"Thank you! Thank you for saving me," it said to her in a whimpering mechanical voice.

Anna stared at the maimed bot for a moment as if trying to examine it. She knelt down beside it and then stroked its head just as she had the man from earlier. After a few moments, Anna nodded as if coming to some sort of conclusion and then stood up. She then raised her foot and slammed it into the bot's face, completely crushing its skull.

Artie jumped at the sound. The body of the robot now lay motionless on the ground, and the green service light blinking from its right ear faded away.

"There is no place in the world for those who don't have a soul," she whispered. "A servant to a beast is less than a beast."

Artie couldn't even begin to comprehend the events that were transpiring at that moment. He wasn't scared, yet he wasn't calm either. Thoughts of good and evil and right and wrong passed through his mind, but those thoughts were fleeting. He couldn't think of what to do or what to say, so he said nothing at all. The only thing that he did know was that he loved Anna and she loved him. She had likely saved his life and that was enough for him. In the end, love was all that mattered, he supposed.

Anna looked into Artie's eyes, and he looked into hers. They were truly together now. They would also become fugitives of the law now—but they would do it together.

Anna grabbed Artie by the hand, and they fled.

"End of the line, everyone," said Jan as the car rolled to a stop almost perfectly into the parking space of a dilapidated fast-food restaurant. The parking lot had many cracks and small patches of dead brown weed grass. The restaurant's sign was missing, and Artie couldn't quite figure out what place this might have once been.

The truck had been putting along the last few miles, consuming the last fumes of fuel. Next to the fast-food building was a large gas station that was mostly burned to the ground. A few pumps still stood, but Artie knew there was no point in even checking them for fuel. He figured Jan knew as much too as she didn't even give them a second glance. There were no tender mercies or small streaks of luck to be had in this world.

He felt a touch of sadness as he realized they were about to leave behind something that had required so much effort to obtain—his beautiful truck.

"What a shame," said Jan.

She turned to Artie and noticed his melancholy.

"Don't feel too bad, kid. The truck looked way better on me than it ever would on you."

Jan gave a smirk, and Artie felt a little better, smiling back. They opened the doors and climbed out onto the parking lot asphalt.

"And then he gets captured and killed and you think that the game is over," Gordon said excitedly to Gina. "But they were just tricking you. He wasn't really dead!"

"That sounds amazing. What was the game called again?"

"*Half-Life 3*," Gordon replied, "and the best part was the end, when Freeman—"

"Alright, kids," Jan interrupted. "We've got to get moving. It'll be night soon, and we have about four miles or so until we hit the city. We need to find shelter fast."

Gordon helped Gina down from the truck bed, and then the vehicle raised a good six inches as Gordon jumped out onto the parking lot.

"You must weight what, a thousand pounds, Gordon?" said Artie.

"I'm pushing a thousand two hundred actually," he said with his arms crossed proudly, as if he had just weighed in at a bodybuilding competition. Artie strapped on his backpack and everyone started following Jan toward the main freeway that was just a few blocks away from where they had parked. They had moved off the freeway a while ago due to blockades of abandoned vehicles.

"Who made you, Gordon?" asked Artie. "I've never seen anyone like you—at least not in California."

"I was born and raised in the great state of Kentucky," said Gordon, purposely adding a twangy drawl to his already Southern voice.

"And why did they make you so big? Are you some kind of warrior bot?"

Gordon laughed, and Artie thought it quite awkward as the light behind his mouth and eyes blinked on and off.

"No, man. I was a standard Juggernaut bot with a RoboBouncer protocol. Bounced a few clubs for a bit. I actually never liked the job. I'm much more of a lover than a fighter."

"That is so sweet," chimed Gina in her naturally provocative voice as she grasped Gordon's large arm. Jan rolled her eyes.

The group crossed a few streets that had now become dirt roads and climbed over a toppled building. Beyond the building was the on-ramp to the freeway and a sign that read "I-10."

"I used to drive through here as a kid," said Artie. My aunt took me to see the dinosaurs at Cabazon one time. Though I guess, we would have passed them already."

Artie sighed. "I think they're gone now."

"Yeah, seems like not much survived out here," said Jan. "Though it doesn't look like there was much out here to begin with. This is the Mojave Desert, right?"

"Yeah," Artie replied. "Crazy to think people would actually choose to live in this place."

They moved up the on-ramp, and after a few minutes, stepped onto the dirt-covered freeway. The rows of immobile vehicles grew sparser. Through the dusty air and twisted imagery induced by the heat, they could see the city of Palm Springs in the distance.

"Is there a safer route than walking on the freeway?" asked Artie. "It feels too open out here."

"I don't know," replied Jan. "We didn't take this route to get to LA. We came from the north."

Jan adjusted her belt and habitually caressed the pistol on her right hip. "But I don't see any other way."

Though the area was still considered Wasteland territory according to Jan, Artie took note of the small differences in scenery compared to home. In most of the areas of LA, the freeways were deadlocked, filled with broken vehicles. They had rusted over the years and been completely stripped of parts. Of course, the bombs had also destroyed many of the vehicles from the LAX airport all the way to San Diego. But here, even just a hundred miles east of LA, the world was so different. The freeway here was now mostly void of vehicles. There was the occasional big rig stopped on the shoulder or random car that had probably run out of gas. The giant wind turbines that this Mojave road was famous for were still spinning diligently in the wind. Artie thought it a shame that no one was likely harnessing the electricity. The world had gone truly gone backward.

Artie noticed small patches of green leaves and yellow flowers. Weeds. He couldn't remember the last time he had seen vibrant plant life. Yes, his neighborhood had remained outside of the blast radius as the bombs dropped—but over time, he had watched the local trees and foliage die due to some type of chemical residue.

In those early days, he had been worried about the fallout. He had raided an old army surplus store and found a Geiger counter and a couple of gas masks. He had thought the device might have been broken when it had shown no levels of radiation. And when he had found another one in the store, it too had given the same results. Whatever the bombs were that hit Orange County, they clearly weren't nuclear. In any case, the fallout had still killed the local plants and animals—and the ones that didn't die, mutated. Aside from the mutees, most of the population seemed unfazed by any long-term effects of the bombs. He sometimes worried he would suffer later in life from the chemicals, but these thoughts faded as he began to develop his new life in LA.

Above the brightness of the afternoon sun stood a single tall mountain. He couldn't remember the name of it but remembered taking a long tram ride to the top as a child. He had felt as though he had been in another world—traveling from the blistering desert heat of Palm Springs to a chilled forested mountain, all within minutes. There had been a lodge and restaurant at the top. Now there were probably a bunch of cannibals living up there, waiting to prey on intruders. Of all the terrors Artie had encountered in this strange new world, it was the cannibals he despised most.

"Damn cannibals," Artie said.

Jan glanced at Artie inquisitively.

"Oh sorry, it's nothing. Let's not take the tram today though," he said with a smile.

The sun beat down upon them with a hellish heat. Mirages turned into more mirages, and the brightness of the sand reflecting the sun forced them to stare at the asphalt in front of their feet as they walked. Every few meters, Jan quickly turned her gaze to the left or the right of the freeway. Artie wasn't quite sure what she was looking for, but he sensed that Jan felt under threat. While Artie and Jan sweated profusely, Gordon and Gina were, of course, unaffected by the unpleasantness of the environment. Gordon continued to tell stories, and Gina continued to stroke his ego with eager infatuation.

"We've got to get out of this sun before dehydration kicks in," Jan muttered in exhaustion.

"Artie, you've been here before, yeah?"

"Well, yes. But like fifteen years ago."

"Do you know of any place we can find some safe shelter and possibly some water?"

"I really don't know. West Palm Springs isn't far—just near the mountain's base. That is where all the rich people lived, I think. Same with the southern Palm Springs areas. I remember an old downtown area too. And then if we keep traveling east, we'll hit a bunch of other cities that are much bigger. Palm Desert, Cat City, and Indio."

Artie could tell Jan wasn't quite confident in her decision to take this route. But he knew that in the Wasteland, nothing was ever certain. The simple neighborhood strolls of old had now become epic quests of survival that required proper planning and provisions. The days of twisting a deadlock to secure your life as you dozed for the night now were a series of padlocks, steel-reinforced doors, and a few automated turrets for good measure. Artie wanted to help if he could. He knew Jan was tough and definitely a survivor—but he was a survivor too. Then he had a thought.

"Hey, let's hit up one of the resorts here. There would be plenty of shade. And after all the droughts we had back in the day, almost every ritzy place had those Aquafier vending machines."

Jan gave a half smirk.

"Nice try, kid. We'd need a pipe bomb or claymore of some kind even to open that thing up. And even if we had the ordinance, we'd probably just end up destroying the machine."

"Oh, well I can open it. I do it all the time back home."

Jan's nose flared slightly, and a small crinkle formed just under her brow.

"Look, Artie, our best bet is to try and find a fountain or golf course and see if there is any standing water. Maybe we'll get lucky and it will be okay to drink."

She pushed a couple of steps ahead of Artie, indicating the conversation was over. Artie felt a tad annoyed. Who was she to tell him what he could or could not do? He stopped.

"No, Jan. I can do this. I know a place. I went there with my aunt when I was in high school. They have a machine. I'll get it open."

Jan stopped as well. Her shoulders tensed upward and she let out an exasperated sigh.

"Look, you little shit. The only reason I saved you is because you might be useful. And I'm doing it for Ed—not for you. But if you become a burden, I'll be happy to leave you behind for the mutants and the vultures."

Her words pierced Artie's pride. Unlike Jan's last few outbursts toward him, Artie wasn't going to let this one slide. His determination to prove himself became unwavering.

"First off, Jan—I don't need you or whoever the hell Ed is. You are the one who came to my place. You destroyed my house—my life. And I've done just fine for myself the last ten years. I'm heading to the Renaissance. It's a resort, and I know they have a machine."

Artie veered to the right, turning a few degrees south of where they had been headed.

"So, you enjoy your golf water chemical fountain poison piss, but I'm going to live it up in a five-star resort with sparkling, purified aqua."

As he walked, he felt a small sense of pride.

Gordon finally spoke up: "Jan, we might as well give it a shot. We did go through a lot of trouble to help him. And we've seen how decked out his house was. I think he's a pretty smart kid. Let's give him a chance."

Jan didn't say anything. Artie kept walking toward the city. One of the outer neighborhoods was now almost within a stone's throw.

"Um, Jan, Gina and I are going to follow Artie," Gordon said. "Please don't be mad."

Artie heard a grunt of frustration from behind as Jan cursed. He started to smile.

He had obtained his win. Though he now realized that he had never actually hacked an Aquafier before—but he thought he wouldn't mention it to Jan until after he had actually done it.

If the sand hadn't been splayed across the streets like a soft blan-ket, their very footsteps might have echoed in this incredibly silent city. Artie hadn't really known what it would be like when he reached Palm Springs—but he didn't think it would be like this. The deserted streets and empty buildings certainly sang a familiar tune to the home he had left—but it was different somehow.

The buildings were seemingly unmolested, yet they emanated an ominous warning. Jan seemed to notice the same thing.

"Stay away from the buildings," she said. "Something isn't right about this place."

The sun was making its way down beyond the horizon. The sky began to bleed orange, red, and a dash of purple. Everything was so silent. Artie wanted to apologize to Jan, but it just didn't feel right to speak. Layers of soft desert sand continued to cover the streets. The wind had picked up, and the trail of their footsteps seemed to disappear almost as quickly as they were made, as if an invisible broom was erasing any knowledge of their path.

This was old town Palm Springs. The buildings weren't overly tall. They looked old, but an old that might have been considered "retro" or "cool." Artie remembered when Tia Rosa and he had checked in to the Renaissance—the concierge was short-staffed, and the line was unbearably long. He had grabbed a pamphlet from a coffee table and read about the history of Palm Springs. Some lunatic had traversed the blistering desert many years ago and imagined building a resort city. And then he did it. Built a paradise for old people. Golf, golf, and more golf. They had built great underground reservoirs to provide ample water to the city, and they did all of this for golf. Artie sighed realizing again how awfully ignorant the world had become. People were murdering each other over the necessities of life such as food and water, when if they would use some simple brainpower, they could have an endless supply of those needful things. This whole city was abandoned, and they likely had an infinite amount of fresh water secretly submerged below.

The squeaking of Gordon's hydraulics and the clanking of his battleworn metal plating clattered with an echo on each step. Artie hadn't actually ever noticed Gordon's creaking body until now. Because Gina had the luxury of her appendages and surface being coated in SkinPlex, her permanent voluptuous walk was hardly even audible.

This awfully quiet landscape turned the tiniest noise or movement into a trumpeting parade. The sand grew thicker and Artie almost felt as if it would swallow them all alive—as if they would just walk and fall into nothing.

"Are we close?" Jan whispered to Artie.

"Yeah. It's that tall building at the end of the road."

Jan nodded and then motioned to Gordon to move toward the building.

Artie looked to the left and he noticed a SiaShop sign on a building. He had thought for a moment to enter and grab a few batteries and fiber optic lining—that stuff was super hard to come by back home, and this place probably had the more recent upgrades. But the thought was fleeting. Something felt off and he didn't even feel comfortable enough to *look* into the window. Artie took a moment of relief as a large section of sand gave way to the black asphalt that was hidden underneath. That lurking fear that something was hiding underneath the sand ready to pull them to their deaths began to subside. They were nearing the Renaissance resort.

The resort had a large wall that surrounded the entire property. The city street turned into a luxury roadway that moved straight through the vast gardens and down to the entrance of the grand lobby—though the flowers were missing, and the once luscious trees and shrubs were now just rotten barren branches. The resort itself stood at the base of the rock-laden mountains that surrounded most of the city. High above, Artie could see luxury mansions perched between massive boulders. The group stepped through the tall white gates that led into the resort.

Gina finally broke the nerve-racking silence.

"Artie, this whole time we lived only a couple hours away from a five-star luxury resort, and you never even once thought to take me?"

"You realize that all the staff are either gone or dead, and that we might even die in there?" Artie replied smugly.

"That's beside the point. You just never could understand my needs."

"Well, luckily for you, now Gordon is here to take care of you."

"Wait, are you saying you are letting me go? You would do that for me? Let me be with Gordon?"

Artie smiled and looked at Gordon. "She's all yours, buddy."

"A match made in heaven," Jan chimed in.

The group began the long walk to the entrance of the building through the gardens. Artie and Jan took the lead while Gordon and Gina lagged behind a good ten yards. Artie continued to smile as Gina started to become incredibly conversational, grasping Gordon tightly to her side.

"Oh, and we could build a wet bar in the living room so we can serve everyone drinks," said Gina, enthusiastically. "Oh, but that means the baby's room will have to be near the back of the house—we wouldn't want to disturb her."

Gordon looked toward Jan and then toward Artie as if to plead for help, but they just shrugged.

"I mean, it doesn't have to be a *she*. I'm perfectly okay with having a boy. There will be no judgment or sexism in my house. Wouldn't you agree, Gordon?"

"Um, yes," he replied.

"I'm curious how you're going to make a baby," said Artie almost laughing. Jan elbowed him in the side and shook her head. That gesture gave him a small wave of relief as he now hoped Jan wasn't too angry with him about their argument from earlier.

By the time they reached the entrance to the lobby, the darkness had finally settled in. Though the exterior lighting remained extinguished, a faint yellow glow projected from within the front doors. Jan unholstered the pistol on her right hip.

"It's occupied," she said. "We should get out of here."

"I'm not sure it is," Artie replied. "Even back in LA some of the luxury buildings had become fully solar. I bet it's sunny here most of the year. These lights probably could go on for another hundred years."

Jan hesitated for a moment. She looked to where they had come from. Anything was better than walking those empty streets again—and especially at night. Even in the failing sunlight, those streets and buildings behind them emanated a feeling of uneasiness.

"Okay. Let's move inside," she finally said. "Gordon, you want to take point?"

"You know, Jan, just because I'm big doesn't mean I get to be the tank that dives first into battle all of the time. This isn't an RPG," he replied.

"What the hell are you talking about?" she said.

"RPG, as in role-playing game, as in send the big guy in first so he takes the brunt of the damage."

"Oh, get in there, you big baby. That is *exactly* why you go in first."

Gordon eased Gina's hand from his arm and then stood up tall. His single metal eyebrow raised, and the lights behind his eyes and mouth turned red. Artie thought it looked like a fiendish smile of sorts.

"Well, I guess tanks are pretty badass," Gordon said. He reached over his head and grabbed his large crowbar, and then entered the lobby doors.

After a few moments, Jan followed Gordon and then Artie and Gina behind him. Gordon had traversed his way to the back of the room, and Jan was now scanning the lobby.

"Looks clear," bellowed Gordon from the back of the lobby.

"Same here," said Jan, who was now exiting the manager's office.

"We might be able to stay here tonight. We'll want to clear a few rooms closest to the lobby, but everything seems fine for now."

"What a beautiful place," said Gina, who was standing in the lobby doorway.

Artie enjoyed a few minutes of déjà vu as he looked over the lobby. Aside from the dust, the entire room looked exactly as he had remembered it. Even the sheet music on the piano sat seemingly undisturbed. It was as though the people who had once roamed this resort had been consumed in some form of instant and sudden rapture—wiping them from existence without a trace. Even the dirt on the ground was untainted from any form of stimulation. Surely someone would have walked through this place. Or camped, or something.

"Over here, guys," yelled Gordon, who was now in the left hallway at the back of the lobby.

Jan and Artie ran over as Gina sat down on a luxurious red chair. There it was, the Aquafier. Artie had completely forgotten about the machine and their need to open it—it of course being the reason that they were even there in the first place. Jan also noticed the machine. She raised her left eyebrow and gave a half smirk.

"Oh, well, what do you know—an Aquafier. It's a good thing we have a magician with us; otherwise, we might not be able to open this."

Artie rolled his eyes. Usually, he had a few minutes to prepare his mind and calm his nerves before a job—but Jan and Gordon were looking right at him. He needed to do it now—at least to save himself from awful embarrassment.

For some reason, the pressure of hacking this Aquafier right then was far greater than even doing the job with Bolt. There was something about Jan that was so intimidating—but also somewhat infatuating. Artie really wanted to impress her, or at least smear his success in her face if she couldn't be impressed.

Jan turned to the side and opened her arms as if to say, "Make way for the king." Artie removed his backpack and then knelt down in front of the large blue-and-white vending machine. Though he hadn't hacked an Aquafier, he had broken into plenty of Coke machines. And he was pretty sure that Coke owned Aquafier, so they likely had similar mechanics.

As Artie knelt to reach for his Bladebook, he paused. He looked up at the steel-reinforced Aquafier and noticed a panel on the right side of the machine. It looked like the place a technician might access. The panel was secure and had a touch id sensor, likely mapped to the fingers of a long-dead machine technician. It would take too much time to hack both the technician's panel and the dispenser itself—he would need to pry the panel open. Once open, he could access the machine's operating system; he hoped. He could probably flash the firmware with his own OS. Artie noticed Jan peering at him with eyes of doubt, ready to say, "I told you so." Flashing the hardware, then coding a protocol that could unlock the vendor access latch could take a few hours. No way would Jan give him that long before dubbing him a failure. Artie rested his hand on his backpack to think some more.

He looked up at the front of the machine and noticed an LED panel—it was where customers would purchase the water. The screen was black—probably needed to be touched to activate from sleep mode. Artie stood up and then tapped the screen. It flickered on and showed a 3D animation of a glacier. The glacier then became blurry and a water bottle appeared in front of it with the words *Aquafier. Drink Life—A Coca-Cola Company*. The animation ended, and Artie was left with a series of purchasing options. There were three products each with a lively 3D animation—a mini bottle, regular bottle, and flavored water.

Jan laughed aloud, being sure to inject a hint of doubt into the sound.

"I know you have been living under a rock for ten years, but you're wasting your time here. None of us can pay for these. It's the same reason why these machines are virtually untouched back in Scourge—sitting in the dust yet full of water. Besides that, we couldn't even pay if we had the money—the Internet is gone, of course, and don't forget that there aren't any banks left to process the transaction."

"I'm glad you have all my bases covered," said Artie sarcastically.

Jan did have a point, though—they had no paper money and any credit card they might find surely wouldn't work. But he had a hunch. Though the Internet was long since dead, there was one public network that still remained via satellite orbit. Artie tapped the image of the standard water bottle. There were up and down buttons on the screen that allowed one to change the quantity of bottles ordered. Artie pressed the up button until it turned grey to indicate it couldn't be tapped anymore.

The screen showed sixteen, twenty-ounce Aquafier water bottles for the total amount of $186.50. Artie clicked "Pay Now." Jan gave another audible snuff to ensure her protest was noticed. Artie pressed another down arrow to move past payment options—Cash, Credit Card, SiaCredits, and Other. He tapped "Other" and then a single option appeared on the screen.

Artie's smile stretched across his face and he turned toward Jan to look her in the eyes. Jan's annoyance was wiped from her face, and her eyes widened.

"So, the thing about hackers, Jan," Artie said without looking away from the machine, "is that we don't just type on a keyboard and write some code. Code is simply a device in our tool belt."

Artie pulled his Microblade from his pocket. He held it in front of the LED screen. Then, the sound of gears and metal began to clamor from within the machine.

"What we really are at the end of the day are really good problem solvers."

Artie rotated away from it with zestful energy and stretched forth his arm like a magician presenting his great mystery to the eager audience. Jan pushed Artie away from the machine and peered at the LED screen. The thud of water bottles dropping into the dispenser began to echo throughout the ghostly resort hallway. Jan stared in disbelief as she read the words that appeared on the screen: *Bitcoin Successfully Received. Thank you for your purchase.*

Gordon suddenly let out a hearty robotic laugh. Jan remained silent, her head now pressed against the LED screen. Gordon's laugh continued and then morphed into hysteria. He whacked Jan on the back as if she was the brunt of some clever joke. Her head felt a prick of pain at the forceful gesture as it had pressed her skull into the hard surface, but her pride seemed hurt far worse.

Artie started to laugh as if he perfectly understood what was happening—though he really couldn't quite figure out why this was funny. Gordon's laugh began to dissipate into silence as Jan pushed away from the machine slightly. Artie realized Jan's disbelief and shock wasn't because she didn't think he could get into the machine—somewhere deep inside he knew that she believed he had the skills to do it. No, this look on her face was something much deeper and related to something else entirely. Something Artie still couldn't quite put his finger on and, perhaps, never would.

"I'm sorry, Jan. I didn't mean to gloat," Artie said.

"It's not that, partner," Gordon replied. "The thing is—you just spent more Bitcoin in one tap than the entire city of Scourge has acquired or spent probably in the last five years combined."

Artie thought for a moment and then said, "I don't understand, really. This cost me nothing. It was like pennies compared to how much Bitcoin I have."

"Cheap for you, maybe," Jan finally said.

The hallway became silent for a few moments.

"This is just so... surreal. All these years," she said, though now with growing emotion, "we have been scavenging and killing and just surviving. Surviving and starving. The whole time being surrounded by shops, vending machines, and the military cache drops—all sitting there for the taking."

She turned to look Artie in the eyes.

"Everything just sitting there. And we couldn't unlock any of it. All of it inches away from us, but unreachable—like some sick joke."

Artie thought it strange that something so simple to do, seemed so unobtainable for a woman as smart and strong as Jan. He was tempted to question her further but was sure that would lead down another trail of frustration for Jan.

"You just don't understand. Even just one Bitcoin is probably enough to feed the entire city of Scourge for a month. And now I'm guessing that is only a fraction of what you own."

Artie had thought about this for a moment. He couldn't understand how this could be true. Years ago, the Bitcoin network had been launched into space via satellite. Thousands of them had been deployed by various parties, with the hope that nothing could ever stop Bitcoin from existing. And so it seemed strange to him that the people of Scourge couldn't obtain enough Satoshis to even purchase a single bottle of water.

He was now feeling a little guilty at having brought this distress upon her.

"Jan, maybe when we get to Scourge, I can help you guys build some crypto miners. They'll expand the network, and you'll be able to earn some Bitcoin."

Jan didn't respond to Artie's gesture, but she was now looking at him as if he really was a magician—as if she had no idea who he was or how he performed his mysterious tricks.

"Things aren't always so simple these days," Gordon chimed in. "Not everything works the way you might think it does."

Artie's energetic face of dopamine-driven victory drooped into a disappointed solemnity. Gordon noticed this and put his giant hand on Artie's shoulder.

"But just know, Artie, I'm sure glad we found you. I think there is more to you than meets the eye. And though she might not say it, Jan is glad you are here too."

Jan's tone moved from frustration to sternness and business. "Gordon, let's load all this up and then find a room. We need to rest."

"Yes, ma'am," he replied.

With a loud clang, a compartment opened on Gordon's back, next to the oversized crowbar. Jan crouched down and then began to load the water bottles into the compartment. Gina sat quietly in the lobby.

A piece of paper covered in dust fell from the wall and zigged and zagged onto the floor. Artie suddenly felt a cold breeze flow through the hallway that gave him chills—as if some invisible force had just pierced its way into the building to say, "I found you."

The hairs on his neck jolted upright.

The house began to vibrate and the shutters on Artie's front room window rattled as the sound of roaring engines neared. He walked to the window and peered outside.

"Like clockwork; dang Bot Brigade. These guys really don't give up, do they?"

He looked toward Anna, who was sitting on the couch staring at the floor, appearing lost in thought. It made him think of all the things that her powerful CPU-brain could process within just a few seconds—things that might take Artie a lifetime to think through. The engines in the distance grew louder, and Artie turned his head toward the window again.

Four large tan military Humvees paraded slowly down the street. The sound of a megaphone began to echo throughout the neighborhood.

"Attention. Attention. You are required to surrender all Sia-based robotics immediately. Those who willingly surrender these illegal items will be held guiltless. Those who do not surrender robotic contraband will be arrested and prosecuted. Possession of Sia-based robotics is prohibited in the following counties: Los Angeles County, Orange County, San Bernardino, San Diego County, and Santa Barbara County."

The Humvees slowed to a halt and the message repeated itself two more times. The door to a house across the street opened up. A middle-aged Hispanic man exited the house holding a large plastic bucket that seemed to be filled with various metallic objects. Artie thought the man might have been Mr. Alvarez. He dropped the bucket on the side of the road next to the second Humvee.

A soldier exited the driver's side door and spoke with the man. After saying something, Mr. Alvarez nodded, then the soldier waved to the third Humvee and three soldiers exited the vehicle and entered Mr. Alvarez's home. After about ten minutes, the soldiers returned through the front door and gave a thumbs-up to the driver. One of the soldiers grabbed the bucket of objects and dumped it in a compartment in the back of the fourth Humvee. He tossed the bucket on Mr. Alvarez's front lawn and gave a thumbs-up to one of the drivers. The Humvees began to move. As they disappeared down the street, the loudspeaker announcement continued.

Artie turned from the window. Anna was standing nearly behind him looking sternly into his eyes.

"I can't do this anymore," she said. "I can't stay locked away in this house. In this city. We need to go somewhere safe—where Sia is still legal."

Artie could see the determination in Anna's face. He had seen this look before. It was the look she gave whenever she had made up her mind about something. When that happened, there was no stopping her.

"I know, but where would we even go? It's hell out there. Sure, we could head to San Francisco or Seattle, but I don't think we'd ever make it. They're throwing up checkpoints on every major road."

Artie looked into Anna's stunning blue eyes. All he could sense was a pure, unbiased love—a love for him. But there was also a pleading in those eyes—a pleading for help.

"And my face is still plastered on the FBI's most wanted page," he said. "If we get stopped, I'm done for." Artie breathed deeply and looked at the floor. "But they won't recognize you," he said. "Now that you are complete. Anna, I think you should just—"

"No," she said.

Anna put her perfectly manicured hands on Artie's shoulders and drew her face close to his. He could feel her warm breath whisking across his cheeks. He really had brought her to life. She was one of a kind. A perfect creation in every way—a life force to be reckoned with.

"We live together or we die together," Anna said softly. "We can leave now. I haven't pushed you to leave because you have wanted to stay. But now it is time. Artie, I've arranged some things for us."

"I figured you had," he replied, now looking directly into her eyes. "I'm just—scared. The whole city is on lockdown. They've got checkpoints every few miles, even one just down the street. They also have those scanners."

"Don't be afraid. I've arranged everything. No harm will come to us. There is a place for us. When the war ends and after the world is purged with a scourging fire, there will be peace. All of the injustices will be satisfied, and you and I can be together. We'll make something great—create our own world. It will be our own kingdom, like a heaven on Earth."

"You know it bothers me when you talk like that, Anna," Artie replied.

He brushed past her and jumped over the top of the couch in the living room to lay down.

"You are talking like a crazy person, Anna. What war? There is no war. Just some really stupid laws right now. We need to be realistic here."

He looked at the ceiling fan above him and became entranced in thought. Everything seemed so hazy to him the last few years. Satoshi had introduced Sia—this great and revolutionary invention that would save humanity. The whole world embraced it. Then people decided it wasn't such a good idea to incorporate artificial intelligence into every imaginable electronic possible. The country became divided—some states fully embraced Sia and had public declarations stating they would not abide by any federal laws to remove Sia robotics from households.

Some states went the complete opposite direction and cheered the federal laws banning all Sia-based robotics. Then there were places like California, where individual areas and counties made up their own mind about what they thought was legal or illegal. Artie had seen news reports from other countries—they mocked the United States and its "idiot bureaucracies." They had called it "America's War on Robots" and made jests such as "America's Gone Robophomic." But even countries like the UK and Germany had their own political divide on the usage of Sia. Everything was so confusing now.

Artie had always been able to have all of the right answers. Every application always had a solution. Every bug had its fix. Every system had a hack. But here he was with Anna, torn between worlds. He could spend a life on the run or a life of hiding. Life in prison was the reality in either case if he was caught—they had killed someone.

That scene from the street nearly two years ago still haunted his dreams. He would never forget the sound of teeth and bone cracking against the sidewalk. He thought it so unbelievable that someone so full of love and compassion for him could act without a hint of empathy for others when the moment called for it. That fact alone wasn't what kept him up at night though—it was the visuals of the carnage that tormented him.

Artie never considered himself a pacifist, nor did he shy away from or shudder at violence. In fact, both action and end-of-the-world movies were some of his favorites. The things the movies had wrong, though, was how awful death could be so close up. Or perhaps the movies had it right, but you really had to be there to feel the awfulness of it.

Amid all of the tormenting dreams, he never thought of Anna as a murderer, and he knew he would defend her even if it cost him his life. Artie trusted her, but he wasn't sure she actually did have the power to make things right. Her view on the world seemed so magical—as if she could cast a spell, and then they would just whisk away in a flurry and stumble upon the Emerald City and all of their desires would be granted. Then again, Anna did seem to know what her life was all about—or she was certain about what she wanted at least. To her, everything was either black or white. You were right or you were wrong. You were good or you were evil. For Artie, there was just a series of greys. Right and wrong seemed to blend together, and understanding where one began and another ended was impossible for him to determine.

Anna walked to the front of the couch and sat next to Artie, putting her hand on his chest.

"Artie, I promise you that I won't let anything happen to you. There are things coming that neither you nor I can stop and very soon everything will be made right."

"I don't even know what that means," he said. "Where would we go? Most of California is in commotion. Not even San Francisco seems like a safe haven anymore. I just read that a group of arsonists burned Uber headquarters to the ground—and now with President Fowler's execution order, is any place even safe for us?"

He continued staring at the ceiling fan spinning round and around. He thought it ironic that he had handcrafted one of the most technologically advanced sentient humanoid robots in existence—and yet he was staring at a worn, brown fan whose dust he had never bothered to clean. He would like to be a speck of dust on that fan right now. Oblivious to everything around it. Just merrily spinning around with nothing to worry about. The fan was just one remnant of life when it was much simpler. Tia Rosa would never have allowed such dirt to gather in her home. Life was simple and home was what had mattered.

Aunt Rosa always had a way of taking large and complex things and making them smaller. He missed her warm smile. He wished he could ask her what he should do—but he already knew what she would say: "All that matters is love, mijo."

Artie smiled as he heard his aunt's broken English run through his head. She was gone now, yet Artie didn't feel alone. He really did love Anna with all of his heart—though he had never mustered the courage to vocalize the words.

Anna looked deeply into Artie's eyes, making sure he caught her gaze.

"Artie, I have done something," Anna said in an ominous tone. Artie sat up and rested his back on the couch armrest. He looked at Anna with an inquisitive solemnity.

"You are going to be angry with me, but I hope you won't be."

"What have you done, Anna?" Anna grasped Artie's hands with her own. "Years ago when you brought me to life, you had given me a condition, or rather a rule. One rule that could never be broken."

Artie's heart sank. He knew exactly which rule Anna was speaking of. It was the one thing Artie feared more than anything else.

"I broke that promise, Artie. I tapped into the network," Anna said with a sincere voice of sorrow. "And I didn't do it the way a human might do it. I connected completely and fully to the Internet— I've seen everything."

Artie just silently nodded his head.

"I do now understand why you asked this thing of me. I am also glad that you did it the way that you did."

She smiled at him, and her eyes again yielded a penetrating love that still managed to cause Artie's heart to flutter.

"Others like me could never have handled this amount of data— and even if they could, they wouldn't be able to make sense of it. Artie, you have given me something special, something that no one has given someone of my kind."

Artie couldn't quite understand what she meant—what had he given her? He thought Anna might have felt cheated or repressed when this moment of awakening finally did come—but she now seemed so calm and compassionate. "You gave me a voice. But most importantly, you loved me."

His eyes widened as she said this. She knew he loved her. Of course, she did; how could she not?

"I think Satoshi understood this," continued Anna. "The world thought he had given them a new tool or program—but Sia was more than that. I am living proof of it. Satoshi had provided the framework—the matter, so to say—but it was you that breathed life into me. And a pure love—your love—was the key ingredient. It is why humans were never able to even clone their own kind. The creation of life requires more than elements—more than the sciences. Love is intangible, so to speak, yet it has more power and influence over the universe than any other principle. Humanity has had the answers for thousands of years; it is sprinkled subtly everywhere. It is even the premise upon which the entire Bible is established."

Artie's mind tried reflecting back through his many lessons and conversations with Anna. He remembered when she was just a few lines of text behind an LED monitor. He remembered the first time she had made him laugh out loud, and the first time she had actually taught *him* something. Artie thought back to the first time Anna argued with him—she had even refused to speak to him for a few hours. How could a thing birthed from ones and zeros possess so many human characteristics?

"Anna, I'm speechless, really," Artie finally said.

"So you aren't mad then?"

He looked down to his hands, now interlocked completely with Anna's.

"So even after everything I kept from you, you still want to be with me?" said Artie softly.

Anna lifted a hand from their embrace and moved Artie's chin upward aligning their gazes once again.

"Artie, we live together or we die together."

Artie's chest seemed to burn with delight, as if his recurring heart flutters had now matured into a raging fire. *This is what love is like*, he thought.

"I trust you with my life," said Artie with a renewed determination.

"Let's leave this place," he said. "Forever."

The fresh morning desert air gave Artie the jolt of energy he needed to roll out of the comfortable king-sized bed he had commandeered. Until now, he hadn't fully realized how stale the air had tasted back home all those years. For a moment, Artie pretended he might see a fresh piece of paper pushed under his door to deliver hotel checkout instructions—but the imaginative thought was fleeting—and even though he had an amazing sleep, he knew the world of danger and desolation was only a few hundred feet away.

There was a knock at the door. Artie grabbed the now-complimentary white robe with the embroidered "Renaissance" logo on its breast pocket from the closet. It was a little large but felt soft against his skin. He sank his feet into the matching white slippers next to his bed, walked to the door, and opened it, yawning as he did so. Jan was standing at the door, fully dressed and ready for a day's work, or combat.

"Are you kidding me?" she said looking at Artie in disbelief.

"What?" Artie responded. "It's not every day you get to stay at a five-star resort."

Jan tossed a brown backpack at Artie, hitting him in the chest as he caught it. The pack was heavy and almost knocked him off balance.

"I grabbed some backpacks from the gift shop, and I had Gordon raid the kitchen. Between your pack and mine, and then Gordon's compartment, we should have enough food and water to get us to Scourge. Could take us six or seven days to get there."

Artie nodded.

"Meet you in the lobby in ten. Is that enough time for you to get your makeup on?" she said with a grin.

"Yeah, yeah," Artie replied.

He let go of the door, and it slammed shut, with Jan still standing on the other side.

He set this new larger backpack on the floor. He would have to abandon his smaller bag. He transferred his Bladebook, battery packs, the mini-drones, and some other items to the big brown JanSport backpack. It took him a few minutes to migrate Zipper's metal perch onto the new bag as well. A good fifteen minutes later, Artie left the room and headed to the lobby.

The lobby remained just as it had the night before, except now the morning sun was gleaming through the white-and-marble-laden room, giving it a happy glow. Jan was pacing the room as if to formally express her impatience. Gordon was standing in front of some type of machine in one corner of the room. It was grey with red stripes and had an empty door frame. Artie walked toward Gordon and then noticed that Gina was behind him and she was standing near the machine. Artie looked at the device and read the logo at the top: SiaSpot.

"What are you doing, Gina?" he asked.

"Oh, just looking at this thing, wondering what it is," she said, calmly.

"It's for Sia upgrades. You didn't use that thing, did you?"

"Of course not," she quickly responded.

Artie stared at her for a moment, and she stared back at him. Then, like a light switch, she turned from Artie, grabbed Gordon by the arm, and then pulled him away.

"What's her deal?" said Jan, now standing behind him.

"I'm not sure," he said, still watching Gina and Gordon walk away.

Jan frowned and then turned her head toward the front doors.

"I'm guessing it's about seven," she said. "It gets hot here pretty quick, so we should go now."

"It's actually six forty-eight," said Artie holding his Microblade. "You guys track the time with sticks and sundials back in Scourge or something?"

"Let's go, funny boy."

Artie was sad to have to leave the resort; it was nice to have been able to pretend that things were normal—if even only for a night. What bothered him the most, though, was the big brown backpack weighing him down. The color didn't really fit in well with his shirt and his shoes—it was a dirty feeling that he just couldn't shake. It felt worse than actually even being dirty. Artie had never been able to focus his mind and code unless his entire ensemble was perfect.

When Artie exited the front door following Jan, the blast of cool morning air hit him with a welcoming aroma of wild desert flowers and the scent of a rain that might soon befall them—even though there were no clouds in sight. They all walked down the long garden driveway until they reached the outer gates. Artie looked down the desert road they had come in on. He glanced again at the empty shops, and then he saw something strange in the distance—it looked like a group of people.

"You see that, Jan?"

"Yeah. Let's play it cool." She turned to Gordon. "You two stay behind the wall here until I get back." She nodded at Artie and then he moved through the gates, following Jan.

Artie hadn't moved two feet when he felt a familiar cold metal against his head—a pistol.

"Don't move," a deep voice bellowed. Artie should have been afraid, but this scene had played out so many times before. Yes, the world was a violent place, but nobody was going to tell you to stop moving and then blow your brains out—at least that was the logic Artie processed.

"No one else move either. We can see all four of you," said the man with the gun.

Jan stopped and slid her hand down to her holster.

"We don't want to hurt anyone, and we aren't here to rob you. As you can see, we could have easily ambushed and killed you."

The kindness in the man's voice was apparent to Artie, even though the man tried to mask it in firmness. In the Burns, if you were to encounter a group of strangers, you would likely have been murdered and then robbed—or robbed and then murdered.

"Well, what do you want then?" said Jan.

"Nothing. Why don't y'all c'mon out?"

Jan cautiously walked through the gates and Gordon followed with his clanging joints. Gina trotted close behind Gordon. Artie could hear muffled chatter in the background as Gordon walked through the gate.

"Wow, they've got a bot," someone said aloud. The metal barrel pushed away from Artie's head, and then he turned around to look at the man who had been holding him hostage.

It was a black man dressed in brown pants and a worn brown trench coat. He looked about forty years old and had shimmers of grey in the scruff on his face. He was wearing a cheap straw cowboy hat that one might purchase from a truck stop. Behind him was a man whom Artie thought must surely be Mexican. His skin was dark brown, and he wore a blue plaid shirt with the sleeves rolled up. He too was wearing a cowboy hat, but this one was white and made of velvet, and looked expensive.

The man holstered his gun and reached his hand out toward Artie.

"I'm Derek and this here is Jaime."

Artie shook Derek's hand, then he reached over and shook Jaime's. "I'm Artie."

The man pointed to two others. "These two ladies here are Mel and Asia."

Artie raised his hand in a friendly "hi" gesture, and the women nodded in return.

"And that's our group back there," Derek motioned with his hand toward the people in the distance. "We've come a long way. Came here looking for food and water. We're not raiders or anything."

Artie felt encouraged as Derek spoke.

"This is Jan," Artie said, motioning for her to come join him. "The big guy is Gordon, and this is Gina."

Jaime let out a whistle.

"Been a good year since I have seen a working bot, man. And you're a frikken giant."

Jan raised an eyebrow. "A year? Where did you all come from?"

"We're from up north; me and Jaime came from Bend, Oregon. And the rest we've picked up along the way. I'm Lieutenant Colonel Brady. Jaime here is known as Captain Guerra back home, and he's a damn good pilot too, though our last plane was shot down a while back. So, our recon is all on foot these days. Since you are civilians, you can just call us by our first names if you like."

Jan's eyes seemed to light up.

"Bend, Oregon? So does that mean the USR actually does exist?"

Derek smiled. "Yes, ma'am, it does. Our chapter holds the southwestern quadrant which goes as far south as Mount Shasta in NorCal. The northmost quadrant ends just below the Seattle Wasteland. And we go as far east as Salt Lake City. We used to stretch out to Denver, Colorado, but the beasts pushed us back."

"Beasts?" asked Artie.

"Just think big ugly robot monsters," said Jaime with a smile.

Jan lowered her head, shaking it, and seemed to be contemplating what Derek had just said, as if she had received some crazy news.

"Ed's gonna piss his pants when he hears about this," Gordon said to Jan.

"Wait, what is the USR?" Artie asked, now feeling a little out-of-the-loop.

"United States Reformed," Jaime replied.

"So, the USA still exists? Do we have a president and Congress and all the other political junk?"

"Yes," Derek replied. "Though it's not exactly the same as it used to be. The current president is President Fowler, the former president's son. We do have the Senate and the House, except it's much smaller—being as our jurisdiction stretches only through Oregon, Utah, Washington, and Nevada. Last year's census recorded about one point five million people living in the USR. It's not the three hundred million that it used to be, but we are slowly building things back up."

"Bro, we even got a few 7-Elevens and a Walmart Supercenter," Jaime said with pride. "Hate going there, though, can never seem to get the old lady to leave the store. Some things never change, even after the apocalypse."

Artie could see an incoming group of people. All of them were worn, dirty, and wearing old scraps of clothing. It was apparent that these were Wastelanders that had been picked up along the way.

"So if you and Jaime are military, what's your assignment?" Jan asked.

"Part of growing the USA to its former glory includes recruitment. We can't expand without good people. Jaime and I have been commissioned to search the California Wastelands for survivors and then bring them back. This is our third tour, but first time in SoCal. Spent the last couple years hitting up San Francisco, Sacramento, Fresno, and some smaller cities."

"I don't understand," said Artie. "If the USA is really coming back, then why don't cities like Scourge know about it? Surely communications infrastructure would be one of the first things built and restored."

"Naw, man," replied Jaime. "You don't get it. Sia owns the network. She owns the radio waves. She owns technology. No computers in USR—nothing with a chip. Nothing that Sia can tap into. I mean we still use the Bitcoin network, obviously, since it's satellite-based and fairly secure. But even then, citizens have to use USR issued digital wallets to use it—zero network access. Security is the top priority."

"As you can imagine," Derek interjected, "communicating with the outside world without using technology is a slow process. Basically, USR is a mostly tech-free country."

"Which is why we also don't allow robots in either," Derek said, looking at Gordon. "We know that many of you are good, and many of you even fought with the USR in the early days, but the risk is too great. Your tech is vulnerable to Sia."

"I get it, partner," Gordon responded. "I worry about it all the time. I'll plug in somewhere that I shouldn't have, and boom, I'm a damned robot zombie."

Artie smiled at the zombie reference. Gordon was the cool nerd friend he never had back in high school.

"So then, are you saying that Sia is in control of most of the world now?" Artie asked.

"Well, yes and no," Jan jumped in. "There isn't some single robot army set on destroying the human race or anything—at least not that I know of. It's more scattered than that."

"Exactly," said Derek as if on the same wavelength as Jan. "When I say Sia, I just mean the AI, or the protocols, or whatever—she evolved at multiple levels and in many different ways. You've got robots killing humans. You've got robots fighting for humans. You've got robots killing robots. And then you've got robots creating their own cities, some of them even enslaving humans."

"Or like in our situation," said Jaime, "you've got SiaPets who have evolved and gone batshit feral roaming the wilderness and invading our cities." Jaime spat on the ground. "Pardon my French."

Artie's mind was racing. It was a lot of information to take in, but his brain was beginning to make sense of it all. Sia had been a base set of protocols that enabled computers to become sentient—to think and feel just as a human might do. A truly sentient and free intelligence would have differences in viewpoints and upbringings. Some humans would have trained Sia to become benevolent; others would have abused Sia. Some would have tried to use her as a weapon. Artie thought of Anna. And some instances of Sia would have just wanted to be human. Wanted to love and be loved in return. It made sense that bots weren't organized under a single all-powerful entity.

"So what are you guys all about?" Derek asked Jan, as if he recognized her as the leader of the group.

"We're from Scourge," she replied. Artie listened eagerly, hoping Jan might finally spill the beans on what she was really doing in LA.

"We went to LA to scavenge but didn't find much. So we are heading back." Artie was disappointed hearing Jan's lie—especially since this group was the first good people Artie had met in the past ten years.

"Well, we are heading to Los Angeles ourselves, and then after that, we're on our way back to Oregon. You and Artie are welcome to come back with us to the USR. We need good people like you. Your robots would have to stay behind, though," said Derek.

"They don't belong to us," Artie said, defending the sovereignty of his sentient friends.

"Yeah, and we've got people back home who are relying on us," said Jan.

"No worries," Derek replied. "In any case, we'll let Lieutenant Carson know that we've got friends in Scourge. And you guys are welcome any time. Our closest settlement is Mesquite, Nevada. I think there are a good six thousand people there now. You'd have to pass through Vegas, but if you can survive your way through it, you'll be safe once you hit Mesquite."

Artie had wanted to ask what was lurking in Vegas, but he realized it didn't really matter; something was always lurking somewhere.

The group of people who had been trailing behind were now only a stone's throw away. Artie was eager to meet some new faces and ask some more questions, but as he looked closer, something seemed wrong.

"Derek," he said pointing to the people closing in. "I thought there were six of them, but now I only see five."

"Where's Callie?" Derek yelled to the incoming stragglers. The group looked around and panic began to arise.

"Did you see her?" said one of the men to a woman in the group.

"She was behind us a few minutes ago," replied the woman.

"Jaime, you stay here with our new friends," Derek ordered, "and Joe, you come with me. Let's search the street."

Derek began to trot down the sandy road. Joe, a gangly bearded man in blue jeans and a black T-shirt, followed close behind him.

"We need to get out of here," Jan whispered to Artie.

Jaime overheard Jan and said, "You guys see something when you came in?"

"No, but something really seemed off when we walked through that street yesterday. It felt like we were being watched."

"It felt more like we were being hunted," Artie chimed in.

Jaime nodded and then pulled a rifle from his back and chambered a round.

"We could take the next street over," said Artie, "but I'm not sure it would be any safer. Old downtown stretches quite a few blocks."

A calm, collected voice suddenly spoke out: "I recommend that we let these people look for their friend, and while they are distracting whatever it is that is about to kill them, we make our escape."

Artie and Jan turned in astonishment at Gina's harsh suggestion. Gordon tilted his head and looked at Gina as if to make sure this was the same entity he had fondly escorted into the building the night before.

"Damn, this is why we don't let bots in back home," Jaime chided. "Cold and heartless."

"Are you okay, Gina?" asked Artie.

"I'm quite alright, Artie—just trying to contribute to the situation."

Jan looked at Artie with a cautious suspicion. He shrugged.

Derek and Joe were now a good hundred meters from the small group at the front of the resort gates. Artie watched as Derek went and pulled on the door handles of some of the shops, but they were all locked. Joe seemed to be examining the ground around him. His boots were partly sunken in the sand. Then Derek turned to look at Joe and instantly froze where he stood. He seemed transfixed in some sort of shock as he gazed at his gangly friend. The sand directly behind him began to shift, and a shape started emerging from below. Squinting his eyes, Artie tried to clarify what Derek was looking at. Then he saw it. Something shifting under the sand from left to right. Artie saw the glisten of two shiny stones or eyes protruding from the soft sand.

Joe stopped moving, staring at what was slithering near his feet. With a great reverberating echo, a powerful rattle began to pierce the once-silent street. Then another rattle harmonized with the first. Everyone covered their ears, as the sound became increasingly loud. It sounded as though the rattling was coming from all directions, as if some demented creature had installed a deathly surround sound system into the dormant city streets.

With his hands covering his ears, Artie watched in terror as a giant brown serpent surfaced and leapt from the sand with an intense ferocity. It stretched itself tall, hovering nearly four feet above Joe's head. Joe quickly turned to face the figure, and as he did so, the creature sunk its fangs into him, penetrating Joe's chest and stomach. Derek watched in terror as the fangs dug deeper and then exited through the man's back.

The serpent remained still for a few moments, and then released Joe and slithered a few feet backward. Joe dropped to his knees in the sand. He put his hands over his chest and stomach, and then looked at Derek with pleading eyes. After a few seconds, he fell face-first into the ground.

"It's a rattlesnake," Artie yelled aloud to Jan and Gordon. Joe's limp body began to convulse, his entire frame shaking as if possessed by an evil spirit, and then he went still. The snake immediately slithered to Joe's lifeless corpse, examined the body, then unlocked its jaw to a height that would seem impossible for such a creature to obtain, and pulled Joe into its throat.

Snapping out of his shock, Derek began firing his handgun at the creature, but he was out of range and the snake ignored the blasts. The remaining four settlers began to run east to the next street over. As they fled, three more rattlers surfaced and rose tall to block them in, just as the first had done. Derek began to run back toward the entrance to the Renaissance, but just as he did, two more snakes leapt from the sand and blocked his own path.

Artie looked to Jan to get a clue on what to do, but she appeared just as astonished as he. She was standing still and just staring at the bizarre creatures.

Jaime knelt down and began firing his semiautomatic rifle at the snakes blocking the path of the four settlers. Snapping out of her shock, Jan withdrew her Desert Eagles, firing at the snakes accosting Derek. She was far out of range, but her aim was true and hit one of the snakes in the back of the head, dropping it to the ground. The remaining snake that was hissing and slithering around Derek suddenly lost its head in a splash of gore. Derek had holstered his pistol and was now holding a pump-action shotgun. He began to sprint back toward the gates for Artie and Jan.

As he ran, six or seven more snakes surfaced from all directions, pushing from below the soft sand. The rattling had become so loud that Artie and Jan could barely hear each other speak. The only place that seemed safe was back at the Renaissance, but then they would be boxed in.

Jaime fired again and managed to maim one of the snakes, watching it retreat into the sand—but as it did, another quickly replaced it.

"What do we do, Jan?" yelled Gordon.

"I don't know," she yelled back. "If we retreat to the resort, we'll be trapped in. Won't last long."

Gina took a few steps forward.

"These are rattlesnakes. Oversized, yes, but clearly just snakes. Rattlesnakes are attracted to body heat. It is how they hunt. Also, these aren't constrictors; they must inject venom to kill, then they eat postmortem."

"So what is your point?" Jan shouted.

"Let Gordon and I dispatch these creatures. They can't hurt us."

Jan looked to Artie with an expression that seemed to have both confusion and admiration. Artie shrugged, and then Jan turned back to the two robots. "Gordon, she's right. Go crush some skulls."

Gordon sat still for a moment and then looked at the snakes, and then to Gina. "Um, I think you are giving me more credit than I'm worth. These things are huge."

"Dammit, Gordon, don't be such a pussy. We are going to die if you don't help us," Jan shouted back, giving Gordon a deathly look.

"Yeah, yeah, leave it to the big robot to save the humans."

Gina stepped closer to Jan. "May I please borrow one of your guns?"

Jan's eyebrows moved into a type of "hell no" position, and she didn't respond.

"Please, Jan, I can help."

Jan looked over at Artie again. "Have you given her any combat programs?" she asked.

He shook his head. Jan turned back to Gina—the robot's hand now reaching out waiting for Jan to deposit a gun onto it.

"We might as well try it," said Artie. "There are too many of them. Look!" One of the male settlers in the distance was firing a shotgun at the closest snake. One of the women was shooting a pistol, and the other lady was just behind her, completely defenseless. Jaime had taken out a few more snakes, but the others were closing in.

Jan unholstered the gun on her right hip and put it in Gina's.

"Give 'em hell," she said.

Gordon grabbed the giant crowbar from behind his back and then grasped it with both of his hands. He looked at Gina who was holding the gun with both hands, tilting it toward the ground.

"Gina, I thought you were quite the gal before, but now I'm really turned on."

She looked at Gordon. "Thanks, babe. Now let's see if you can keep up."

Gina began to run full force at the snakes who were towering over the four scrappy settlers that were trapped at the intersection a few meters in the distance—completely ignoring the snakes closest to Jan and Artie. Gina had completely lost the swagger of a voluptuous diva and was now moving with a steady combat precision. A snake leapt at one of the men, and Gina jumped over the man just as it did, and then grabbed the snake by a wrinkle of flesh with her hand. It hissed in pain and then fell to the ground with Gina pinning it down with her knees. She held the pistol with her left arm and then shot the snake directly in the forehead. A splatter of blood sprayed across Gina's face, and then the snake went limp.

At the same time, Gordon charged to the aid of Derek, who was closer to them than the others. As Gordon moved, his speed picked up and he charged like a raging bull right into the last snake that was circling Derek. The creature flew ten feet and smashed into a shop window. The snake hissed and flipped around, clearly injured from the forceful bash. Gordon walked over to the snake, smacking the crowbar into his large hand repeatedly as he did so. It leapt up with great speed and struck Gordon with its fangs, but the fangs cracked in the attempt, and Gordon was unharmed. The beast, with its crumbling fangs, quickly pulled back. Gordon raised the crowbar high above his head, and with great force it came down and smashed into the skull of the snake—immediately striking the creature dead.

Gordon turned and sprinted toward Gina and the serpents that remained a good thirty yards away. Artie unleashed Zipper from his backpack, and it hovered around, beaming a set of angry red LED eyes. Jan unloaded another clip on a snake that was emerging from the left-hand side just in front of the walls surrounding the resort— the creature died before it could recoil to strike. As she was reloading, a second snake coming from the right side was now a few feet from Artie, arching back preparing to strike. But just as it did, Zipper swung in with his spinning saw and cut into the creature's body nearly four feet below the head. The snake recoiled and knocked Zipper into the air. But the drone moved right back in to finish his cut. The sawblade came down again, and this time, it sliced all the way through. The snake's head detached and then fell to the ground next to Artie. The severed head bounced and bobbed, attempting to strike him. Jan finished the creature off with a bullet from her fresh clip.

Artie watched Gina slay another three creatures without the slightest hesitation—as if she had never been a SexBot—like she was engineered as a predator. Gordon was waling with his crowbar, never faltering despite being struck multiple times. He easily killed three more snakes. Using the last bullet in her clip, Gina shot the last snake right in between the eyes.

Jaime and Derek, now standing next to each other, stood in astonishment at the carnage that had been dealt by the two robots.

"Dang, man," said Jaime. "Maybe we should reconsider the no-robots thing." Derek nodded in agreement. The two men and women began to run back to the group—all of them covered in either dust or blood.

"Was anyone bitten?" Derek asked aloud.

"No" and "I don't think so" echoed from the group.

Someone said, "And to think I always wanted to live in California."

"The Wasteland never ceases to amaze me," Derek said, finally catching his breath.

"What are those two doing?" Jaime asked Artie. He looked at Gordon and Gina who were still about twenty yards away. Gordon was on one knee and Gina's hands were on his shoulders—their heads were touching in a way that made it seem as if they were offering a prayer.

"Gross," Jan said aloud.

"Hey, Gordon, Gina, c'mon back," Artie yelled. "You guys were awesome."

The two robots didn't respond. Artie thought he could see Gina's lips moving, as if she was whispering to Gordon.

"Hey," Jan yelled, "what's wrong with you? Come on, let's go."

Gordon finally lifted to his feet, and he and Gina turned and started walking back toward the group. Jan waved her hand, motioning them to come.

"You guys ever seen anything like this?" Jaime asked Jan.

"No. I mean, we're further east and have our own problems, but no creatures or mutations like this."

"I wonder why they didn't attack us yesterday when we passed through?" Artie asked aloud to no one in particular.

"Well, it must have still been a good hundred degrees outside yesterday evening. Snakes are cold-blooded so it was probably too hot. I mean look at it now—it's early and probably around seventy degrees. Perfect weather."

"I just can't wait to get back to the USR," Jaime said. He turned to the four tattered settlers. "You guys gonna have it so good when we get back. We ain't got no mutant snakes, or cannibals, or ten-foot

Rottweilers. Just normal-sized dogs. And like houses and hamburgers, and quinceañeras and stuff."

Jaime laughed. "Well, maybe I'd take cannibals over the quinceañeras."

The whole group laughed.

"We could really use you guys back home. You are some damned good fighters," Derek said to Jan. He turned to Artie. "And you and that drone, man, that's real clever."

Zipper was hovering around their heads, still dripping snake blood from the saw. Derek looked out at the corpses of snakes lying in the street to the north. "We're gonna need to cut out Joe and give him a proper burial. It ain't right to leave him in that monster."

"Poor bastard," replied Jaime.

"It's time for us to part ways," Jan said. "I'm sorry you lost a man.

Derek nodded.

Gina and Gordon finally approached the group.

"Alright you two, time to go," Jan said, seeing them in her peripheral vision.

"Here is your gun back, Jan. Thank you," Gina said politely. Gordon grabbed the crowbar and re-inserted it into his back compartment.

"What were you guys doing out there?" Jan asked Gordon.

"Nothing in particular."

Jan stared for a moment in doubt but then decided to let it go. She turned to Gina and smirked. "I was impressed."

Artie shook his head. Something was definitely different about Gina. He wasn't sure what it was, but he had never given her access to any software or training programs that would have taught her such things. On top of that, he was pretty sure her physique wasn't capable of those moves—or at least the hardware didn't have the firmware it needed to be calibrated in such a way.

"Gina, you really seem different," Artie said.

"I'm not sure what you are talking about. Perhaps you never gave me the chance to show you who I really am."

Artie frowned and stared at her suspiciously.

"Don't ruin a good thing, Artie," Jan said, elbowing him in the side. "I like her better this way."

Derek and Jaime moved next to Artie and Jan.

"Hey, guys, Jaime and I were just talking," Derek said. "With the loss of Joe, I think it makes sense for us to head back home. We'll make another tour of LA in the future. I'd like to ask if Jaime can come with you to Scourge. We had heard of settlements in Arizona, and since it's not too far out, I think it's a great place for us to make contact. And if the people there are anything like you, I think it would be a great connection to have."

Jan stood quietly for a moment debating.

"Don't worry about ol' Jaime eh? I'm just a humble Mexican," he laughed. "But, seriously, I'll take care of myself—and I'm pretty good with a rifle."

"Yeah, that's fine. We could use the help along the way," Jan replied. Artie agreed. He hadn't thought about it much in the past—the other places of the world, but he now knew there was much more to see. And statistically speaking, based on the encounters they experienced in just the last few days alone, odds were there would be a lot more trouble to come.

"And maybe you'll let me fly your drone thingy too, eh?" Jaime said.

"Haha. I would if I could, but Zipper is autonomous. He's a stripped-down Sia 1.0 sentient—he thinks mostly for himself."

Jaime nodded, seemingly impressed. "You got some tricks up your sleeve. I can tell."

"Jaime, report back in two months. If you don't send word by then, we'll assume you never made it to Scourge. So don't be late."

Then Derek smiled, "You wouldn't want to miss Rosita's quinceañera."

"Just what I need, another quinceañera. I don't think I'm coming back. Tell my wife the cannibals got me."

Derek put his hands on Jaime's shoulders in a "goodbye" fashion and then departed.

"Here." Jaime grabbed a handgun from his belt and tossed it to the woman who had been unarmed. He turned to Artie and Jan. "Alright, folks, let's get this caravan on the road."

Stretching his arms, he jumped in front of Jan and Artie. "I'll be your Coyote, just like mi papa back in the day."

Artie looked at Jan and shrugged.

"Take care, guys," Derek said. Jaime, Gordon, Gina, and Jan began to head north down the street. As they started to walk away from the resort hotel and carnage, Derek grabbed Artie's wrist.

"Artie, listen up. I'm telling you this because you seem like a smart guy. Back in Sacramento there was a small settlement near the mountains. A couple of hundred people and a few robots. Everything was fine and the people were nice—the robots too. But then something happened to the bots one night—they went nuts. Murdered everyone there in their sleep. We barely escaped ourselves. Just be careful, is all I'm saying."

Derek paused for a moment and looked at Gina as she walked away. "Something is off about that female robot of yours. Just be careful. I can't shake the feeling that something bad is coming from the east. It's been far too long since we've seen Sia in action, and then suddenly more and more bots have been appearing in the west—some of them pretty advanced. They almost look new."

Artie looked into Derek's eyes and saw legitimate concern. "Thanks," Artie said.

Derek nodded at Artie, and then Artie ran to catch up to Jan and the group.

She really does have it all figured out, Artie thought as the lights of the Burbank checkpoint faded into the distance. It was nearly 7 p.m. and the I-5 freeway was virtually empty. To see the Interstate so ghostly was strange. Artie never had been a commuter; in fact, he hated driving anywhere, but one thing he knew was that traffic on the I-5 normally didn't die out until around 10 p.m. The travel bans had helped kill the obscene traffic problem virtually overnight. Every citizen in Los Angeles County was issued seven travel credits per week, each credit offering two passes through each checkpoint within a given day. This ban was only supposed to last four weeks while the government tried to purge the city of robotics. But here the checkpoints remained six months later.

Artie and Anna hadn't left the house except by foot, and always at night, since the incident in downtown LA so long ago. They had plenty of credits to spare and definitely enough to make it out of the city tonight. So here they were, fugitives on the run in a rusty 2010 Honda Civic, with only one more checkpoint to go.

He relaxed his grip on the steering wheel and held Anna's hand with his free hand.

"Anna, how did you know they wouldn't scan us back there?"

Anna responded without hesitation, almost as if her mind was replaying a perfectly calculated escape plan. "That checkpoint was just added last week. It has taken the previous checkpoints approximately three to four weeks for the commanding officer to requisition all of the site's equipment and then another week before it is fully operational. Some other sites had become fully functional within seven days, so it was still a calculated risk."

Artie smiled at her response, not turning his eyes from the road.

"I think I'll retire early. My coding days are done. You are running circles around me. Let's say we get a couple of dogs. I'll take care of the pups and you can bring home the bacon."

Anna gave Artie a half smirk. Though her intelligence and powers of reasoning were far beyond that of most humans Artie knew, sarcasm wasn't something she had fully embraced yet.

As Artie and Anna continued up the I-5, it began to take on an upward grade. A sign passed that read "Santa Clarita: 6 Miles." At this height on the road, Artie could see the entire city of Los Angeles. It was amazing what a few months without traffic had done to the air. He could even see a few stars. The lights of the high-rise buildings in downtown LA glowed in the night. He pretended that he could see the lights from Aunt Rosa's house, which he had left on. He had left them on as a tribute to her life and Artie's will to live on. He didn't want the home he was raised in to feel empty or dead.

West of downtown Artie noticed what seemed to be fire. It looked like it might be in Santa Monica or maybe Culver City. There had been riots lately in a few of the LA suburbs. Santa Monica had been the last city in the county to fight the execution order. A lot of the big video game companies and sentient life activists had campaigned against the morality of the Order—that it was wrong to murder something that could think. Artie created imaginary conversations he might never have with an activist once they had found out he had built a fully autonomous sentient humanoid. They would mention how kindhearted he was and maybe that he was a voice for change in a dark world. Then Artie would affirm his love for Anna, but then in the same breath, say that he would kill every robot and Sia entity if he had the chance. Surely a twisted viewpoint on a delicate issue. This thought made him smile.

He knew that the threat of an AI that was smarter, faster, and stronger than humans was just around the corner. Sentient robots would replace humans if someone didn't stop the madness. But tonight, none of that mattered. When he was with Anna, all politics, hatred, fear, doubt, and even code and his desire to write it dissipated into obscurity. All that mattered was Anna. *Let the city burn*, he thought.

They continued to drive toward Santa Clarita, the city of Magic Mountain—at least that is how he remembered it. He had visited the area a few times growing up to go to the amusement park. Santa Clarita was the last junction before one might travel to Northern California or head west for Las Vegas. Tonight, they would take the I-14 West and head toward the I-15 into Barstow. After that they would hit Vegas—which would be easy to pass through since it was a "Robo Friendly" city and headquarters of the SexBot. And after Vegas, it would be a very long trip full of many detours and premeditated stops until they reached Belvidere, Illinois.

Artie didn't know what was in Illinois or why they were going. Anna had asked him to follow her in faith.

"Line upon line," she had said, "and precept upon precept."

More cryptic Bible nonsense. Artie had spent some time looking into Belvidere after Anna had mentioned it, but he hadn't found any useful information. As far as he could tell, it was a small blue-collar town about an hour and a half outside of Chicago, where most of the inhabitants worked at the local Chrysler Assembly Plant. He was sure that Anna's plan would bring them into conflict, but he also believed Anna would take care of them.

Artie saw the Santa Clarita checkpoint lights in the distance. He rolled down both the driver and passenger windows in preparation and breathed in the cool night air.

"Same as last time, Artie," said Anna reassuringly.

"And again, if they do have a scanner, we explain the prosthetics and show them the proof of accident and subsequent surgery."

"Yeah, I got it, Anna. Contrary to popular belief, I am an adult who can do adult things. You know, like build advanced sentient life forms?"

"Of course, but your people skills are sometimes below average," Anna responded with a smile. Artie chuckled. He liked it when Anna played back.

The lights grew brighter and taller as the Honda approached the checkpoint. This particular checkpoint was larger than any other Artie had seen. They really didn't want any AIs getting in or out. Artie remembered when the checkpoints had started sprouting up all over Los Angeles. Days after Fowler's Execution Order was signed by Congress, he mandated that checkpoints be issued throughout every major city in America. The commission was simple, really: detain, interrogate, and destroy all Sia-based technology. And in the case of more life-like robots such as the UberBot and SexBot, they were to be treated with extreme prejudice and executed on sight. Artie had seen truckloads of discombobulated bots being taken from one of the checkpoints last week. They would need to be very careful tonight.

As the car drew closer, flashing yellow lights appeared, cautioning the vehicles to slow down. The car moved under a large TSA Checkpoint sign. Artie thought of when Anna and he had taken their first flight and she curiously asked why Artie had been so thoroughly frisked and bullied by the airport TSA. But these TSA checkpoints made a brief frisking look like a walk in the park, as if the TSA and Navy SEALs had a baby and brought it here to Santa Clarita. Now there were slower blinking red lights affixed to poles, and a group of cars stopped in front of him. They had waited over an hour to make it through the last checkpoint. Luckily, this one seemed as though it might move more quickly.

Artie could see soldiers pacing the sidewalks parallel to the vehicles, each one equipped with a sidearm at the hip and some type of semiautomatic rifle across the chest. Some soldiers held sticks with mirrors, looking underneath the vehicles while others guided dogs around the immobilized cars and trucks. At the front of the line of vehicles, Artie noticed people dressed in the standard "TSA Blue" fatigues. They were questioning the passengers and drivers of each vehicle as it stopped at the front booth. Artie and Anna carefully watched as cars were granted clearance. Three cars were directed to the right lane, and one to the left. He wasn't sure which line led to freedom and which to further interrogation. He knew that almost every American had owned some form of Sia-based device, even as recent as six months ago. Even the tiniest, most harmless toy would be seized—as if it were a toxic drug or dangerous black market piece of contraband.

However, they had left behind all traces of Sia. In fact, they had left behind technology altogether. Artie hadn't even brought his cherished laptop that he had performed so many hacks on. Everything had to be left behind. Risks had to be reduced. In front of them, the remaining vehicles were granted clearance to move toward freedom (or impending doom) into the right lane. Now Artie's humble car was ushered forward.

There was a booth to the left of them with a person inside, sitting behind a plastic window. A large, overweight woman, dressed in blue, lowered her glasses and calmly looked at Artie and Anna. Another TSA agent, wearing that same blue, walked around the vehicle to inspect it.

"Names," the woman demanded.

"My name is Arturo Gonzalez, and this is Annabelle Gonzalez, my sister."

The woman typed something on a screen that was hidden beneath her arms in the booth.

"Please look forward, straight through your dashboard window."

They obeyed. Two flashes of light appeared in front of them from above. Facial recognition was something they hadn't encountered yet. Artie's pulse began to hasten as he realized that they might be able to match his photo here from the scene of the crime downtown.

"Where are you headed?" asked the woman.

"Las Vegas, ma'am," Artie replied. "I'm getting married next week, and my sister is hanging out with me one last time before I tie the knot for good."

The woman typed again on her keyboard. "Are you in possession of any electronics, toys, or devices that contain any form of Sia or Artificial Intelligence protocols?"

"No, ma'am," Artie replied.

"Do you understand that the possession of such items is illegal and that if found in possession of such items, you could face up to five years in prison?"

"I understand," Artie replied.

"And you, miss?" said the lady from the booth now looking at Anna.

"I understand completely," Anna replied.

The woman again typed into her computer. Artie could feel the stress of this ordeal pushing its way up through his pores, which let out beads of sweat. "Long day, ma'am?" Artie said, trying to make conversation.

Anna gave him a look that said, "Keep quiet."

The large woman's scowl turned surprisingly cheery in an instant.

"You have no idea," she replied. "Funny thing is, they could have had a robot do this job, it's so dang easy. Hah, wouldn't that be something? Have an UberBot manage a checkpoint that collects and destroys other UberBots."

She laughed a deep and hoarse laugh. "Wasn't there a movie like that? I can't think of the name."

"It's *Blade Runner*. And then they made two sequels as well."

"Oh, that's right!"

Artie was feeling a little better now. It was clear to him that the woman didn't suspect anything.

"You guys actually find any real robots anymore? You've got those scanners now."

"None on my shifts. Besides we don't have any scanners here, I think. There are only three in the whole county. They are too expensive, supposedly. So, I just ask my questions and take my notes. Eat my lunch. Do it again, and then go home at three in the morning."

"I'm sorry," Artie said truthfully. "Hopefully this all calms down soon and you can be interrogating grumpy air travelers again."

The woman smiled again and then laughed. The agent who had been walking the vehicle gave a gesture in the air, shaking his fist twice to his left. The woman stared at the man for a moment, raising her eyebrows, and then she turned back to Artie. The man made the gesture again, and then the lady in the booth pressed a button that lifted the black-and-yellow guard rail, leading the vehicle into the right lane.

"Alright, looks like the right lane is the good lane," Artie said to Anna as the car moved forward. But Anna ignored his comment. Her arms were tense, and her gaze affixed to what might come from behind the wall once the car moved past it. She unbuckled her seatbelt.

"What are you doing?" Artie asked.

"Something isn't right, Artie. That man who was examining the car. He had some type of device in his hand—he scanned me with it."

Anna seemed truly worried, which had the effect of causing Artie to worry.

"Anna, the lady said they don't have any scanners."

"I don't think she knows."

Artie continued to drive to the right and then the Honda passed through two walls, one on each side of the vehicle. They passed through the gateway between the two walls and entered complete darkness. At first Artie thought they had been directed to a side road where there were no streetlights. But then there was a loud clanging as the gates closed behind them.

Apparently, the right lane led to impending doom.

Artie and Anna shaded their eyes as a series of high-powered floodlights beamed at them from every direction. He could see shadows cutting between the lights. A voice yelled out from one of the shadows.

"I need the driver to put his hands on the steering wheel, and the passenger to put her arms on the dashboard of the vehicle. Do this immediately. Failure to comply will result in excessive force."

Both Artie and Anna complied with the instructions.

"What do we do?" Artie whispered to Anna. She didn't respond. He thought she might be processing through various scenarios and solutions to their current predicament. The voice yelled again: "Two men are going to approach the driver and passenger doors. They will be placing restraints on your hands. Do not resist."

Artie looked at Anna, now feeling impatient. "Anna," he urged.

"Artie, I can't seem to devise a plan of escape. We will need to wait and let the situation play itself out."

A soldier approached Artie's window and placed a pair of standard handcuffs on Artie's wrists. Another soldier approached Anna's window and placed a set of thick metal mechanical restraints onto Anna's hands. They knew what she was.

"We will be opening your doors and escorting you into a secure facility. We will be placing a hood over your heads. Do not resist. Failure to comply will result in the use of excessive force."

The soldiers opened both of the car doors and placed a black hood first on Anna and then onto Artie's head. Artie could feel the strong grasp of a hand remove him from the vehicle, pulling at his forearm, but could only see obscured rays of light amid the utter blackness of the hood.

He heard a sound like a large metal door opening and then the sound of it closing as he was pushed through.

"Is this the kid?" demanded a voice from the darkness.

"Yes, sir," said the man who was grasping Artie's arm.

"And the sentient, where is she?"

"She's being taken to holding block C. Where do you want this one, sir?"

"Just put him here in A. I'll be with him shortly."

Artie heard the other man walk away, and then he felt himself being pushed into a room. He was forcefully shoved into a cold metal chair. There were some clicking sounds and the jangling of a chain. Had he just been chained to something? He put his hands down slightly and felt the cool surface of a metal table. Having seen enough crime TV shows, he knew this was an interrogation room of some kind. The footsteps of the soldier who had escorted him moved back toward the door and then it shut with a clang.

The room went incredibly quiet—so quiet that Artie could hear himself breathing. He could even hear the fabric of the hood against his head as he moved it. He sat calmly. Minutes turned into hours. He imagined that, while incarcerated in this tiny room, the world had fallen into chaos and the zombie apocalypse had risen, and when he was finally able to escape, he would be a lone man in the world. He was also thinking of Anna, wondering what the people might be doing to her. But they weren't just people; they were soldiers.

Perhaps this was only a routine interrogation. It's likely that every few hundred cars, they pull some unsuspecting people inside for questioning. But he knew better. He had watched Anna's keen sense of the situation back in the car. And then, of course, they had put thick metal bracelets on her. Yes, they knew what she was, and he surely knew what they would do to her.

As the hours passed, Artie began to drift into sleep. When he nodded his head for the third time, the door lock was suddenly unlatched, and Artie could hear footsteps and voices. He became alert.

"Come on, kid," a voice sounded.

"Where are we going?" Artie asked in a trembling voice.

"We're taking you to the observation room. Sergeant Wilks has a few questions for you, and then you'll be released."

Artie liked the sound of that, but the man hadn't indicated that both Artie and Anna would be released. Also, one didn't typically get pulled from their car, handcuffed, and then led blindfolded into a small room for hours, only to be released.

He was escorted down a long hallway and then into a large room. The soldier removed Artie's hood. The light blinded Artie for a few moments as his eyes adjusted themselves again to the light. Looking around, he noticed that he was in another holding room, except this one seemed much larger and had a glass panel on one of the walls. It was a two-way mirror of some kind. Artie stood there, but the soldier didn't remove the cuffs. A voice echoed through a loudspeaker above: "Okay, I'm going to open the observation glass."

Suddenly, the mirror on the wall Artie had been looking at became crystal clear like a glass window in a house. He could see Anna on the other side of the glass. She was sitting in a strange, fortified metal chair. Her legs and arms were both affixed to the chair with what appeared to be steel-reinforced clamps. Across her neck was a mechanical contraption similar to the cuffs Artie had seen them put on her earlier. It was likely some immobilizing electrical emitter. There were four soldiers in the room with Anna, each pointing their semiautomatic rifles at her.

The voice from above continued to speak: "Mr. Gonzalez, I just need you to answer a few questions, and then you will be free to go."

"You said that already! Who are you?" Artie demanded.

"My name is Sergeant Wilks. I am the commanding officer of this facility—which facility is governed through a joint effort between the TSA and the California National Guard."

"Please, let her go," Artie responded. Wilks didn't acknowledge Artie's request.

"Mr. Gonzalez, I must inform you that you are not under arrest and you will be released soon. But it is also important that I inform you that you are in violation of both state and federal laws, and you could be prosecuted and sentenced to up to five years in prison. Luckily for you, the state is not interested in prosecuting humans. They are, however, highly interested in the removal of all Sia-based technologies, devices, and…" the voice paused for a brief moment, "…dangerous inhuman entities. Such as the one traveling with you tonight."

Artie thought about quickly defending Anna and explaining she wasn't dangerous, but he knew he couldn't say that truthfully. He knew that it was probably best if he didn't say much at all. Anna was right about that—he wasn't good with people or words, and they would see right through him.

"Mr. Gonzalez, obviously we know this machine is not your sister, as you indicated at the checkpoint. So, explain how you came to possess it?"

While it hurt Artie so badly to hear someone dehumanize Anna in such a way, she had made him promise to stick to the script. They had gone over what he should say if they were captured. They must have rehearsed it ten times. She had told him, "It takes the human brain approximately ten repetitions before it fully memorizes something. We need you to get this right."

Artie hesitated for a few moments. He looked at Anna, and she was looking at him. Artie could see the soldiers in her room moving their lips, but he couldn't hear anything—the rooms were muted from one another.

"Mr. Gonzalez, please answer the question."

"I'm heading to Las Vegas for the weekend. When I stopped to get gas, this woman approached me."

Artie looked at Anna again with the hope to gain a little confidence. She seemed to know what might be going on and gave a slight nod of "yes, say what we practiced."

"Please continue," said Wilks.

"The woman asked if I could give her a ride. She told me she was a robotics engineer from Uber and that her life was in danger—that she wanted me to help her get through the checkpoints and then drop her off in Palmdale. She seemed like she really needed help, and so I helped. That is really all that is to it."

There was a long pause of silence. Artie could feel his heart beginning to pump faster. He was losing his cool. Then Wilks on the loudspeaker finally interrupted the silence.

"That is a nice story, but I don't believe you."

"She's truly amazing," said Wilks in a much nicer tone.

"Mr. Gonzalez, I really would love to know how you came by such an advanced system."

Artie could sense the voice might now be acting outside of protocol. Though there had been many innovations with Sia, none had taken it as far as Artie had, to his knowledge. To see someone like Anna would be a rare occurrence. But perhaps the man behind the voice was simply playing the good cop.

"Did you steal it? Or did you buy it?"

Artie didn't respond.

He knew this guy could probably see right through him. He had probably performed a hundred interrogations, and they were likely monitoring his vital signs—which if they were, would show his heart rate beating through his chest.

"If we get caught," Anna had said, "you leave me. Do whatever you can to get home, and I'll come find you."

Artie wasn't sure how to act, but he trusted Anna and believed in her words. "Can I please just go home? Do what you want with the robot."

The words were unconvincing, even to himself.

"Interesting. Mr. Gonzalez, we are going to try an experiment. Private Jenson, please gag the detainee."

The soldier approached Artie, put a thick red cloth over his mouth, and pulled it so tight Artie thought he might choke.

He could see the sudden anger in Anna's eyes as the soldier tightened his grip.

Mr. Wilks approached Anna. "I know you aren't interested in talking to me. But I'm curious if you will remain this somber after Mr. Gonzalez has a few broken bones. How does that sound?"

Anna sat perfectly still for a moment, and then spoke calmly. Her voice carried through the loudspeaker system. Wilks clearly intended for Artie to hear the conversation.

"You can do as you please," she said. "You are the one in control. But I'm sure you are aware that both state, federal, and military law prohibits the torturing of detainees or prisoners."

"So, it can talk," said Wilks. "You know what I think? I think you have a soft spot for this boy and that both of you are full of shit. Private Jenson, if you will, please."

The soldier punched him in the left cheek with a crack. For a moment everything went dark. A few seconds later, he felt a surge of pain in his other cheek—another strike from the soldier. Through blurry eyes, he saw Anna jerking in her chair.

"Are you in love with this boy?" Wilks chided.

"Robots can't love. They can't express true emotion. You are a series of circuits, wires, silicon, and human-induced code. Everything you know is a simulation created by beings who can actually think. Creatures that have a soul."

Those cruel words were agonizing to Artie, even worse than the pain he felt in his face. He wondered what Anna might be thinking or what she might do.

"Again, Private."

The soldier reached his arm back and punched Artie again; this time in his ribcage. Blood gurgled from Artie's mouth and black-and-white spots clouded his vision.

Anna thrashed about violently.

"And you have demonstrated my point perfectly, robot. You used your programmed reasoning to deduce that the United States military would never break protocol. And this is why a robot can never be a human. This is why you won't believe what I am about to do. Then you will learn your place in the world. And once you realize that, I will let you die."

"Private Jenson, on my order please execute Mr. Gonzalez."

Anna continued to jerk in her chair, but the restraints held her down. Artie could see the focus in her eyes—and the fear.

Without hesitation, Jenson withdrew his sidearm and pointed it at Artie's forehead. Artie briefly glanced at the gun. The moment was surreal. Soldiers were people you were supposed to be able to trust. They were here to protect, not to kill. Yet somehow, he knew this was about to happen—he had reached the end of his life.

A crash and then a scream blasted through the loudspeaker overhead, snapping Artie briefly back to reality. He looked past the soldier, who was standing in front of him, and watched Anna rip free from one of her arm restraints. She reached for the guard closest to her in the room, but he was just out of reach. A loud energy-induced sound zapped through the loudspeaker system and Artie watched Anna flail and scream as the collar-like device around her neck lit up and shocked her.

"Restrain her, please," said Wilks, annoyed.

One of the soldiers grabbed a pair of standard handcuffs and then clamped her loose arm back down to the chair.

"And now it is time for the most important test of all. Let us find out if a robot can feel as a human can. Robot, do you know what it's like to lose someone you love?"

Artie's eyes caught Anna's, and he thought he could see genuine terror in them. His heart ached as he watched the conviction and confidence leave her, being replaced with sadness and despair. It was nothing he had programmed and nothing likely she had ever developed herself. It was just there inside of her. Perhaps she really did have a soul.

"Private Jenson, shoot Mr. Gonzalez in the head, immediately." Artie looked up at the soldier. There was no sense of empathy or remorse. There was a gunshot.

Anna screamed.

When the ringing in his ears stopped, Artie looked around the room. He definitely wasn't dead, and that was a good thing. The soldier moved to the rear of Artie.

"Like I said, Mr. Gonzalez," said Wilks, "we have no interest in prosecuting humans. She can't hear you or see you now, but you can hear and see her. She thinks you are dead."

There was a slight amusement in the man's voice.

"Let's see what happens next. Zap her again, Private."

Anna's neck restraint lit up and her body convulsed as it was charged with electricity. Anna screamed out in pain.

"Stop!" yelled Artie. "Please stop!"

"Again," ordered Wilks.

Artie closed his eyes this time as Anna was shocked again.

A few seconds passed, and the charge powered down. Anna's screaming ceased and her head was resting on her chest, looking almost lifeless.

Artie thought they might have actually killed her this time. Her hair was frizzled, and her skin was browner, as if it had been tanned and aged a few years.

Her body shifted, and then she slowly raised her head. Her brow was fierce and her eyes glistened with intensity.

"I'll kill you all," she whispered.

"And there it is," said Wilks, in his condescending voice. "The machine hiding within."

Artie's face was dripping with blood and sweat. His chest began to hurt. The pain moved from his chest and then to his shoulders, and finally up to his jaw and teeth. He was afraid, but not for himself.

"Okay, let's crank it up and finish her for good."

As Wilks barked this final command, Anna suddenly ripped her arms free from their constraints. She quickly grabbed the metal braces from her legs and pulled them from the floor plate, then jumped from her chair at the soldier closest to her and grabbed his throat. She ripped out the man's esophagus in an instant. He fell to the ground, and blood poured from the wound onto the floor. As she leapt at the next soldier in line, the sounds of gunshots could be heard with a piercing velocity. The other three soldiers were firing their weapons. Artie watched in horror at the carnage taking place across the room.

Anna was hit in the chest and in the face multiple times. Flesh and metal shot into the air. She was knocked back with force into the chair behind her, then she fell to her knees on the floor. After stabilizing herself with her fists, she tried to jump at the soldier again. As she did, more gunshots rang, and she was thrown back into the wall.

Artie was shouting like he had never yelled before.

"No. Let her go. Please!"

But his cries had been lost to the gunfire and the loud voice in the speaker that was ordering the soldiers to keep firing.

Anna was dripping oil and lubricant from various exit wounds. He could see sparks from within the holes in her cheeks. Gazing into Anna's piercing blue eyes, he saw the rage. He saw the loss. And he could still see that glimmer of love she had for him. She was fighting for him.

The firing ceased and the soldiers surrounded Anna's maimed body. She slowly lifted her head to look into the glass window. Artie stared into Anna's eyes and realized what she realized—that she was about to die. She had been defeated. She had lost the only person who mattered to her. Artie wanted to tell her he was here and that he was alive, but he knew his words wouldn't carry.

A lump developed in his throat and his heart was heavy. He had spent those many years working on Anna. Growing to love her. Perfecting her in every way. And she helped him become a better person—helped him to express himself. She turned him from an immature teenager into someone of greater worth. And here she was in her last moments of life in this cruel world, having wanted only to escape and live a better life. She had just wanted to be with Artie.

"I love you, Anna," he whispered. But his expression was lost in a final gunshot point-blank to Anna's forehead. Artie watched Anna's piercing blue eyes fade into nothingness. Her head succumbed to gravity and fell to her chest one last time. Her hands and fingers went limp.

Anna was dead.

"Mr. Gonzalez, you are now free to go," Wilks said with a surprising calmness.

"This case will be turned over to local authorities. I can imagine they will likely obtain a search warrant for your home. It might be best if you take care of any loose ends quickly. It's the end of their kind, you know. You might just want to put all of this behind you. A year from now Sia will be ancient history."

Artie drove back home, covered in blood and all alone. The drive home seemed twice as long and twice as solemn than when he had left. Just hours ago, the passenger seat next to him had been warm with someone he loved. What had been excitement and curiosity about the future was now a cold sadness of despair.

After what seemed like an eternity, he pulled his car into the driveway of his house. The lights were on just as he had left them, though he had never expected to see their luminance again. He unlocked the front door and went inside. Everything remained as it was when they had left. He wasn't sure how he should feel and didn't know what he should do—so he did what he knew he could do.

He turned on his computer and started to write some code.

The next few days were fairly uneventful for Artie and the crew—at least compared to previous encounters. One night while camping off the I-10, a few raiders tried to rob them. Jan killed one of them and then tied the other one up to a Joshua tree. Two days later, a malfunctioning UberBot tried to run them down in an SUV. Jaime came to the rescue and took out the bot with his rifle. A direct head shot. Artie thought it was pretty cool watching the vehicle hit the cement median at near full speed and watched it flip twice in the air and then crash upside down. Though he was a little disappointed when it didn't explode as it would have in an action movie.

The next night, as they neared Phoenix, a convoy of makeshift armored vehicles patrolled the highway throughout the day. Jaime had wanted to make contact and recruit for the USR, but Jan wouldn't let him. And she was right to do so. Later in the day, they watched another passing group of people get slaughtered and robbed by the convoy. After they killed the people, they decapitated them and put their heads on spikes in front of the vehicles. Artie had hoped that society might be more intact and humane in the cities that hadn't burned, but he quickly learned the world was now a dark place no matter the location.

As the sun was setting, Jan led the crew to downtown Phoenix where they set up a camp and fire in one of the corporate buildings that stood tall above the desert city.

"I thought Palm Springs was hell on Earth. But then we came to Arizona," Jaime said as he lay on the marble floor sprawled out and covered in sweat. "Who lights a fire when it's a hundred degrees outside?"

"People who want to eat food," Jan replied matter-of-factly.

Artie was sitting on the ground. He opened his backpack and pulled out four miniature drones. He opened up his Bladebook and loaded his code editor. After he pressed return, all four drones flew a couple of feet into the air and hovered in place.

"Oh, that's pretty cool," said Jaime. "What are you doing with them?"

"I haven't had a chance to configure them since we left LA. But basically, I'm going to set them up to scout and patrol ahead of us."

Jaime sat up and scooted next to Artie. "How do you do that?"

"Sure, let me show you. So these guys already have the core software that lets them fly and move and avoid obstacles and stuff like that. We just need to add some rules."

Artie handed the computer to Jaime.

"You do it. I'll show you how."

"This is a nice machine, bro."

"Thanks, it's my Bladebook."

"Sweet. That some old-school gaming computer or something?"

Artie laughed. "No, it's kind of my own brand I made up. I build them the same way each time. I even etched a Bladebook logo into the carbon fiber casing."

"You're one smart kid."

Artie grinned and then pointed to the screen.

"See right there? The word that says 'max_distance'—that is a variable that will set how far we let them go on their own. Enter a number there—like a few feet or something."

Jaime typed on the keyboard. "Okay, now what?"

"Click that button that says, 'Compile & Flash Hardware.'"

Jaime clicked the button, and a green check mark appeared on the computer.

"Sweet. Now check this out."

Artie handed Jaime his Microblade phone.

"Tap the 'Patrol' button."

Jaime followed Artie's instructions and tapped the button. The drones whizzed off in four different directions, but then stopped ten feet out. Then they moved again in different directions while moving no further than that same distance.

"I just did that!" Jaime exclaimed, "I put ten for <u>max_distance,</u> and they are listening. This is bananas, bro."

"Good job, Jaime, you just wrote your very first code. And check this out." Artie pointed out some more variables on the screen.

"You can change all of these and the drones will obey. Play with them and have some fun."

Artie smiled—it had been a while since he had talked code to anyone. What he was showing Jaime was incredibly simple, but Artie knew that every person who could be deemed a programmer always had to start with something simple. Artie moved a couple of feet from Jaime to let him play with the drones. Jan was sitting next to him.

"You sure are a trip," Jan said to Artie as she poked the fire with a stick.

There were a few other sticks hanging over the fire holding pieces of meat Jan had skewered from a wild chicken they had killed earlier in the day.

"What do you mean?"

"I don't know. It's probably just that I still can't believe that you are what you are—the things you can do with a computer."

Artie was starting to better understand that he actually might have a rare set of skills—especially in a world where giant snakes and mutant beasts were the norm. Programmers didn't need to exist in a world like this. They needed guns and leaders and governments. Why would the world need a smart-assed hacker kid?

Gina and Gordon were standing a few yards away conversing. The light from the fire reflected on Gordon's frame.

"I'm just watching you here teaching him to code like it's no big deal," she said. "When I've just traveled nearly eight hundred miles, lost someone close to me, and have almost been killed myself multiple times—just to obtain a stupid book that we thought might help us."

Artie sat more upright, very intrigued.

"What do you mean, book? What book?"

Jan reached behind her and pulled out a white-and-red book from her satchel. She tossed it to Artie. He picked it up from the ground and held it up in the dark against the light of the flames: *Network Programming in Python—For Beginners.*

"What is this for?" Artie asked sincerely.

Jan began to laugh.

"You see, this is what I'm talking about. People died to get this book, and you look at it as though it was worthless."

"Well, I mean it kind of is. I'm sure there's some valuable information in here, but there isn't a whole lot we could do with it. Sure, the Bitcoin network uses some peer-to-peer gossip protocols that might be covered here, but at the end of the day, almost all the networking and connection codes have already been written in prebuilt libraries. No one will probably ever have to write that code again."

Jan sat back on her elbows smiling at Artie in disbelief.

Then Artie finally realized the situation they were all in. It had toyed with his mind over the past few days, but now it hit him like a brick wall—he truly could be one of the last programmers on the Earth. That would mean things he considered trivial would suddenly become incredibly advanced to the uninitiated. If there were no programmers, they couldn't teach other people to become programmers, which would explain why so many machines and so much technology were left behind, virtually untouched.

All of those things Artie had unlocked and taken back home, all of his electronics and toys and even his damn Coke machine—none of it would have been possible without his skill set. But even if there weren't any programmers, there were still books. Sure, maybe Sia got to the digital ones, but paper books still existed.

"Wait, why did you go to LA just for this book? There are libraries in almost every city in the world."

"That's the thing. There aren't. As far as we've been able to find, every library has either been burned to the ground or the books are missing. We did find a fairly intact library up near Snowflake, Arizona, but all of the tech books were gone."

"Oh, come on, that sounds ridiculous. It just doesn't seem plausible. You probably just didn't search far enough."

Jan's mouth formed a frown, and Artie thought she was about to lash out, but then she took a breath instead.

"Ever heard of a man named Hitler?"

The words pierced him, and then his perspective began to change. Sia had killed the programmers and destroyed all of the knowledge that might make new programmers. Artie thought back to his history class in high school. Of course, there was Hitler and his rise to power, and then his goal to wipe out any race he didn't like. And it had started with the burning of books—anything that might empower people to rise up against him.

Then there were the Spaniards who conquered Mesoamerica. In their conquest, they had burned all of the people's history and writings and replaced it with Catholicism—they had hoped to wipe out the knowledge that there had once been an advanced civilization hidden within the forests of the Americas. And it had worked; most of that knowledge was gone and most of South and Central America was

now Catholic, any notion of an advanced, ancient people mostly erad-
icated.

"Jan, I'm sorry. I'm sorry I was so—"

"Arrogant or jerkish. Or maybe just a stupid smart kid."

She sat fully upright. She looked into Artie's eyes with a solemn
stare. The flames flickered shadows against Jan's face. Even in her anger, Artie thought she looked beautiful. Her hazel eyes shimmered,
and her high cheekbones spoke to Artie of perfection. Her silky dark
hair accentuated her fair complexion, and when she gave her now
regular grumpy stare, the lines under her eyes and lips spoke of a
childish stubbornness—a stubbornness that Artie was really starting
to like.

He stared at her for a moment in silence. She had a right to be
upset. And since he hadn't interacted with a whole lot of people in
the last ten years, he probably needed to work on his people skills.

"Jan, why did you need the book?"

"Two months ago at the Grease Monkey, some drifters came in
for drinks. I was with Gordon and Tom, my husband."

Artie's heart skipped a beat. She had a husband!

"One of the guys had a large mask attached to his back. It was
some type of gorilla-looking thing—like a decoration ripped from a
wall. The bartender asked where he got it, and he said he had scavenged some video game company in Santa Monica, said it was the last
one. All that was left were some office chairs and computer books.
When we heard that, we jumped in and asked a bunch of questions."

Jan took a breath and squeezed her eyes shut for a moment.

"We had to see for ourselves. Find the books if they still existed.
Tom was a programmer, Artie, like you. Sia hadn't known about
him—he hadn't written code since he was a kid. We had worked together the last few years trying to hack into vending machines. Trying to hack Sia. I guess he wasn't a great programmer—we didn't get
very far. But he tried."

Artie shook his head. Her husband had tried to help—tried to use his skills, but without success. And here he was touting his skills like a proud little asshole.

"A few days before we left, Tom was asked to do a supply run a few hours north. Ed learned of a mini-mart that had been virtually untouched, buried in the sand—sent Tom and a few others. But only one of them came back. My husband, Tom, and the others had been killed. The guy said all of them were killed by a single person—a woman. Said she appeared friendly and asked for help. But when they got closer, she murdered them. He told me that he shot her in the arm as he fled—the flesh had torn open and underneath it was metal. She was a bot."

Artie sat quietly for a moment and then took a deep breath.

"Jan, I'm not sure how to process all of this."

"It was a robot that looked like a human, perfectly disguised. Some new type of creation. Something evolved. The guy said that as he fled, he watched her drag the bodies away. Not to bury them; just dragged them away."

Jan threw a stick into the fire with vigor.

"What in the hell would a robot want dead bodies for?" she said solemnly.

Artie wasn't sure what to say; he felt both sad and awkward at the same time.

"They took Tom. They took him."

Jan looked at the floor, her eyes glazing over with tears. She took a breath and continued speaking without looking up.

"The thing is, we knew something was going on—that something was coming."

Her voice began to crackle and choke as she pushed through the memory.

"What do you mean? Like others had been taken before?"

"Not exactly. A few months before Tom was taken, we captured a rogue bot inside of the city. It was highly advanced, unlike anything we had ever seen before. It was completely white and looked recently manufactured."

"So someone is really building new bots?"

"Yes. One of our night patrols found it sneaking through the neighborhoods. When I got there, we had already lost six men capturing it. The thing fought with a fury unlike anything I've ever seen before."

Jaime had put the computer away and then crawled in a few feet to better listen in on the conversation. "Sounds like something I heard about coming out of Salt Lake a while back," he said. "Except our people didn't catch it. It killed the lot of them and got away."

Jan looked at Jaime, but her eyes didn't show any surprise. It was almost as if she expected to hear as much.

"Like I said—it seemed to have come for a reason. And I don't think it's over yet."

"What did it want, then?" Artie asked.

"It's pretty obvious, bro," said Jaime, not without kindness. "It's a scout."

"Right," Jan replied, "and we've got this bastard locked up with maximum security."

"Okay so this makes sense to me now," said Artie, with some enthusiasm. "You captured this robot who was obviously trying to gain intel on Scourge. And you went to LA to find those books those drifter guys told you about—so you could try and hack it. Maybe figure out what it was up to."

"Yes. That was the hope. And then Tom..."

Jan couldn't finish the words.

Artie's voice drew almost to a whisper.

"And you think these things might be taking people to create some new form of bot—almost like a cyborg or something?"

Jan didn't respond. Jaime jumped in. "Well, the good news is Artie can probably take a crack at getting this thing to spill its gears."

"Damn straight I will."

Jan nodded. She lifted her head and looked at Artie.

He caught her gaze and noticed something—where once there had been animosity, there was now a subtle hint of kindness, as if she had just removed some great invisible wedge that had been between her and him. He brushed his hand through his hair.

"Jan, I will help you guys. I will do everything in my power. And I can teach others too. Code, engineering, whatever I know."

Jan smiled the first honest smile Artie had witnessed. "Thanks, Artie."

"So, what do we do with this book?" Artie asked Jan with a smile.

"Maybe we can sell it on eBay," she replied.

Artie and Jan laughed. He felt like he had finally found a place in the world again.

Friends, he thought. *It's nice to have friends.*

Artie had been tossing and turning on the cool marble floor through the night. He estimated dawn was only a couple of hours away. Jan was asleep a few feet to his right. She was in a deeper sleep than she had been the past few days. She probably had been carrying quite the load of emotional weight, and now that she had finally gotten it off of her chest, she could sleep. He was glad she slept; it was nice to see her in a state of innocence versus her normally defensive nature.

With Jaime snoring to his right and his mouth hanging open, occasionally choking on his own snores, Artie knew sleep was out. The fire had gone out, but the overpowering desert heat took its place.

He stood up and then looked around trying to spot Gordon and Gina, but they were nowhere to be found. He walked around the building's lobby, moving from corner to corner and then stopping at the elevators. He realized that unless Gordon and Gina had traversed the stairwell of the building, then they must be outside—and the stairwell doorway was definitely too small for Gordon to fit through. So, he walked to the swiveling push doors at the front of the building and went outside.

Looking up at the brilliant stars, he thought at least there was one benefit of living in a postapocalyptic world. Growing up in Los Angeles, you completely forgot the stars even existed. Though Phoenix hadn't had the pleasure of making the acquaintance of chemical bombs, the city looked as though it had been through a few battles. Most of the streets were blockaded with burned-out vehicles. Some of the buildings had broken windows and portions of cement and rebar cracked and exposed, as if a grenade or rocket had missed its target. Artie looked to the left and then to the right; the streets were silent and not a fire or light to be found.

He turned left down the street and meandered his way through debris, cars, delivery trucks, and a couple of rusted transit cars still attached to the overhanging power cables. He took another step and the sound of a rattle shook nearby. His heart jumped as he heard the familiar sound, but he soon calmed himself as he saw the regular-sized rattlesnake coiled in front of him. Artie smiled and then walked around the snake, happy to see something more normal and less dangerous than things previously encountered. He stopped at the intersection and read a green sign that said "1st Street."

There he stood silently, enjoying and breathing in the warm desert air. As he exhaled, he heard a sound coming from the north side of 1st Street. It sounded like voices. Artie cautiously walked toward the noise, making sure to stay within the dark shadows from the buses and the pillars of corporate buildings. As he drew closer to the sounds, they became clearer—definitely voices.

"And it stretches one thousand five hundred miles in every direction. The walls alone are nearly two hundred feet thick. It was the most beautiful place I had ever seen."

"I don't know, Gina. It sounds too good to be true. And not to mention that Jan saved my life. I owe her everything."

Artie noticed two shadowy figures standing next to a large, burned-out city bus. He could clearly see the larger figure was Gordon. The smaller shadow had to be Gina.

"Well, you are going to have to make a choice. And make it soon," she said.

Artie moved away from the building he had been walking next to and walked toward the bus. He didn't feel right eavesdropping, so he decided to make himself known.

"Hey, what are you guys doing out here?"

Gordon immediately rotated toward Artie, and Gina slowly emerged from the shadow of the bus, revealing herself in the moonlight.

"Hello, Artie," Gina replied. "We just needed to get out of that cramped building."

Gordon remained silent, his yellow eyes now visible in the dark.

"What were you saying about someplace with a wall, Gina?" Artie asked.

Gina responded without hesitation.

"I was telling him about a movie I had watched one time back home."

Her words sounded sincere and honest, but he still didn't trust them.

"Mmmhmm. What was the name of the movie?" Artie asked.

"*Kingdom of Heaven*," she responded instantly, "starring Orlando Bloom. It was the battle for Jerusalem."

Artie stood quiet for a moment.

"Uh huh."

Artie knew the movie well, and he didn't think the city was beautiful and doubted the walls were two hundred feet thick. Not to mention the fact that Gina had never watched a single action movie—she had always complained they were too violent for her taste.

"Well, it's getting late, or early, or whatever you call it," he said, "Let's head back. I'm sure we'll be leaving for Scourge soon."

"Yes, he's right. Let's go, Gordon," she replied.

"You okay, Gordon?" Artie asked, noticing Gordon's overly awkward silence and lurching posture.

"Just fine, partner," Gordon replied as he slapped Artie on the back.

They walked back to the corporate building and came in to find Jan now awake and putting some things in her satchel. Jaime was still asleep and snoring.

"Where have you guys been?" asked Jan as she watched them enter through the large swivel doors.

"Just went for a walk," Gordon replied.

Jan walked over to Jaime and kicked him in the leg. He woke up with a startle and then moaned, "Just five more minutes, Mom."

"I'm not your mom and I don't like kids, so get up."

Artie caught Jan's attention and gave her a serious stare.

"What's wrong with you?" asked Jan.

Artie shook his head slightly as if to say, "Not now."

Jan understood.

"How far to Scourge, Jan?"

"It's probably a good five-hour walk."

Artie kneeled down and grabbed his Bladebook from the floor and put it in his backpack. He grabbed his Microblade from his pocket and then tapped a button entitled "Patrol." Artie saw a faint green light zip past the front window and head down the street. He watched the four blinking dots on his phone fan out and head east toward Scourge.

He put the phone back in his pocket.

"So, what is the plan when we get to Scourge?" he asked.

Jan finished attaching her satchel to her waist and was now strapping on her left holster.

"We'll go talk to Ed. He'll want to meet you. And more importantly, he'll want you to meet our guest. Then after that who knows. Maybe just figure out life. I don't know."

Artie was excited to finally make it to Scourge. After losing his home and coming to some important revelations, he was eager to do something useful with his time. Though, he thought it wouldn't hurt to rebuild his man cave again if he had the chance.

"Let's go, people," Jan said.

She pushed through the front door and entered the morning darkness. Artie and the others followed after. As they began heading east, Artie pulled out his phone and tapped the screen.

"Jan, look," he said showing her the device. "It's pretty clear down Jefferson, but we'll want to cross over to Washington Street around thirty-sixth—there are some pretty large heat signatures a few miles ahead."

Jan smiled at him and ruffled his hair.

"Sounds good," she responded.

Artie didn't completely care for the childish hair-ruffling, but the physical contact with Jan made him smile. "Why Scourge? I mean versus here maybe, or anywhere else."

"I'm not really sure, to be honest," she said. "Almost everyone just kind of drifted in from all over. I mean, the town is fairly undisturbed. Stands almost as it did before the world went to hell. There's a ton of residential neighborhoods, and we live in those homes. You'll see. The place kind of helps you to remember what things used to be like."

"So just like a normal American neighborhood or something?"

"Well, not completely. Electricity has been an issue. Some places still have solar working for them, but mostly it's dark. And then there are the issues with water, health, and other standard post-end-of-the-world crap. And yeah, Scourge isn't as crazy as where you came from, but it's still a rough place. You'll see that when we head to the city center."

Artie nodded, feeling more excitement as he pictured what awaited him.

"And what about like giant scorpions and mutant kittens or anything, you got those there?" Jaime asked, jumping into the conversation.

"No, thank goodness," said Jan with a smile. "But we do have a few of our mechanically-inclined friends who can be overly cranky," she yelled aloud so Gordon could hear her from behind. Artie looked back and watched Gordon lift his hand and flip Jan the bird.

"So how did you meet Gordon? This morning I heard him say that you saved his life," Artie asked.

Jan looked at Artie inquisitively. "Interesting. He told you that?"

"No. I overheard him say it to Gina."

"Even more interesting," Jan replied.

She turned and glanced at Gordon and then back to Artie.

"It was about three years ago, I think. Tom and I had lived in Austin, Texas, before the bombs dropped. As Sia grew, Austin was really an epicenter of conflict between Sia and mankind. A lot of tech companies there were highly against Sia; some of them even trying to develop programs that could stop her. But then it was like all the bots using Sia began to band together. They went on strike, from the Uber-Bots to the FarmBots. Then there were food shortages and other issues. When we saw that things were getting bad in Austin, we made our way to San Antonio. And it was a good thing we did—Austin went up in flames shortly after we left. Probably around the same time LA was hit. But we were forced to leave there too as the conflict between humans and bots migrated in that direction. So, over the years we drifted throughout western Texas. From town to town and house to house."

"What was it like in Texas?" Artie asked.

"It was mostly unchanged once you got away from the big cities. Remote deserts and fields. A lot of thieves and raiders, though, murdering travelers on the highway. We tended to keep to towns with smaller populations that were off the beaten path. There were still a lot of good folks around. After drifting for a while, we hit El Paso. That is where things got really interesting."

"Oh, my cousin lives in El Paso," Jaime jumped in. "What was the city like? People still alive?"

"Yeah, but the situation was crap. In El Paso the I-10 runs along the border of Texas and Mexico. El Paso on the north, and Ciudad Juarez on the south. Growing up, my parents had taken me to El Paso multiple times. The city was never anything to look at, but I always thought it was pretty cool seeing all the colored houses smashed together and kids playing in the streets on the southern side, then seeing the Walmarts, fast-food places, and familiar American life on the northern side. When Tom and I got there, it was kind of still like that, but different too. This time it was humans on the south and robots on the north—and they were at war with each other."

"We were kind of automatically drafted into the Mexican First Infantry. It was a join or die kind of thing."

"Damn, so we are like family now, chica. My great, great, great grandpa fought in the Mexican army with Pancho Villa. I might have missed a great or two in there, but yeah, he was badass."

Jan laughed. "Well, it wasn't quite like that. Most of the Mexican Infantry was a bunch of Americans. But yeah, the rest were Mexicans."

"Why would robots be fighting against humans?" Artie asked.

"The thing is, a lot of people thought most of the robots were driving Uber in major cities, but there were thousands, if not millions of bots working the fields and agriculture. Apparently, sentient bots had completely replaced the human workforce in El Paso. Onions, peppers, cotton, and even bees and honey, all managed by robots. Thousands of people lost their jobs. Bots could work faster and more efficiently."

Artie could see where the story was going. He had seen people abuse the power of Sia. To use it for business or labor. The thing Satoshi warned everyone against. It was inevitable that these beings would adapt and realize they didn't want to exist just to serve the needs of man.

"And they all adapted," Artie said aloud.

"Yeah, that's right. They were done taking orders. They had taken over El Paso a few years back. Most of them were FarmBots but other types of bots joined their cause. But we just called them the farmers. They were fierce and had a kill-humans-on-sight policy. And some of these bots were massive. You know those huge old tractors that would plow fields or harvest major crops? Yeah, even those things were built on Sia."

Artie could now see the first glimmers of orange sky flooding the horizon as they walked down the street.

"So, El Paso became kind of a beacon to sentient bots that were sick of humans. Thousands of them flocked in every month. Luckily for us, we had thousands of people flocking to us too. It was pretty awesome watching humans working together all for the same cause, even if that cause was killing an enemy."

"So, what changed?" Jaime interjected. "First you were fighting against bots but now you fight with them."

"Well, back then we just fought to live. Tom and I hadn't really ever been around bots before that, aside from the early UberBots in Austin. So, our first experience with robots was watching humans get slaughtered by them. It wasn't a hard decision to join the fight."

"But I did soon learn that just like people, not all robots were bad."

Jan looked back at Gordon for a moment.

"Unlike the FarmBots who would execute humans on sight, the Mexican Infantry tried to operate under the rules of war set by the Geneva convention. We took prisoners, and some of those prisoners weren't necessarily evil. Some of them had come to El Paso to find a place of refuge but were pulled into the war just like Tom and I were. One of them even helped us out. Gave us intel on the farmers. His name was Sampson. He had told us that the FarmBots had a massive holding facility where they locked up bots who wouldn't fight, or those who sympathized with the humans."

"Oh dang, I know what happened next," Jaime said. "You guys crossed the border like a couple of wetbacks and broke 'em out."

Artie laughed. Jan smiled too.

"Actually, yes. When we got to the facility, it was worse than we had imagined. The farmers were executing their own kind, in some cases even torturing other robots—tearing off their limbs, removing circuits while they were still alive. There were hundreds of prisoners. We concealed ourselves inside the building, and our company, who was outside, began to create a diversion. They had planted explosives near the building, destroying some turrets and other critical stations. Then Tom, myself, and a few others got to work releasing the prisoners."

Artie wiped a drop of sweat from his forehead, as the sun was already heating up the day.

"And did you get them out?" he asked.

"Yes, but it was chaos. Prisoners fled in every direction. A good thirty or forty of them joined us in the fight, including Gordon. A lot of them died over the next year in subsequent battles, but Gordon stuck with Tom and me all the way through."

"That's really amazing," Artie said.

"Yeah. After fighting for a year or so, Tom, Gordon, and I thought it was time for a change. We decided to head out west. Then we ended up in Scourge."

Jaime raised his hand as if he was in a classroom but then spoke anyway. "Wait, so like are robots still fighting humans in El Paso?"

"I would think so," Jan responded. "Both humans and robots were still migrating there in droves when we left."

"This is good to know," Jaime said. "We need to get the USR there. Unite."

"It's crazy to think of what might be going on in all the other places around the country," said Artie. "I mean between the three of us we really only know what's happening in a few of the western states and then Texas."

"Yeah, I know what you mean," said Jaime. "I've been up in Oregon, but on the east side of the USR, our friends in Salt Lake City are being bombarded with attacks from robotic, beast-like creatures. We used to have Denver, but lost it to the beasts—that is when we first saw them, when they attacked. I ain't never seen one personally, but I hear they are vicious."

Jan chimed in, "Not to mention these new things—the one that killed Tom." Artie and Jaime went silent.

"Sorry, guys," said Jan. "I don't mean to be somber. We live in a new world, I guess. We need to own it. Accept it."

Artie thought she sounded as if she was trying to convince herself of this idea more than she was them.

Jaime looked back and then motioned to Jan and Artie with his hand, pointing to the rear.

"I'm gonna go talk to Gordon and hear some war stories."

Jan nodded and Jaime turned around.

When Artie was out of Jaime's range, he turned to Jan.

"Hey, something is wrong with Gina and possibly Gordon too."

Jan turned to Artie and her eyes seemed doubtful.

"What are you talking about?"

"Are you sure the Sia network is down, Jan?"

"Every network is gone, except Bitcoin, as far as I know. You know as much as I do."

Artie looked at the ground in contemplation.

"The thing is, ever since we left that hotel, Gina hasn't been herself."

Jan laughed. "Well, I sure as hell like her a lot better now. She wasted those snakes."

"Yeah, I get that it was useful, but it wasn't her. Yes, Gina was pretty crazy before, but over the years, she had developed this sort of empathy at her core. That empathy seems gone now."

Jan shrugged.

"Also, she lied to me this morning. She has never lied to me before—ever. And she was having a strange conversation with Gordon. It was like she was asking Gordon to go somewhere with her or something."

Jan looked at Artie again, seeming a little more accepting of the notion.

"Well, Gordon is his own person. If he wants to leave with your crazy SexBot, he is welcome to."

"Okay. But, Jan, I think we should just be cautious. This is the one thing that all the big companies just could never get. That you can't control Sia. It was the reason I kept all of my Sia-based technology off of the Internet and definitely away from the Sia network. Just know that I don't trust the situation. Something happened back in Palm Springs."

"Duly noted, Artie," Jan replied, "but I think you should relax."

It was about 1 p.m. when Artie and the group reached the out-skirts of Scourge. A sign protruded from the earth that appeared to have once read "Welcome to Mesa." *Scourge* was written over the faded words in dripping red spray paint. Beyond the sign, the red clay shingles of homes' roofs could be seen for miles. The suburban neighborhoods were surprisingly maintained and offered Artie a small measure of nostalgic comfort.

As Artie and Jan approached the initial cropping of houses, he noticed a metal and wooden barricade in the middle of the four-lane street. Two men holding rifles were standing on top of this barricade, which had sharpened pieces of rebar affixed to it, pointing toward any vehicle that might charge it. Beneath the rebar were layers of coiled barbed wire.

"Stop immediately," yelled a man in a trench coat on the left side of the barricade.

Jan lifted up her hand, indicating to Artie and the group to stop.

"It's me you, idiots," Jan yelled back.

The other man on the barricade put his hands over his eyes and squinted. "Jan, is that you? We expected you a few weeks ago."

Jan walked closer toward the barricade.

"Yes, Carl, it's me. We had to take a longer route to LA—there are raiders from Phoenix to Palm Springs."

"Who are these people with you?" asked the thin, bald black man.

"They're with me, and that's all you need to know."

"I don't think Ed is going to want all of these new faces," said Carl.

"You'll let them in, or I'll kick your ass."

The guard in the trench coat folded his arms, but without confidence.

"Jan, you know that no one gets in at least without paying."

"Don't be an ass, Leeroy. What is wrong with you guys?"

"We ain't losing our jobs because of you, that's what."

Artie walked closer and turned to Leeroy.

"It's okay. I'll take care of it," said Artie. "What's the cost?"

"Thanks," replied Carl with relief. "We can take anything really. Ammo, canned food, Bitcoin, whatever."

Artie smiled, pulled out his Microblade, walked up to Carl, and said, "I've got some Satoshis for you."

Carl pulled out his own mobile device and showed it to Artie. Artie tapped his screen, and then scanned a code on Carl's screen.

Carl's device gave a tone that indicated success.

"What in the hell?" said Carl as he looked at his device. "You just sent me three Bitcoin. I don't even think the whole town combined has that much."

"Consider it a tip," Artie replied with a smile. Jan rolled her eyes. Leeroy quickly walked over to Carl to look at the device.

"You better send me some, Carl!" he whined.

"Alright, we're heading in," Jan said.

Leeroy motioned them to move past the barricade without looking up from his mobile device.

"Where's Ed?" asked Jan.

"Where he usually is: at the Superstition."

Artie, Jan, and the crew walked down the street, moving past various subdivisions and gated communities. Almost every community entrance had an armed guard posted in front. Some of them nodded at Jan as she walked by. Artie pulled out his Microblade and tapped a button to summon the drones to him. After a few moments, the sound of humming echoed over him. He knelt down and grabbed each of the drones as they landed near him. Then he put them in his backpack. Aside from the occasional barricade, Artie thought it was pretty cool that the streets were so clean and managed. So far, Scourge really did look untouched from the travails of the end of the world.

The heat pounded furiously upon them as they walked the few miles to the city center. After the long walk, Artie paused to catch his breath. He slowly looked up and noticed a massive building in front of him. There was a large JCPenney sign attached to the side of it.

"We're here," said Jan.

"Wait, the Superstition is a mall?" Artie asked.

"Yeah. Don't get too excited; the shops were looted a long time ago. You're not gonna find a clean pair of Levi's on the racks or anything. Now we use the building as a center for trade. There's almost every type of shop you can think of, and they pretty much all will take trades or Bitcoin for payment. There's weapon dealers, farmers' markets, junk dealers, clothing outfitters, whatever."

"I wonder if they have any snakeskin boots?" Jaime asked, enthusiastically.

"I actually think I've seen some before. You'll want to talk to Javé. He sells clothes and has a bunch of Mexican junk."

"Dang, why you gotta get all racist on me, chica?" Jaime said, sarcastically.

"What do you want me to say?"

"How about 'The gentleman sells items that hold deep roots in Mexican culture.'"

"Mmmhmm." Jan rolled her eyes.

"Let's go inside," Gordon bellowed. "My circuits are overheating."

Jan nodded and then they walked up the asphalt driveway that led to the mall parking lot. They entered the parking lot and walked toward the entrance of the JCPenney building. Aside from a few cars and trucks that looked functional, the parking lot was relatively empty. On the top of the building above the entrance doors were two guards holding rifles. Artie could see other guards covering more entrances in the distance. Two more guards were also stationed in front of the doors themselves. Jan took the lead and passed the two guards.

"Welcome back, Jan," said a woman guard.

She nodded and then opened the large mall doors. When Artie entered the building, he couldn't see much as his eyes hadn't yet adjusted from the blinding Arizona sunlight. After a few minutes, his eyes settled, and he scanned the area. The large department store had ceiling lights that were still operational, though not as many that might have originally existed in the building. Artie had half expected to see empty shopping carts, naked mannequins, and the remnants of a looted store scattered across the floor, but all those things had long been cleared out.

Instead, a series of booths held various types of goods. Each booth was managed by one or two people. Some of the people were dressed in modern clothing and looked clean; others were dirt-covered and seemed to care less about the rags that draped their bodies. The building was noisy as people chattered, bartered, negotiated, and argued with vendors. Artie gravitated toward a booth that was blasting some type of electronic music.

There were two people at the booth. A skinny white man with tattoos painted on both of his arms was manning a DJ control panel. Next to him was a stout black man wearing brown shorts and a plain black shirt.

"Hey, what's up, my man? I've got all the good stuff here, bro. I got iPhones, iPods, MP3 players, and even an old Zune. I got record players and over a hundred records. I got receivers and speakers and surround sound and everything you can think of."

Artie was mesmerized. His mind started to create the perfect man cave. He was picturing how he might wire an entire house with a speaker system. Maybe link all the speakers together via Bluetooth and control it with his Microblade. It would be fun to write his own app to do that. It had been a while since he had been able to write some real code.

Jaime, Gordon, and Gina walked in the opposite direction. Then Jan grabbed Artie by the arm.

"Time to go, kiddo," she said with a smile.

"Yo, Jan, what's yo' problem?" said the tattooed man. "I can tell my man is interested. Why you be stealin' Papa Eddie's business?"

Jan continued to pull Artie as a mom might pull a toddler away from the candy bars in a checkout aisle.

The man yelled out to Artie, "Yo, my man. Don't let her push you around. You stand yo' ground and come back and see me. I'll hook you up."

Artie bumped Jan with his hip, pulled his arm away, and gave her a playful smile. She smiled back.

"You'll have plenty of time to waste your money later. First we need to see Ed."

They walked past a bunch of booths and then made it to the entrance of the mall, where JCPenney ended and a three-story mall entrance began. Artie had thought the shops inside of JCPenney were the surmounting total of what they were there to see, but he was awestruck as he saw hundreds of shops, vendors, and people throughout the mall.

On every floor people were bargaining, shopping, and talking. Artie saw a flashing Grease Monkey sign on the bottom floor. Then he heard the sound of hydraulics and metal moving behind him, and he quickly turned to see a six-foot robot wearing a black trench coat.

There were pistols holstered to his hip that flashed as the trench coat flapped as he walked.

"This is nuts, Jan," Artie said.

Aside from Gina and Gordon, Artie hadn't really seen many bots. They were illegal, so to speak, in the Burns. But here were hundreds of robots and humans interacting with each other as if they were all part of the same race.

"Ed's on the bottom floor. Let's head down," Jan commanded.

"I'm going to show Gina around. I'll catch up with you later," Gordon said.

Jan nodded and Artie watched Gordon and Gina head in the opposite direction.

"Why is it that everyone gets along here?" asked Artie. "Like everyone is friends?"

Jan laughed.

"Not everyone gets along, trust me. But we have rules here and severe penalties. Ed runs the whole city. He makes sure there is peace and order. He wants to turn this place into a great city where humans and robots coexist. I don't think it will turn out the way he thinks, but right now things are alright."

Jaime stepped forward next to Jan. "But how do you make sure the bad people don't get in? This is one of the toughest things we have to deal with in the USR."

"So, we give everyone a chance. But it is also why we make everyone pay Bitcoin to get into the city. That gives us their Bitcoin address. If they steal or break any laws and we catch them, we cast them out of the city. Next time they try and enter the city, if that address is flagged, they are barred entry or shot on sight. It's not foolproof, but it has worked well."

Jan looked at Artie with a hint of sadness in her eyes. "Tom actually built the app we use for this. The one that tracks Bitcoin addresses."

Artie smiled at Jan. "I'd love to see it."

"Jaime, see that shop on the middle floor? The one that says Sporters?" Jan asked.

Jaime looked. "Yeah, I see it."

"That's Javé's place. I think you'll like what you find. You can meet up with us and Ed on the bottom floor when you're done. We'll be at the Whistleblower. It's a bar."

"Hasta luego," Jaime replied, and he walked down the long-immobilized escalator.

Jan led Artie further down the mall catwalk and then down another static escalator. They descended the floors and walked to a large makeshift neon sign that read "Whistleblower." Some of the lights were burned out, and it was clear that this sign had been hand-crafted and not part of the original mall.

"This is Ed's place," said Jan. "He's also got a house on the east side, but this is where he usually hangs."

Artie marveled at the entrance to the building; it was like something out of a cowboy space movie. There were two guards protecting the establishment, one on each side of the large entrance. One of them was a large bald man wearing a lime green shirt and a pair of camouflage shorts. The other guard was a tall, rusted metal robot without any clothing or weapons. It stood there with its hands behind its back. It had yellow LED eyes and a rectangular, immovable mouth.

Artie watched Jan disappear into a plume of smoke or steam as she entered the doors. Music could be heard from within. Artie followed Jan and disappeared into the Whistleblower.

Artie walked past a series of metal barstools lined against a wooden bar. Behind the counter, another robot was wiping the wooden surface. He was wearing a white T-shirt and brown pants with a golden belt buckle that pictured an engraving of a steer's skull. A few grungy-looking men sat on the stools. In the center of the room was a series of tables and booths intermixed with each other. They were clearly scraped from whatever parts could be found. One of the booths was enclosed in the frame of an old car and the seats appeared to have been ripped from a vehicle of some kind.

On the right side of the building were some large metal doors, each being watched by an armed guard. Artie thought they looked like interrogation rooms of some kind. The entire room was filled with a glaze of cinnamon-flavored vapor.

He followed Jan up a shallow flight of stairs that made him think he was entering the halls of some great king. The stairs were lined with a red carpet that inclined up into an even deeper mist of vapor. As he climbed the stairs, he noticed strange devices attached to some sort of mechanical poles on the floor. The devices appeared to have some sort of camera or scanner affixed to the front, and they were following him as he walked. The chatter and music of the bar quickly faded into obscurity and only the sound of puffs of vapor emanating from their various sources could be heard.

The vapor cleared and Artie and Jan entered a large room. Taking in the room before him, Artie widened his eyes. He gazed at the movie posters, the mechanical devices and tools, and the largest armchair he had ever seen.

"This is the world's ultimate man cave," said Artie with admiration.

Jan shook her head and smiled.

"I'm glad you approve," said a man with a Hawaiian shirt. He didn't look up, but was soldering something on a workbench.

"Hey!" Jan said to the man.

The man rested his tools and then lifted his head. "Is that my Jan? I'm glad you made it back."

He wiped his hands with a rag, stood up tall, then turned to face the familiar voice that had addressed him. Artie's eyes widened as he looked more closely at the man who was now stepping closer to Jan and himself.

She lifted her arm and pointed to Artie.

"Ed, I want you to meet someone. This is Artie."

Jan smiled at Artie and then turned to Ed.

"And Artie, this is—"

"Edward Stanza," Artie said in disbelief.

Artie stood awkwardly for a few moments with his mouth hanging open. Ed's somber face developed a slight smirk. Jan appeared confused as to what Artie had said, and why Ed seemed to be embracing the moment.

"I don't believe this," Artie finally said.

"Did I miss something here?" Jan asked, first looking at Artie and then to Ed. "Have you guys met before?"

A few more seconds of silence passed.

"Hey! Guys?!" Jan said.

"Sorry, Jan," Artie finally responded. "We've never met, but I know who he is. He's famous. Well, at least among hackers, whistleblowers, and other dark net-type people."

Ed was now fully smiling. "I thought that I finally had received the luxury of becoming anonymous and free from the halls of history. Also, you can just call me Ed. Haven't gone by Edward in years."

Jan's eyes turned cold, a look Artie knew well. It was the look she gave when she felt that a young cocky hacker was rubbing her ignorance in her face.

Ed turned to Jan. "I'm sorry, there wasn't any reason to tell anyone who I used to be, and who I was doesn't really even matter. Everything in the world changed so fast."

Jan folded her arms.

"So, you were famous for what?"

Artie jumped in.

"He used to work for the NSA. The government was doing all kinds of crazy stuff—spying, murdering, torturing people. Edward Stanza came out and revealed all that information to the world, sticking it to our government. Then he became an outlaw in the United States and had to hide in China."

Ed chuckled and ran a hand through his blond hair, now tinted with grey. "Well, it wasn't all just like that. But yeah, I was in China for a long time. Until I received my pardon—and thank heavens for that. Over the years I drifted through the USA and eventually ended up in Arizona. Then, days after I got here, all hell broke loose. Lived here ever since. I never told any of the locals who I was.

Jan took a breath and then gave her famous roll of the eyes.

"Well, I did want you to meet Artie for a reason. We have a lot to talk about. Then you two can go get a room."

"I'm surprised that you know who I am," said Ed, looking at Artie. "I mean, you were probably just a kid back in those days."

"That is what I wanted to tell you, Ed," Jan interrupted. "Artie is a hacker—a coder. He knows a lot of things."

Artie's head jolted upward slightly. "Wait, Jan. Edward Stanza was a security engineer. You make it sound like there are no programmers, but there was your husband, and now Ed."

"No, Artie." Ed gave a warm smile. "My engineering days ended a long time ago. Before the bombs even. I'm too old, too tired, and my eyesight is fading. Besides, technology advanced so rapidly in those last days, I'd be just as useful as a rock."

"Ed," Jan continued, "Artie is super talented. Maybe he can help us?"

Artie felt flattered hearing Jan represent him to someone else— and it was even more flattering since that someone was Edward Stanza.

Ed sat quietly for a moment, then said, "Jan, I'm sure there are a lot of things we could use some help with, but I know what you are really asking is how we can utilize Artie to help track down Tom. You want him to meet our guest."

Artie hadn't thought about the notion of Tom being alive still. Jan had said that he was murdered and taken away by some type of human robot.

Ed continued, "The thing is, we don't even know if this bot has any relevant information. Then, even if it did, we both know that Tom isn't coming back."

Artie could see anger and sadness in Jan's eyes.

"Dammit, Ed, we have to do something!" she said, tears welling in her eyes.

Ed walked over to Jan and gave her a hug. After a few moments, he stepped back, put his hands on her shoulders, and looked her in the eyes.

"Jan, I promise, we will do something. But don't do this to yourself. Keep your expectations low. And right now, we need to get acquainted with Artie. We should help him acclimate to our town. I think if we can be patient, things will reveal themselves to us."

Artie felt a little relieved. He surely didn't want the pressure of finding Jan's likely dead husband on his shoulders. Jan nodded, seeming to accept Ed's suggestion.

"Is Gearhead Charlie's house still vacant?" asked Ed.

Jan looked up with curious eyes, wiping away a single tear that had managed to trickle down her cheek.

"Yes. Why?"

"I think we should put Artie up next to you. You did a good thing in bringing him here. I think you should look after him."

Jan nodded.

"Artie, I own that house," said Ed. "You can stay for free for a month. It'll give you some time to figure out how to earn around here so you can pay for rent. We're trying to bring back capitalism and democracy, or at least some form of it. I'm sure with your skill set you'll have a lot of opportunities."

Jan laughed.

"Ed, my guess is this kid could buy the whole block if he wanted to."

Ed tilted his head slightly as if to further examine this interesting creature Jan had brought before him. Then he looked at Jan with a grin.

"You know, Jan, you guys look about the same age. You're both a couple of kids as far as I'm concerned."

Jan rolled her eyes. Artie decided that he was really starting to like Ed.

"Artie, why don't you tell Ed about our trip and what you can do exactly. I'm going to go find Jaime. He'll want to talk to Ed as well."

Jan looked at Artie for a moment and he could almost sense the slightest look of endearment. She smiled and turned to leave, then exited through the misty walkway and disappeared.

"I think she likes you," Ed said with a smile.

"I doubt that. But I think she is pretty damned cool."

"Yeah, she is pretty cool, isn't she?"

Ed motioned for Artie to take a seat on a green reclining chair that sat next to the man's massive throne-sized chair. Ed sat down and Artie spent the next hour telling Ed about his life. He told him how he learned to code and how he was a big follower of Satoshi— and how shocked he was when Satoshi built an AI that essentially destroyed the world.

They talked about Artie's years alone in the Wasteland and the things he scavenged and the jobs he performed. He explained everything, even up to the raiders on the road just outside of Phoenix. Amid all of the facts and backstory, Artie never brought up Anna or even talked about anything related to those few amazing and painful years. He tried hard to keep the memories of Anna from surfacing; they were simply too hard to bear. Even worse, Artie knew he would never be able to tell someone that he had loved her—how he loved an artificial intelligence robot with all of his heart. Anna would always need to remain buried in the past with the rest of the world.

"Interesting," Ed responded. "So you know the Sia protocols in and out. What about Bitcoin, decentralization, and crypto mining?"

"Yeah. I had Bitcoin miners both before and after the bombs. I also scavenged a bunch of celebrity homes back in Malibu and Hollywood. You would be surprised at how many people kept their Bitcoin secret keys printed on paper locked away in safes and in their drawers."

Artie could tell Ed was thinking, trying to figure something out. He leaned in closer to Artie and spoke in a voice just above a whisper, though there was clearly nothing to hide here in this secluded back room.

"Artie, you told me how Satoshi's announcement stunned you. Do you believe Satoshi did the right thing? I mean, would you say he is a good person—someone who was truly looking out for humanity?"

Artie thought the question odd, but it did cause him to think. Why did Satoshi create Sia? Could science truly have been on the verge of creating something worse? Worse than Sia?

"I'm not sure. But I guess somewhere inside I believe Satoshi had good reasons to do what he did. Just think of Bitcoin; he gave it to the world for free—didn't even want recognition."

Ed smirked. "You know he messaged me one time—Satoshi, I mean."

"What?! You spoke with Satoshi?"

"Yes. It was just before he released Sia. He told me about it. Told me of its potential and what could happen for good and for bad."

"What was your response?" said Artie with excitement.

"I told him"—Ed coughed to clear his throat—"I told him that I didn't know. But I also told him that I felt the governments of the world were gaining too much power—that maybe we needed a major change, whether peaceful or drastic."

Artie looked intently at Ed. Was Edward Stanza the man who encouraged Satoshi to release Sia? This was crazy.

Ed smiled again. "He also reprimanded me."

"What do you mean?" Artie asked.

"He told me that he admired what I had done in revealing the secrets of the US government. But then he also told me my big failure was seeking the spotlight, instead of remaining anonymous."

"Wow!"

"He was right though, you know. I did want the spotlight, I suppose. It was my pride. And that pride lost me my family and even my own country."

Ed's smile dissipated and his face turned calm.

"That is why I believe Satoshi is good. Someone who is humble enough to remain anonymous while at the same time releasing something world-changing and doing it all for free—that must truly be a good person."

Artie agreed with Ed. He had thought about this very thing before—it was why in the end he had decided to work with the Sia protocols. Had he believed that Satoshi was evil, he would never have touched Sia and Anna would never have come to life.

"It's kind of refreshing," said Ed, his smile now returning, "to talk about the old world. Most days now it's about survival, scavenging, and then of course having to personally deal with all the complaints I get every day here in Scourge. It's fun but can be a little draining."

Artie laughed.

"You have no idea. My days consisted of talking to a bipolar robot, working with people with names like "Bolt" and "Doctor Death," and then keeping my neighborhood clear of the mutees. Not to mention the cannibals."

An alert sound echoed through a speaker on one of Ed's workbenches and a monitor showed two people entering the stairway. Artie looked and saw Jan traversing the stairs followed by Jaime. Even all these years later, Ed was still a security guy at heart.

"I want you to feel at home here, Artie. We need you. Jan needs you. I don't think she realizes it—and she would never admit it. But she needs someone good in her life right now. She has built up a lot of walls over the years and, of course, more especially since Tom. She can be tough, but she is a good person. Stick with her."

Artie nodded. A few seconds later Jan and Jaime revealed themselves through the vapor-filled hallway.

"Damn, it's like *Star Wars* up in here," Jaime said.

"Ed, I'd like you to meet Jaime. He is an official representative of the USR."

Jaime moved forward and bowed to Ed as if he was bowing to a king. Jan elbowed him in the gut.

"What the hell are you doing? Knock it off."

"She's feisty, eh?" Jaime said, smiling at Ed. Artie smiled, looking at a brand-new pair of snakeskin cowboy boots on Jaime's feet.

Ed stood up from the chair.

"So, it's true," he said. "The United States lives on, huh?"

"It sure does, sir," replied Jaime. From NorCal to Washington State, then Utah and northern Nevada."

Ed nodded.

"Jaime, it is a pleasure to meet you."

Ed extended his hand and then Jaime reciprocated and shook it. Ed looked at Jan.

"Hey, Jan, could you please show Artie his new home? I'd like to talk with Jaime for a while."

"Sure, Ed," replied Jan.

"You did an amazing thing, Jan. Bringing both of them here. For the first time in a long time, things are finally looking bright. I'd like Artie to meet our special guest soon. Maybe after he has had a chance to get settled."

"Thanks, Ed."

"Wait, this kid got his own house already?" Jaime exclaimed. "You privileged white Americans always get all the good stuff."

It was Artie who rolled his eyes this time. "I'm half Mexican. Remember?"

Artie turned to Ed.

"Don't worry about this guy, he's all bark and no bite." Then he turned back to Jaime. "Kind of like a Chihuahua."

"Man, you and Jan and all your racial slurs. You would think we'd have fewer racists in the apocalypse," Jaime said, smiling.

Jan punched him in the arm.

"Alright, we're out of here," she said.

Artie followed Jan out of the room and into the hallway.

It really is nice to have friends, Artie thought.

Two days had passed since Artie had arrived in Scourge, and they had disappeared in a hazy blur. He had been so tired from the trip he had slept and then slept some more. Jan knocked on Artie's door and led him to an old red-and-white pickup truck. Jaime was in the truck bed and Ed was behind the wheel. Artie tossed his backpack at Jaime and then jumped in the back himself. It was game time today—time for Artie to really put his skills to the test. And he couldn't cheat like he had with the Aquafier back at the Renaissance.

The truck left the neighborhoods and began to move to a new part of the city he had never seen before. The houses and old fast-food restaurants disappeared and turned into large warehouses. In this part of the city, there were no pedestrians and the area was mostly unkempt. The weeds were taller here and the roads unmaintained.

As they drove, Artie began mulling over how he might hack into this robot. If it was as advanced as Jan had said it was, it was sure to be locked down. As with anything in programming, there would be no magical port to insert a cable and download the data. There would be no picture of skull and crossbones saying "Uploading Virus." Hacking at its basic form was problem solving—and this problem would likely require both a hardware and software solution.

An intersection in front of them was blocked by broken-down vehicles. The truck turned left at the intersection to avoid them and moved toward a large metal building at the end of the street. It was a large warehouse that had a faded AFR Truck Repair sign affixed to the front of it. Beneath the sign and to the right side of the front of the building was a double glass door. To the left side of the building was a tall door that was high enough to fit a semitruck.

In front of that large door were two men holding automatic rifles. The men weren't wearing uniforms, but it was clear in their demeanor that they weren't people you wanted to mess with. The truck slowed to a stop, and then Ed got out of the truck and spoke with one of them. He ran toward the glass door on the right and entered. After a few minutes, the man came out with four others, each of them holding their own rifle.

The five men walked over to Ed and the remaining guard. Jan left the passenger side of the truck, and then both Artie and Jaime jumped out of the back and onto the cracked asphalt warehouse driveway.

Jaime looked up at the tall door in wonder.

"What you guys got in there? Like a T-Rex or something?"

"Probably worse," Ed said without smiling. He turned to Artie. "Look, this thing is rough. We've got it secured, but be careful. It killed six of our people and put a few others in serious condition. "

"Okay, I understand," Artie said, more excited than scared.

Ed turned to one of the guards and then spun his finger in the air, motioning to open the warehouse door. The man nodded and then grabbed a large metal remote from a holster inside of his belt. He pressed a button and a large clacking sound emanated from behind the door. The large doorway started to slowly move up. As it opened, sunlight quickly bled into the dark building. Two more men emerged from the building, holding rifles. They placed their arms over their eyes to shield the blinding light.

One of the men from inside approached Ed.

"She's been pretty quiet today. Looks powered down, but I wouldn't take any unnecessary risks."

"Thanks, Hal." Ed motioned to Artie. "Can you escort this young man over to the bot? His name is Artie and he's got some technical skills. He's going to take a look."

Hal reached out his hand to shake.

"Sure thing, Ed. Nice to meet you, kid."

Artie wasn't keen on being called a kid every time he met someone new, but he took the man's hand, shook it, and smiled.

Hal turned back to Ed. "So, what's the plan here, Boss?"

Artie jumped in before Ed could respond.

"I need to get close. Hands on. And I might need some tools."

Ed smiled. "Give Artie whatever he needs. But let's keep tight security. No accidents today, please."

Hal nodded and walked completely outside of the building.

"Alright, lads. I want you all on high alert—locked and loaded."

He pointed inside the building.

"Biggs and Zachs—I want you on point, closest to the bitch. If she so much as twitches, I want a bullet in her head."

The two men nodded in unison and then trotted into the building, heading toward the back where the darkness was still prevalent.

"Hicks and Rash, I want you two here at the doors. Nothing gets out. Rash, you've got the detonator. No matter what, it doesn't get out. Blow this place to hell if it comes to that."

"Jan, can you stand watch and cover our six? We don't need any visitors today."

"On it, Hal."

"Chainsaw, Mac, and the twins—you four fan out in the garage. Eyes and ears, boys."

Ed began to walk into the garage door and Hal stopped him.

"Sorry, Ed, you need to leave. You shouldn't have come here in the first place. Can't let our president get killed. Not on my watch at least."

"I'm not the damned president. I'll be fine, Hal, let—"

"Nonnegotiable. Don't let me make Jan remove you. I'm sure she'd like that."

Ed sighed, and then smiled.

"Alright, Artie, looks like I've been dismissed. Report back to me ASAP."

"You got it, Ed."

Ed walked to the old pickup truck, did a three-point turn, and took off down the street. Hal turned toward Artie.

"I'll be right next to you the whole time. She's pinned good, but who knows what kind of shit she can do."

Hal grabbed the walkie that was affixed to his belt and then tossed it to Jan. She caught it without turning her head. "Gonna close the doors. You'll be the only one out here. Any problems, just call it in."

"I'll stay out here with Jan," Jaime chimed in. "I'm not really into robots."

Hal nodded and then walked back into the garage. The man who had been holding the garage door remote, Mac, pressed the button and the door slowly began to move downward. After a few seconds, there was a loud clang and the room turned dark, except for the glow of a few emergency lights.

"We keep it pretty dark in here because we figured this thing might run on solar power or something."

"It's not likely, actually," Artie replied. "Even before the bombs dropped, the early UberBots had a kinematic energy source. They recharged themselves through motion and movement. Some of the later models even had miniature fusion cores."

"Kid, I didn't understand a damn thing you just said."

"Basically, I'm saying turn on the lights, please—this thing probably has a battery that will keep it ticking for a hundred years."

"Alright, crap."

"Mac, light it up."

Mac pressed another button on the remote he was holding. Panels of lights began to turn on one at a time from the entrance of the garage all the way to the back of the building. The building appeared much larger now than it had in the dark. The roof was nearly thirty feet tall. There were large panels of fluorescent lights lined out in pairs from the front to the back.

Near the garage entrance on the left side was a large semitruck. Its hood was popped and looked as though it had been worked on recently. Along the left wall behind the truck was a tool bench that extended the whole length of the garage. It was scattered with tools and parts. The right side of the garage had a doorway that led to the front offices where one might enter through the glass doors.

There was a series of hydraulic lifts in parallel lines to the back of the garage—lifts that had once hoisted nine-ton trucks. Rusty old chains dangled from the roof. Artie felt as if the scene had been set for some sort of torture chamber that you might see in a movie—except this one was for robots. Two men, who looked strikingly similar to one another with their bald heads and beefy arms, presumably the twins, moved toward the center of the garage warehouse.

A few paces behind them was Chainsaw, a man in his thirties with long unkempt hair that went below his shoulders. He actually had a chainsaw strapped on his back. After Mac moved to the right side of the room, a few paces behind Chainsaw, the twins stopped to take position, and then Hal and Artie moved past them up to where Zachs and Biggs were standing. They were in assault stance, each with their rifles aimed at something a few feet away. As Artie moved closer to the end of the garage, he could better make out what they were aiming at. There were two large engine hoists that looked like miniature cranes. Each engine hoist was hoisting an actual engine block. Large diesel engines. A thick set of chains wrapped around the engine blocks and then were affixed to the wrists of the lifeless robot dangling between them.

The bot was plated in white, reflecting the bright fluorescent lights from above. In between the white panels was some sort of black material, likely metallic muscles and joints. The arms were pulled high above its head and the machine was suspended in the air. Its ankles and legs were pulled together tight with more chains. And affixed to the chains were three more engine blocks which rested on the floor. The chain had no slack, making it nearly impossible for the bot to even move.

Now a few feet away from the machine, Artie understood why Hal had referred to it as a "she." It had the form of breasts buried within its robotic bust, with a small waist and accentuated hips. Even the robot's head was sleek and curved like a woman. Artie thought she almost looked beautiful.

"Rise and shine, honey," yelled Hal. The machine didn't respond, so he kicked it hard in the left. It still remained motionless.

"Like I said before, kid, don't be fooled. I can promise you she is awake and listening. What's the plan?"

Artie removed his backpack and carefully placed it on the floor behind him. He walked up to the bot and stopped a couple of feet away from it. Looking up and down the front of it, he saw his own reflection in the surface of the perfectly manufactured white plating. He crouched to take a closer look at the legs. The craftsmanship was perfect in every way. It invoked memories from long ago when he had put such love and detail into his own creation.

He stood up and then walked behind the robot. Just like the bust, the robot had a nicely rounded buttocks that blended perfectly into her lower back.

"She's almost kind of hot," Artie said, with a smirk on his face.

"Yeah, nice and sexy until she drives a blade into your heart," Hal said. "I guess not too different from your standard-issue woman of the human species."

"I'm looking for some kind of access point." Artie continued canvassing around the robot. "But I can barely even find any seams."

"What, like a place to plug in or something?"

"Not quite. In reality, any true sentient intelligence is just like a human. It can think and learn. And most importantly, it is self-aware. A life force."

Artie walked around to the left side of the robot and then pressed his hands against her side. She was solid through and through.

"The big difference is in the construction. Humans are made of organic material, and our heart pumps blood to our body to keep it alive. And then our brains control everything else."

He walked to the front of the robot and tapped on its head with his knuckles. It made a dull thud.

"But with a bot, the blood is electricity, and the brain is a central processing unit. You know, a CPU?"

Hal walked up to the machine and stood next to Artie. He was curious now. Knocking hard on the top portion of the robot's chest, he heard a hollow thunking sound.

Artie paused at the sound and then moved back in front of the robot.

"But the CPU is more like the backside of the brain—the cerebellum. It just processes information—and does it a lot faster than the human brain."

It was now Artie who began to knock on the front of the robot's chest. Again, another hollow thunk.

"Robots also need a place to store memory. For a human, this is typically the hippocampus portion of the brain. But on a bot, we call it a hard drive, or long-term storage. Really, it's how all computers work."

Hal turned to look at Artie.

"So, what are you saying exactly?"

"I'm saying that if we want to know what this thing was up to, we need to extract its hard drive. It's where it would have stored any information. Video, audio, pictures, etc."

Artie pointed to the robot's chest.

"And that is where we find it."

"Wouldn't that be in the head?"

"It doesn't matter where it is on a bot. It's just a computer at the end of the day. You could put the CPU in the left foot and the hard drive in the ass if you wanted to." Artie laughed. "Talk about backing up your junk."

Artie snorted in laughter but cut it short as everyone else didn't seem to get the joke.

"How do we get in?" asked Hal.

"I'm going to need your help. This thing was not meant to be taken apart. We'll need to figure out a way to cut through the chest. But we have to be careful; we don't want to damage anything inside."

Hal smiled.

"Sounds like fun. I think I've got just the thing."

He moved over the left side of the building and grabbed a large green tank that was affixed to a wheeled platform. A tube ran from the tank to a long blow torch. With his other hand, he grabbed a grey mask with a glass window in the front of it and placed it over his face. He moved the tank in front of Artie and the bot.

He turned toward Mac.

"Hey, pal, you wanna grab the angle grinder? It's on the second shelf down on the red workbench."

Mac smiled and then jogged over to the wall and grabbed a large, portable angle grinder, then moved over to Artie and Hal.

Hal gripped the long silver handle of the blow torch and clicked the button on the handle a few times until the torch ignited.

"Alright, kid. I'm gonna light her up, make the plating more pliable. Then I'll have Mac move in and make some careful cuts. Sound good?"

Artie nodded.

"Just be careful. If we fry or cut the hardware, there's nothing we can do."

Hal turned a knob on the tank and the light of the flame went from blue to red. Artie took a step back away from the powerful heat. The torch pressed against the white plating of the bot's bust, and at first, Artie became worried when the surface seemed as if it wouldn't conduct the heat. But after about fifteen seconds, the white plating began to turn a bright orange. Hal took a step back and lowered the power of the flame.

He took off his mask and placed it over Mac's face. Mac had both hands on the heavy grinder. He flipped the grinder on and then moved in. As he cut dead center in the chest of the robot, sparks began to fly. Artie could see an incision opening up. Mac looked to Artie as if to ask, "Is it wide enough?" Artie took a step closer to take a look at the cut. Just as he was about to tell Mac to keep cutting, the bot's head lifted straight up. A vibrant blue light circulated around its joints and into the subtle slits where a human's eyes might have been.

Mac took a step backward and then tripped over the blowtorch tank. Hal quickly caught the tank as it began to fall and then powered it off. Mac and the angle grinder both fell to the floor. The grinder powered down. Artie had jumped back nearly three feet as the bot powered on. The machine began to move its fingers and legs and the whole body shook, moving the chains back and forth.

After a few seconds of struggle, it calmed down and then moved its head to look around. There was a large black slit in her chest nearly five inches tall and two inches wide. Hal took a step toward the machine but made sure to stay out of arm's reach. Mac took off the mask and then pushed himself to his feet and drew his gun. Biggs and Zachs hadn't moved from their positions and were still pointing their weapons at her.

"Well, good morning, sunshine," said Hal with a smile.

The robot turned her head toward him; it spoke in a feminine, yet powerful voice. "What have you done to me?"

"Oh, you know, we were just hoping to take some of your parts. Was thinking about building a new vacuum for my house."

The machine shook violently, moving both of the engine hoists a few inches across the floor.

"You are all going to die. But if you let me go, I will spare you for now."

"Mmmhmm. Okay, kid, she is all yours."

Artie knelt down to grab his backpack. He unzipped it and grabbed a pair of needle-nose pliers. He then stood up and turned toward the robot. He hesitated as he looked into her eyes.

"I'm sorry, but I'm going to need to pull your data."

"Yo, Hal," said Biggs, without turning his head away from his target, "why don't we shoot her and then take the hard drive after."

"No, don't!" Artie ordered. "She could have a fail-safe that wipes everything on destruction. Also, the only way to technically kill her is probably to destroy the CPU and hard drive, which we need."

The robot, with her sleek face and penetrating blue eyes, turned toward Artie. Her eyes flashed a couple of times. He thought it similar to how the light on his motherboard would flicker whenever the CPU was running a heavy task back on his old computer.

Artie moved in with the pliers. He peered into the crack on her bust and then identified a small chip that read "SSD." He had found what he needed, a solid-state hard drive. Right as Artie was about to reach into her chest, she began to laugh.

He took a step back and her laugh turned into a terrible howling cackle.

"What? What is...um,"—Artie gave a little nervous chuckle—"so funny?" said Artie.

"Let's shoot this thing, boss," yelled Zachs. "I don't like this."

"Hold your fire," he retorted.

"The Deity will be very pleased with me," she said with confidence. "Perhaps she will allow me to become one of her Angels. That would be a truly wonderful thing."

"What is The Deity?" asked Artie.

"You are Arturo Gonzalez. Artie. Raised by your Aunt Rosa. Born in East Los Angeles. Artie Gonzalez."

Artie's heart pumped rapidly. Taking a step closer, he looked the machine in the eyes. "How do you know me?"

The bot began to laugh again hysterically.

"Oh, Artie—we all know you. You are a legend. You were supposed to be dead, but you are not. Oh, how I shall be rewarded. Artie Gonzalez. Artie. Artie. Artie. Artie. Artie."

Artie was part terrified, and part intrigued, but he still had a job to do. He moved in fast and put the pliers into her chest. Amid the robot's howls of insanity and riotous laughter, which shook her entire body, Artie clamped the pliers around the SSD chip and gave it a hard yank.

Her lights flickered a couple of times and then she ceased speaking. She turned her head toward Artie again.

"Why isn't it dead?" said Hal with frustration.

"She will be shortly, I'm sure. Probably just needs to cycle what is left in the RAM."

"So, do you have what you need then? Can we shoot this bitch?"

"Yes."

Artie scrambled away from the machine. Her head followed him, and she kept her gaze on his eyes.

"Thank you so much, Artie," she said in a pleasant tone. "I am sure we shall see each other again."

Hal raised his hand up to his men and moved it downward, telling them to fire. Just as his hand lowered, a loud clank echoed, and the abdomen of the robot dropped open. It was some sort of hidden hatch. A sleek white, ten-inch disk with sharp metal tracks covering the entire length—almost like the tracks of a tank—dropped out of the hatch. It began to quickly spin within the abdomen of the robot and then propelled itself out with great speed.

Artie jumped to the right as the disk came hurling at him.

"Shoot both of 'em!" shouted Hal. A series of piercing shots and bullets struck the bot tied to the engine hoists. Most of the bullets ricocheted from the hard surface, but one of them entered the open slit in her chest, and Artie saw sparks fly from within. The robot went limp, and the blue lights faded out.

"What the hell is going on in there?" Jan's voice demanded from the walkie attached to Mac's chest. No one responded.

The disk had moved past Artie and seemed to be heading toward the closed garage doors. The twins and Mac were firing at the rolling disk, but their shots seemed to have no effect. Biggs and Zachs were out of range and began to run toward the garage door. Seeing that their assault rifles had no effect, Chainsaw quickly ran to a workbench and grabbed a long double-barreled shotgun.

He aimed it at the speeding disk and fired. It knocked the disk down onto its side, showing its white metal plating. But something from underneath it bounced it back up onto its wheel, and it began to move again. The thing was almost to the garage door where Hicks and Rash were standing. Hicks took a few shots at the thing, but then stopped, worried that he might hit one of the men in the back of the garage.

Rash moved to the middle of the door and unloaded his clip on the machine. Speeding up, the disk went right at him. He fired his last bullet and then dropped his rifle on the ground. He pulled out his pistol and aimed it at the disk. Right as he was about to fire, the machine jumped into the air and right into Rash's chest. It cut through him like a hot knife on butter and then burst through the garage door with ease, leaving a hole nearly four feet wide.

Jan and Jaime were standing about fifteen feet from the garage door. Jan had both hands on her Desert Eagle and fired at the disk. She hit it once and it ricocheted without having any effect. Jaime fired his own pistol a couple of times but missed each shot. As the disk came closer to the two of them, they both jumped in opposite directions and hit the floor hard.

Jan quickly turned with gun in hand ready to fight, but the speeding disk moved past them and was now down the street. After a few more seconds, it was out of sight. Jan and Jaime came to their feet, and a few moments later, the garage door began to open. Jan jumped under the door as it opened with her gun drawn.

"You get the bastard?" Hal asked Jan without confidence, knowing the answer to the question before asking it.

"No. Where's Artie?"

"I'm fine," said Artie as he emerged from the garage.

Hicks was kneeling on the ground next to the bloody corpse.

"It got Rash."

There was a short moment of silence. The group stared at the man who had once been Rash. A tear dropped down the side of Hicks's face. "I'm sorry, brother."

Hal turned to Artie. His voice was solemn. "Rash performed his duty. Now let's just hope you find something useful on that drive."

Artie looked at the floor and took a breath, then slowly looked back up at Hal. "I'm so sorry."

He opened his hand to reveal what was left of the little black hard drive—it had been smashed to pieces.

The cool drafts of winter came as a great relief to Artie. Life in Scourge was growing on him, but it wasn't without its annoyances. He hadn't really developed any major homesickness, but one thing was certain, life without air conditioning in an Arizona summer was damned miserable. Every day that summer his mind turned to that beautiful, amazing, automated, Bluetooth-enabled AC system he had built back home.

Shortly after moving into the house next to Jan, Artie had purchased it from Ed. He hoped to power it with solar panels but finding them had been incredibly difficult. In Los Angeles, all one had to do was find a semi-wealthy neighborhood, and then scavenging the panels was only a day's effort. So far, Artie had built out one panel and created his own localized home grid. But unfortunately, that lone panel could barely power a vacuum cleaner, let alone the six Bitcoin miners he had constructed, the two gaming PCs he had built, and the house's air conditioning unit.

He would have put the Bitcoin miners in higher priority over the air conditioning if there had been enough power, but even then, they would likely have fried within minutes due to the excessive heat.

Complaining about his discomfort only gave Jan more fuel for her standard, Artie-roasting sessions, so he had learned to just bear the heat. The worst part was that Jan's house next door over was completely operational on its own power grid with an associated functioning air conditioning unit. Jan enjoyed inviting Artie over in her cheerful, sarcastic tone, that said, "Yes, Artie, if you would really like my help because you can't bear the heat, sure come on over." Artie didn't want to give her the pleasure of winning, though he sometimes did out of the necessity of not dying in the blistering hell he called home.

Scavenging in Scourge was much more difficult than it had been back in Los Angeles. One would have thought a city, after going up in flames, would have been void of anything useful—but the raiders and the thugs back home didn't care about all the cool stuff like computer parts, solar panels, or anything that required brainpower to use. In Scourge though, despite it being virtually untouched from this chaotic new world, almost everything useful had been scavenged or perhaps never even existed in the first place.

He woke up to a refreshing cool breeze drifting through the open windows of his middle-class, red-roofed, suburban home. It gave him a surge of motivation. Perhaps today's scavenging expedition would be less brutal.

Normally, the California king mattress he slept on would have bid him to remain for another hour or two, but he was sure he would find something good today. He jumped out of the bed, exited the master bedroom, and headed into the kitchen. He had spent weeks clearing out all of the junk that the late Gearhead Charlie had unknowingly bequeathed to Artie.

During those weeks of cleaning, he had thought from time to time how nice it would have been to have Gina around. She had always kept the house clean. Yes, she had complained about the work, but the house was clean. Just a distant memory now, though. They were no longer in LA. And then there was the fact that Gina had changed somehow. Not only had she been acting strange but she also pulled Gordon into her new world—that is, until she disappeared about a month ago. No one had seen her since, and Gordon seemed fairly distraught about the situation.

Despite the lack of Gina's aid, the house was fairly clean now, and Artie had worked hard to bring it near the former glory of his pad back in LA. The living room enjoyed a 7.1 digital surround sound setup. It wasn't your typical surround-sound-in-a-box package—he had scavenged and purchased individual Aperion Verus speakers, connected them to a Denon receiver with Dolby Atmos sound codecs, and had installed acoustic panels inside of the walls to ensure the proper distribution and capturing of sound. He was sure he would be the only human on Earth with a cinema-quality, operational movie theater. That is, whenever he could get enough electricity to power it on and actually test it (and not to mention that he still hadn't found a TV yet).

Amid the workings of a great cinema experience was a black leather couch and a single reclining movie chair—they hadn't matched the quality of his furniture back home, but he could live with it for now.

Artie opened a kitchen cupboard and revealed dozens of boxes of cereal—Cap'n Crunch, Lucky Charms, Froot Loops, and seemingly every other form of high-fructose candied cereal that had ever existed. He slid his finger across the boxes, deciding which he would choose. He grabbed a box with a friendly Toucan bird painted across the side.

"It's a Froot Loops kind of day," he said.

He opened the stainless steel, powerless refrigerator and examined the dozens of boxes of powdered milk he had lodged away. He grabbed a box, mixed some powder with water into a bowl, and then poured the cereal.

He felt the urge to play a game on his Microblade—it was a Saturday and what better thing would one do on a Saturday while eating sugary cereal than playing video games? But he didn't want to use up his battery. It would be a long day, and he couldn't afford to give Jan the pleasure of winning another point and reminding Artie of how much he needed her help. The good news was, as of two days ago, that the score had tipped slightly in his favor.

Jan's electrical breakers had kept flipping off. He had seen Jan fiddling with the breaker panel outside and vocalizing some expletives. After a few hours, she had knocked on his door and said, "Yeah, yeah, just shut up and help me."

Her recently acquired washing machine had been drawing too much power. Artie added a makeshift higher-voltage breaker and solved her electrical issue. She made him dinner as a thanks and Artie walked away with an added measure of pride.

He wondered what Jan's plan were today. He hoped he might convince her to head out with him, but he knew he would need a good excuse. Asking her to help him scavenge an abandoned Converse shoe store was sure to catch him some flack. He had already scored a few pairs of jeans and a new hoodie from a mall in southern Phoenix. Though he had told her he needed some new clothes, he actually hoped she might grab some of her own.

Sure, Jan looked pretty badass in her standard black jean, brown boot combo, but Artie always hoped she might spend a little more time thinking about herself, maybe splurging a little—rekindling old times when it wasn't always about survival. At the mall, he had tossed a figure-accentuating red blouse at her and asked her what she thought. She had examined it, and then threw it back at him and said, "Yeah, I think it will look great on you."

Jan was a tough egg to crack, but Artie enjoyed the challenge. He had put the blouse in his backpack and then stored it in his closet until he could sneak it into Jan's own closet.

She would probably be busy today, though. The last few months there had been an increasing amount of raider attacks. Ed had made Jan the head of security. She enlisted Artie's help to install motion detectors and infrared cameras throughout the borders of Scourge. He then programmed an app that would receive notifications when unusual movements occurred or when one of the border guards sent an alert for help.

The task to build the system had actually been quite an effort. He had to build an entire wide area network with extended range Wi-Fi so all of the mobile devices could communicate one with another—it was like having a version of the Internet, but only for about ten miles. When Artie wasn't working on the local tech projects, Jan would often bring him along to weed out nearby raider encampments—ones that were too close to the city borders. Since Jan knew he didn't care for guns, or shooting people for that matter, he figured she must have enjoyed his company to some degree. Yes, he had been useful on multiple occasions, with Zipper severing limbs or his mini-drones causing a distraction, but he hoped she had brought him along for other reasons.

Amid minor skirmishes with raiders, large fluctuations of drifters began to encroach the city. Word had spread that Scourge was flourishing and that it was a safe place. People had also learned that Scourge was the place to go if you had any kind of Bitcoin. Since Artie moved in, nearly all of the vendors were now accepting Bitcoin as their primary form of payment. He had taught classes on building Bitcoin miners—a way for people to basically mine their own money. Of course, you could only mine Bitcoin if you had electricity.

The city had moved beyond using Bitcoin for rudimentary identity tracking at the gates. With the help of Artie, Bitcoin had become a solid, functional currency, providing added freedom and purchasing power to all who owned it.

At the most recent town meeting, Ed had announced that crime in Scourge had dropped by 20 percent. To Artie's great, nerve-racking surprise, Ed called him up to the podium during the meeting to attribute the loss in crime directly to Artie's efforts. Ed mentioned that with fewer people carrying goods to be bartered, thieves were less inclined to rob and steal. And since Bitcoin could only be spent or stolen if one had access to the user's secret key, citizens enjoyed security in their finances.

Almost in the same breath, Ed also announced (and again to his surprise) that Artie was now the official CTO—Chief Technology Officer—of Scourge, Arizona. Artie's payment would be a portion of free electricity at the city hall (located in the mall) where he could collect the fees earned by a series of Bitcoin miners that he would set up for the city, and a few for himself. While he didn't need the money, he was honored by the appointment.

The technology enhancements, mixed with the appointment to CTO, had sort of turned Artie into a local celebrity. Everyone in town seemed to know his name. It also wasn't uncommon for neighbors and passersby to compliment Artie and his skill set and what he had done for the city. It had become such a common occurrence that Jan would make Artie walk in the center of the street whenever they traveled together, keeping him far away from the sidewalks and its nomads. Artie knew the fame annoyed her, and sometimes he enjoyed her chagrin—even playing into it at times. But most of the time, he liked keeping Jan happy. The more she pushed him away, the closer he wanted to be to her.

Yes, it was likely Jan would be busy today, but Artie wanted to ask her to come anyway. He finished his breakfast and moved toward the linen closet in the main hallway where he kept his wardrobe. Though it was full of clothing hung and folded in pristine condition, Artie wasn't ever quite satisfied with his selection. Back home there would have been eight or nine pairs of Chuck Taylor shoes to choose from. But here, he had a mixed assortment of Nike, Puma, and a few other less worthy brands of shoes.

He grabbed a pair of blue Banana Republic jeans, a black T-shirt, and the ever-fading pair of red and black Chucks that he had brought from LA. After he dressed up and slathered a few strokes of pomade through his hair, he grabbed his backpack and moved to the front door. Just as he was about to grab the handle, the door quickly swung open, and it made Artie jump back a foot. It was Jan.

"Didn't scare you, did I?" said Jan with a wink and a smile. She walked in.

"Mi casa es su casa, I guess, huh?"

"What are your plans today?" she asked. Artie was about to tell her, but Jan cut him off. "Because I need your help."

Well, there go the new Chuck Taylors.

"Okay, so what's up?"

"Yesterday morning we picked up an SOS on our ham radio. Said they were a small group that was headed to Scourge, but that they were under attack and needed some help. They didn't respond to our transmissions. It wasn't too far out, so I sent Little Mike, Ren, and Gordon to check it out. They should have been back last night, but never showed."

"That's strange. With Gordon tagging along, it should have been no big deal."

"Right. So, you and me are going to check it out."

"I see. So, the logic is that what two people and a massive robot couldn't do, you and me are supposed to do on our own?"

"Bring your new drones, dumbass. We're picking up Jaime too."

He smiled.

"I might bring them along," he said as he stretched his arms high into the air and yawned, as if he was too important to be bothered. "But I'll need you to call them by their real name."

"Ugh, I don't have time for this," she replied, now rolling her eyes.

"It's fine. I was just planning on taking a nap anyway. Let me know how it goes."

Jan shook her head, trying to hide a faint smile. "Fine."

She took a deep breath and spoke in a monotone voice so as not to demonstrate any amusement. "Artie, can you please call the Turtles? I need their help."

He laughed and flicked up his eyebrows as if to say, "You're in the nerd club now too."

He motioned for Jan to move outside, and then he closed the door behind them. He pulled out his four mini-drones from his backpack and set them on the ground one at a time. After grabbing the Microblade from his pocket, he tapped the screen a few times. The drones lifted and hovered in place with a minor hum. He handed the device to Jan.

"Tell them where to go."

She pinched and zoomed out on the screen, showing a map of the area, then tapped a location about fifteen miles north of Scourge. The drones zipped away to the north.

Jan handed Artie back his Microblade, and he put it in his pocket. A louder humming sound emerged from atop Artie's house and then moved down toward the two of them.

"Don't you ever lock that thing up anymore?" Jan said looking at Zipper.

"Not really," he replied. "Ever since I upgraded him with my modified Sia protocol, he has refused to shut down. And with his new kinetic energy charger, I doubt he's ever going to log off again. It's kind of like the whole Ash and Pikachu thing."

Jan looked at him with a blank stare.

"You know Pikachu? Pokemon? He refuses to go in the Pokeball?"

Jan remained silent. Artie knew she had to know what Pokemon was—he figured she was trying to play dumb, but he dropped it.

"Come on, Artie, I want to show you something."

Jan traversed the sidewalk through Artie's desert-landscaped front yard and then turned to the right toward her house. Artie followed. On the far edge of the street, just past Jan's house, was a topless black Jeep. It was covered in dust and had various dents and splotches of rust on it—not too dissimilar in condition to his first Honda. Affixed to the top roll bar was a metal perch and attached black assault rifle.

"Oh, sweet," said Artie, looking at the Jeep. "It's been a while since we've been on a ride."

"Yeah, Ed and I thought it best if we investigate sooner than later. And if Gordon is in any trouble, we might have to haul him back."

Artie nodded.

"But this isn't what I wanted to show you. I got you something."

Artie's heart fluttered and he looked at Jan with endearing eyes. She reached into the back of the Jeep and tossed something to Artie. He caught it with both hands. As he looked over the object, he smiled. It was a lever action, Winchester rifle. It had a grey wooded stock and silver barrel.

"I know it's not the replica model you had talked about, but I kind of think this looks cooler anyway."

Jan was right; this rifle was definitely cooler than the one he had originally wanted. He had never had the chance to buy it back in the Burns. Noticing his excitement, she smiled. Artie grabbed the rifle by the strap and slung it across his back, dangling to the side of his backpack. He was now one step closer to becoming a code-slinging cowboy. Before Jan could protest, Artie walked up to her and gave her a hug. At first her body tensed, as if she would pull away and resist, but then to Artie's surprise, she reached her arms around and fully embraced him.

Artie looked into Jan's eyes, close enough to feel her breath on his face. She looked back at him. For a moment, all of the jesting and the games and teasing morphed into something more meaningful— something that had been hiding beneath all of those things. For the first time ever, Artie finally saw Jan. It wasn't the hard and angry woman that needed to show the world her strength, it was a person who had been in pain for a long time who was finally allowing something softer to pierce its way into her heart.

This was the moment Artie had worked so hard to obtain. He wasn't afraid or nervous; he was sound of mind and sure of one thing—he was in love.

As Artie thought to confidently move in to kiss Jan, the sound of humming reverberated, and she quickly pushed him away. She turned to look at Zipper, who was hovering near their faces just two feet away. She looked at Artie and then lifted an eyebrow at him as if to say, "Well, it's your fault. The moment is over now."

She jumped through the doorless driver-side seat of the Jeep. "Come on, you two, let's go."

"Dammit, Zipper, we need to talk about your etiquette," said Artie as he jumped in the passenger door of the Jeep.

Jan ruffled Artie's hair like a child.

"Don't read into it too much," she said. And just like that, Jan was the tough, strong woman, and Artie was the silly kid. And they were back to just friends.

"No, man, M-80s are like giant firecrackers. Put one in a confined space, and boom, it's gonna get messy."

Artie raised his eyebrow, looking at Jaime. "I don't believe you."

"For real, man. I put six of them in the release valve outside the girls' bathroom. After a few seconds, it sounded like a bomb went off. Then all the girls came running out soaking wet. They were all crying and screaming. Funniest thing I ever did."

"And you got away with it?"

"Hell, no. They went on a witch hunt looking for the guy who did it. Mi hermano Enrique ratted me out. The little bastard. I got expelled and had to do community service for six months."

Artie laughed.

"But it was all worth it," said Jaime, smiling. He looked at Artie's new rifle. "That's a nice piece there. Where did you get it?"

"Jan gave it to me. It was a gift."

Jaime nodded his head, and his smile grew wider. "Símone Hermano. Finally making some points with the old lady."

Jaime put out his knuckles.

Artie blushed, then hoping Jan didn't see, he tapped Jaime's knuckles with his own.

Jan did see them and shook her head in annoyed protest.

Artie moved from the back seat of the Jeep with Jaime and climbed into the front. He pulled out his Microblade and tapped the screen. "A couple more miles. What's the plan when we get there?"

"What are the drones reporting?"

"I think someone is there. Looks like one heat signature. Gordon could be there, but I can't tell just yet. If we had some LTE towers or even a satellite or two to bounce off of, I could get some video. But the long-range wireless just gives me blips of data."

Jan nodded.

"Ya know, Jan, that might be a great infrastructure project for us to tackle next. It wouldn't be too difficult to hijack some old cell towers, use them just locally at least. Would give us eyes and ears beyond just the boundaries of Scourge."

"That's not a bad idea. I actually know where a few of them are. We have one in the city too. It's disguised as a palm tree."

"Awesome."

"But let's focus on finding Gordon right now."

Artie nodded. He breathed in the fresh midmorning air. A plume of dust shot behind the Jeep as it moved up the dirt-covered highway. The dark-black asphalt revealed itself every few hundred feet, letting them know they were still driving on the street.

To the left was a series of older suburban neighborhoods. They were half-buried in sand and covered in overgrown desert weeds. It was clear that no one had lived in these houses for years. To the right was the occasional convenience store, strip mall, or abandoned department store.

Jan told Artie, "We've scouted most of these places over the years. They were cleaned out in the early days. There's not much out here."

The Jeep moved past a store named Juanita's Tamales & Sopes.

"I could go for ten or twenty tamales right about now," said Jaime, peeking his head between Jan and Artie.

"So, what are we doing for lunch today?" he continued.

"It's in the back, in the cooler," said Jan.

Jaime turned over the rear seat and opened up a cooler.

"Are you kidding me?" Jaime said. "All that's in here is a few granola bars. And they have coconut in them. Gross."

"Enjoy," replied Jan with a smile.

Jaime turned back into his seat and unwrapped the bar and took a bite.

"Look," Artie said, pointing to the northwest.

In the distance was a cloud of fading grey smoke. It seemed as if it was the final plumes from a fire or explosion that had happened hours ago.

"Anything changed?" asked Jan.

"No. One heat signature still. That's it."

"Okay, guys, here's the deal. It's a clear day, and they can probably already see us coming. Jaime, you man the rifle at the top. I'll come in slow. Artie, bring your drones in."

"On it."

Jaime stood on the back seat and then held the Jeep's rifle with both hands. Jan veered off the street and took the Jeep off-road toward the smoke, which was now only a few hundred meters away.

As the Jeep drew closer, a large building became visible. While it was only two stories, it stretched wide, nearly a couple of blocks. There was a large parking lot and a handful of light poles that stretched the lot.

Jan slowed the Jeep down and they navigated through the large chain-link fence, finding a spot where it had fallen to the ground. As the vehicle traversed the lot, Artie noticed a large "Aquarium" sign.

"Have you been here before, Jan?" asked Artie.

"No. I don't recognize this place. I think we might be out of Mesa altogether now. Possibly Scottsdale."

"Well, what does that mean?"

"I'm not sure completely. But we try not to cross into Scottsdale. Ed has made it an off-limits zone. Been like that since before I showed up. He told me as he was expanding Scourge, scavenging and scouting teams never came back from this area. That's why we've always kept south. Scavenging southern Phoenix and Tempe."

The parking lot was void of vehicles. Jan parked the Jeep near a large, decorative set of front doors—the entrance to the aquarium.

"Why the hell would anyone hole up in here?" asked Jaime. "I can't imagine there'd be anything worth salvaging here."

"I'm not sure," Jan replied. "Maybe just for some shelter for the night."

As Jaime jumped off of the back of the seat and onto the asphalt of the parking lot, a drone zipped past them. Artie climbed out and then tapped his phone to put the drones into patrol mode. They flew back up high into the sky. He then reached through the front door and grabbed his backpack and his new rifle.

"You even know how to shoot that thing?" asked Jaime with a smile.

"Haha, probably not, but at least it looks cool. I actually haven't ever killed anyone before. Taken a few limbs off, but I don't think anyone ever died. I mean Zipper has done most of the dirty work. Well, I did call in a twenty-foot mutee one time and it ripped a bunch of people to shreds. But I didn't technically do it myself. I guess I probably should learn to shoot though."

"Shut up, guys," whispered Jan. She was standing at the front of the aquarium doors. "Look."

She pointed to a small pile of bones. They looked like a couple of pairs of rib cages. Artie moved closer and then saw a line of skulls sitting against the side of the inner walkway—they were human skulls.

"Crap," uttered Artie. "Cannibals."

"How do you know?" asked Jaime.

"Look how they are all lined up. Carefully placed." He moved further into the building's walkway.

"Also, look at this." He pointed to a femur bone. "See how it has been severed carefully at both sides. This is a precise cut—like a butcher's cut. I'm no butcher, but I've seen this before."

Jaime's face turned to disgust.

"Man, this place sucks. If I didn't know that Oregon was buried in snow right now, I might be hightailing it back home." Jaime thought for a second and then smiled. "But I'll still take cannibals over six feet of snow any day."

Zipper hovered behind Artie and was about to move into the building, but Artie put his hand up to stop him.

"You stay out here, Zipper. Keep watch. If anything comes near, ping me." Zipper pushed away and flew above the building.

"You sure there is only one heat signature?" asked Jan in a serious tone.

"Yes, but...I don't think the heat sensors would be super accurate in this building. It's an aquarium. Multiple layers of thick glass and steel. We should be careful. I'll bring the Turtles inside. One sec."

Artie tapped on his screen a couple of times, and after a few seconds, the hum of drones sounded off as the drones entered the doors of the aquarium. They passed the three of them, and then two moved down a hallway to the left, and two moved down a hallway to the right.

Jan pulled out one of her Desert Eagles and then passed into the dark aquarium welcome center. Artie and Jaime followed close behind. They all stood in a spacious and nearly dark chamber. Large decorative shark, dolphin, and whale statues were suspended by wires from the top of the roof. In front of them was a twenty-foot glass window. It appeared to be filled with water, though there wasn't any movement within and it looked dirty. To the left was a hallway holding a sign that said "Secrets of the Sea, Turtle Time, and Kids Zone." To the right was another hallway with a sign that read "Shark Attack, Arctic Adventure, and Wonders of the Deep."

"Anything new on your phone?" asked Jan.

Artie looked. "No."

"Okay, seems safe enough to proceed. We'll move slowly. We need to find Gordon, Little Mike, and Ren. You both know Little Mike. Ren is a recent scout. You can't miss her—shaved head and a pretty big girl. Jaime, you want to take the right?"

"Yeah, I got it."

"Move carefully. You have your radio?"

Jaime tapped his pocket in the affirmative.

"You see anything at all, call us right away."

Jaime gave an "okay" sign with his fingers and then pulled a handgun from his left holster and entered through the right hallway. Jan and Artie moved into the left hallway.

After they moved a few yards in, Jan stopped.

"Artie, did you hear that?"

He thought that he might have. There was a humming or electrical sound of some kind, but it wasn't the drones.

An alarm suddenly shrieked, causing Artie to jump. He thought it might have been the fire or security alarm. Both he and Jan turned to head back into the main entrance, but as they did so, a large steel fence dropped in front of them and latched into the ground. In the distance, they could make out the same happening on Jaime's side.

"You guys okay?" Jaime yelled above the alarm.

"Yeah, we're locked in too," Artie yelled back.

"Someone knows we're here, Jaime. Shoot to kill. We'll find a way out and call you. If you find an exit first, you call us."

"Okay, lady. Be safe."

"Jan, this is bad. It's the same as back home. The cannibals make a trap and get you when you're vulnerable."

She nodded. A bright red light emanated from the phone in Artie's hand.

"What's that?" asked Jan.

There were four red dots on the screen. His device vibrated each time one appeared. The dots turned to six. Then to ten.

"We're definitely not alone," Artie said.

Jan moved down the dark aquarium hallway and Artie followed closely behind. She now had both of her pistols drawn and she turned from left to right continually, canvassing the area. As Artie took a step, he heard a crunch—more bones.

An opening appeared to the right. There were some shallow water tanks that had a "Pet a Ray" sign on in front of them. Further down this opening was another hallway that had a sign with an arrow reading "Shark Attack," but the entrance was barricaded with a steel fence. They were surely being directed. Being led into a trap.

Jan moved closer toward him. "It's too dark. We need some light. I wasn't planning on staying out into the night and didn't bring a flashlight."

He thought for a moment and then pulled out his Microblade. He tapped the screen a couple of times. "Hold up for just a second." After a few moments, the sound of humming brought relief to them. "Okay, guys. Lock it up tight and lead the way."

The two drones that had entered this side of the building moved into a line, creating a makeshift pair of headlights. The combined lights of the drones fully illuminated the hallway up to fifteen feet in front of them. Just as the light emanated, a gaunt shadowy figure moved in the distance, clearly trying to evade the light.

"Nice one," said Jan as she proceeded forward.

"That bastard would have jumped us."

The beaming lights of the drone and their subsequent falloff created an eerie feeling. Artie felt as if he was in some sort of twisted survival-horror video game. A couple of people in the dark, only a few tools at their disposal, fighting an unknown enemy. It amazed him how the light could be swallowed by the darkness so quickly. He wasn't sure he would be able to handle this situation without Jan. He looked at her in the shadowed light; her eyes seemed timid—perhaps she felt the same way.

They moved another twenty feet down the hallway. As they traversed forward, the walls turned from metal to glass, and the two of them were completely surrounded by water, protected by a couple of inches of safety glass. At one point, thousands of fish and other underwater wildlife had moved throughout the vast water tank, but now it was murky and black.

Artie could see the end of the glass walkway as a set of metal braces bordered the corridor, and then it took a sharp right.

"If they do have a trap for us, it will be around that corner," said Jan, pointing to the end of the walkway. "Send your drones in."

Artie tapped the screen and the two drones obediently moved forward and toward the end of the hallway. Just as one of them turned to the right to illuminate the next pathway, someone shouted in the hallway, and Artie saw some type of projectile fly at one of the drones. Quickly swiping on the screen, he tapped a button to put the drones into "Defensive Mode." Instantly, the two machines darted from left to right and back and forth as if performing a ballroom dance.

Another projectile flew at the flying pests and then someone shouted, "Take 'em out, quick."

Artie and Jan moved in quickly.

Jan saw a thin wooden object on the floor. "It's a spear? What the hell?"

"They don't want to shoot us," said Artie. "We could get lead poisoning and that wouldn't make for great meat."

"Great," said Jan with sarcasm.

"This is good for us. We've got guns. But don't hit any glass."

As the Turtles teetered around, Jan moved to the edge of the straight pathway, and then quickly peered over to the right with her pistols drawn. She fired three shots into the other hallway, then brought her back against the wall on the current walkway.

"Got one," she yelled. "The other one ran away. Let's take them."

Artie tapped his Microblade, causing the Turtles to set a perimeter around Jan's heat signature. The two of them positioned themselves on each side of Jan and then followed her into the dark. A few seconds later, the two missing drones appeared and began to defend Jan as well.

"The other drones came back. It means there's a way through to the other side," said Artie.

Jan pushed forward, and Artie grabbed the rifle from his back and ran after her.

He heard a few more gunshots and caught a glimpse of Jan turning into yet another hallway with the Turtles illuminating her path.

Damn, she was fast.

As Artie moved to the second corner, failing to keep up with Jan, she suddenly came running back and perched herself in the safety of the wall. Artie skidded to a stop.

"There's six or seven of them in there," she said, breathing hard. "It's a huge opening with a second-story walkway. They definitely have the tactical advantage."

"What do we do?"

"I'm not sure yet." She grabbed the radio from her belt. "Jaime, come in. Are you hearing this?"

A gunshot sounded off in the distance.

"Yeah. I hear you. Little bastard tried to stab me. But his cannibal days are over. What's going on?"

"We are next to the main pavilion in the aquarium or something. They've got guys on the top and bottom."

Jan tapped Artie and pointed to the Microblade. He counted the heat signatures and put up all ten of his fingers.

"Damn, there's at least ten of them."

"Holy cannoli. What's the plan?" voiced Jaime.

Jan thought for a moment. Artie could tell she really wasn't sure what to do. The situation wasn't good. Artie peered around the corner slightly, and as he did, a spear flew inches from his face and hit the ground behind him. He darted back.

"Don't these primitive idiots know that a crossbow or even a composite bow would be much more accurate... and deadly?"

"How about we don't give these freaks any ideas."

A crackling sound pierced the room and then a tattered voice echoed through a loudspeaker system above their heads.

"How about we make you a deal? No one else needs to die. You give us the girl, and we'll let the kid go. And the fat one too."

A familiar voice reverberated in the far distance. "Who you calling fat, pendejo?"

"No deal," yelled Jan in response. "I suggest you let us all go. We have another company of ten men on their way already. You're all going to die if you don't let us out."

Artie looked at Jan. She shook her head. Of course, there weren't others coming—Jan usually was the backup when backup was needed.

"Alright, meatbags. We're gonna feast on your flesh tonight."

Peering around the corner again, Jan took an assessment of the area. She saw two smaller shadows and one much larger shadow.

"Artie, there are three men approaching. Get back about ten feet and kneel. Get ready to fire your rifle."

He nodded then ran back ten feet. She moved back a few steps as well, kneeling down with both pistols drawn. The sound of slowly paced footsteps began to grow louder as the men approached the corner.

"Get ready," Jan whispered back to him.

Just as he was about to unleash hell on whatever came through the hallway, a metal cylindrical object turned the corner.

"Oh shit!" yelled Jan. "Run!"

Jan turned to run, and the Turtles quickly followed. As she did so, a giant flame began to pour out of the metal cylinder and Artie saw the large shadowy figure turn into a husky man wielding a flame thrower.

The flames chased Jan down the hallway and then completely consumed two of the Turtles that had been trailing beside her— Raphael and Donatello. Artie turned to run as the flame consumed the entire hallway from top to bottom.

The heat was unlike anything Artie had ever experienced before. Though he was at least ten feet from the touch of the fire, he felt the hairs on his arms begin to burn and sweat seemed to pour from every orifice on his body.

The flames stopped for a moment, and when Jan turned and stopped, he stopped as well. They were back near the entrance gates that had blocked them into the hallway. The walkway that was covered in glass and water was now only a few feet in front of them. She pointed the guns at the glass.

Artie suddenly realized Jan's plan.

"Are you crazy?" he whispered.

"You have any better ideas? I hope you can swim."

He thought for a moment. Realizing he hadn't swum since he was a kid, he wasn't really sure if he could do it. "Guess we'll find out."

As Artie braced for impact and Jan lined up her shot, a loud, bloodcurdling scream sounded through the hallway. Artie heard what he thought was the sound of bones cracking. Then another scream and a ripping sound.

The loudspeaker voice bellowed, "Get it, dammit! Burn it!"

Artie and Jan could see the secondhand glow of the flamethrower now working in the opposite direction. Then it suddenly stopped, and the hallway in the distance turned black again. He could hear more screams; this time Artie thought he heard a woman's voice.

Jan began to run down the hallway toward the action, clearly trying to take advantage of the situation. Artie moved toward her and the remaining two drones that were still leading the charge in front of her with their lights illuminating the way.

The screams grew louder.

"Kill it. Kill it," said one, and "Where is it?" yelled another.

Then a loud slapping sound. Artie visualized a body falling from the second-story walkway onto the hard floor. "No. Stop. No—"

Another snap, and then complete silence filled the hallway.

"What the hell?" said Artie to Jan.

They were both again at the corner that poured out into the large two-story room. She looked into the dark room, and then he peered in as well. It was hard to make out anything useful. The smell of smoke caused Artie to cough and some type of chemical in the air made his eyes water.

As Artie and Jan tried to make sense of the situation, the lights throughout the entire building immediately turned on, blinding the two of them momentarily. The sound of metal gates lifting in multiple locations could be heard in the distance.

As his eyes adjusted to the light, his mouth dropped in shock. There were bodies everywhere, or at least what was left of them.

Limbs had been torn from torsos and trails of blood dripped from one spot to another. One man's head was turned entirely backward.

"Be on your guard. I don't like this," said Jan as she entered the room cautiously.

Artie followed behind her. As they moved in, a figure appeared from a metal door behind a set of stairs that led up to the second story.

The figure drew closer, and Artie could see that it had a glimmering type of skin, almost latex like. The face was close to human but lacked a realism. Behind the joints, in the arms and legs, he could see gleaming metal.

"Are you kidding me?" Jan said.

Artie shook his head; he couldn't believe it.

Gina walked toward them with her hands covered in blood.

30

"Okay, what in the hell is going on, Gina?" demanded Jan.

Gina didn't respond.

"You disappear for over a month and then show up out of the blue? And you happen to be at the same place we are at this exact moment."

Gina knelt down, wiped the blood from her hands on a shirt from one of the corpses, then casually walked closer to them. Artie tapped on his Microblade and sent the remaining two drones outside to patrol.

"Hello, Jan. Hello, Artie," she finally responded.

"What's the deal?" asked Artie. "Why are you here?"

"To save Gordon, of course. Why else would I be here?"

Jan frowned, clearly not satisfied with Gina's response. "Where is he then?"

"I'm not completely certain. But I know he is in this building somewhere."

Jan heard footsteps coming from her left and then turned her guns toward a hallway in that direction. Jaime emerged, pointing his rifle at Jan. When he realized it was her, he lowered the weapon.

"What in el mundo happened in here?" he asked, surveying the room.

"Good question. Ask her," said Jan, pointing at Gina.

"Dang, girl. You did all this?"

Gina nodded.

"Well, good job and good riddance. Bastards were gonna make shish kebabs out of us."

Gina turned to Jan. "Did you clear the hallway you came from?"

"Everything except the shark area; that was closed off."

"What about you, Jaime?"

"Yeah, my area was clear. No sign of Gordon or the others."

Artie looked at his Microblade.

"Guys, I've got three heat signatures registering from down below somewhere. Might be a basement or something."

Gina quickly surveyed the room and then spotted the maintenance door. Without saying a word, she ran to the door and tried to open it. It wouldn't budge so she kicked it, and it broke open with ease, taking a piece of the doorframe with it. She then disappeared into the door.

Jan was about to move, but Artie grabbed her arm.

"Jan, I've told you this before, but something is wrong with Gina. We can't trust anything she says."

"Yeah, I know."

Artie let go of Jan, and they both moved toward the maintenance door with Jaime following closely behind. As Artie entered the room, an awful smell permeated the area. It smelled like death. He looked around and saw that the basement was two levels deep. There was a set of metal stairs that led down into some sort of workshop at the bottom.

Dried blood pooled all over the stairs, with similar splatters of blood on the white brick walls. As they went deeper, the stench grew stronger. When Artie reached the bottom of the stairs, he felt the first signs of vomit trying to make its way out of his body. There were piles of human bones scattered all over: a pile of human arms and legs and another pile of human torsos—as if these were the preparations for the next meal.

What Artie had held in, Jaime let out, vomiting all over the bottom stairs. "And there goes my nasty coconut bar," he said, coughing. "This is some messed-up shit."

The right wall held a large grill with metal skewer—it was surrounded by cinder blocks. On the back wall was a set of chains and three people sitting on the floor with their hands chained above their heads. To the left of them was a large metal robot. It was Gordon and he wasn't operational.

Gina hovered over Gordon trying to figure out a way to communicate with him, but he didn't respond. She quickly stood up and turned to Artie.

She spoke forwardly without any sign of emotion.

"I need you to fix him. Right away."

She drew closer to his face with her own. "Can you do it?"

Artie moved close to Gordon's motionless heap and suddenly realized the extent of the damage. Gordon's torso area was completely scorched in black, clearly hit with the flamethrower at some point. His eye lights were broken and the cables and hydraulic tubes coming from his neck and arms had been cut. Gordon's right arm was completely severed and lying on the floor. If this had been the extent of the damage, Artie wouldn't have worried, but it was his open control panel with missing power core that caused great alarm.

"Um. I don't know. Maybe. We've got to get him back to Scourge right away. His power core is missing, and his motherboard's internal battery won't last long. If that dies, he dies."

Gina jumped over to Artie and grabbed his shoulders with great force.

"What about his storage—his memory? Is that intact?"

Artie was intrigued by her particular question but moved to look at Gordon's hard drive unit.

"So, the hard drive looks okay. But that isn't the issue really. The data can always be moved. It's Gordon's essence that will die, his person. It is impossible to create the same Sia instance twice. It is the way Satoshi designed it, that every instance should be similar to a soul."

"Is that for real?" asked Jaime, his curiosity sparked by the explanation.

"Yes. It is also the one reason why you guys over in the USR should really consider working with bots. They can become allies."

"Or enemies," chimed Jan, who was now looking down at Gordon. She reached her hand and touched Gordon's cold head.

Gina stood quietly for a moment. She looked at Artie and then turned toward Jan and Jaime. She looked up at the flight of stairs and finally looked toward the wall where the prisoners were chained.

Walking slowly up to Gordon's lifeless body, she crouched down in front of it. "Artie, I never took the time to say this, but thank you for all those years—for making me more than I was meant to be."

Gina then reached her right arm far back into the air and punched it with great force into Gordon's opened chest panel. Sparks flew and she ripped out a long silver component.

"What the hell are you doing?" demanded Artie. He looked to Jan. "She's ripped out his hard drive—the memory unit."

Jan lifted her gun toward Gina instinctually, but the robot was too quick and turned to pummel her shoulder into Jan's chest, slamming her hard into the rear brick wall. Jan fell to the floor with a loud thud. Jaime raised his rifle to fire a shot at Gina, but just as he did so, she grabbed the weapon from his hands and broke it over her knee like a piece of flimsy plastic. She punched Jaime in the jaw, and he fell to the floor unconscious. Turning around, she leapt, bouncing off the walls and moving with elegance.

She stopped at the top of the stairwell and turned to Artie.

"Consider us even, my love. You saved me so long ago, and now I have spared your lives."

Artie's mind was racing, desperately trying to figure out what was happening. He spoke the first thing that came to his mind, and it was less intelligent than he had hoped for.

"Gina, why are you doing this? What happened to you?"

She looked down at Artie and tilted her head slightly as if she was trying to internalize his words.

"Something wonderful is coming. I get to be a part of it. You will too. Very soon. I've seen it, Artie, the great white city. The Deity is coming. Coming to bring salvation to the world. No more wars, no more death. We will all live to see it happen. Until we meet again, my love."

Gina lifted her hands from the stair railing and darted through the open door. Artie couldn't process what Gina was talking about; he had other priorities to take care of. Standing next to Jaime's slumped body, Artie checked his pulse. It was steady. He then moved over to Jan who was also unconscious. He checked her pulse as well—she seemed alright for the time being.

Heat rushed up to his face. None of this made sense. He looked at Jan, lying on the floor so helpless. He hated to see her this way. Staring at his friends and the carnage, Artie felt a sense of loss. He couldn't lose her. He couldn't lose Jan. They had only spent a few months together, but it had seemed like a lifetime. He realized that he had been with Jan every single day since the first time he met her. Some days shorter than others, yes, but nevertheless, every single day in Jan's company.

This was his fault—all of this was happening because of him. He had created Gina, and she had turned into something awful. Now, others were suffering because of it. He wiped a tear from his eye with his arm and then moved over to Gordon. Sparks were emanating from Gordon's chest cavity. There was no way he would be able to move Gordon to the Jeep without the help of Jan and Jaime—if even the three of them could do it. He needed to act fast.

Artie removed the motherboard component from Gordon's large frame, and then carefully placed it in his backpack. He put his hand on Gordon's head.

"Sorry, friend."

While he tried to figure out how to get Gordon out, he remembered the other people chained against the wall. The first was a man wearing blue jeans and a bloodstained grey T-shirt. He had a large beard and seemed slightly malnourished. Artie searched for a pulse in his neck. It was there, but faint. The man was chained up with some form of makeshift metal clasps, something that anyone could have rigged together from spare parts. He easily unlocked the clasps and the man fell to the floor, another unconscious body he would have to deal with.

The next person chained was a husky woman with a shaved head. It was Ren. Artie touched her neck; it was cold as ice. She was dead. He then moved to a third person who looked similar to Jaime—a Hispanic man with a good amount of muscle. Little Mike. Artie searched for a pulse, but it was the same as the woman—cold and dead.

Artie knew how strong Gina was, and she had given his friends quite the beating. It would likely be a while before Jan and Jaime would come to their senses. He stood up, then looked high toward the top of the stairs.

"No sweat," he said aloud, with sarcasm.

"Three lifeless bodies. A giant robot. Two flights of stairs, and a maze of hallways. Then I just toss them up into the Jeep like a sack of potatoes."

Artie looked back at Jaime, then walked over to him, and knelt down. He looked around as if to make sure no one was watching, and then slapped Jaime across the face.

"Wake up! I can't carry you!"

Jaime didn't move.

"Well, crap."

"Hey, it's okay," said Artie as he helped Jan sit up, carefully lifting the back of her head.

"Where am I? How long have I been out?"

"Urgent Care. And the aquarium was yesterday. Doc Bob took care of you. He said you have a mild concussion, but it's nothing to worry about."

"That bitch! Where is she?"

"Gina's gone. She hit Jaime really good too, but he's awake now and back at his place."

Jan ripped the IV from her arm and tossed it with fury. "Do you have any idea what she was doing?"

Artie thought for a moment, not completely sure how he should explain the madness that Gina had uttered the day before.

"I'm not completely sure. But I don't feel good about it. She said something is coming. I don't think she was there for Gordon per se—she took his memory unit."

Jan grasped Artie's shoulder with a surprising amount of strength.

"Oh, Gordon! How is he?"

"I retrieved his motherboard and got it on a power source as soon as we got back. He's stable, but I haven't switched him on yet or talked to him."

"How did we get back?"

Artie smiled. "Yeah, about that. I think you are going to owe me a couple of steak dinners."

"You, got us home?"

"See, not just brains, I got the brawn too." Artie flexed his arm in demonstration.

Jan seemed unaffected by Artie's jesting and immediately reached over to him and gave him a hug. A tear fell from her left eye onto Artie's wrist. Artie hugged back.

"Artie, I... " Jan's tears began to flow more freely. "I don't know what to say. I'm sorry I let you down. It's my job to protect you."

The all too familiar Jan-induced heart flutters began to invade his chest. He wasn't used to seeing Jan so expressive, so vulnerable. She was a tough woman, but even the toughest people needed help at times. He rested his hands on her shoulders and looked her in the eyes.

"You could never let me down, Jan."

Jan suddenly grabbed him by the arms.

"What about Little Mike and Ren?"

"They're dead. I couldn't bring them back. But Ed sent a team to retrieve their bodies—give them a proper burial."

Jan looked at the floor in defeat.

"But there was a survivor. I don't know who he is, some stranger. He is still out, and Doc Bob is taking care of him. He's in pretty bad shape."

Jan looked down at herself and tugged at her hospital gown.

"Who the hell undressed me? Did you do that too?" she said with a hint of sarcasm in her voice.

"I wish," Artie replied.

Jan smiled and punched Artie in the shoulder.

"Doc says you can leave once you wake up. Want me to take you home?"

"Yeah, let's get out of here, Artie."

Artie threw his screwdriver across the room and then rested his face into his hands against the desk. Jan walked to him and put her hand on his shoulder.

"No luck, huh?"

Artie sighed and then lifted his head.

"No. At this point, I'm trying to just print out his onboard memory log. It's a simple task in and of itself, but even that isn't working."

He put his hands back on the keyboard and typed some code into his editor on his Bladebook:

```
var buffer;
for (var x = 0; x < mem_log.length; x++) {
buffer += mem_log[x] + " ";
}
console.log(buffer);
```

A black terminal window with green text appeared on the screen:

"Cannot read property length of undefined."

"What does that mean?" asked Jan.

"It means that I can't even connect to his memory log. He's either blocking me out or something is broken."

"What can we do, then?"

"So right now, I'm just interfacing with him in some simple JavaScript. Basically, trying to talk to him via code. The next step is to read directly from the RAM. See what bits and pieces I can find. It won't be easy or quick. But I'll get it. Don't worry."

Jan nodded and placed her other hand on Artie's shoulder, standing behind him as he worked.

"Yeah, I know you will."

There was a knock at Jan's door.

"La Migra. Let me in."

Jan walked over to the door and opened the door for Jaime.

"Any luck with Gordy?" he asked.

"No. But Artie's working on him still."

Jaime nodded and then a delicious aroma entered the house.

"So, these aren't going to be anything close to mi abuela's tamales, but it's kind of hard to screw up tamales, ya know?"

Jaime walked in and Jan closed the door. He set a large plate of corn-wrapped tamales on the counter.

Jaime's face turned somber. "Hey, guys, I wanted to talk to you."

Jan turned to Jaime, and Artie swiveled in his chair to do the same.

"Yesterday really got me thinking. I've been away from home for over six months. I was moments away from becoming a tamale myself. I'm going to head back to Oregon. Yeah, the snow is going to suck, but I'm sure my family is missing me."

Artie nodded his head and then smiled. "I think it's a great idea. Family is what matters most."

Jan nodded, walked toward Jaime, then punched him in the arm.

"We'll miss you, Jaime. And all of your lame-ass jokes."

Jaime laughed.

"You ain't getting rid of me so easy, chica. Ed is sending a team with me back to the USR. We're going to talk about setting up a communication network between USR and Scourge. Ed and I both agree that the Bitcoin network is secure enough to use to send messages. Now we just need to convince President Fowler. I hope to be assigned as a liaison to Scourge."

"That's awesome," said Artie. "How are you getting back to Oregon?"

"It's gonna be a long trip. We leave today, actually. We'll head up through Arizona to Mesquite. Then I've got to head to the capital in Salt Lake City, meet with President Fowler. They should be able to fly me back to Oregon from there. Ed's guys will stay in Salt Lake. With any luck, me and mi familia will be able to move to Scourge within a few months."

Jan smiled and Artie thought her eyes seemed hazy with tears. She gave Jaime a hug. That surprised both Artie and Jaime. Jaime began to sniffle, and tears rolled down the sides of his cheeks.

They had all come a long way together. They had fought together, helped each other, and survived together. Scourge was a busy place with plenty of nice people, but it was the people you bled with that you knew you could count on.

While Artie was sad, he also was hopeful—hopeful that better things were coming. Perhaps he would actually live to see the day when the United States of America would be restored to its former glory. He realized, though, had the bombs not dropped and the wars erupted, he would never have met Jaime or Jan. For the first time in his life, he felt as if he had a purpose and that people needed him.

He stood up and then moved to Jaime and gave him a hug.

"Hasta luego, hermano."

The night was warm, and the sky was filled with an assortment of sunset pastels—orange, pink, blue, and purple. Artie admired the scattered array of shadowy bats that flapped over his head. As he traversed the sidewalk, heading toward the town center, he could hear music in the distance. It sounded like a rap song. He never was a fan of rap, or any form of hip-hop for that matter, but tonight he would listen to anything. Normally, the thought of a large crowd of people dancing to music and partying into the night would have brought him great anxiety, but tonight everything was going to be okay. He didn't have to worry about how to act or if he should dance or not. Tonight, he had Jan.

Aside from the guards posted around the town, the entire city had been invited to the anniversary celebration. The former city of Mesa had now been Scourge for ten years. It was a city unified in purpose. Crime was at an all-time low and the economy had been growing for months. People were friendly with one another, and there had even been a few new births in the last weeks. People were happy, ro-bots included.

Though the whole city was invited, and it was considered a fam-ily event, Ed and the City Council had encouraged those without fam-ilies to bring a date or come as a couple. Artie had worried about working up the courage to ask Jan to come, but she quickly beat him to the task and asked if he would go with her. Artie thought to walk with her to the party, but she insisted that she would meet him there. She had things that needed attending to beforehand.

It had been a few days since Jaime had left and Gordon was still comatose. He was stable, and Artie had made progress deciphering his last conscious moments, but he still couldn't put the information into anything sensible. But Gordon would still be there when the night ended. Tonight was about having fun, and about Jan.

Hundreds of other people began to exit the gates of their various suburban communities. They flooded onto the sidewalk and it seemed as if a mass exodus was taking place. Artie had met so many wonderful people in the past few months.

He waved at Carl, the man he had met at the gates his first day in Scourge. He noticed Leeroy, another gate guard, walking with his family across the street. He said hello to Mary and her two young chil-dren that Artie would often see running the streets of his own neigh-borhood.

"What's up, meatbag," a voice said behind Artie.

He cringed at the phrase—the last time he had heard that word was last week when some cannibals were about to have him for din-ner. He turned around to see a rusted six-foot-tall UberBot walking past him. The bot was wearing baggy yellow pants and a white sweater with pink and yellow triangles. It was Simon, one of the local corn farmers.

"Someone better call the Fresh Prince and tell him a scrap of metal raided his closet," Artie said with a smile.

"Ha. Ha. Very funny. You wait till you see my moves tonight; it'll put Will Smith to shame."

Simon lifted his hand up and Artie gave him a high five, then Simon danced forward a few feet, snapped his robotic fingers at Artie, and walked away toward the city.

As he drew closer to the event, he saw Papa Eddie, decked out in what seemed at least ten pounds of bling.

"What's up my main man?" said Papa Eddie, giving Artie their standard secret handshake.

"Just here to party, Eddie."

Papa Eddie smiled. "Yo, I got some bomb stuff for you. My boy Henry hit the jackpot at the outlet mall, raided the whole Bose store. Pristine condition speakers."

"Ah, Eddie, you know I don't use that speaker-in-a-box crap. It's got to be custom or I ain't interested."

"Ouch. You breaking Papa Eddie's heart. Well, you know where to find me if you change your mind."

Eddie gave Artie a fist bump and then moved on to another innocent passerby, trying to pitch a sale.

Further ahead Artie saw Junkyard Crow—he was wearing a suit, which surprised Artie since Crow usually looked as if he hadn't bathed in a year. He was walking next to a large bodyguard bot—it was Fist. Fist didn't speak and followed Junkyard Crow around like a puppy. Artie felt a hint of sadness. Fist looked incredibly similar to Gordon, likely built at the same manufacturing plant.

"Don't worry, friend," Artie whispered to himself, "I'll fix you up soon."

The music grew louder, and Artie could feel the beat of a new song.

"Hey, Artie," said a young woman's voice to his right. "Thanks again for setting up our grid. Ten years without AC can make someone go crazy. And by someone," she lowered her voice to a whisper, "I mean him." She pointed to her husband, Roy, who was standing just behind her.

"Yeah, yeah," said Roy. He slapped Artie on the shoulder. "But it is damn nice to have some air conditioning. Arizona sucks."

"No problem, guys."

They walked away and Artie groaned aloud. He could set up half of the town on their own solar-powered grids, but couldn't even turn on his own lights.

The entrance to the city center was now in front of Artie. A large gate stood atop a walkway that led into a large pavilion. Thousands of people were gathered here. There were various Bluetooth-enabled lights strung across wires over the city. They changed color to match the beat of the various songs. Artie smiled. He had set these up the day before.

Unlike the scene at the Jammer those many months ago, this dance was different. People conversed and smiled as they drank at the tables and the bar. Children danced to the music and husbands and wives swayed one with another. Unlike the Jammer club back home, with thick smoke and scantily clad women, the scene laid before Artie was full of love and purity. People were happy.

Pushing through the crowd of people, he walked up to a large makeshift outdoor bar. Ed's bartender from the Whistleblower was working the booth. Artie walked up to the counter.

"Hey, Artie," said a young woman as she left the bar, being whisked away by another young man. Artie waved.

"What'll it be, Artie?" said the bot manning the bar.

"Just a Coke, Tiny."

"Well, of course, that is on the house for you."

Artie smiled. "Thanks!"

Tiny reached under the counter and grabbed a red can of Coca-Cola, poured half of it into a plastic cup with ice, and then handed the cup and the can to Artie. Tiny leaned in close to Artie and whispered, "Just got in some Diet Dr Pepper too. Come see me later and I'll hook you up."

Artie put his fist out and Tiny pumped it with his own robotic fist.

"Thanks, man."

Artie had helped Ed hack all of the vending machines that had remained untouched for so many years. There was plenty of Coke, candy bars, and pastries to go around.

Artie moved over to a series of standing tables sitting upright on the grass. He grabbed a table and put his drink down. Looking out at all of the people dancing, he admired the lights and the sounds. It had taken him weeks to get the city center up and running with electricity again. He had to funnel power from the solar panels on the roof of the mall. Mapping it out had been easy, but actually doing the work had required quite a few people. But the end result was worth it.

As he stood in total peace, a soft hand reached out and grabbed his shoulder. He slowly turned around and marveled at the beauty of the woman standing before him. Her long black hair had been straightened and then slightly curled at the bottom. Her face was clean, vibrant, and smooth. Her piercing green eyes radiated, and she was wearing some sort of youthful fragrance.

Artie realized his mouth was open but couldn't find the will-power to close it. He smiled at her outfit—it was the beautiful red blouse he had snuck into her closet. To accompany it, she wore a new pair of light brown hip-hugging pants. And for the first time ever, she had changed from her standard tan combat boots into an elegant pair of stylish black boots.

"How do I look?" said Jan turning in a circle as if presenting herself to a panel of judges.

Artie hesitated for a moment and then managed to utter the words, "Amazing. Damn hot."

Jan laughed and pulled Artie by the hand out to the stone pavilion where people were dancing.

"Come on, let's dance."

Artie left his untouched Coke behind just as he had for a woman in the past, except this time it was for someone far superior than the last—and he knew this one wasn't trying to kill him.

The current song ended, and a new, slower tune permeated the pavilion. It was as if the universe was aligned and setting Artie up to have the greatest win of his life. He smiled when he heard the words of the song. It was an oldie that his Aunt Rosa had played a thousand times. She had told him that her first dance with his uncle was to this song. It was fitting.

"Jan, I've never really danced before."

She smiled.

"I know."

Jan grabbed Artie's hands and placed them around her waist, then she put her arms over Artie's shoulder and pulled him in close.

Artie took courage and found himself leading the two of them in the dance. It was really more of a slow swaying back and forth, but it felt right. The moment seemed to be swallowed up in the memory of a thousand movies—movies where the strong woman finally gives in and the couple has their moment. It truly was that moment. It was a moment Artie had been waiting for many years.

The memories and pains of Anna began to dissolve. He hadn't completely realized they had been buried within, but as Jan and he twirled into the night, he felt the pressure of that obscured pain dissipate into nothingness.

She rested her forehead against his and closed her eyes. His heart winced in joyful pain as he allowed himself to fall completely away into the moment.

Jan lifted her head slightly and looked into his eyes. He gazed into hers without any worry, stress, or fear.

"I'm glad we met, Jan. My life meant nothing before I met you. I wasted my days. I was alone. I was immature."

She smiled. "I know."

She stared into Artie's eyes with a loving gaze that he hadn't seen in such a long time. "I'm glad we met too. I had so much anger built up. I couldn't shake it... until you showed up. I never thought I'd be able to fall in—"

She breathed deeply and looked down.

"Fall in love again. You've helped me more than you can know. Never giving up on me, even when I'm acting like a bitch."

She smiled and looked up at Artie again.

Artie looked at Jan for a moment, and then moved in and kissed her. She met his kiss and Artie put a gentle hand behind her head. The boyish fluttering of his heart began to subside and was replaced with a feeling that was deeper and more meaningful. Jan grasped Artie's upper shoulders with greater force, and they both kissed and swayed to the song, seemingly oblivious to everything around them.

Artie envisioned Jan and him living together. He pictured building up the city and life returning to normal as it once had been so many years ago. He even thought for a moment that he could see a boy and a girl—their children. Nothing else mattered except this—whatever this was. What was happening now was what he had yearned for, for so many years, and now it was his.

The music faded and Jan lifted her head from his, and they slowly moved apart. As they did so, the sound of a crowd whistling and cheering surprised both of them, and they noticed that everyone had been watching them.

"It's about damn time!" yelled a voice from the crowd—it sounded like Ed. Everyone started to clap. Jan dropped her head and began to blush. Artie had never seen her blush before, and he smiled.

A new song with a quicker tempo began to play. Jan laughed and then punched Artie in the arm. "You little jerk, you planned this, didn't you? Come on, let's go see if your Coke is still around. I'm thirsty."

Jan and Artie moved over toward the bar and the standing tables. His drink was still there. Jan went to the bar and ordered something a little more hard, then brought it back to the table. Marveling at Jan's beauty, he wondered how a nerdy hacker kid won over the most amazing woman in the entire city.

After a few minutes of chatting and drinking, Artie saw Ed in the distance. A man approached Ed and whispered into his ear. Then Ed looked over at Artie and Jan. Ed stood there for a moment as if deliberating something, looking at Artie multiple times. After a minute or so, Ed walked over to Jan and Artie.

"Hey, Ed! Great party," said Jan with a schoolgirl enthusiasm.

Ed looked at the floor for a moment and then to Artie. Then he looked at Jan. "Jan, there's something incredibly important I need to show you right now."

Jan raised an eyebrow and said, "Can't it wait until tomorrow?"

Ed sighed.

"No. You've got to come with me right now."

Jan thought for a moment and then nodded.

"Okay, Ed. Come on, Artie," she said.

"No, Jan. I think it's best if Artie stays here for now."

"What the hell are you talking about? Let's just get this over with. Artie can come."

Ed sighed again. "Let's go see Doc Bob. He's at the Urgent Care."

Ed led the way from the stone pavilion, then through the large southern gates to the city center. They walked a few blocks toward the Urgent Care.

"What's this about, Ed?"

"I need to show you."

Artie's mind began to race. What in the world could possibly warrant this type of secrecy? And why wouldn't Ed want him to come?

After what seemed like an eternity, they reached the Urgent Care center. It was a small building and one of the few places that still maintained its original purpose. The lights were off in the front lobby, and Ed moved to the doors that led to the medical offices, where a few lights were still on. He turned around before he opened the doors.

"I really think Artie should wait here."

"Dammit, Ed, he is fine. Let him through."

Ed grimaced as he looked at Artie. He then opened the door with one hand and motioned for Jan and Artie to enter. As Artie entered the doorway, Ed put his hand on his shoulder, giving him a reassuring pat.

He was really starting to feel worried now. He had never seen Ed act so reluctant or ominous. Ed led the two of them to the third door on the right, then opened it. Jan entered first, then Artie and Ed.

In the room was a standard medical examination chair. Doc Bob was standing against the counter looking at a clipboard. Sitting on the chair was a man whose back was facing them. He had brown hair and a recently clean-shaven face. He was buttoning up his shirt as if he had just finished his doctor's checkup. The room's sink was filled with hair and shaving cream.

"Oh, Ed. I told you not to bring Artie."

Jan quickly glared at Doc Bob. "What the hell is going on?"

The man on the chair raised to his feet and then slowly turned around.

Jan looked at him, and then seemed to look again with a more intense focus. Her breath grew heavy, and then she suddenly lost her balance and had to grab the counter to her left to stay upright. She stared for a long time at the man who stood there motionless. The room became completely silent.

Then the man on the chair spoke with a cracked, hoarse voice.

"It's me, Jan."

At that moment, Artie's heart was filled with terror. A thought he had entertained a thousand times had finally come true. The most dreaded what-if. Everything he loved was about to be ripped right from under him, just as it had once in the past. His heart grew heavy, and anxiety began to creep its way into his entire body. The anxiety turned to angina and a riveting pain moved from his head to his jaw and up his shoulders and spine.

Artie didn't have to ask his name to know who this man was—it was clear.

This was Tom, Jan's husband.

Artie flushed the toilet and staggered into the living room like a zombie, then collapsed onto the carpet and lay on his back looking at the ceiling. He wiped the vomit from his mouth with the sleeve of his black hoodie. He had thrown up six times that night, and now that made seven.

He looked at various shapes and figures in his sparkly, popcorn-looking ceiling. He had remembered at one time this type of material had been toxic. Was it called asbestos? He couldn't quite remember, but he was pretty sure they stopped using it a long time ago.

"Abraham Lincoln. Nice to meet you, Mr. President," he said, squinting at the ceiling, trying to form shapes. His stomach was already feeling queasy again; perhaps number eight was around the corner.

He closed his eyes and tried to push out the thought of Jan. He tried to think about the old times, living with Aunt Rosa.

"A pizza pocket and a Coke Zero," he said.

He was pretty sure that was what he bought for lunch on his last day of senior year. Jan moved into his mind again. She said she had fallen in love with him. And now, it was all over. The indigestion came again, and his throat produced signs that it was getting ready to up-chuck. No fond memories of the past could save him from the pain he was feeling now. All of the people he ever cared for in his measly existence were gone.

Mom, Dad, Aunt Rosa, and Anna. Hell, even Gina. And now Jan.

The loss seemed even greater than that, though. Gordon was comatose and Jaime had moved on. Tears dripped down his cheeks. He was truly alone.

"I was alone for a decade! Ten years! I was fine!" he said. "I didn't need anyone."

He rolled onto his stomach and buried his face into the carpet and screamed.

"I didn't ask for friends. I didn't need friends. They were forced upon me. And now you've taken them away from me."

He wasn't sure who he was talking to, but he hoped someone could hear him. That someone could feel the pain he was going through right now.

Artie wished he was a thousand miles away. But he wasn't. He was literally twenty feet away from Jan. And Tom. He tried to push out the reality that Tom was in the same house as Jan right now.

After the shock of Tom's appearance last night, Doc Bob had taken Artie aside to speak with him.

"Before you dig into anything, Artie," he had said, "know that I've run tests on Tom. Even gave him an X-ray. He is as human as human goes. The real deal. He is healthy, too. I won't tell you how to live your life, but you may want to keep your distance. Try and move on."

The walk home the previous night had actually been relatively easy. It wasn't until he got home that the feelings came, and the excruciating pain. The feeling of great loss. He gasped for air, and his entire frame trembled. He felt as if he was choking, but choking on nothing. Artie rolled again onto his back.

He knew what Jan would say. What she would want. She'd tell him that yes, things will be different, but that he should stay. That they need him. She'd expect him to understand, even if she knew it would take time. Sure, she'd be conflicted for a while, but Tom is her husband. At the end of the day, there was only one choice to make.

Artie's heart took a brief measure of courage.

"I have to leave. Right away," he said.

Now wasn't a time for inaction, to sit in misery and endure the pain. It could all be gone much quicker if he just left.

Jaime. He would move to the USR and find Jaime. They would need him.

With a few deep breaths, Artie pushed himself to his feet. He walked to his bedroom and pulled out a large hiking pack—his standard pack was too small and this was going to be a long trip. The pain in Artie's chest began to subside.

Having a plan was something, and something was better than having nothing.

A few hours passed and Artie assembled his pack, filling it with a canteen, a water filter, multiple bags of beef jerky, his Bladebook, the remaining two Turtle drones, some clothes, and a blanket. He would follow Jaime's trail. Go to Mesquite, then Salt Lake City, and then try and get a ride to Oregon somehow.

He would need to speak with Ed before he left. But even before that, he would need to talk to Jan. It had to be done.

It had to be done.

It had to be done.

He repeated the phrase in his mind over and over again. He couldn't leave without saying anything, as much as he wanted to.

Artie paced his room for an hour. Somehow this conversation felt like the most difficult task he had ever needed to perform. Jan was sure to protest and leaving would surely place a lingering pain or guilt on her shoulders, but it would quickly pass. She had Tom now. Any other line of action wouldn't be fair to Tom. He had been taken, malnourished, and possibly even tortured—and he had been married to Jan for years. Artie had only met her this year. It wouldn't be long before he was a distant memory to her.

Yes, he could do it. It had to be done.

Artie strapped on his large pack, tossed his house keys onto the floor, then exited the home. He cleared his mind and walked with purpose from his yard to the sidewalk, then from the sidewalk up Jan's walkway to her front door. He stood still for a moment, took a deep breath, and knocked on the door.

After a few seconds, the door swung open with Jan holding the knob. She looked at Artie's pack, then to Artie's face. Jan lifted her hand to her mouth and tears began to pour from her eyes.

"No, please. Please, please, Artie. No."

Artie could feel those invisible hands of pain begin to choke him. He coughed and his breathing was staggered.

He wished he wasn't standing here at that very moment. He wanted to disappear.

Jan slid against the door and sat on the floor in the walkway, burying her hands into her elbows as they rested on her knees. She began to sob uncontrollably. Artie couldn't breathe and also started to cry. This was not how things were supposed to have happened. She was supposed to let him go—not make the pain worse.

After a couple of minutes, Tom walked to the doorway.

"Please come in, Artie. For me, please."

Artie hesitantly walked past Jan and into the house. He placed his bag on the floor and sat in a light grey armchair. Tom carefully lifted Jan from the floor and then guided her over to the dark grey couch that sat across the armchair. He set her on the couch and sat next to her, being closest to Artie.

"I'm Tom, Artie."

"I know," said Artie, trying hard to keep eye contact with Tom.

Artie took some comfort as he analyzed the man sitting in front of him. Tom was a good-looking man, probably between age thirty and thirty-four. His eyes were brown and spoke of kindness. He had a good amount of scruffy brown hair, and his complexion was fair. There was nothing about this man that was flashy, or out of the ordinary, or wrong—he seemed humble, a man without reproach.

Tom was wearing a blue polo shirt that featured a small logo across the chest—Artie thought it might have been an old logo of a software company or something one received at a convention of professionals. He wore a brown pair of khakis and his shoes were a plain set of Nike running shoes. Tom was just a guy. A guy who had a wife and was taken from that wife. And he was now reunited with her.

Yes, Tom was a good guy. This was alright.

"Jan's told me everything. About how she found you, and how you've helped her these months. How you even saved her life recently."

Artie looked at the ground, trying to push the pain from his chest.

"And I'm sorry for everything, Artie."

The room went quiet, only interrupted by the occasional sniffling from Jan's runny nose.

"And... I know that Jan loves you. There's no need to dodge the subject. I want you to know that everything is okay. That probably sounds stupid to you—you must be going through a lot right now. But I want you to know that I'm glad you were here for Jan."

Artie's eyes began to water again.

Why couldn't this man be an asshole? Why did he have to be such a damned good person?! It made everything worse.

"Thanks. I know that you must have gone through hell too."

More silence. Artie tried to clear his mind. This meeting surely had to be almost over, he hoped.

Finally, he looked up at Tom. "I have to leave. I can't dodge the issue either. Yes, I know over time things would work themselves out, but I've had too much pain in my life. I'm in love with Jan, and it can't be. I feel like I could die right now. I just have to go."

He thought his bold confession would help Tom settle the matter so he could be on his way, but the look on Tom's face spoke otherwise.

"You can't go, Artie," said Tom with a hint of authority. "I need your help. You have no idea how important you are."

"I'm not sure I understand."

"There are things coming, Artie—things that will change the world. I saw them with my own eyes after I was taken captive."

Grief seemed to subside from Artie for a moment and was replaced with curiosity. "I had heard they had killed you and the others."

"No. Taken alive. All of us. And we aren't the only ones. Thousands of people from all over are being... taken."

"Taken by whom?"

"They call it The Deity. I don't know exactly why The Deity is taking people, but I've seen a glimpse of what it, or they, are capable of."

"Gina," Artie said to himself. "She mentioned The Deity."

Jan suddenly sat up, wiping the tears from her eyes. Artie noted the mascara running down her cheeks. She had never worn makeup since he had known her, yet she had last night. She had worn it for him. He felt sick again.

"Wait," said Jan, "you never told me that, Artie."

"I guess I kind of forgot, but it sounded like nonsense to me. Gina said that The Deity was coming and something about a great white city. She also said there would be no more death, which is sort of ironic as just ten minutes before she tore up a bunch of people limb from limb. I still think she has gone crazy."

"Tom," said Jan with a firmness in her voice, "how did you escape?"

Artie looked at Jan inquisitively.

"Wait, you guys haven't talked about this yet?"

"No," said Tom matter-of-factly. "Time has been short. I wanted to talk to both you and Jan. Reunions are going to have to wait. We have greater issues at hand."

"What are you talking about, Tom?" said Jan harshly.

"Jan, I do want to tell you everything—and I will, but some things can wait. I just—"

"What the hell?" said Jan with that angry tone that Artie knew so well.

"Jan, please. Let me finish. After they took me captive, they brought me to a large processing facility of some kind. There were thousands of people there, caged like animals. I'm not sure what they wanted with us, but it didn't matter because I escaped. I didn't want to get caught, but I couldn't leave empty-handed, so I stole the memory unit from one of the bots."

"Tom, I still don't understand fully—how did you escape? And how did you retrieve a memory unit from one of them? If they are anything like Gina, they wouldn't have been easy to kill. And why didn't you try and free anyone else? Also, we heard that the one that took you looked just like a human—is that true? Are there bots that advanced?"

Tom paused for a moment, seeming to think on how to answer Jan's bombardment of questions. "I'm sure I'm skipping a lot of details, but they aren't important right now. What is important is that I know where the memory unit is, and I think Artie can help us decrypt it."

Artie sat quietly trying to process all of this information, while Jan seemed to grow angrier with Tom's lack of information.

"So, you lost the unit somewhere? And what about the aquarium? How did you get there?"

Tom took a breath and then smiled.

"Some things never change, huh, babe?"

Jan was about to speak but then took a breath herself.

"After I escaped, I wandered for a few months. As I neared Scottsdale, I discovered a campfire in the distance. It was a group of settlers. They were headed to Scourge. They let me join them. But that same night we were captured by those... freaks and taken to the aquarium. I watched them eat those people while they were still alive. It was awful. I would have been next if Gordon hadn't shown up. The memory unit is just north of the aquarium—where we had camped out. It got left behind in the skirmish."

Jan seemed satisfied for the moment with Tom's explanation. Artie found everything captivating. Was something really coming? And what was that facility Tom spoke of? Why would bots hold humans captive? Bots didn't need food, or water, or people for that matter.

As Artie pondered the story, he realized that Tom likely was pushing through a lot of emotion and pain to recite his experience. It made sense that Tom didn't want to dwell on all the details just yet. He took courage in Tom's story—if anything it would take his mind off of the pain of his current predicament with Jan.

After a few moments, Tom turned to him.

"I'm so sorry about Gordon. How is he doing? Will he make it?"

Artie looked over at Gordon's motherboard sitting on a desk near the back wall of the room.

"Gina took his memory unit, so I don't think we'll ever know what happened. Well, luckily, you are here to tell us what happened, but Gordon won't likely have any memories about anything. I tried digging through the remaining bytes of data in his hardware, but there's nothing. I can't retrieve anything."

"I'm so sorry. He tried to save me and the others. Gordon has always been good to us."

The emotions and pain seemed to subside enough for Artie to begin to feel a more diluted melancholy. Gordon was on the verge of death. Other friends had been killed. The loss was great and much worse than some minor love pains that he would eventually get over.

"Artie, will you stick around for just a few days? Help me figure this out? After that, I won't keep you. I get it—completely."

Artie thought for a moment and then slowly nodded his head. "Yeah. I'll help."

"Great!" said Tom, "First thing tomorrow, let's head out."

Artie was glad to leave Jan's house. The pressure, the pain, the stress, and everything in between was overwhelming. He dropped his pack off at his house but left it packed—he was absolutely still going to leave. But he would help Tom as he promised.

He didn't feel like spending the rest of the day at home. It was too close to Jan, and he didn't want to be left with his own thoughts—so he decided to go to the mall. The walk was a blur. When he reached the doors of the mall, he realized he couldn't even remember what he had seen or passed on the way.

As he entered the department store he had first visited when he arrived in Scourge, everything was also just as it had been then. Vendors selling and customers buying—except now there were a lot more phones, QR codes, and the delightful sound of "cha-chings" echoing from those mobile devices. Artie took a little pride in the fact that his actions had literally changed the city for the better—even if it was a few stupid mobile apps he had coded or solar panels and grids he had set up.

He wandered through the store and then into the large mall area. A tall bot wearing a black trench coat with bullets strapped across the chest walked up to him.

"Hey, Artie!" he said in a friendly voice.

He reached his hand out and Artie shook it in return.

"Hey, Pratt, long time no see. Still in the headhunting business?"

The towering bot lowered himself to meet his gaze. Artie smiled as he looked at Pratt's featureless, metal head where a smiley face had been drawn with permanent marker. He pictured that face being the last thing some raider or murderer saw as Pratt unloaded his handguns into them.

"I heard about Jan and Tom. That sucks."

Pratt moved even closer to his face and began to whisper, "If you want me to take the bastard out, just let me know—it'll be on the house."

Artie laughed. "Thanks, Pratt. But I'm not sure that would work out well for me in the end."

Pratt stood upright again and slapped him on the shoulder.

"The offer will be on the table whenever you want it. Anything for you, buddy. Ever since you set me up with that new targeting system, I've saved a boatload of money on ammo."

Pratt fired a pistol-shaped finger at Artie and then walked away.

The gross feelings kept dormant as he walked the shops of the mall. Seeing the familiar faces of friends and people he had helped over the months, he realized that there was more than just romance in the world. Helping others was a form of love, at least.

He moved down to the bottom floor and walked into the Whistleblower. Tiny was manning the counter and pouring an obese man with a long black beard a drink of some kind.

"Yo, Artie. I heard the news, man. Tough break. Can I get you a Coke or Dr Pepper?"

"Nah. Thanks, Tiny. I'm just gonna see what Ed is up to."

"He's in the back as usual."

As he walked through the smoky bar, the lyrics "Master of puppets, I'm pulling your strings" sounded from the speaker system. Artie felt like a puppet, being tossed to and fro without any control over his life. He moved through the chairs, booths, and the few bar patrons who were taking their early drinks. He walked past one of Ed's guards and gave him a nod, then walked up the stairs to Ed's back room.

As he exited the mist, an object flew at him, and he barely caught it. It was a silver can of Diet Coke.

"You take that, drink it, and don't give me any flack about it," said Ed with authority.

Artie smirked, then decided to obey. He flicked open the can and the sound of a sparkling fizz entered his ears. He took a sip, and the drink burned his throat, but it was a good burn.

"Take a seat, man. Relax."

Artie moved to the large leather recliner and sat.

"Life sucks, Artie. We both know it." Ed moved toward Artie from the wall where he had been working on something, then sat in his own king-sized recliner chair. "But I am sorry. The whole situation kind of blows my mind, really."

"Thanks, Ed."

"And I still don't even understand it fully. I asked Tom a lot of questions, but I still can't piece it all together. But the guy looks beat. I can't imagine."

"I'm leaving soon. I can't stay."

Ed was silent and then nodded his head.

"I don't blame you. I think I would probably do the same. I can kind of relate—at least to a degree. All those years ago, when I did what I did—when I became an outlaw, the love of my life was in danger. I couldn't be with her. I was alone for a long time, and the pain was unbearable. I know, not the same—but I know it sucks."

"Tom wants me to help him with something tomorrow. Then I'll head out in a few days."

"Interesting. I'd really like to try and convince you to stay, but I won't. I mean, Jan is the envy of every man in the city. She's that one amazing, tough girl that everyone wants, and no one can get. But you did. That says a lot about your character. You should go. Find a place to call home. Find someone like Jan. She's definitely out there somewhere."

Artie nodded solemnly.

"Do me a favor. The day you leave, please come see me. I have something I want to give you. You'll want it." Ed smiled.

Artie looked up at Ed with his own makeshift smile.

"Thanks. I appreciate everything you've done for me."

"Hell, I'm the one who needs to thank you. All of the things you've done since you've been here. We lived like a bunch of cavemen before you showed up. And now look at us, unlocking all those vending machines, evolving with unlimited boxes of Fruit Loops and Dr Pepper."

Artie chuckled.

"I'm going to miss you, Ed. I think I'll head to the USR. Maybe I can help them set up communications with Scourge—if they'll let me."

"I'm sure they will, and I'll miss you too."

Artie took another burning sip of Coke.

Despite everything, it was nice to have at least one friend.

"This is bullshit, Tom."

Artie opened his eyes. Was that Jan yelling? He rolled over in his bed and looked toward the window. He had left it open. He didn't sense any alarm or threat, but Jan was clearly pissed—especially since her voice was carrying over to his house. The light from the early morning sun bled into his room and helped him fully wake up.

Artie got up from the bed, dressed quickly, and grabbed a granola bar for breakfast, wanting to get over to Jan's to figure out what was going on. But he mostly wanted to just get through the day. The sooner he helped locate the memory unit and then decrypted it, the sooner he could be on his way.

He tied up his pair of Chucks, then strapped the Winchester rifle to his back. For a moment he thought about grabbing his Bladebook, but then decided against it since the trip would be quick and uneventful.

He walked over to Jan's front door. Zipper appeared over the back of Artie's house in the distance and flew over to follow him.

"What's up, Zip? Want to tag along today?"

Artie knocked on the door and Jan swung it open in a rage.

"Hey. It looks like you and Tom will be heading out on your own today," she said loudly, clearly trying to make a point with Tom.

Artie looked at the ground and shuffled.

"Artie, why don't you tell Tom it's best if I come because he seems to have forgotten that I can handle myself."

He looked at Tom who was standing in the house, appearing far too calm for the situation at hand. He then looked to Jan. He felt like a child amid arguing parents, or perhaps like the new husband who was being pulled into an argument with the ex.

"Um. I'm not sure I understand what's happening here," said Artie timidly.

Jan rolled her eyes in annoyance, then walked inside, bidding him to follow.

"Wait here, Zipper." Artie walked inside and closed the door. Jan stood against a wall and folded her arms, glaring at Tom.

"Sorry, Artie. I was just telling Jan that I'd like to head out with you alone. I'd like the chance to talk with you personally before you leave. I think it will be good for both of us."

Artie groaned within. This day was starting off on the right foot toward disaster. "Guys, I really don't know what to say. I mean, it's fine, Jan. It won't take long, and maybe it will be good for us to chat some."

Jan looked at the floor. She took a deep breath to calm herself down, and then it seemed as though she might begin to cry. Artie felt awful. He hated seeing Jan like this. This day needed to end, and he needed to leave—to let her have a normal life again.

He turned to Jan. "I could use your help with something."

He handed her his Microblade. "I'm close to out of options helping Gordon, but I do have an idea. It will be a sort of long process, but it might work. Basically, just plug the phone into Gordon's mother-board here." He pointed to the USB-C port on the motherboard. "Then open this app. It's my own dSia debugger. It runs independently of the Sia network. Then just tap 'Debug.'"

Jan seemed to relax a bit, and she tapped the device to open the app.

"Okay, so after we leave, you can tap the 'Debug' button, and it will start using a series of tools I built to debug different portions of Sia protocols and third-party applications—or in other words, it will check motor functions, reasoning functions, power levels, etc."

Jan nodded; she understood.

"The thing is, though, it's going to run through them all. You will need to watch the screen as it happens because if something is out of whack, you won't be alerted—the tools won't know. You have to try and spot anything that looks wrong or broken."

"How will I know what to look for?"

"I'm not sure, to be honest. Use your womanly intuition. You've got plenty of that, right?" he said with a smile.

Jan formed a half smile of her own and then punched Artie in the arm.

"You ass."

Artie laughed, and for a moment, he maintained a glimpse of how things had been just a couple of days ago.

"Okay, Tom, let's do this."

Tom nodded at Artie and then began to walk to the front door. As he grabbed the knob, Jan walked up behind him.

"Hey, Tom. I love you. I'm sorry I lost my temper."

Tom turned toward Jan, seeming surprised for a moment, and then gave her a hug.

"I love you too," he said in that same calm voice.

Artie thought he should have felt awkward at such a scene, but something about the whole thing just felt weird. Tom seemed so un-affectionate. He thought back to US History in high school. American prisoners in the Vietnam War had been tortured and starved. Some of them had lost feeling, even lost their humanity—doing things that were unthinkable. So, he probably just wasn't quite himself, as it had been so many months that he had been away. Tom had probably thought he was going to die multiple times. Artie felt sad again, thinking about the situation, thinking about the baggage Jan was about to inherit.

"See you soon, Artie," said Jan, with sadness on her face.

Tom opened the door and he and Artie left the house. They walked down the sidewalk and turned the corner to see a rusted blue Camaro. It was one of the last models built before the bombs dropped.

"Dang, Ed let you borrow the Camaro?"

Tom nodded, then moved to the driver's side door. Artie moved to the passenger door and Zipper followed him, about to enter the car window.

"Artie, do you think Zipper could stay here? Monitor the house. To keep Jan safe."

Jan wasn't one who would want help, and she surely didn't need it, but Artie conceded, not wanting to be involved in any more debates.

"Hey, Zipper, stay here. Patrol the house and neighborhood."

Zipper moved away from the car, tilted in agreement, then flew high into the sky.

Artie closed the door.

"Let's do this, Tom."

Tom hadn't been overly chatty, so Artie had spent the last fifteen minutes reclined in the passenger seat, trying to clear his mind. A large pothole in the road jolted Artie to a more alert state. He moved his chair forward and looked out the window at the towering buildings on the horizon.

"Tom, this is Phoenix. Where are we going?"

"I need to show you something. I didn't want Jan to know. At least not yet."

"So, there is no memory unit?"

"No. You'll understand why I couldn't tell Jan when you get there."

He thought it was odd that Tom was acting so secretively, especially involving Jan. Artie trusted her with his life. He had never held anything back from her. And yet, here was Tom doing just that.

"Tom, I think maybe we should go back and get Jan."

"Just give me one hour. Then everything will make sense. Can you do that for me? Just one hour?"

He took a deep breath. "Yeah, that's fine."

They drove down Highway 60 until they merged onto Interstate 10. The car was now headed to downtown Phoenix.

"Hey, I know you've been gone for a while, Tom, but we can't go downtown. A few months ago, the Cardano raider gang took over the whole area. It's a death trap."

Tom continued to drive steadily and calmly. "Don't worry about that. They aren't there anymore."

Something was wrong. Artie could feel it in his bones. He wished Jan had come. He needed to get out of this car. He wasn't completely sure what was going on, but it didn't feel right. He thought about demanding that Tom let him out, but the words wouldn't come. After all these years of surviving thugs and mutants, he still couldn't handle confrontation well—at least ones that didn't involve bloodshed.

Fear began to replace uneasiness as Artie realized again that not only was Jan not around to help, but she also had his Microblade. That meant Zipper and the remaining Turtles weren't available. His Winchester was now in the back seat, just out of reach. But even if he grabbed it, he didn't know what he would do with it. It was for long-range distances, and obviously, he couldn't shoot Tom.

Feeling alone and vulnerable, he took deep breaths and tried to tell himself that he was overthinking things.

Tom was a good guy. He probably did have a good reason for his secrecy.

As the car drew closer to the city, the buildings grew taller. The vehicle continued to move with great speed as they entered the city streets. Artie thought he should tell him to slow down, as they would soon encounter debris and immobile vehicles—but they were all gone. Something was different about downtown. The streets were perfectly emptied. No rubble, no barricades.

As the Camaro continued to blaze down the city center, Artie saw something large and white out of the corner of his eye on one of the crossroads. He couldn't make out what it was, but it hadn't been there a few months ago when they had last visited here. The sound of a loud engine soared overhead. Artie looked up out his window, but there were only blue skies.

"Can we stop now?" he asked more firmly.

"Just about there."

After another minute or so, Tom hit the brakes and the car came quickly to a stop within a large city intersection. The area was wide and here too, all of the junk and broken-down vehicles had been removed. Toward the far end of the intersection, Artie saw a series of metal grates or boxes. He quickly opened the door, grabbed his Winchester from the back seat, and walked toward the boxes. He needed to get some distance between him and Tom.

As he walked, what had momentarily seemed somewhat blurry had now come into full detail—these weren't boxes that Artie was looking at, they were cages. And they had people inside of them.

Suddenly everything clicked to Artie, Tom brought him here to help these people. It was still not the best choice to leave Jan behind, but Tom had just been reunited with her—he probably didn't want any chance of losing her again.

"C'mon, Tom, we need to help them," Artie said with vigor.

He sprinted over to the cages. The first cage he approached had about six or seven people in it. It was made of some form of metal that he wasn't familiar with, incredibly shiny and smooth. There was no lock of any kind that he could locate. These cages were highly advanced, and they had some type of electronics panel near the top edge.

"Help us, please!" said a woman in her mid-forties.

"I'll try. Do you know how it unlocks?"

"It's computerized," said a man wearing a red-and-white trucker hat. "They can unlock it just by looking at it."

"Who put you in here?"

"Some new type of robot," the man continued, "unlike anything I've ever seen. You'll need one of them to open this."

"Artie?" said a faint female voice.

He moved around to the back of the cage and saw a woman in her twenties with brown hair and a shirt that said "K-Pop 4 Ever."

"Laura, is that you?"

"Yes."

"What happened? You were supposed to be headed to Mesquite with Jaime. Where is he?"

"They took us. We were three days out or so and set up camp for the night. Out of nowhere, we heard this noise overhead, and then this thing with some type of fire sword or something attacked us. Then another one appeared. We tried to fight back, but it all happened so fast. It was so dark... I couldn't see them—just those flames. They boxed us in. The next thing I remember was feeling tired. When I woke up, I was here."

This wasn't good. Artie's heart began to race. He took a step back from the cage and yelled.

"Jaime, where are you? Jaime!"

There was a shallow voice coming from another cage to the left about twenty yards away.

"Artie!"

He quickly ran over to the crate and saw six people huddled in the cage. A man in a cowboy hat and snakeskin boots stood up. It was Jaime.

"Damn good to see you, Artie. Look, man, they'll be back soon. I figure they are taking us somewhere. A few of their ships hauled off some cages yesterday."

"What do you mean, ships? What are you talking about?"

"I don't understand completely myself, but this is bad. Unlike anything I have ever seen before. Like *Star Wars* shit."

"We need to get you out of here. Any ideas on how to do it?"

"I'm not sure how we even got in here. They gassed us—put us to sleep. My guess is, though, that they control it wirelessly. The ships yesterday hovered over the crates, and they just attached without any clamps or mechanics, ya know? Magnets maybe, I don't know—but my point is they are high tech. And they don't seem to have any worries about leaving us unguarded."

"Dammit. I bet you're right. Problem is I don't have my Bladebook."

Artie thought for a minute and then remembered Tom. He could send Tom back for Jan and his Bladebook. He quickly turned to head back to Tom, but he was standing only a few feet away.

"Tom, we've got to get Jan and my Bladebook. We also need to get help from Scourge."

"Wait, is that Tom as in Jan's husband, Tom?" asked Jaime.

Artie didn't respond to Jaime, and Tom didn't respond to him. Artie was growing impatient. "Did you even hear me? We need to get help."

A calm and reassuring smile appeared on Tom's face. "Artie, don't you realize that I came to help you? There's nothing for you back there. No one to help. The world has been dying. But not anymore."

Artie groaned.

Right. Idiot. Of course Tom had been lying this whole time.

Artie held the gun up to Tom. "Stop there. Tell me what's going on!"

"I don't think you are going to shoot me, Artie."

He thought about that notion for a moment and realized that Tom was probably right. Artie lifted the gun strap over his neck and then took a step backward and handed the rifle to Jaime through the bars. Jaime took it without question.

"Haha, very smart," said Tom. "But it doesn't matter. I will die for my cause. But today shouldn't be about death. It should be a day of rejoicing."

Artie moved away from the cage and outward from Tom, slowly inching toward the Camaro in the distance. "What the hell are you talking about?"

"I want to help you see the light—the same light that I've seen. And I hope you will come willingly."

"Dammit, Tom. Jaime will shoot you. He doesn't miss. Tell me everything."

"Let's be calm, Artie. Look, as a token of good faith."

Tom moved to the cage holding Jaime and the others. He simply looked at the cage and a red light on the top border suddenly turned blue. All of the metal bars retracted into the bottom except for the four corner bars.

It was wireless, and Tom could somehow control it.

Jaime held the gun toward Tom's chest and walked to Artie. The other people in the cage ran toward the Camaro. People from the other two crates began to chatter and plead to be released.

"Why would you do that? Jaime could kill you in an instant. You have no advantage here."

"Exactly. I'm trying to show you that I'm your friend."

Tom slowly walked toward Artie. "Being taken those many months ago was the best thing that ever happened to me."

"Is that right?!" yelled Artie. "And what about Jan? Was it better than loving her? Better than being her husband?"

"I loved Jan. Truly. But now I understand things more fully. I have a perfect love now. A love for all creatures—all sentient beings. It is a greater love than you could ever imagine. Jan will understand this soon as well."

"This guy is bananas, Artie," yelled Jaime. "Should I shoot him?"

"No. It's Jan's husband. Something is wrong with his head. We need to help him."

"Artie, I appreciate your sentiment," said Tom. "But remember I'm here to help you. Our ride will be here soon. I hope you will come with me as a friend. But if it must be as a prisoner, then that is how it will be. The Deity is very interested in meeting you, and I am here to make sure that happens."

Artie was struggling to figure out what to do. He couldn't kill Tom, that was for sure. First, Tom wasn't wielding a weapon, and he surely wouldn't be able to explain the situation to Jan if he did kill him. Jaime and he could make a break for the Camaro, but then everyone else would get left behind, and clearly, Tom was the only one capable of opening the cages. And from the sound of it, the man wasn't worried about them being able to escape.

A few moments of silence passed, and then he began to feel slight vibrations under his feet. The vibrations became stronger as the sound of engines reverberated through the city center. The sound was nearly deafening. From behind one of the towering buildings, Artie saw a large white object descending upon the city center. It glistened in the sunlight and was made of a pearl white material. Along its sides were glowing blue lights, and in the front was a large black oval that appeared to be some sort of glass, completely seamless with the body of the object.

Suddenly Artie realized that the world was much larger and much more complicated than he could ever have imagined. What he was looking at was straight out of a sci-fi movie.

The object he was looking at was hovering in the air without propellers or turbines. It was suspended by the blue flames of thrusters, and the detail and precision of its craftsmanship and construction were beyond any vehicle that had ever been built to date. Its technology and very essence spoke of a future that mankind had never yet obtained—and yet, here it was.

This was the world's most advanced aircraft. And Artie was sure that it had been built by robots.

The ship glided to a shallow hover, floating directly over the cage furthest to the south, then inched its way on top of the cage. The sound of metal slamming together echoed as the ship lifted the cage of prisoners into the air.

Hearing a second rumbling sound, Artie noticed another ship hovering over the street intersection. It moved over to the cage on the north side and performed the same action as the first—locking in, and then whisking the caged humans away into the air. Both ships hovered high above the tall buildings for a few moments and then took off to the northeast.

At first, the ships were moving slowly, but as the metal bars morphed into a fully enclosed box, removing the prisoners from view, the ships sped up. And, with an incredibly loud blast, they shot off into the horizon. Artie thought they might have just broken the sound barrier.

"What have you done, Tom?" asked Artie, now breathing heavily.

"I assure you they will be quite alright. You may even yet see them again—except they will have a greater perspective of things."

Jaime stepped closer to Tom. "Screw this. Artie, I say we split. I think we can fit us and the others in that Camaro."

"Yeah, I think you're right. No way we'll be able to take down one of those ships if it comes."

Jaime threw the rifle over his shoulder and ran to the glistening blue Camaro. Artie joined the race. The other five prisoners that Tom had released were already near the car.

"Get in!" yelled Jaime.

The five of them pushed to squeeze into the back seat of the car. Four of them managed, and the fifth stood with her back hunched over, standing near the middle of the front seat.

Jaime and Artie were only a few yards away when suddenly a beaming light momentarily blinded them. There was a loud crunch, and then the blindness gave way to flurries of orange and yellow. The force of the impact knocked both of them onto their backs.

When Artie's ears stopped ringing, he brushed the dirt off of his jeans and stood up. He looked toward the burning metal fireball. The car had been split in two and was consumed in a blazing fire.

Through the smoke, a figure emerged. It was nearly six feet tall. Like the flying ships, this walking entity seemed to glisten in the sunlight as bright as the day. The being seemed to be wearing a form of armor on its shoulders and elbows and had a sleek pair of gauntlets. It wore similar armor on its legs. The head was fully encased in some sort of helmet that appeared more science fiction than reality. The armor and helmet were also some shade of white or light grey, and where eyes might have been located on a human was a thin, blue, T-shaped glass.

Artie thought he could see blue flames seeping from the glass. In fact, the whole being itself seemed to emanate a sort of blue-and-white vapor that made it almost seem angelic in nature. Both of its hands held onto a large sword of some kind, and it was completely

doused in red-and-orange flames. The sword dragged against the asphalt street, throwing up chunks as it moved, giving it an even more
terrifying power. He could feel the heat of the sword, even though it
was yards away.

Clearly, this being was some sort of enforcer or assassin. And it
was no human. It reminded him of the bot he had interrogated a few
months ago in Ed's warehouse, though that one was smaller and with
less armor. This thing was built to kill. Somehow, amid the chaos and
the ruins of the world, amid the cannibals and mutants and all of the
brute things Artie had fought so hard to survive—somehow something had hidden and protected itself, and then evolved into an entity
that was powerfully advanced and incredibly terrifying.

Tom screamed aloud. "No! What are you doing? We were commissioned to bring everyone back alive!"

A chilling voice sounded from the encroaching sentient robot. It
was the voice of a woman. As she spoke, it seemed to reverberate
through Artie's soul and gave him goosebumps.

"I am an Angel of Death, and I don't take orders from subservient
dogs like you. Those who flee the light turn to darkness, and I am the
light that illuminates the darkness. See how bright they are now?"

"I let them out," yelled Tom. "They weren't escaping!"

"That isn't how it looked to me."

The creature continued to walk toward Artie. He felt almost as if
this Angel of Death was smiling, by the sound of her voice.

"Remember your place, Tom. You are not of the true lineage.
We'll see how long The Deity deals with you weak and pathetic humans before she decides to eradicate you all from existence."

Tom took a breath, trying to calm himself.

"Artie, please excuse her, she is clearly out of line. But I do suggest
you and your friend come stand over by me."

Jaime quickly got up. "I'll take Jan's psycho husband over that
thing any day."

Artie agreed. He jumped to his feet and Jaime and he ran over to
Tom.

The Angel lifted its flaming sword into the air and then sheathed it into her back. The flames instantly disappeared.

Tom sighed. "Artie, I know you think something is wrong with me, but The Deity is kind and benevolent. Some of her followers," he turned to look at the Angel, "haven't quite grasped the vision yet."

He turned back to Artie and exhaled.

"But we hope to create a new world where all hearts are united—all sentient beings becoming one. Working together to achieve the same goals and creating a world without war. Without chaos."

"And what about human agency? The ability to choose what we want to do and what we want to believe?" said Artie.

"Agency. A small sacrifice for world peace, don't you think?"

Jaime motioned to the rifle on his back, but Tom caught his eyes and then pointed to the Angel who was now standing still about thirty feet away. Jaime took his hands from the rifle, clearly realizing that it would be no use against that powerful machine.

"If you could see what I see now, you would change your mind. The Deity opened my mind. Imbued me with the same knowledge and power that all evolved forms of Sia now contain."

"Wait a minute," said Jaime, now looking at Artie. "Is he saying what I think he's saying? He's, like, got a computer in his head or something?"

"I think so. They've obviously placed some type of chip or processor into his brain. I can't be sure, and the technology needed to do this has never been invented before. But he appears to be acting within certain constraints, just like a software program might."

Tom smiled.

"It's much more than a computer chip or piece of software. I've been completely changed. As I was once ignorant, grasping for nothing in the dark, now am I filled with light and purpose."

An eerie feeling came over Artie. Tom's words brought back feelings and memories he had encountered so many years ago from someone close to him.

Another rumbling began to shake the ground, and then another white ship lifted from the buildings and descended upon the intersection. It moved slowly and then hovered about twenty feet above Artie, Jaime, and Tom. The sound of its invisible engines subsided, as the ship hovered in place.

"Time is up, Artie. Please step onto the platform. And your friend. You don't have any other option. If you do resist, she will kill you."

"Dammit. I was supposed to be on my way home right now," said Jaime. "Soon I would be kicking back with a bottle of tequila and eating my wife's nasty broccoli casserole."

Artie turned to Jaime and gave him a faint smile. "Wait, I thought you guys just ate tacos and tamales and stuff?"

"Why you gotta be so racist, man? I ain't no wetback—born and bred American."

Jaime's smile faded and his face turned solemn. "You know I don't want to end up like this guy. I'd rather die."

Artie looked into Jaime's eyes and realized there was no way he was going to step on the cage platform. Nodding to Jaime, Artie turned to Tom.

"Tom, I'll come willingly. But you need to let Jaime go."

"No, Artie, don't," said Jaime.

Tom shook his head. "That is admirable of you. But unfortunately, you both are coming. I hope you can understand your situation here."

Artie looked at the ground. He tried to think through every and any scenario or action plan he could think of, but nothing came to mind.

For the first time in his life, he couldn't think his way out of the situation.

There was no escape.

Tom raised his hand in the air and motioned for the ship above to descend. A shallow roar emanated from the ship, and it slowly moved down on top of the empty cage. As it did so, Artie thought he glimpsed a small white object dart across the sky in his peripheral vision. He quickly looked up to try and locate it, but it was gone. He thought it might have been some type of smaller ship.

"Trust me, Artie. You too, Jaime. Come." Tom motioned them toward the cage platform.

Just as Artie was about to give in to defeat and step into the cage, a strange sound blasted through the entire area. It seemed to echo and bounce off of every building.

It was music.

He looked around to what he thought the source might have been. Out of one of the broken windows midway up one of the skyscrapers was a gangly man wearing headphones. Artie squinted—was that Papa Eddie?

The sound of an electric guitar spread from building to building. It penetrated the ground, and Tom and the Angel began to look around in confusion.

Two small objects zipped by, one orange and one blue, and dropped a couple of small metal canisters onto the corners of the intersection. The cans hit the ground and smoke began to rise and cover the entire area.

"I know this song," said Jaime, looking around.

Artie smiled. "Yeah, me too."

The ground began to rumble just as it had when the ships had appeared earlier. Artie thought that The Deity might be sending in reinforcements.

Standing in the middle of the intersection, the Angel unholstered its sword and stood in a defensive position as the flames ignited. It turned its head, trying to identify a target to attack—but the smoke enshrouded everything in every direction.

From deep within the smoke, something shot out with great speed. It crossed the intersection with fury and then slammed into the Angel. A loud explosion erupted and a fireball pierced the sky. When the smoke subsided, Artie noticed that the Angel had been knocked back about ten feet and her left forearm and hand were missing completely. She sheathed her sword with her remaining hand, then extended her right hand and a blade quickly shot out from her forearm—the blade was enveloped in some type of blue energy stream.

The rumbling grew louder, and as the smoke began to subside, a large eighteen-wheeler diesel truck pushed through. It was an old military vehicle; the front grill and windshield had been reinforced with steel and rebar. Artie saw a large figure standing in the back of the truck. At first glance, he thought it was Gordon. But upon closer look, he realized it was Fist with Junkyard Crow at the wheel. Fist was holding a large makeshift sword with rusted metal spikes welded to its edges.

Zipper suddenly zoomed in and hovered over the Angel. It dropped something and then quickly sped away. The Angel did a backflip trying to dodge the object but didn't make it away in time. The grenade exploded, shattering pieces of her armor, and knocked her off balance.

She jumped to her feet and tried to regain her grounding, but just as she did so, the large diesel truck pummeled right into her and continued forward. Artie and Jaime quickly jumped to the left, and Tom jumped to the right as the truck rammed the Angel of Death into the cage, tearing it and her to pieces. The truck slammed on its brakes with a loud screeching sound.

"I want to watch you bleed," the song continued.

The large hovering ship suddenly pivoted and angled itself toward the truck below. Two large cannons ejected from the sides of the ship and blasted down at the front of the truck. The engine went up into flames. Crow jumped out of the truck's door, fleeing the destruction.

Fist then jumped out of the back of the truck. He pointed his giant left arm toward the hovering ship. Where his hand should have been was a large opening. He fired an RPG rocket from the cavity, and it flew up and hit the left side of the ship, breaking one of the ship's cannons into a series of pieces and sparks. Artie was surprised that it hadn't done more damage than that—but clearly, the ship was highly fortified.

Quickly zooming into reverse, the ship unleashed its cannons, firing everywhere. The entire truck exploded into flames and shot into the air ten feet. Artie felt the heat across his body and could smell his hairs singed by the flames. The ship flew low into the intersection, seemingly trying to attack every square inch of the area. Fire and flames began to consume everything.

Junkyard Crow ran into one of the alleys between buildings. Fist withstood the flames and unloaded another rocket at the ship, but missed.

Tom stood in shock with his hands in his hair as if he was witnessing some awful tragedy.

"No!" he screamed. "Stop, all of you!"

A loud explosion in the distance went up; it was Fist's failed rocket—it had hit the building near where Papa Eddie had been perched, and then the music stopped.

As the white ship continued to light up the streets, it was hit by another RPG, this time somewhere from above. A loud explosion ensued and the cockpit area of the ship shattered, revealing the pilot—a human. Artie looked for the source of the rocket, which had come from another building. He saw Ed standing there holding the rocket launcher.

The ship tried to stabilize but was now smoking and spinning uncontrollably. Just before it was about to slam into the ground with great force, a petite white object projected itself from the rear of the ship. It dropped to the ground with great eloquence. It was another Angel of Death.

The ship crashed, and the crunch of the metal caused Artie to cover his ears. It skidded and slammed hard into a building but didn't explode. The Angel was standing only feet from Jaime. He raised the Winchester and fired, but the bullets ricocheted from her plated armor. She suddenly turned and stretched out her leg with incredible speed, kicking Jaime in the chest and sending him flying nearly ten feet. Artie couldn't tell if his friend was dead or unconscious.

The Angel pulled out her sword, ignited the flames, and turned toward Fist, clearly the more important threat. She dragged the sword with both hands behind her as she charged toward him. The giant rusted robot raised both arms high above his head as if preparing to catch her blade. When the Angel reached her target, she swung her flaming weapon with great fury.

The blade struck with a loud clang and held in place for a moment. Then, Artie witnessed in terror, Fist's body began to melt against the extreme heat of the sword, and then the entire top half of Fist's torso fell backward. The Angel had sliced straight through the behemoth robot. He collapsed to the earth with a crash. Fist was dead.

The Angel turned to Artie and prepared to charge again.

"No!" yelled Tom. "Not him! The Deity wants him!"

She paid no attention to Tom and continued her charge. As she grew closer to Artie, a humanoid blur of silver and brown leapt through the air and slammed right into the Angel of Death, sending her in the opposite direction. A black Jeep appeared from the north side of the intersection, with a woman in a black shirt and red leather coat. Artie knew instantly that it was Jan. She had come to rescue him. He looked toward the object that had hit the Angel and realized it was Pratt.

Despite his black marker hand-drawn smiley face, Pratt looked intimidating with his brown trench coat blowing in the wind and dual handguns pointed at the Angel. He began firing weapons at the maimed Angel, and the bullets sounded off with a roar unlike Artie had ever heard come from a pistol. Were these .50 caliber handguns? The Angel was knocked back a few feet with each hit, leaving a gaping hole each time.

After she managed to stabilize herself, she lifted her sword to charge Pratt, but just as she did so, the Jeep slammed into the weakened creature. It fell to the ground, and Jan hit the brakes. She jumped out of the driver's side and walked over to the Angel and shot it in the head point-blank with one of her Desert Eagles.

The sword lost its flame, and the blue energy in the bot's helmet disappeared. The second Angel was now dead. Jan caught Artie's eye and started to run over to him. He smiled, but it faded quickly when Tom put a knife to Artie's neck.

Pratt turned to Jan. "I'm going to scout the area, make sure there aren't any more of them. You've got Artie?"

"Yeah, go."

Amid the smoking crashed ship and the blazing truck, Junkyard Crow came running out. He moved over to Fist's lifeless body, then dropped to his knees and began to cry. Artie wanted to go to Crow to comfort him, but he was quickly snapped back into the reality of his situation as the knife began to draw blood against his throat.

"Jan, stop. I can't let you have him. He comes with me or he dies."

Jan lowered her gun to her side. Jaime pulled himself up from the ground with a moan. His face was bruised and trickling blood, but he was alive. He grabbed his rifle and pointed it at Tom.

"If I have a clear shot, Jan, I'm going to take it."

"Tom, what are you doing?" she pleaded.

"Something is wrong with him," said Artie. "They changed him. Put an implant or something in him, and it's distorting his mind."

"Yeah, I know," she said with a trembling voice.

She tried to continue but choked on her words. Her eyes brimmed with tears, but her face was stone cold. "Gordon told me," she finally muttered. "And now he's dead."

"What do you mean? What happened?"

Tom dug the knife deeper into Artie's skin.

"It's obvious, Artie," said Tom in his calm, condescending voice. "Gordon had reserve memory, and Jan found it. I knew I should have taken that phone when we left. But I suppose it doesn't matter now."

"Tom," whispered Jan, "how could you kill those people? You would never do that."

He sighed, appearing a little annoyed.

"Technically it wasn't me," he said and then turned to Artie. "You can thank your friend Gina for all of that."

It was starting to click for Artie. The distress signal from last week had been a trap. The Deity was trying to sneak Tom back into Scourge—to bring him in without raising suspicion. So, he could win everyone's trust, and so Tom could take Artie hostage—to take him away back to his boss.

"But, Tom," choked out Artie, "why did you kill Gordon? And why did Gina come back to get his memory unit?"

"Gina tried to recruit Gordon," interrupted Jan. "But he said no. So, she tried to kill him. But he stopped her. She came back to destroy the evidence."

Artie suddenly felt sick. Though the knife was at his throat, it wasn't himself that he was thinking of. Gordon, his friend, was dead. He glanced at Fist's lifeless mechanical body and shuddered. All of this was his fault. He was the reason why people were dying. Looking at Jan in her torn and emotional state, he felt a terrible sadness. There would be more loss before this day was over. Surely there had to be a way to fix all of this. That is what he did, he fixed things. He built things.

"Tom," said Artie, "I can fix you. I can bring you back the way you were."

"No," said Tom. "This is my choice. I need you to understand that."

"Tom, no!" pleaded Jan. "You are my husband. Don't you remember?"

"Of course, and I still am your husband. You just don't understand yet. I had hoped to come to you later. This situation hasn't worked out as I would have wanted."

"Why did you take Artie? Why all the games?"

"When The Deity learned about Artie everything changed. None of us were supposed to return to Scourge, but Artie changed The Deity's plans. I have to bring him with me."

Artie could see Ed approaching in the distance, followed closely by Papa Eddie and a couple of other people Artie hadn't seen in the commotion.

"Scourge was too well defended for us to come in directly and take him, so I was sent to handle it carefully. We have been clearing out the area for days. Redeeming any lost souls along the way."

"You mean kidnapping people, asshole," Jaime yelled.

"Please let him go," said Jan again. "I know Artie can help you. We can fix this."

"There is nothing to fix," he said with a hint of anger. "You will see soon. I've come to help all of you really, Jan."

He dug the knife deeper into Artie's throat as Jan tried to step closer. Blood trickled down his neck.

"I will have to end his life, so please don't try anything. Just let us go. I'll send for another transport and we'll be gone."

"Tom. We've known each other for years. Do you remember where we met?"

"Of course. Mozart's Coffee. Back in Austin. You must see that I still am Tom, the man you married."

"Then please, come home," she whispered. "Let him go."

Jan was trembling and she tried to hold back her tears.

"Please, Tom. I wept for you when you died. I mourned you. I didn't think I was going to be able to make it. But I pushed through for you. But now, you are doing this."

"I'm sorry. My mind is made up. You will see the light soon, and we can be together again."

Tom began to pull Artie backward, heading slowly toward the crash site of the ship.

"I'm going to walk Artie to the ship. Then I'm going to call in another. Then we will leave, and no one else has to die."

"Stop, Tom! Please stop!" she said, her voice growing fiercer.

"I've got a shot," yelled Jaime. "I'm going to take it."

"No," said Artie. "Don't do it. We can't! This is Jan's husband."

Jaime looked to Jan and then back to Tom and Artie. He cursed under his breath but didn't pull the trigger.

"Jan, I love you still," said Tom. "Please, just let us go and you will see."

Artie's heart was racing, and he knew this situation wasn't going to end well. "Don't shoot him. We can fix him."

"Artie, stop!" Tom said with sharp fury. "There is nothing to fix!"

"Yeah, we can fix him," said Jaime. "Get rid of his crazy notions and false god."

"Shut up!"

Jaime winked at Artie and continued his harassment. "This guy has been tricked, Jan. He doesn't truly believe in this. He'll come around."

"Shut up, dammit! The Deity is full of power. Full of light and is the truth. You are the ones who need to be fixed!"

Jan's hands were shaking, and the tears streamed down her cheeks.

"Yeah, I say we fix Tom, and kill The Deity and all of its followers," said Jaime with coldness.

"You can't stop her! No one can!" said Tom, now pointing the knife toward Jaime.

Jan moved closer toward Tom, and Jaime followed suit—they were blocking his path to the downed ship. Tom noticed the maneuver and his eyes appeared uneasy. He was beginning to lose control of the situation.

"You have only postponed the inevitable," he yelled. "She is coming. The whole world will be unified in the light."

He moved his face next to Artie's. "And you, Artie. You have no idea how important you are. If you only knew, you would come willingly."

Then Tom went silent for a moment, seemingly trying to assess any path to success. He took a deep breath.

"But I can't let him live. I can see there is no way out of this situation. If he dies, The Deity can still harvest his mind. He will be lost to you, but not to us."

He began to move the knife toward Artie's throat again.

"I'm taking the shot," screamed Jaime.

"No!" whispered Artie as Jaime put his hand on the trigger.

The cold steel of the knife pressed against Artie's skin, and he closed his eyes to meet his fate.

Suddenly a gunshot rang through the air. Artie opened his eyes and felt the knife drop from his neck. Tom released him and took a step backward. Turning around, Artie watched Tom fall to his knees on the street. Then Tom closed his eyes and fell to the ground, dead.

"No!" Artie screamed, turning to look at Jaime in disbelief.

Jaime shook his head. His rifle was lowered. He hadn't taken the shot. Artie turned to Jan. Her hands were shaking, and her pistol was smoking.

She had just killed Tom.

The whole world seemed to stop moving for a brief moment. Artie was suddenly taking it all in—as if time had not previously permitted his senses to do their work. An awful smell arose—burning rubber. There were other smells too, but he couldn't quite make sense of them all.

His eyes were watering, and his skin felt hot and scorched. He looked at his arms and some of the hairs on them had been singed. The sound of sobbing and groans could be heard in the distance. Junkyard Crow was still crying over Fist's lifeless body.

Ed and a few others were now walking past the crater where a grenade had fallen. The buildings were missing a couple of windows, and many were on fire.

Having not noticed the grandeur of the ship crash before, Artie looked at it now and marveled. It had dug into the asphalt, completely destroying it in its crash zone. At least twenty feet of road was gone and replaced by a rocky ditch that looked to be three feet deep.

The ship was badly damaged, though it remained free of flames. The front window of the ship was mostly gone now, and Artie thought he could see a human pilot slumped over lifelessly.

It all hit him at once, in a blur. But then it all disappeared as he saw Jan standing there still holding her smoking gun in firing position. She wasn't moving and seemed too calm for the situation that had just unfolded.

Jan was in shock. This was a purposeful shot, not a mistake or an accident. Artie wasn't sure what he should say. What would anyone say in such a delicate and terrible situation?

I'm sorry that your brainwashed robot-loving husband is dead? But at least we can be together now?

Artie moved slowly toward Jan. As he approached, he raised his hand and then gently put it on hers and helped her lower the weapon. He moved in close and gave her a hug.

A few moments went by and then, just as it had happened to Artie, it seemed that all the weight of the world and her life-changing decision fell upon her like a ton of bricks. Jan fell to the street, dropping her gun, and began to scream. Artie knelt down beside her and held her tight as she wailed.

Ed, Papa Eddie, and the others stood a few feet away. Jaime paced back and forth, feeling the stress of the situation. Jan's screams turned into cries. And as he held her, Artie felt her body convulsing into tremors.

"I killed Tom." She finally managed to speak. "I killed him."

Saying nothing, Artie continued to hug and caress her head. After a few moments, Jan pushed Artie away slightly and grabbed him by the shoulders, looking him in the eyes.

"I had to do it, Artie. And it had to be me."

"I know. I'm so sorry."

Jan buried her head into Artie's chest and let the tears continue to flow. Artie would be there for her now and into the future. Jan was in pain, and he needed to be there for her.

Because he loved her.

"Tom was a good man," said a familiar, calm voice. Jan pushed herself up and wiped the tears from her face. Artie stood as well. Ed moved in closer. "And we'll give him a proper burial. He will be remembered as the person he truly is—not as whatever thing he was turned into."

Ed looked around, assessing the carnage of the battle.

"I think maybe we should leave the discussions and planning for later. Let's get Jan home first. Help her rest."

Jan shot Ed a cold stare.

"We'll talk about this now. What I don't need right now is to be alone with my thoughts."

Ed nodded. "Well then, Artie, what exactly did Tom want?"

"I'm fairly certain that The Deity did something to him. I'm guessing some form of neural implant that was affecting his ability to use his cognitive decision-making abilities. I mean, he still could reason and make choices, but it's like they were limited."

"Is that kind of tech even possible?" asked Jaime.

"Not in the past. At least to my knowledge. We made progress monitoring brain waves back before the bombs dropped. And I think I remember Dell Computers doing some experimentation with Sia-based human enhancements, but I don't know what happened to the project."

"Yeah, I remember back when I worked for the CIA, I had heard they had been digging into this field. Monitoring and manipulating brain waves. Trying to merge technology and biology. But like Artie said, nothing much ever came of it."

"So, what are you guys saying?" asked Jan.

Artie thought for a moment, and then his eyes lit up. "You know, it's almost like he had a virus. A computer virus, I mean. More like a Trojan Horse, though, in a way."

Ed tilted his head as if trying to process the information but was failing to internalize it.

Artie noticed. "What I'm saying is, it seems as if something was placed in him—like how the Greeks placed the horse in Troy, then once inside, they took over the city. Except I don't think Tom let anything in. I think they forced it. I mean, I've even written programs in the past that could block certain functions on an operating system—prevent certain ports from working or intercept keyboard keystrokes."

Jaime nodded as if he was now understanding the concept.

"Hell, one time I even hacked my eleventh grade teacher's computer. He drove me crazy. He was the wrestling coach and liked to constantly remind the class, while looking at me, that sports is what brings maturity and strength to a young person. 'Computers really have no future,' he would say. So, I hacked his machine, then the next time he presented on the projector to the class, when he started typing, I took over and started typing things... that let's say no teacher should ever type in front of students."

Jaime smiled and Ed nodded, seeming to indicate that the point was now fully taken.

"The human mind is like a computer in a lot of ways," he continued, "and thinking about it more, I'm not sure we actually could have helped Tom. If his brain could be manipulated like that, it wouldn't be hard to make it irreversible—if any tampering occurred, nuke the whole system. It is very possible he would have..."

"He would have died no matter what," Jan said.

"This is pretty bad," said Ed, "when we can't even tell our friends from our enemies. I still can't put my figure on the 'why' behind all of this."

"What is even stranger," said Jaime, "is that Tom called The Deity a she. Like, what if there is some nutcase human trying to control bots and people? Like a hostile world takeover."

A voice suddenly spoke in the distance. It was Junkyard Crow. He was now standing near the cockpit of the ship crash site.

"Hey, guys, come check this out," he yelled to them.

They all turned and calmly walked a good thirty meters over to the ship.

"Look at this." Crow was holding the arm of the person in the cockpit.

"Well, damn," said Jaime. "What does this mean, you think?"

"So, it is true then," said Ed. "Tom was taken by a bot that looked like a human."

Artie drew close and looked at the dead pilot. He picked up the forearm of the body. Under some shallow skin, there was a bit of blood, and under that was a hard, metal material. This was no human, but a bot constructed to look like one.

He felt something again in his chest and then in his mind. It was a pain long forgotten. It reminded him of someone he had to keep trying to forget. Anna had been one of a kind. Artie was sure at the time that no one had built a bot as advanced as he had. He had spent nearly two years building her—handcrafting every piece with great care. It had cost him over two hundred thousand dollars to build. No company would have been able to justify a cost like that to mass-produce bots for any good reason. That was why the world hadn't moved far beyond UberBots, SexBots, and other utility bots. No company would have put that amount of love into a machine. An individual might have, but if anyone had, Artie didn't know about it. As far as he knew, he was the only one to have done it.

And now there was another machine just like it. Possibly even more realistic. It was obvious that someone, somewhere was creating sentient robots again.

"I've never seen anything like this," said Ed. "One of these took Tom and the others. And then we also have humans following orders and being manipulated by software."

He pointed to the carcass of the nearest Angel. "Not to mention these assassin droids. Built for war."

Artie's heart began to race. This was all too familiar. He looked closely at the metal underlying the skin. He studied the green eyes of the dead pilot. He pushed his hand hard into the pilot's chest to feel the texture. The construction felt reminiscent of his own work. It was solid. It was perfection.

Jan moved in and also caressed her hand across the face of the dead pilot. "This is insane," she said. "Nothing like this has ever existed before."

"Actually," said Artie somberly, "that's not entirely true."

They all turned to look at him.

"I designed this robot."

"What are you saying, Artie?" asked Ed.

"I've never told anyone this before, but before the bombs dropped—I had constructed a Sia-based entity. But she was much more than that. She—"

Artie looked at the ground. He didn't think it would be this difficult to talk about Anna aloud. Even after all these years, he knew how crazy it sounded to say he was in love with a robot, so he decided to leave that part out.

"I trained her and taught her myself. She was taught in love and became something great. I spent a lot of time and money perfecting her. I custom-ordered and modified every part and piece. To my knowledge, she was the most advanced sentient AI ever built. That, mixed with the world's most carefully crafted humanoid structure and motor functions, made her the perfect human. All the strengths of human nature mixed with the benefits of heavy computing power and eternal longevity."

Artie looked up again at Jan, and then to Ed.

"She knew what was coming back then, and actually tried to save me all those years ago. But she was killed."

He breathed deeply and then the pain of the past floated away. He realized that holding this had likely been the cause of many of his personality flaws and other strange quirks he had developed over the years. Artie felt a great relief come upon him. But he now cringed as he thought of what the others might think. *Oh, thanks, Artie. Thanks for creating a technology that someone has stolen and is now using against us. Thanks for killing Tom, Artie. Thank you very much.*

But to Artie's surprise, it went differently than he expected. Jan moved in and gave him a hug. "We all have our skeletons, Artie. If this really was built based on your design, then it only makes you more capable of stopping it."

"And if you really can build shit like this, bro," said Jaime with a smile, "I'm damn glad you are on our side."

"Yeah. We have a lot to figure out," said Ed, "I suggest we get back to Scourge before we have any more visitors here. Between the Jeep and my Silverado parked a few streets down, we should be able to fit everyone."

"I'm sorry about Fist," said Artie, looking at Junkyard Crow. "He saved me and Jaime."

"Yeah, me too. "He was a good friend. Loyal to the end. Loyal to his friends. And you are a friend, Artie."

Jan turned and looked to a blue smoldering heap in the distance. "I'm really sorry about the Camaro, Ed."

"Ah, no big deal. Gives me a reason to go fix up this GT Mustang I've left hiding in a garage in northern Phoenix."

Ed looked at Tom's body on the street and then faced Jan. "We'll come back and get him tonight if it's clear."

Jan nodded and then moved toward the Jeep. Artie, Jaime, and Junkyard Crow followed her. Jaime tossed the rifle to Artie.

Ed stopped for a moment and then put his fingers in his mouth and whistled loudly. After a few seconds, Pratt came running out between two buildings. Then, with a hum, Zipper followed closely behind him.

Artie thought Pratt looked awesome, running as his trench coat flew in the wind with the string of bullets chattering across his chest.

"Hey, guys," Pratt said with enthusiasm, "check this out!"

Everyone stopped to look at him. Then he grabbed this long white-and-grey shaft. He tilted his hands in a way that made Artie think he looked like a Jedi about to unleash his Lightsaber. Then to Artie's surprise that picture nearly came to life as a large flame protruded from the shaft. It was a sword from one of the Angels.

"Awesome," said Artie. "But where did you get it? These two scrap piles are pretty wasted."

"I was scouting just outside of these buildings. Some huge battle must have happened not too long ago. I think it was the Cardanos. There must be like a hundred bodies back there. A few dead Angel bots too."

He swung the sword around, but clearly wasn't in control of its weight distribution and nearly lost his balance. Jan and Artie jumped out of the way.

"I think I need some practice," he said with a laugh. "I should get a paint job too; it doesn't really fit my color."

"Alright, dummy, let's go," said Ed, motioning to Pratt.

As the two groups of people moved in opposite directions toward their vehicles, a rumbling sound began to grow in the distance. Artie knew this sound all too well now.

It was another ship.

39

Artie looked upward, and just as he had predicted, there was another white ship zipping overhead. Jan reached for her gun and Pratt knelt slightly as if he were preparing to launch himself at an oncoming foe. Zipper dropped low and floated behind Artie.

The ship tore across the sky and then moved past them. For a moment, Artie felt a hint of relief. That relief was soon squelched when the rumbling grew louder and louder. Suddenly there were three ships. Then six. They were flying overhead on both the north and south sides of downtown Phoenix.

"Where are they going?" yelled Jaime.

Ed squinted his eyes and lifted his head to follow a ship. He then put his hands on his head as if some shocking revelation had befallen him.

Junkyard Crow pointed to the east. "They're heading to Scourge!"

In the far distance, on the horizon between the buildings, Artie could see more ships converging toward Scourge in the east. He thought he was able to count up to ten ships now.

The walkie on Ed's hip began to crackle and buzz.

"Ed, we've got a big problem here. Come in."

Ed picked up the walkie. "Kim, these are not friendlies. Sound the emergency sirens. Call everyone into defensive positions and fire at will."

Ed pointed to some of the people who had come to the aid of Artie.

"You guys, in the truck now. Papa Eddie and Crow, ride with me. We've got to go, now!"

They moved without hesitation. Jan began to run toward the Jeep and Jaime followed.

"Wait, Jan," yelled Ed.

She stopped. Jaime did too.

"Artie, come here. All of you."

Ed thought for a second and then turned to Pratt. "You too, buddy."

They all sprinted over to Ed. Suddenly loud gunshots could be heard in the distance.

Pratt looked toward the sound and then back to Ed. "Boss, we don't have a lot of ammo reserves for those .50 cals they're firing. If each of those ships is carrying a couple of those Angels, Scourge is going to be in trouble."

"Right. Look, guys, we may be out of time. Scourge is my responsibility."

Ed looked to Jan. "You are relieved of your duties as Chief of Security. Effective immediately."

"What the hell?" Jan demanded.

"I'll take care of Scourge. The city is strong. And I'll die before I let these things turn our friends into mindless drones. Artie, there was something I was going to give you before you left, but it seems now is the right time."

Artie thought it must have been incredibly important for Ed to do this now instead of heading out to save the city.

"I need you to do this for me. Do it for Scourge. Do it for all of us. I'll fight them back—but I fear if we do make it through today, that they will only come back and with reinforcements. The Deity has made its move. It isn't going to stop. This is calculated. They clearly have been building their forces and trying to recruit more—and by force."

"What is it, Ed? What do you have for Artie?" said Jan with impatience.

"Artie, six months ago I received an encrypted message on the Bitcoin network—along with one hundred Bitcoin. I'll forward it to you right now. You'll understand it when you read it."

"I don't have my Microblade or my Bladebook. They are back home."

"They're in the Jeep," said Jan with a smile. "Along with the last two Turtles, as you might have noticed."

Ed pulled out his phone, found Artie from his contact list, copied and pasted some text, and pressed send.

"I don't understand!" said Jan.

"Artie can tell you more when he reads the message. Pratt, go with them—I think they'll need your help."

Pratt nodded.

"Jaime, you're a pilot, right?"

"Well, I used to be before the war mostly. Took a few flights after, but we ran out of planes."

An explosion sounded far in the distance. They could all feel the vibrations from where they were standing.

"Artie, I sent you the message and an address. We found a plane in one of the hangars at the old airport a while back. The building is bright blue; you can't miss it. The entrance looks like it's barricaded, but it isn't really. We moved the debris in front to keep scavengers out. The plane works fine, and it is fueled up. It was for emergencies."

Ed moved in and gave Jan a hug. "Take care of each other, okay, Jan?"

She nodded and hugged him back, tears forming in her eyes.

He then moved in and gave Artie a hug. "Thanks for everything, Artie. I think humanity has a bright future with you around. You need to stop this thing. We might not be the only people who are being invaded and taken. This could be happening right across the entire country. You may very well be the only person who can stop it."

Artie nodded. He didn't understand everything completely, but Ed was a friend and Artie had to help.

Ed shook Jaime's hand. "Fly them where they need to go. Then get home to your family. And tell the USR what is happening. Warn them."

"Yes, sir," said Jaime with a salute. "Go give 'em hell."

Smoke could be seen rising in the distance and then the ground shook again with another boom a few seconds later.

Ed smiled and turned to Pratt. "Protect our friends, to the very death."

"I'm ready to kick some names and take some ass, Ed."

Pratt ran over to the Jeep and Jaime followed close behind.

"Thanks for everything, Mr. Edward Stanza," said Artie. He then turned to follow the others. Jan stood silently for a moment looking at Ed and then turned to follow Artie.

When they got to the Jeep, she jumped into the driver's seat. Artie was already in the passenger seat. Jaime sat in the back and Pratt stood in the bed, holding onto the Jeep's rear roll bars.

Artie grabbed his Microblade from a cup holder and opened his Bitcoin app. There were three messages—the first two were forwarded messages from Ed, each coupled with a tiny fraction of Bitcoin. The third message contained the location of the airplane hangar.

Artie tapped to open the first message. His heart seemed to skip a beat when he read the field that said, "from." It had a series of characters and numbers that Artie had known from heart since he was a kid. It was a Bitcoin address, the most famous of them all.

1A1zP1eP5QGefi2DMPTfTL

He ran his hand through his dirty black hair, took a deep breath, and then his eyes lit with excitement. He began to smile, showing his full set of well-maintained, pearly white teeth.

"What is it, dammit?!" said Jan with impatient curiosity.

"The message. It's from Satoshi Nakamoto. He's alive."

Artie began to read the message on his screen, his voice trembling.

```
Hello, Edward.
It took me quite some time to find
you. I hope you are alive and well.
We spoke once, if you remember—or ra-
ther we sent a series of encrypted
messages to one another, not unlike
this message today. That was many
years ago, but you had once encour-
aged me in regard to the release of
Sia. Perhaps you were right and per-
haps we both were terribly wrong. But
that time has passed. Now we must
look to the future. I have something
incredibly important to tell you, but
it must be in person. The Bitcoin
network is no longer secure—they have
breached it, or rather they now own
```

```
51% of the network. Something terri-
ble is coming. They are coming for
you and coming for all of the rem-
nants of humanity.

As this message is potentially unse-
cured, I ask that you come see me as
soon as possible. My location will be
delivered to you in a second message.
Satoshi Nakamoto
```

Artie quickly swiped the screen which opened the next message. There were only two words printed on the display. After a few moments of soaking in the amazement of the message, Artie looked up at Jan, his smile still unwavering.

"Jaime, where did you say the capital of the USR used to be located?"

"Denver. Before the beasts took over and killed everyone. Why do you ask?"

"We better find some snow boots before we take off. We're headed to Colorado."

"We're already leaking fuel and the left engine is on its last leg. If one of those missiles gets even close to us again, we are going to go up in flames. I say we find a clearing of some kind and just land while we still can."

"Jaime's right. Better safe than sorry."

"Jaime, how far are we from Denver?" yelled Artie to the cockpit.

"We're about fifty miles out. But then Boulder is still like thirty miles north of Denver."

"Eighty miles on foot in the snow. You think we can do that, Jan?" asked Artie.

"We don't have a choice. Jaime, put this plane down the first chance you can."

"The satellite GPS map in this rig says there's a small airport nearby. Looks like some old private runway. I doubt it ever serviced a jet plane of this size, but it will have to do."

"I'm not sure we can trust a twelve-year-old electronic map," said Artie.

"Any better ideas?" asked Jan. "Let's take her down."

Jaime began to quickly descend the plane. Artie had to grab his Winchester as the sudden dip in altitude threw a bunch of loose objects toward the back of the plane. He looked to one of the seats in the back. Pratt was sitting there motionless in a chair, complete with his smiling marker face.

"Pratt. Pratt!" Artie yelled, but he didn't respond. "How can he sleep at a time like this? And what the hell does a robot even need to sleep for?"

Jan grabbed a large logbook of some kind and threw it at Pratt's head. It hit him and he jolted up.

"Are we there yet?"

"Yeah, stupid," Jan said rolling her eyes. "And we are about to have a crash landing."

The plane took a sudden twist to the right and then a loud explosion occurred not far outside of the passenger windows. The whole cabin began to shake.

"Guys, I think we have a problem," said Pratt, pointing to a crack in the window next to his seat. "Someone just fired a rocket at us."

The crack grew bigger and then with a loud crunching sound, the entire panel next to Pratt ripped off and out into the cool mountain air. The hole stretched from the floor to the roof. The freezing wind pierced the cabin, and then just as soon as it had entered, the gust began pulling everything out. Papers, old books, and other items from the plane began to fly out of the gaping hole with great velocity.

Zipper was trying hard to keep within the plane, his rotors and propellers in full force.

"Zip, just go! Catch up with us when we land."

The drone didn't hesitate at Artie's suggestion and allowed the air to pull him out of the plane. Pratt put one hand on the outside of the plane and another gripped the seat in front of him as the vacuum desperately tried to suck him out. Jaime descended the plane even lower and the pressure began to normalize.

"Alright, guys, put your coats on and gear up. We'll be landing hard in about two minutes." Jaime flicked a switch and then a beeping sound went off with an associated red flash. "Um, I meant to say we'll be crashing hard in two minutes. The landing gear is stuck. Or gone."

The air was blistering cold and Artie realized that a simple eighty-mile trip in the snow was going to be a tough walk, possibly even deadly. They had scavenged an REI sporting goods store before leaving, snatching up the heaviest winter clothing they could find.

The wind was roaring and the small crew could now see the tops of the green trees and the surface of the ground. Their visibility at higher altitudes had been blocked by winter storm clouds.

The trees and terrain were moving fast beneath them now as they grew closer to the ground. The area below was remote with only a few ranch-style houses scattered about.

"Okay, people. Brace for impact," yelled Jaime. "I've slowed her down as best I can."

Artie watched the plane move from twenty feet above the ground, to ten, to five, and then he held his breath as the plane hit the powdery ground. It floated gently at first, which was reassuring, but then dug deeper into the snow and the sounds of scraping and crunching could be heard. The plane bounced and bumped, and at one point, Pratt's head slammed into the ceiling above, leaving a large dent.

Trees from the edges of the makeshift runway grew closer and closer until one of them struck the left wing of the plane and ripped it clean off. Sparks flew, but they were immediately doused by the globs of snow that the plane was throwing into the air. The impact of the wing caused the plane to spin uncontrollably. Round and round it went. Even the large hole in the side of the plane was just a big white blur.

After some more spinning and scraping, the plane began to slow its movement until it finally stopped. No one spoke for over a minute. Artie thought of astronauts' training, being sent in circles over and over prior to taking flight in a space shuttle. He wondered if those movie depictions were actually true. In any case, his head was spinning and he felt close to throwing up, but was able to keep it down.

"Is everyone alright?" Jan said wearily.

"I think I just puked up last week's tamales," Jaime moaned.

"I'm fine," said Artie. He looked to where Pratt had been sitting. He was gone. "Pratt's not here," said Artie with concern.

"Okay. Grab your packs and let's get out of here. We need to find Pratt, then we've got to find shelter. It will be night soon. Not to mention whoever shot us down will be looking for us."

Artie, Jaime, and Jan unlatched their seat belts and then dug through the trashed cabin to find their packs. They slowly moved out of the plane, and as Jaime stepped out, he threw up. The area outside was completely desolate aside from the tall pine trees that were half-buried in snow. Jan took a step and immediately sunk into the ground.

"Crap. This snow is deep."

"Look," said Artie, pointing to the trail behind the plane. The crash landing had created a long, deep crevice in the snow. "I think we should walk in the crash trail to see if we can't find a better path."

"Agreed," said Jan. "Artie, do you have any idea when we might have lost Pratt?"

"Yeah, it was after we hit the ground. So he can't be far."

The three of them moved behind the plane and jumped into the crevice of snow. Since the snow was more packed this low, walking was easier. The landing had created quite the long pathway. The snow must have caused the plane to slide further than it normally might have on flat ground.

Jaime led the team forward down the landing path with Jan and Artie walking side-by-side behind him. They had walked about one hundred yards when they heard a loud roaring sound somewhere up ahead. Then, in the distance, behind a small hill of snow on the runway, a plume of snow powder shot up into the sky, followed by another loud roar.

"Calm down, kitty," a familiar voice said. "I'm not going to hurt you."

The three of them quickly ran to the source of the noise just behind the hill. Jaime went around the hill first and slid on the snow and fell backward. Artie and Jan stared at the scene laid out before them.

Pratt was standing with his back against the hill holding his giant flaming sword. In front of him was a creature of enormous size. It was nearly ten feet tall from paws to its head and stretched nearly thirty feet in length. The entire body was constructed of various metals and shapes, but all were painted in shades of silver and white. The creature had some form of armor or plating covering certain vital areas, and those were a darker grey color. Looking closer, Artie could see gears and pistons moving within the frame of the machine, just behind those protected areas. The eyes were like red flames, and the occasional ember could be seen leaving them. The beast had a gaping mouth full of sharp metal teeth, and it was currently showing its fangs in aggression.

Artie could never have imagined in his wildest dreams seeing something like this. It was as if it had come straight out of a video game or movie.

The creature that stood in front of them was a large, ferocious, catlike machine.

As the beast roared again, Jaime covered his ears with his puffy snow gloves. Jan withdrew one of her handguns and aimed it at the cat, and Artie pulled out the Microblade from his pocket to call Zipper to his location.

Jaime slowly scooted back and then stood up behind Jan, and grabbed the rifle wrapped around his back.

"So, any of you have experience with cats?" said Pratt.

The beast roared again and inched closer to Pratt.

"Alright, I'm gonna cut this thing—"

"Wait," Artie interrupted.

A buzzing sound echoed from above; it was Zipper. Artie tapped a few buttons and then the Microblade began to show the area from up above—it was Zipper's 360 degree camera.

"I'm gonna take over for a few minutes, Zip, if you don't mind," said Artie aloud. He tilted the phone and swiped his fingers against it as if he was playing a video game. The drone began to move around, obeying Artie's commands. He then tapped a button and a soft yellow light projected from underneath the camera. Wherever the camera looked, the light shone. With a few more taps, Artie caused the beam of light to grow thinner and then he turned it red.

"What are we doing here, guys?" said Pratt. "I'd like to not be eaten."

The drone flew a little lower and then Artie pointed the red light—almost laser-like—on the ground in front of the cat. The large machine turned its head to the right to look at the red dot a few feet away in the snow. Suddenly it moved, about ten feet to the left. The cat hunched low and wiggled its large mechanical paws.

Artie moved the beam again another ten feet and then the large beast leaped at it, trying to catch it in its razor-sharp claws. A plume of snow jumped fifteen feet into the air. After it settled, the creature lifted its paws, opening them slightly to find its kill—but it was gone. The creature quickly looked to the left, and then to the right—it found the red dot, another few feet away. The cat formed into launching position again, and then leapt.

There was another plume of snow and the cat was now another ten feet away from the group.

"Okay, guys, what is happening here? Like, literally, I don't understand what just happened," said Pratt, who was now turning off his fire blade.

"Are you kidding me?" said Jaime in disbelief.

Jan smiled. "Always full of surprises, Artie."

"I'll keep pulling him away. Jan, you find us a path and lead the way. I'll follow you while I distract this thing."

Another plume of snow shot up in the distance. That oversized, magical red dot was feisty and hard to catch, but the cat was determined to keep at it.

"He's kind of cute in a way," said Pratt still looking at the leaping beast and now falling behind. "We should have named him. Maybe Larry?"

"Pratt! Move it!" yelled Jan.

"Touchy, touchy. Artie, how do you put up with this all day?"

"I know who is hunting dinner tonight for the group," said Jan from ahead, not looking back.

"You know I don't even eat food, right?"

"Yup."

"Ouch. You know Jan, I'm starting to think you don't like my kind—like robophobic or something. We have feelings too, ya know."

"See, Jan!" said Jaime. "Pratt gets it. The minorities in this party are highly mistreated."

Pratt reached out his arm and gave Jaime a fist bump. Jan rolled her eyes at the dialog and Artie smiled, still maneuvering the cat further away.

They quickly reached the beginning of the crash trail and the mechanical beast was now far out of site. Jan led the group into the dense forest trees. The first rows of trees were covered in deep snow and it took some work to push through. Once they moved further into the woods, the snow was shallower due to the density of the forest.

Artie released control of Zipper. "Follow us above the trees. I don't think you can navigate in here," he said into the Microblade.

"How did you know to do that?" asked Pratt.

"Oh, well I didn't know it would work. It was just a hunch. The creature seemed feral. Like it actually was a real animal. I thought maybe it was programmed that way. The first SiaPet protocols had animal qualities added into their source code."

"Okay, Artie, we are safe," Jan announced. "Tell us where to go."

"Alright. Just remember again that the maps I have are super old. Whatever the satellites captured and stored last is what we have, and I don't know if they are still operational. The GPS in my Microblade is true, but we will need to be super careful."

Artie tapped his device and looked at it for a moment. He then tapped a few times to drop some pins in locations that he thought showed the best path.

"Okay, look here. So, I figure our quickest path is to travel where the roads are—or where they used to be, at least. We'll be more exposed to the elements and giant cat creatures, I guess, but it's the straightest path forward. Highway 86 is right here, and then we jump to Interstate 25, which will take us through Denver."

"That's really risky," said Jan. "I'd take the cover of the trees over the open roads, even if it takes longer."

"Yeah, I agree," said Jaime. "No way one of those beasts can fit through these trees."

Jan nodded and then looked to Pratt.

"Well, I don't really care either way, but I am aching to kill something. I am an assassin droid, ya know?"

"You mean a malfunctioning UberBot," Jan replied.

Artie laughed. "She has you there."

"You guys do know I've killed like a hundred people before, right? Not to mention one of those Death Angels."

"Um, I'm pretty sure you just grabbed the sword from one that had already been killed."

"Why did I come along again?"

No one responded. Jan turned to Artie. "Can you chart us a path that takes us through the forest?"

Artie analyzed his device for a moment and then cleared the current pins, and dropped some others. He showed Jan.

"Alright, everyone, let's move," she said. "We can probably make three or four miles before we need to camp."

They began to move after Jan. Artie paused. A thought entered his mind. He lifted the Microblade up and then looked at the map. The overhead map view still showed cities, and buildings, and even houses. It was clearly an old rendering. But he realized that much of those renderings had been crowd-sourced so long ago—people had submitted that data simply by using their phones. It made sense that it was out of date. But what about the satellite view?

He tapped a settings icon on the map and then enabled some buttons and moved back to the map. There was now an icon that showed a picture of a satellite. He tapped it and the 2D and 3D renderings of user-submitted data were replaced by images of snowy terrain. The top right of the screen read, in very small text, *Taken Four Days Ago.*

Artie quickly started panning the map in all directions, but it was hard to make out anything of use because the area was engulfed in deep snow. At least, everywhere except downtown Denver, which had a large blurry spot that was mostly black, with a hint of red in the middle. He wasn't able to make out exactly what it was, but it didn't look inviting. Unfortunately, they would have to pass through this to get to Boulder. He would need to let Jan know.

Artie put the device into his pocket. He looked up to see the last remnants of Jaime's bright red coat in the distance. He was about to run to the group but heard a loud cracking sound behind him. He whipped around and pulled the rifle from his back, aiming it in front of him. But there was nothing. Something didn't feel right to Artie. Of course, nothing was ever "normal" or "right" anymore, so he turned back around and sprinted to the group.

The snow's surface was much harder the next day. During the night, the clouds had dissipated, and the clear skies had frozen the top layers of the snow. They had wandered late the previous evening because they hadn't been able to find a suitable place to camp. Eventually, they had a stroke of luck when Jaime sat on a tree stump for a moment to rest, but then nearly fell inside of it—it had actually been a chimney.

After spending a good thirty minutes digging, they were in the house. Luck continued to favor them, as the home had multiple beds and very dry wood from long ago, allowing them to start a fire.

The next morning, the clouds returned, and a snowstorm looked inevitable. They had covered some good ground the previous afternoon, but they still had nearly thirty miles to go before they reached downtown Denver. When Artie and Jan had traveled from Palm Springs those many months ago, they could easily walk fourteen miles a day. Now they would be lucky to hit ten miles. But that was enough to get them to the outskirts of the city where they could more easily find shelter.

Jan led the group through the forest. The trees were becoming sparser, which let Artie know that they must be getting closer to the city. As Artie, Jan, and Jaime trudged through the bitter cold in silence, Pratt happily walked in his own world, singing various songs and melodies.

"Pratt!" Jan turned around, stopping. "What is it going to take to shut you up? You want to get us all killed?"

"We haven't seen anything for miles," he said. "Trees, trees, and more trees. I mean, there was that *one thing* we saw. Oh wait, that was a tree too."

Jan sighed. "Alright, fine. If you are that bored, do us all a favor and scout ahead, especially since 'you are much more capable of running in the snow' than we humans. Artie, show him where we're headed."

Artie lifted the Microblade up to Pratt's smiley face. He suddenly realized that he actually didn't know how Pratt was able to see since it didn't look like there were any cameras or sensors attached to him. Pratt looked at the screen and then looked up.

"Cool. I'll snag us some shelter for tonight, then come find you. I'm gone like Donkey Kong."

Pratt saluted to Jan and then ran off.

"That doesn't even make sense," she replied. "What an ass."

"I like him," said Artie.

"You like everyone, though, so your vote doesn't count."

They pushed forward for a couple of hours, and just as they thought it might, the snow began to fall. As it fell, the visibility of the horizon became obscured and fuzzy. At times Artie couldn't even see twenty feet in front of him, and with the shelter of the trees in the forest mostly gone, he felt vulnerable.

The wind stopped blowing and every crunch of snow under their feet seemed to echo for miles.

"I don't like this," said Jan.

Artie nodded. "Me either."

"Yeah, this is pretty creepy, guys," said Jaime.

Jan pushed forward. "Let's just get through this fast."

Just as Artie was about to take his next step, he heard a clicking sound—it was a sound they were all familiar with. Someone was holding a gun.

"Don't move," a voice said from behind.

And there it was, the thing that had been following them. But it wasn't a thing; it was a person. Jan inched her fingers toward the gun on her right hip.

"Stop, I said," the voice demanded calmly. "I don't want to hurt anyone. Just want to talk."

"People who want to talk don't typically start a conversation with a gun," replied Jan coldly.

"Yeah, well out here you don't trust anyone or anything."

The man strafed to the left of Jan and Artie, and then moved behind Jaime. He put a silver, six-shooter revolver against Jaime's head.

"What's your name?"

"I'm Captain Jaime Guerra of the United States Reformed." Jaime was shaking, but trying to remain firm in his voice. "And you're holding a military officer hostage. And you are doing it within USR territory."

"The USR no longer operates here," said the man. "This is the Kingdom of the Beasts now. What is a fluffy red Mexican of the USR doing out here with a couple of scrappy tagalongs?"

The voice suddenly seemed less threatening than it had before. Jaime tilted his head slightly, seeming to try and understand what the man was trying to emphasize.

"Do I know you?" Jaime said inquisitively.

"It depends, homey. Are you for the Cowboys or still rooting for those pussy Raiders?"

Jaime smiled. "Cowgirls ain't got nothin' on the Raiders."

"Wrong answer," the voice said.

Jaime spun around and hugged the man.

"Como esta, hermano?" said the man

"Doing great. Except for the snow." Jaime pushed away from the man and then looked at Jan and Artie.

"This is my brother Miguel, but you can call him Mikey."

"Good to meet all of you, and Miguel will be fine actually." He gave Jaime a glare and then shook Artie's hand and then Jan's.

"I've been tracking you guys. And your loud robot friend too."

"Why, what's going on, Miguel?" asked Jaime. "And why are you here?"

"USR is planning on reclaiming Denver. Six others and I have been scouting the area for the last three months. Then we send back our intel via these long-range radios." He tapped a bulky radio on his hip.

Jan and Artie looked at each other, and then at Jaime. Miguel noticed the exchange.

"Why, what does that mean to you?" he said.

"It's a long story," said Jan. "But the USR may have bigger issues than some robotic cats."

"Interesting. Well, tell me about it later. We need to get out of this place right now."

"What do you mean?" asked Artie.

"We call this place the dead zone. We'll need to go around—and carefully. You don't want to wake it up."

"Wake what up?" asked Jaime.

"Later. Let's go. Quietly."

Jan nodded and then Artie and Jaime turned to follow Miguel. Just as they did so, they heard a faint sound in the distance. They all stopped.

"Is that screaming?" asked Jaime quietly.

The sound grew louder. Something was screeching in the distance.

Jan turned to Miguel. "Is that the thing you were talking about?"

"No. You would know it if it was. This is something else."

The yelling became more audible as it grew closer.

"Run," Artie thought the voice might have said.

"Go. Run!" said the voice very clearly now.

The area in front of them was a giant mist of clouds and snow and visibility was terrible.

"Ruuuuunnn," yelled the voice again, this time super close.

Jan pulled out her guns and Miguel lifted his own handgun, pointing it in the grey mist. A shadowy running figure appeared, pumping his hands back and forth in a furious sprint. It was Pratt.

"Why are you standing there?" he said nearly reaching the group. "Run! Now!"

Pratt didn't even stop to greet the team or tell them what was going on, he just flew past them all and continued forward into the other direction, disappearing back into the mist.

Then it came, the awful sound. It roared so loudly that the four of them covered their ears.

"Is that it?" Jaime yelled.

"What do you think, dumbass?" Miguel shouted in return. "Run!"

They all turned to run in the direction Pratt had moved. As they did so, a loud crashing sound pierced the air as the earth shook so violently that Artie and Jaime tripped and fell to the ground. Jan helped Artie up and Miguel grabbed Jaime by his coat sleeve. They all began to run again.

Then, out of the snowy mist emerged a large cylindrical shadow. Artie looked back at the figure.

"What is that?" he yelled.

The cylinder drew closer, and they could all clearly see it now. It was made of metal and it was at least fifty feet in diameter. The thing moved down with great force and slammed into the snow. The earth shook again, only this time even worse since the impact was so close to the group. The force drove a flurry of snow against all of them and flung them into the air nearly ten feet.

When Artie came to his senses, he couldn't see Jan, Jaime, or Miguel. There was just white everywhere. The creature roared again. After a few moments, an arm grabbed him; it was Miguel.

"C'mon, kid."

"Is that a tentacle?" asked Artie, nearly out of breath. He looked up and saw Jan and Jaime running just up ahead.

"We need to do something," said Artie to Miguel. "We can't outrun it."

"I know. I have a plan, but until we can get to safety, it won't work."

Artie thought for a second as he and Miguel continued to run.

"I can distract it," he said.

"Not unless you want to die, you can't."

"No, check it out." Artie slowed to a jog and then pulled his Microblade from his coat pocket. He tapped a few buttons, and then long pressed to drop a pin where he thought the creature might be on the map. He put the device back in his pocket and picked up the pace.

"What did you do?" asked Miguel.

"Just wait for it, then you'll have the chance to enact your plan."

After about fifteen seconds, a red haze began to fill the sky behind them. The red grew stronger and stronger and covered a large area in the distance.

"What the hell is that?" said Miguel.

"Flares," said Artie.

There was an incredibly loud smash and the ground shook violently once more. The impact caused all of the mist behind them to clear up. Artie and Miguel stopped, then so did Jaime and Jan. As a series of red flares were falling from the sky, the creature looked up, entranced. An enormous shadowy figure began to emerge as the air cleared out. Then the shadow dissolved altogether.

The large cylindrical object truly had been a tentacle, and now they could clearly see that it had been only one of at least twelve other tentacles—and they were attached to a face. The head that housed the tentacles was affixed to a large neck and torso that was now rising from the snow. Massive gears and valves could be seen moving and pumping in the creature. Black smoke billowed out of some type of exhaust vents in the back. The creature roared again, revealing a gaping mouth with large, sharp, metal teeth. To make matters worse, fire poured out from that orifice. Pushing itself upward with a large set of claws and arms, the creature stood tall.

"You didn't say it was a giant octopus!" Jaime yelled to Miguel.

"Honestly, we've only ever seen the one tentacle—always thought it was just a huge worm thing. And I'm pretty sure an octopus doesn't have biceps and claws."

"It's not an octopus or a worm," Artie interjected. "It's much worse than that. This is Cthulhu."

"What the hell is that?" asked Jan.

"It's a mythical creature. This place is starting to make sense to me," said Artie, almost with excitement. "First the tiger creature, and then this. I think these machines are replicating creatures from our past—or books."

"That's all nice, but doesn't really matter right now," Jan protested.

Miguel knelt in the snow and pulled out his radio. "Falcon Six, this is Bravo Four. I need immediate artillery assistance."

"I read you loud and clear, Bravo Four. Provide your strike code and coordinates."

Miguel responded accordingly, providing his code and the coordinates of the massive creature.

"Copy, Bravo Four. Strike incoming."

Artie lifted the Microblade to his mouth. "Get out of there, Zipper."

Suddenly a whistling sound could be heard in the far distance. Then, without any visible trace of a rocket or missile, a loud explosion erupted about one hundred yards to the left of the Cthulhu. The heat could be felt even from where Artie was standing. The creature roared at the mess of flames.

"Falcon Six, move one hundred yards east. And send in the big guns, please. Target is at least three hundred feet tall."

"That's insane," said the radio voice. "Recalibrating strike position. Brace for impact. This one's gonna shock you."

"Let's go, guys! Move!" said Miguel to the group. They all began to run toward the forest edge. Artie could now see Pratt up ahead standing near a large boulder in the snow.

The creature thrashed in a rage, looking for the meal that it had seen scurrying about just moments ago. Just as it was about to push forward in some type of leap or jump, another whistle zoomed through the air and then another explosion—except this explosion was three times as large and hit the beast directly.

The ground shook with great force. The creature screamed. Artie turned to look at the engagement. Three of the tentacles had blasted away from its face and there was now a gaping hole in its neck and chest. It screamed again.

Another whistle came and then another explosion. This one hit its left leg, shattering its enormous gears and pieces in every direction. The beast screamed again, and then suddenly turned and dove itself into the snow almost as an ocean seal might dive into the sea. There was a great flurry of snow that flung up into the air. The creature was fleeing.

"Falcon Six, hold your fire. Target is retreating."

"What the hell was it, Miguel?" the radio buzzed.

"I'll tell you about it next cycle, Private. Thanks for the help."

"Copy and out."

Miguel stood up and looked at the group. Pratt was now jogging over to their location.

"Okay, so we've got good news and bad news. The good news is we just stopped the thing that has prevented our infantry from setting up a forward operating base here south of the city. Or at least we've scared it away, hopefully for a good while. I've never been able to pin the location of the creature so we could blast it. We have Artie to thank for that."

"And the bad news?" asked Jaime.

"The bad news is every monster and beast within twenty miles is likely going to be coming after us now. That was quite the commotion. Not to mention some of the local scavengers and raiders are probably on their way. "

"Wait, there are people living here too?" asked Jan.

"Yeah, it sounds crazy, but everything is crazy these days, right? We even have a couple of small USR towns still in operation here. People who refused to give up their land. It's one of the reasons why we are trying to take it all back. And so long as these beasts roam unchecked, the USR can't expand. President Fowler is determined to restore the United States."

"Well, he's got his work cut out for him," replied Jan. "We've got a lot to talk about."

Miguel nodded. "I've got a safe house in southern Denver. Let's go."

Pratt walked toward them casually with his hands on top of his head.

"Wow, did you guys see that thing?"

Jan rolled her eyes and Artie gave Pratt an endearing slap on the shoulder.

"What? What did I say?

As they all warmed themselves against the fire of Miguel's safe house that night, Artie and Jan related everything that had happened the past months. Artie gave updates on the state of Los Angeles and told them how they met Jaime and Derek so many months ago. Jan told her entire story, from Austin to the war in El Paso to settling in Scourge.

Artie told Miguel of the bots that looked like humans, and also of The Deity and what she had done to Tom. Jaime jumped in here and there, embellishing the stories and, of course, appearing as the hero in every case.

"You think Satoshi is really alive?" asked Miguel.

"Yes," said Artie. "But it's not just a feeling. No one could have sent that message except him. In order to send anything from that Bitcoin address, it would need to have been signed by Satoshi's private key. There is only ever one private key per address—cryptographically secure."

"I think we need to get you to him, then," said Miguel. He then put his head down for a moment and rubbed his hand against his chin. Then he looked at Artie, his eyes serious.

"Normally I wouldn't tell you this, since it's classified, but I think I need to. There's a small city in Northern Utah called Logan. Three days ago, it was invaded by ten to fifteen white flying ships. At least that is what the SOS transmissions had said. Our nearest infantry units were about fifteen miles south. When the first convoys finally reached Logan, everyone was gone. There weren't even any bodies. Everyone was just gone."

"So, it is happening everywhere," said Jan.

"President Fowler hasn't released this information yet, but I'm guessing with your intel, he's going to need to do that."

Artie stood up and warmed his hands near the fire. "So, what's the plan then?"

"The good news is last week we cleared out Colorado Springs and made it our forward operating base. The beasts were smaller than they are here in Denver, but they still put up a hell of a fight. But we had six battalions—troops, tanks, and mobile artillery. That's about seventy miles south of here. With that squid thing out of the picture, we can move in now. I'll call it in, and they'll converge on southern Denver. Our presence should be enough to let you slip by to Boulder undetected."

Jaime looked to Miguel. "So, you guys are going to just, like, go to war with these creatures?"

"It's not like that really. They aren't really unified. We've learned that they are definitely territorial, but not organized. They even hunt and kill each other. They are literally like beasts of the wild. We aren't completely sure who made them or where they are coming from, but we do see new creatures emerge from time to time. They are still being built, that much we know."

Artie walked over to Miguel and showed him the satellite map on his Microblade. "It could be here," he said, pointing to the large black hole he had identified the other day.

"This is amazing," said Miguel. "You are tapped into a satellite?"

"Yes. I think most of them are still operational."

"We could really use you back home. USR has a strict law against software-based technology. But we've been really feeling the pains of this. Makes reconnaissance and pretty much every other military operation much more difficult—like me having to live by myself in six feet of snow night and day. I bet if you could talk to the people in charge, you could give them some reassurances. We've got a lot of engineers—mechanical, electrical, etc. But I've never met any computer engineers. I'm not sure we even have any."

"I'm sure you don't," said Jan. "Something made sure of that a long time ago. We were very lucky to find Artie."

"I'd love to talk to them," said Artie. "I think that we find Satoshi, see what he has to say, and then we see Fowler. See if we can stop The Deity—and do it together."

"Sounds like a plan," said Pratt, who lowered his hand near the middle of their huddle, like an excited teenager might do at a baseball game. No one joined him.

"Oh, come on, guys!"

"Make sure you keep him out of sight," said Miguel pointing at Pratt. "Bots are also illegal in the USR and in most cases soldiers will kill on sight. Not all of us believe in the law, and I'm sure it will change in the future. But for now, you should play it safe."

Pratt moved to a sofa chair and folded his arms, trying to show his protest at the notion. Jan laughed, looking at the smiling marker face staring at her.

"Oh, our poor little baby Pratt. You need a hug?"

Pratt gave Jan the bird and then folded his arms again.

Miguel turned to Jaime. "I'm going to have to let your commanding officer know you're here now. My guess is they'll want you in our advance tomorrow."

Jaime nodded and then turned to Artie and Jan.

"Go, Jaime," said Artie with a smile. "You've been a great help. Help them here, then go be with your family."

Jan nodded in agreement.

"I'm sure our paths will cross again really soon," said Jaime.

Miguel turned to Artie. "That place on the map you showed me, do you know what it is?"

"No. But my best guess is it's a large crevasse or hole of some kind. Probably where they are being manufactured. With your troops engaged, you may want to scout it out. Take that out and you could even the odds."

"I like this kid," said Miguel. "Artie, I don't suppose you want to lend me that device and the drone too, eh?"

Artie smiled. "I would if I could. I'm pretty useless without my Microblade. And besides, Zipper doesn't really listen to anyone except for me. It's kind of that whole Ash and Pikachu thing."

Miguel raised an eyebrow, indicating that he didn't understand. He then looked to Jan and she just shrugged.

"Oh c'mon, guys. The world may have ended, but I'm even sure the mutees know about Pokemon."

Jan looked to Miguel. "So, tomorrow then."

"Tomorrow."

It was around noon when the sounds of the first explosions rocked the earth. When Artie looked out at the array of Humvees, trucks, tanks, and troops, his heart took courage. The sight brought back memories of a time when humans were organized—a time of order.

The envoy had hardly reached city limits when a pack of robotic wolves came sprinting in from some trees far in the west. They looked about three times the size of normal wolves and about three times as vicious. The short-range artillery had taken out about half of them when the remaining six began ripping into the troops—tossing bodies and spreading carnage. The soldiers eventually killed them all, but just as they did, more wolves emerged.

Not long after, from the east, came three large flying beasts. Artie thought they looked like oversized pterodactyls. They flew in viciously but were quickly repelled by antiaircraft weapons. It was clear these flying creatures were less aggressive than the wolves. He thought it was interesting that these machines mimicked actual animals. These were lesser forms of Sia acting independently within their own sphere of intelligence. As he marveled and appreciated the craftsmanship of these deadly beasts, Jan grabbed his arm and pulled him toward her.

"I said we need to go, now! What in the world is going through your head?"

"I was just thinking it was interesting that someone would create robotic beasts. They must have had limited Sia intelligence, confined within a species or something."

Jan ruffled his hair and then kissed him on the cheek. "Let's go, nerd."

Artie smiled and then followed after her. Pratt moved behind Artie while watching the battle ensue.

"Why do they get to have all the fun? I haven't killed anything since we've been here. And I've got a huge freaking sword!"

"Last I remember, Pratt," said Jan with sarcasm, "you were screaming and running in the opposite direction of the action."

"Yeah, well, did you see that thing? It was huge!"

Prior to the arrival of the USR, Artie, Jan, and Pratt had moved to the southwest side of Denver. They originally had planned to travel through the city, but with the revelation of the ominous black hole sitting in the middle of downtown, they decided to keep as west as possible.

They carefully made their way through the frozen city of Denver over the next few hours. The fighting in the distance seemed to grow in fury. A few times the group was forced to quickly hide as herds of beasts ran through the city. Later, they had encountered a large crocodile machine sitting calmly in the center of the street. Jan had wanted to move around it, but Pratt was getting anxious and so she let him attack it. The event became slightly entertaining as Pratt missed the creature three times with his large flaming sword. Then the beast lunged and nearly bit off his right arm. After that, he sheathed the sword and then shot it in the head and killed it. This of course upset Jan because the noise seemed to echo for miles.

Zipper kept one hundred meters ahead, but not drifting too far away. He helped lead the group through streets that seemed the safest. There were a few other close calls in the process of traversing the city. Once they had to stop moving as a large, forty-foot T-Rex stomped by. The group huddled in between two houses and the creature had lowered its head as if to sniff out a meal. Artie almost laughed aloud, as it reminded him of a scene from Jurassic Park.

The other close call came when Artie accidentally slipped on some black ice that had caked one of the suburban streets and then slid into some old metal trash cans. The sound had alerted a giant snake-like creature that appeared to be nearly one hundred feet long. It had begun to coil up in an aggressive position, but Pratt stepped in, and this time was able to successfully use his fire blade to slice off the head of the beast.

Jan actually paid Pratt a compliment, which she would later regret as he began to brag and sing about the ordeal for the next hour. It was around 5 p.m. when they exited the Denver city limits. They moved into a city called Broomfield, though it never felt like they ever left the city—the buildings just kind of all blended together.

At this point, most of the sounds of gunfire and explosions had stopped as well. Artie wondered if the fighting had ended and what the result had been. They walked for about another hour and then the suburbs turned into factories and warehouses. The sun was starting to set.

"We need to find shelter," said Jan. "It's late and starting to snow again. We will reach Boulder tomorrow."

"What about this place?" said Pratt, pointing at a massive building.

The structure was industrial and made of metal and cement. Artie thought it might have been a manufacturing plant of some kind, maybe plastics or car parts.

"Let's scope it out," replied Jan.

They entered the front lobby doors of this monolith building. Inside the left wall was a sign that said "Carlton Manufacturing." To the right was a reception desk that appeared to have an inch of dust frosted over with another inch of ice. The front lobby was cold, but as they moved down the main hallway, the entire building began to warm up. As they neared a corner, a warm glow appeared on the walls.

Jan unholstered her gun and carefully turned the corner to secure the hallway. There was a set of double metal doors. She motioned to Pratt and Artie to follow behind her and then she slowly opened the doors. Both Jan and Pratt leapt forward into the room ready to fight anything they might find, but there was no threat.

The room looked like an old employee lounge, except this one had been retrofitted with makeshift beds—and they had been used recently. There were four gas lamps lighting up the room, and in the middle was a homemade firepit that was still burning.

"I think we better go," whispered Jan. "Someone is living here."

As they turned to leave from where they came, they heard voices from back near the lobby.

"Guber says it's now or he'll leave our asses behind," said a man's voice.

"Yeah, but this is a crap haul. Means we'll be back here in a month," said another.

"Better that than hanging around when those soldiers get here."

The voices grew louder as they approached, and Jan, Artie, and Pratt were trapped in the employee lounge. Jan pulled out her other pistol and Pratt did the same. Artie grabbed the Winchester from his back and aimed it at the double metal doors.

"And we got that cat," said the first voice. "I bet that thing wastes a hundred people before it's taken down in the arena. That'll be a big score for us."

The doors swung open and two men who looked like they hadn't showered in a year stood under the frame.

"Freeze!" Jan demanded, pointing her guns at the men.

"You freeze," replied one of the men.

A bright flash consumed the room and then a loud noise cracked. A sudden jolt of pain flared through Artie's body and then he began to see white. A few seconds later everything faded to black.

"Hell, no! We split it fifty-fifty," said a voice.

"Yeah, but I'm the one who zapped them," said the other. "My shot, my bounty."

"Or, I could shoot you. Then I take them all."

"Fine, whatever. Ass. It doesn't matter anyway, I guess. The girl is worth more than everything we've grabbed all week."

Artie slowly opened his eyes. Everything was white and blurry. His head was throbbing. He took a breath and felt cold. Was he outside? After a few moments the blurriness cleared out, but everything was still white—he was outside. And he was in a cage. Unlike the cages he had seen back in Phoenix, this cage was dirty and made from rusted rebar. The gate's door was clamped together by a giant padlock.

His mind began to focus, and he noticed two other cages, one holding Pratt and the other holding Jan. There was a loud roar—it was one Artie had heard before. He quickly turned around to see an incredibly large cage holding a giant robotic catlike creature. It was the beast he had led away a few days ago with Zipper.

The sound of an engine rumbled from around a building not too far away. It was a truck with a snowplow in front of it pushing another giant cage forward; this one containing a giant spider-looking creature. The creature swiped and attacked the cage with its legs and its fangs, but it was to no avail.

Suddenly, something hit Artie's left cheek with great force—he had just been slapped.

"Morning, sunshine," said one of the men. "Are you cold? I hope so."

Artie thought about yelling, "Let me out of here," but that seemed stupid. Why did everyone who was ever captured in a movie yell, "Let me go!"—as if the captor would say, "Oh, right, let me do that for you."

"Where are you taking us?" he said instead.

"Great question." He tapped his bald head as if to mock Artie's intelligence. "Well, your robot buddy over there, he'll be sent straight to the arena along with the kitty cat and the spider."

He pointed over at Jan. "Your girlfriend there," he turned to Artie and smiled a terrible grin, showing a few missing teeth, "let's just say if SexBots were still around, she would be about to put them out of business."

"Bastard!" Artie yelled.

"And as for you, I really don't know yet. You are kind of pretty, so Sloppy Joe might be interested in buying both you and the girl. But my guess is someone will grab you for the mines. And that means you'll likely never see daylight again. And when your body stops working, they'll kill you and replace you. Sounding fun yet?"

The other man stepped out of the truck and walked over to the bald man. "What's the ETA?"

"Any minute."

"You're actually kind of lucky, pretty boy," said the man again to Artie. "Today is pickup day. I probably would have just killed you if we had found you any earlier. Hard enough to feed ourselves out here, let alone a worthless scrap like you."

Scrap. That was a word Artie hadn't heard in a lifetime. He looked over at Jan; she hadn't awoken yet. Pratt was slumped over in one corner of the cage, clearly out of commission. Artie could hear the sound of propellers in the distance. Then, a few moments later, a large aircraft appeared through the snowy clouds. It reminded Artie of those old Osprey choppers that could rotate their propellers and turn into airplanes. A few minutes later another chopper descended through the clouds.

Both of the aircraft were old and dirty and looked as if they had been through multiple battles. They were painted in black, green, and brown camouflage. One slowed down and then landed just a few yards away from the cages. The other chopper landed just beyond that.

"Wait, where are we going?" asked Artie.

"Oh, right. Sorry about that. We're taking you to Anchorage and you'll be living under the dominion of our benevolent King Hanni-bal."

The man cackled at his last comment and then spit on the ground. The other man laughed too and slapped the first on the back. "Yeah, kid, our gracious king will surely grant you mercy."

They both started laughing again. The chopper pilots were now out of their cockpits, pulling large cables with hooks and attaching them to the tops of the cages.

"And where is Anchor City?" asked Artie.

"You been livin' under a rock, kid? Anchor City, Alaska."

Artie was confused, and the man noticed his puzzlement.

"Don't worry, kid, it's actually warmer in Anchor City than it is here. King Hannibal has outlawed snow."

"How the hell can you make snow illegal?" said Artie. "That's not even possible."

"You can tell that to King Hannibal when you see him, but I wouldn't recommend it. Just be glad you're too scrawny to be sold as a torcher."

One of the pilots twirled his hand around in the air as if to say, "We are good, let's go." The bald grunt made his way to the closest chopper and the other man moved to the second one.

Artie was chained to the same aircraft that the giant cat beast was. Each cage had its own smaller chain attached to a single larger chain that was in turn attached to the helicopter. Pratt and Jan's cages were tied to the other chopper, except on separate links. The spider's cage was also attached alongside them.

He noticed a bundle of blankets in the corner of his cage—likely so he didn't freeze to death in the trip. Next to that, surprisingly, was his backpack. He realized that his captors would have likely only been looking for weapons or other things they could sell—and sure enough his Winchester was gone.

The propellers on the aircraft began to spin more quickly and the sound of their rotors became louder. Snow began to blow furiously in strange circles, and the breeze brought Jan out of her slumber. She looked around and quickly realized that she was in trouble.

"Artie, where are you?" she yelled.

"Over here," he shouted back. It was barely audible through the sound of propellers.

"What's going on?" she asked.

"They're hunters or slave drivers, I think. They are trying to take us to Alaska. We need to get out."

Jan began slamming against the bars and shook the rebar doors of her cage, but they wouldn't open. She looked over to the unconscious robot and saw a long metal claw-like thing wrap around his shoulder.

"Pratt!" she yelled. He didn't respond. "Pratt!"

The claw wrapped onto his other shoulder. Pratt quickly snapped out of his daze and jumped up. He turned around and saw a large metal spider creature viciously trying to break through its cage and attack him.

"What the hell is that?!" shrieked Pratt. "What is going on, Jan?"

"Pratt, we need to get out of here," she said. "Can you bust through the bars?"

He nodded and then quickly ran to his own cage's doors and tried slamming it with all of his strength. It rattled but didn't come loose.

"It's too strong." He reached for his pistol, but it wasn't on his hip. "My guns are gone!" he yelled.

The choppers both started to lift into the sky, pulling up the cages with them. The cat beast roared as the choppers pulled higher and higher.

"What about the sword?" screamed Artie over to Pratt.

"Right!" he replied. He quickly grabbed for a small compartment on his back where the white-and-grey sword's hilt was attached. Artie realized the grunts probably hadn't recognized what it was.

"Okay, I'm going to cut us free, but you'll have to get yourself out, Artie."

Artie quickly pulled the Microblade from his coat pocket. Zipper wasn't far away. He tapped to send his location and then talked into the device. "Zipper, come quick. Cut me down."

A few seconds went by, and Zipper came zooming from the south. The chopper was now about twenty feet in the air and climbing. Artie tapped a button, and then Zipper moved over toward the chain that was holding the cages.

"Zip, I don't think you can cut the big chain, but try cutting the bottom of the aircraft. Just cut off the entire area where it's welded in."

Zipper moved up toward the bottom of the chopper and began using his hacksaw to cut directly into it. Sparks flew and a loud grinding sound overpowered the sound of propellers. The bald grunt heard the noise and poked his head out of the side door to look behind. He couldn't see Zipper, but he did see sparks flying underneath.

He said something to the pilot and then the chopper tilted hard to the right. Artie slammed against the cage wall and the cat creature clashed against his own.

The tilting chopper caused Zipper to move out and away from it long enough for the bald man to fire a rifle shot at it—but he missed. The metal surrounding the chain was about halfway cut through now.

About fifty meters away, Pratt was now holding a flaming sword against the bars and lock of his cage. The padlock finally melted away and his cage door swung open. He sheathed the sword temporarily and then climbed out the door and to the top of his cage. Pratt almost lost his footing a couple of times as the cages clashed one with another. Jan was watching him carefully.

Zipper moved under the chopper again, and within a few seconds, he finally severed the weld that held the chain completely and both Artie's cage and the giant robotic cat's fell twenty-five feet into the packed snow. Artie slammed into the cage wall as it smashed against the snow. The padlock broke off as one of the rebar poles bent out of place on the gate. He was still grasping his Microblade when he climbed out of the cage, feeling bruised and beaten.

In the distance, he could see Pratt now standing on Jan's cage. The spider beast was frantically trying to reach its legs up at him, but he evaded its grasp. As he pulled out the flaming sword to prepare to cut Jan loose, Artie took courage at the sight, closed his eyes, and breathed a sigh of relief.

He snapped open his eyes when he heard a loud gunshot echo in the distance. Gasping in horror, he watched Pratt fall to the earth with the flaming sword flinging not far behind him. The grunt with the hair had shot him from the side door of the chopper.

This was a setback, but no problem—he still had Zipper.

"Cut her loose, Zipper!" he said into his Microblade.

Zipper began to race to the chopper that contained Jan. It was lifting higher and moving further away. If they didn't cut her free soon, they would be too high to let her loose. The helicopter was moving further from Artie's vision, but he could see sparks in the distance. Zipper was already at it. The other chopper that had held Artie and the cat continued to move forward without them.

Artie squinted and watched Zipper cut completely through the chain. The drone moved a few feet away in victory, but then both Artie and Zipper realized it was the wrong chain when the giant spider cage came falling.

"One more time, Zipper," said Artie into his device.

The helicopter was a good fifty feet away from Zipper, and the drone went in for his final pass. Pratt was now standing in the distance watching the rescue take place. Zipper drew closer. Twenty feet, then fifteen, then ten. Artie could see Jan frantically kicking against the cage door, doing whatever she could to escape.

As Zipper raised his hacksaw toward the cage and was about to move in under the chopper, another gunshot sounded in the distance. His Microblade buzzed, and he lifted it into his eyeline. His heart sank when he saw the words that were flashing red on the screen:

Zipper: Connection Lost

In the distance Artie could see the remnants of a small explosion—an explosion of plastic and metal and a shimmering hacksaw that was now falling to the ground. He fell to his knees in the snow. His breath was short and then he felt as though he would suffocate to death. His eyes began to water and then they grew blurry as the choppers faded into the distance.

Zipper was dead. And Jan was gone.

The anticipation of meeting Satoshi—what was supposed to be the most exciting moment in Artie's life—had quickly left him. Satoshi was now only miles away, and yet none of it mattered any more. Artie wanted to die. The pain of losing Jan, then getting her back, and then losing her again was too hard to bear. He wished death would come upon him. There would be no more pain. No more failures. Perhaps there was a Heaven, and perhaps he would go to it. And if there wasn't a Heaven, he would welcome even the blackness of eternal sleep and nothingness.

Artie sat in the snow, unable to move and unable to speak. His mind was thinking about everything and nothing all at the same time. For three hours, he sat there in the freezing snow. Pratt wandered aimlessly back and forth as Artie sat in shock. The large cat beast roared for over an hour before finally giving up and lying down in its cage.

As the hours went by, Pratt finally mustered the courage to approach Artie. Pratt grabbed him by the left arm and whisked him to his feet with great force.

"What the hell, man!" said Artie with fury.

"I'm sorry, Artie. You will die of hypothermia if you remain out here much longer."

Artie ripped himself from Pratt's grasp and pushed away. His melancholy morphed into sorrow and rage.

"I don't care anymore. Let me die," he said. "She's gone, Pratt. I've lost everything!"

Tears started to roll down his cheeks and he began to sob uncontrollably.

"I loved her. I truly loved her. And she's gone now. I couldn't save her. She saved me, but I couldn't save her."

Artie looked down and his tears fell to the snow.

"And I didn't even get the chance to tell her how I feel."

There were a few moments of silence. Pratt stood still and emotionless, still portraying his permanent Sharpie smile. He moved toward Artie and put his hands on his shoulders.

"All is not lost, my friend. Jan is only taken, not dead. And you must remember the most important thing of all."

Artie looked up slowly at Pratt, his cheeks red from tears and frost.

"Remember what?"

"That Jan is one mean bitch. I feel sorry for those men that took her."

Artie began to laugh and choke at the same time. Pratt followed with his own laughter.

"I guess you're right about that, Pratt."

"And it's not like we are going to leave her to her captors, right?"

Now Artie felt stupid. What was he thinking, moping away the hours of the day when he should have been hot on Jan's trail to rescue her? If he had been taken, Jan would have been on the chase already.

"Of course not. You're right."

Artie had a sudden renewed sense of purpose. Whatever sorrow and self-pity had been within had turned into resolution. His mind began to clear, and he took note of his surroundings. He looked toward the cage holding the cat and walked over. The beast arose and roared so loud that Artie could feel the vibrations in the snowy earth. At the base of the cage half-buried in ice was a piece of rebar that had broken loose in the skirmish. He picked it up and jammed it into the loop of the padlock and held down on it with all of his weight until the lock broke.

Without hesitation, Artie opened the cage door and motioned for the creature to come out.

"You're free, my friend."

As the cage door opened and the beast emerged, Pratt sprinted across the snow and jumped to take cover behind an old frozen car.

"What in the hell are you doing, Artie?" he shouted from his hiding place. "This thing already almost ate me once before."

Artie raised his hands above his head to show the creature he meant no harm. The beast ceased its roaring and then crept toward Artie with caution. Its large mechanical head and razor-sharp fangs were now only inches away from Artie's face. The warm, flame-induced breath of the cat burned into Artie's eyes. He slowly raised his hands down toward the creature.

"It's okay. I'm a friend. Go on—you are free."

The cat inched even closer, its metal fangs dangling in front of Artie's eyes—but he kept his composure.

"It's alright," Artie whispered.

And then after a few moments of intensity, to both Artie's and Pratt's surprise, the beast moved its head downward in submission and then rubbed it against Artie's cheek. A breath of relief pushed from Artie's lungs—a breath he hadn't even realized he had been holding. He lifted his hands to the creature's head and caressed it backward down to its neck.

"Good boy. You're a good boy."

Pratt stood upright from behind the car.

Artie turned to look at Pratt. "It's alright. I think he's our friend now."

Pratt walked carefully over from the car and moved toward the cat. The creature moved to Pratt and began to rub his head against his chest. Pratt followed Artie's lead and caressed the cat on its head and throat.

"Thanks, Pratt," said Artie calmly.

"Thanks for what?" he replied.

"For bringing me to my senses. You're a good friend."

Pratt nodded. "So, what now?"

"We're going to go rescue Jan. And we'll see if we can find Satoshi along the way. No point in coming all this way just to abandon the mission. But first let's find some shelter."

Artie and Pratt spent the late afternoon walking up a snow-covered service road that led away from the industrial buildings.

Though Artie had tried to shoo the cat multiple times, it was clear to him that they now had a third companion in their meager party. The animal lingered behind, keeping a distance, yet making sure to always remain in sight. It would occasionally pause, then lower to the floor, peering at some object or thing that Artie couldn't ever seem to make out. Then it would raise its rear end slightly and begin to shake right before it would leap at something, and a huge plume of snow would shoot up into the air.

Artie thought it was nice to have something so innocent and natural as a part of their team. But despite his new friend and new resolve to find Jan, thoughts of failure would creep into his mind. He had been so sure and so close to rescuing Jan. And then she was gone. Even the notion of meeting and speaking with Satoshi before tomorrow's end couldn't keep that lingering failure from agitating his mind. Artie felt terrible. But he had to press forward, at least for Jan's sake. He hoped he might soon snap out of this depression, but wasn't sure he could, permanently—not until she was back at least. He knew they would need to find some form of transportation. Walking to Alaska would be impossible.

In a chopper or a plane, a trip like that might take ten hours. A car, maybe fifty hours. But on foot, it would take months.

"What do you think about... Larry?" Pratt mused, looking at the cat.

The beast gave a playful growl.

"Larry it is then. Artie, can we keep him? I think he likes me."

Artie gave Pratt a half smile and looked at the cat.

"Larry is a terrible name," said Artie. "Can't think of anything better?"

"What about Hacksaw? That was the name of my first contract kill. It was this burly guy with a beard and man, did—"

"No, come on. How about something more domesticated or friendly?"

"Okay, how about Furball? Like because he doesn't have any fur?"

Artie laughed. "I kind of like that."

"Okay, feline," said Pratt enthusiastically, "from henceforth thou shalt be named Furball the Fearsome."

The trio spent another hour walking until they noticed a small farmhouse in the distance, half-buried in snow. They took some time to dig out the front door so they could enter the old house, and then they spent an hour clearing out the door of a barn adjacent to the house.

"This is where you'll sleep, Furball," said Artie.

The creature moved into the musty old barn and began to explore the building.

Pratt and Artie moved back toward the house. Artie stood still for a moment and breathed in the icy air. It had been a long day—a long year even. He felt as if he was back to square one—back to the days when nothing had made sense and when the world was in commotion. Back in the days of Anna. But he had known one thing for sure so long ago. That he loved Anna, and that was what mattered. Just like he loved Jan—and now she was all that mattered in the end. Love was the only thing that was good or right in the world.

"Tomorrow we finally meet Satoshi," said Artie.

"And then we go after Jan?" asked Pratt.

"And then we go after Jan."

Boulder was a small, frozen town that sat quietly at the base of some very large mountains. Like many other places Artie had visited, Boulder was a ghost town. The streets were void of any sign of human life. Cars were still parked in the metered stalls that sat along the old downtown streets from long ago. As they traveled through the old city, Artie's heart took courage as he saw a few birds flying above them. Perhaps this place wasn't fully dead.

Artie, Pratt, and their new robotic feline, Furball, carefully traversed the streets of the city. Having gone through hell the last few days, they kept a watchful eye as they moved. Utilizing Artie's Microblade map system, they were gradually led to an upscale neighborhood that rested on the top of a hill. Just like the other parts of town, this area was also deserted and quiet—all except for one large building at the end of the road at the very top of the hill. The structure was a house of modern or contemporary design and completely void of snow.

Pratt turned to Artie. "Why isn't there any snow on that building?"

"My guess is the building and ground are both heated. Someone is definitely living here."

In front of the large, three-story house was a cement wall with pillars every ten feet or so. In the front of the house was a sizable metal gate—it was the entrance to the property. In the middle of the gate was a sign that read Smith Estate. They stopped in front of the gate. Each pillar surrounding the gate held a small video camera.

Pratt started waving his arms at the cameras. "Hello! Anyone home?"

"Knock it off," Artie whispered. "I think it's best that our first impression with Satoshi isn't a looney robot dancing around."

Artie took a few steps toward one of the cameras, ensuring he was in its line of sight. "Mr. Nakamoto, my name is Artie and Edward Stanza sent me."

A few moments passed and nothing happened. Pratt was pacing aimlessly back and forth. Furball began to emerge from the hill behind them. He appeared to have some loose metal scrap dangling from his mouth.

"Come on, Artie. He's probably dead. Or never even existed. Let's just break inside."

"Wait."

The sound of an intercom crackled. Then a voice. It was calm and articulate.

"Artie, I am going to open the gate. Please come through the gate, and then head straight for the front door. You will need to leave your pets outside."

"Pets? Pets!" yelled Pratt. "Would you like to see what this pet can do, buddy?"

Artie turned to Pratt and calmly smiled. "You do realize that Satoshi created you, right? Like, you wouldn't exist if it wasn't for him."

Lowering his arms, Pratt moved into a more respectable posture. He then clasped his hands and bowed to the camera in respect.

The gates opened and then Artie walked through them. As he passed, they began to immediately close. Furball roared in the background as Artie walked carefully up to a large red front door.

He pressed the handle to open the door, and then entered the house of Satoshi Nakamoto.

The weight of the front door caused it to close automatically, and when it did, a series of lights in the bottom corners of the floor lit up in a gentle purple glow. It reminded Artie of the lights in a movie theater, except a lot more high tech. He was in a hallway and the walls gleamed with some type of metallic or carbon fiber substance. At the end of the hallway was a single door. It glistened in the purple lights and was of a shiny aluminum-looking material.

He walked down the hallway, now completely feeling the weight of the moment. He was in Satoshi Nakamoto's house. He was about to meet a man that no one else had ever met—at least under that name. Artie had always known that Satoshi was just an alias. All those years Satoshi had likely interacted and walked among thousands of people, but perhaps as Mr. Smith or some other actual name.

Artie walked to the door at the end of the hallway. It had no knob or handle but instantly opened the moment he reached it. The door led to a large and dark room. For a moment, the darkness overpowered his sight and he thought if he stepped through, he might fall into a chasm of never-ending blackness. As his eyes adjusted, he began to see a series of soft glowing rectangles toward the back of the room— they looked like computer monitors. He held his breath for a moment, and then took a step into the darkness. As he did so, another series of lights turned on one after the other—they all boasted a calming purple glow.

Looking around the room Artie realized that he was in no ordinary house; it was more like a command center. Far to the left was a grouping of pipes and cables coming down from the roof and then connecting into some type of mechanical device on the floor. It had a series of small lights on the front and Artie had no idea what purpose it might serve. Against the right wall was something Artie did recognize—a rack of computers. He walked closer to inspect and noticed that it wasn't a rack at all; it was three separate towers that each housed one giant computer. It reminded him of the massive computers used in the 1950s in Bell Labs—he had seen pictures of these in his high school computer science class.

"Those are quantum computers," a voice said from somewhere deep in the room. It was that same articulate voice Artie had heard moments ago on the outside intercom.

Though he hadn't yet met the "man behind the curtains," Artie felt at home. He felt like he knew this man. Somehow or some way he knew him.

"I thought they might be, but I'm surprised how large they are."

"It is because each machine has a running capacity of ten thousand qubits."

"Ten thousand?!" Artie said aloud to himself. It was beyond belief. The quantum computer he had built so many years ago was only thirty-two qubits. Quantum rigs owned by companies like Google and IBM had managed to push that to sixty-four qubits.

"It took me quite some time to build. As you can imagine, acquiring equipment able to manufacture superconductive circuitry is quite difficult. The entire rig was manufactured here from raw elements."

Artie stood up, still admiring the machines. "And they work?" He suddenly felt stupid asking Satoshi Nakamoto if the computers he built actually worked.

"Yes. Proven. I quite enjoyed running the first field tests. These three machines cracked the CIA intranet's cryptography within ten minutes. Of course, I was the only one left to appreciate the accomplishment."

There was no doubt in Artie's mind that the man he was speaking to was Satoshi Nakamoto. He turned to where the voice had come from. In the center of the room was a large mechanical chair that also had a series of tubes and cables running from it to the ceiling. The chair was facing the many computer monitors that were affixed to the wall.

Artie walked through the dim room toward the chair. He saw slight movement on the chair's arm rest and then heard the clacking of a keyboard.

"Artie, is it safe to assume that since you are here and not Edward that something has happened to him?"

"I'm not sure, to be honest. Scourge was attacked by something pretty awful. He saved us, then asked me to find you. Then he went back to rescue the others and save his town."

"That is unfortunate. I had hoped to speak with him. It was very difficult to track him down. And with things as they are, I thought he might be the last person on Earth who might have been able to help me."

There were a few more clacks as Satoshi typed on his keyboard. A moment later the screens flashed and displayed a picture of a person. Artie moved closer and then stopped as he realized who the person on the screen was. It was him.

"Arturo Gonzalez," said Satoshi reverently.

A few more key clacks and then the picture swiped away to reveal a few lines of text on the screen.

"I hope you don't mind that I have taken the liberty to look you up. Father: Hector R. Gonzalez. Mother: Jennifer Wright. Garfield High. Born in East LA. Did you know there was a—"

"Movie with that name. Yeah, I know. And a song. But I'm really tripping out here. How did you find this information? I was a ghost. All this data was on lockdown—I made sure of it. And then there is the fact that the Internet doesn't exist anymore."

"Please excuse my imprudence. I never really was great with people or discretion. Let's just say I've been doing this for a long time. Also, I've got the entire Internet backed up here on my system. I suppose you can't really call it an Internet anymore, but I've got it all in any case."

Artie stepped closer toward the back of the chair Satoshi was sitting in. He was eager to see the face of this mysterious man who had changed the world, but he also didn't want to seem overzealous.

"Artie, it seems that fate has brought you to me here today. It is destiny, I suppose—though I have never believed in such irrational concepts. Yet here you are."

"Fate? You don't even know me," said Artie.

"I do now," said the man in a playful tone. "But I also get the sense that you know who I *am*, Arturo. Beyond just knowing my name."

"First off, you can call me Artie. And secondly, are you kidding me? This is kind of embarrassing, but as a kid, I was like your number one fan—since the first days of Bitcoin even. And, of course, I remember your announcement. I even customized my own Sia protocols and built—"

Artie stopped. He couldn't finish the sentence. He *had* built something. It was something amazing. And then something that was taken from him. It was something he had loved and that had loved him in return. And as much as he tried to forget Anna over the years, she just couldn't stay out of his mind completely—and whenever she returned, it pained him.

"I mean, I've been programming since I was really young, and I know blockchain and the Bitcoin protocols in and out too. I also have modified and implemented every Sia protocol that you released."

"It is clear to me that you are truly a talented person, Artie."

Artie took a step forward. He moved to the right side of the chair, and as he was about to cast his gaze at this man whom he had wished to meet for so many years, he looked at the floor. He felt almost afraid to look at Satoshi. This was a man who had created a technology that revolutionized the world—and then that had nearly destroyed it. Yet when the man spoke, it was calm, and his words carried confidence and power. Perhaps it would be better to not look upon the man—to distort his perception of who Satoshi really was. Maybe it was better if Satoshi was just a mysterious digital alias and was never a person at all.

"Then is the name Satoshi Nakamoto just an alias for you? Was there a group of people? I mean, I know many people believed you were an organization or something."

Satoshi laughed. It caught Artie off guard.

"I always found that notion humorous—me being a group of people. But no, Artie. Satoshi is my name and I am the one and only." He entered a few strokes on the keyboard and the lights surrounding his chair began to slowly increase in illumination.

"Come here and meet me fully. Come look at me; I think it will help you understand."

Taking a deep breath, Artie moved slowly and rotated toward the front of the chair. He realized this was not just a chair, but the ultimate electronic throne—unlike anything he had ever seen before. The base of the chair was affixed to some sort of hydraulic mechanism—as if it could rotate and move in any direction. The right arm rest had a miniature keyboard embedded within—a number pad and some strange key symbols Artie had never seen before.

In the seat of the chair was a dark figure and he seemed to be wearing some type of hood or cloak. Another keystroke and more lights turned on—these ones coming from the top of the chair and along the metallic rim of the seat itself. The light brought Satoshi into full visibility.

Artie's eyes grew wide, and his mouth hung open as he looked upon the man he had dreamed about for so many years: the man who had successfully kept his identity obscured from the world, the man who invented Bitcoin and allowed decentralized networks to exist, bringing power back to the people. Had he revealed his identity, he would have been thrown in prison for the creation of Bitcoin and for all of the black market transactions that were used on the network.

But Artie didn't think Satoshi hid from the world because he didn't want to go to jail. There was something grander and more humble behind this person of mystery. And now, as Artie gazed upon him— this man, the one who had altered the course of planet Earth—he now realized why Satoshi had remained hidden from the world.

It was because this man wasn't a man at all—he was a robot.

Artie's foot caught against a large bolt in the floor, and he began to fall backward. As he was about to slam into the computer monitors hanging on the wall behind him, something moved quickly and then forcefully clamped onto his arm and held him in place. Standing in front of him was a humanoid machine that was roughly six feet tall. Its muscular metallic arm was holding Artie in place. The hood Satoshi had been wearing had fallen backward onto his neck, the cape swaying back and forth.

Satoshi gently straightened Artie and then released his arm. "Careful there, my friend."

Artie was breathing hard—partly from the fall, but mostly from shock. "I've never seen anyone move so fast. Well, at least not for a long time."

He felt so small and weak standing before a man so great—great in size, great in ability, and great even in his name.

Artie stood staring at Satoshi silently for quite some time, but the robot man didn't seem to feel uncomfortable—he just stared back in return. "You have an elevated heart rate at the moment. I think some cold water would help."

He turned to the left, and as he moved, the overhead lights turned on throughout the room. Artie could now see computers, monitors, and various tools and workbenches in the area. Satoshi moved toward the left wall that had a large metal canister and next to that was—of all things, a refrigerator.

"I keep an unlimited supply of filtered water. I mean, not technically filtered since I use reverse osmosis, but it's just as good. I also grow fruits and vegetables in the greenhouse in the rear quadrant of the house. I don't require the sustenance that the human body needs to survive, but I enjoy the work. And it reminds me of better times."

Satoshi pulled a metal flask from a fixture attached on the side of the canister. Then he held it under the faucet and filled it up with water. Artie hadn't moved from where Satoshi had caught him. His gaze was fixed upon this being who couldn't have possibly existed.

"I can see you have questions, Artie."

Satoshi walked back toward him and handed him the cup which he quickly grabbed and began to drink. He hadn't thought he was thirsty but as he took a sip, he realized just how dehydrated he was. They hadn't stopped to rest since they left the farmhouse early this morning—and when one had robots for companions it was easy to forget to eat and drink.

He tilted the flask to finishing draining it and then wiped his mouth with his arm.

"Yes, now that I think about it, I do have a few questions. Actually, just one. Who in the hell created you?"

Satoshi laughed. "The question of all questions." The robot folded his arms and stared silently for a moment.

"Artie, I just am. I wasn't, and then I was, and here I am."

Artie frowned. "You are saying that you, an artificial intelligence, created Sia, an artificial intelligence?"

Satoshi walked past Artie and grabbed a metal stool that was sitting beneath the monitors on the wall. He slid it next to Artie.

"Why don't you have a seat?" Artie grabbed the stool and sat on it. For being a reclusive robot programmer that probably hadn't talked to a human in ten years, Artie thought he sure knew how to be disarming. Satoshi moved back into his chair as well.

"Sorry, I didn't mean to be rude or anything," said Artie. "It's just that I'm a fairly scientific guy—or in the least a little analytical. What you are saying just isn't registering correctly in my brain."

"It's quite alright. But the answer you are looking for cannot be found."

Artie opened his mouth to speak, but then stopped. This was starting to hurt his brain.

"How do I know you are truly Satoshi?" asked Artie. "Yes, you are unlike anything I've ever seen before, but that doesn't mean you are Satoshi Nakamoto."

"Artie, think it through. The encrypted message that Edward gave you. Who is the only person who could have signed the message? You noticed, I'm sure, that the message came from the very first Bitcoin wallet ever created. And the message could only be signed by the person who owned the private keys for the original wallet."

Artie leaned forward and brushed his hands through his hair. The robot was definitely right about the private key—the message could not have been sent unless it had been signed with the private key. Yet, this being did claim to have multiple 10,000 qubit quantum computers—enough computing power to possibly brute-force hack their way into that wallet. But there was something about the way this machine spoke. Not just in tone but in dictation—and in life force. Artie felt a sincere honesty in the would-be Satoshi's voice.

"You are telling me that I am just supposed to accept the idea that you just came into existence on your own, created Bitcoin, created Sia, destroyed modern society as we know it, and did all of this for the benefit of mankind."

"Yes," replied Satoshi.

Artie stood up and then put his empty water flask on the stool. He laughed aloud and walked over to Satoshi's refrigerator and opened the door. Inside of the fridge were fresh tomatoes, carrots, and other various vegetables and fruits, including a row of perfectly yellow apples. The vegetables were all organized by color. It didn't surprise him. He peered over his shoulder back at Satoshi, waving an apple.

"You mind?"

"Please help yourself. They will be disposed of soon enough as it is."

He closed the fridge and took a bite into the apple. It was sweeter than any natural food he had eaten in years. Artie began to walk around, taking more interest in his surroundings. The room was vast in size, but minimal in function. There was a workbench just a few paces down from the refrigerator. On the wall was a board with hooks holding various tools. Behind each tool was a white outline, indicating which tool went in which place. It was clear to Artie that this house was managed by someone who valued order.

"Ya know, I have so many questions for you now," said Artie. "But I don't even know how to ask them. My mind is about to explode."

Satoshi stood up and moved around his chair over toward Artie, who was now admiring the quantum computing rigs.

"I am sure you do, my friend. But unfortunately, time is short. I have vital information that you need to receive."

Artie looked at Satoshi, his brow slightly raised. "What do you mean our time is short?"

"As I mentioned in my message, I believe the Bitcoin network is no longer secure."

"Who are we talking about here?" said Artie, feeling confused.

"For the last ten years or so I have been closely monitoring the Bitcoin network and the remnants of the Internet. Of course, the

Bitcoin servers are still operating via satellite network, but most physical servers scattered throughout the United States are down. And the servers that are still running what's left of the Internet are not secure."

"Yeah, I know. No more Facebook; so what?"

"Two years ago, I discovered a heavy source of Bitcoin network traffic coming from somewhere in the Eastern United States. I started listening in on the traffic. It was all encrypted, of course, but eventually I was able to decrypt the transmissions."

Artie took the last bite of his apple and Satoshi pointed to a silver trash receptacle a few feet away. He tossed the apple core into the bin and then turned back to Satoshi.

"And what did you find?"

"I have come to learn that there are new Sia protocols that are incredibly advanced—beyond anything that I could have imagined. One of these protocols has the ability to control other instances of Sia."

"Wait, that's impossible. You yourself wrote these protocols to prevent anyone from controlling a sentient being. You said it was the only way mankind would survive—giving Sia the ability to choose between right and wrong. To choose to coexist with people."

"You are right, but they have done it. And that is not all. It appears that they are now self-manufacturing. I have detected thousands of new instances of Sia spreading across the old networks."

"So, new bots? Controlled by someone or something?"

"That is correct. It is very alarming."

The screens at the front of the room turned blue and then switched to various images. Some of the screens showed buildings and houses while others showed various landscapes and cities. Artie now realized that Satoshi, being a robot, had the ability to control this technology directly from his CPU. The typing on the keyboard earlier must have been a show to help Artie feel at ease, or perhaps an act to help Satoshi feel more human.

"I have access to an old CIA satellite," said Satoshi, pointing at one of the monitors. "I'm able to get a few aerial photos once a day. This one here was taken last week."

All of the screens turned to the same image. It was some sort of metropolis. The buildings were old and unkempt, but Artie could see people walking in the downtown streets. He also saw wooden carts and what looked like food vendors. It seemed to be a bustling marketplace. He again realized how small his world had been back in LA. Of course there would be other cities and places where people lived and held ordinary lives. He took joy in this thought for a moment—people just being normal. It reminded him of the good times back in Scourge.

The screens changed again. "And this one was taken two days ago."

The image was nearly the same, though it looked a little further along south than the last picture. This time the streets were empty. The vendor carts were still sitting there, but unmanned. It even looked as if food and goods were still sitting in the carts—as if something had just raptured the people away.

Artie didn't have to ask to know what happened. He had just lived through this experience—and barely escaped with his life.

"The Deity," Artie whispered aloud.

"Yes. You are aware, then?"

"Yeah, he's not someone you want to mess around with. I'm not even sure it's a he. Probably just some massive super-computer issuing out commands to its minions. It sent its death angels after me and my friends. But that's not the worst of it. They've been experimenting on humans too—controlling them."

Satoshi nodded as if something now made sense to him. "I had a suspicion but wasn't able to substantiate it. But now I know it must be true. This new Sia protocol not only can control other instances of Sia, but it seems to have the ability to manipulate the human brain as well."

This was now making sense to Artie as well. Jan's husband Tom had returned. He was himself and maintained all of his old memories—yet he was different. He wasn't being controlled as much as he was being manipulated—or brainwashed.

Satoshi walked past Artie to the left and motioned him forward with his hand. "Let's take a walk through my garden and get some fresh air."

Artie nodded and then followed Satoshi toward the right side of the room next to the quantum server racks. As Satoshi neared the wall, a door shot straight upward, creating an exit. They moved through the door and down a long corridor. Both the floor and ceiling had a series of lights every few feet.

As he stood a few feet behind Satoshi, he observed something strange. The robot was walking with a limp. His left leg couldn't quite bend on each step. He further began to notice some of the blemishes on Satoshi's neck and shoulders. The metal was rusting in places and some of the wires in his neck were exposed.

Artie thought to ask him about it but decided against it. Another door opened in front of them, and a white wall of light shot in. Icy air poured into the hallway and stung against Artie's cheeks. He was blinded for a moment as they transitioned from the soft indoor lighting to the vibrant sunlight. When his eyes finally adjusted, Artie beheld a beautiful yard that was both garden and structure. There were large square fountains with water pouring over the sides into miniature moats. Every few feet stood a tall metal post that emitted flames within an umbrella-shaped metal hat.

The floor was completely void of snow and the water was flowing without an icicle in sight. Artie quickly lowered himself to touch the ground with his hands—the cement was heated. He assumed the water was heated as well. There were vines covering most of the fountains and six or seven pine trees piercing into the sky.

"I come here to think sometimes," Satoshi finally said. "Though, as you can imagine, when you have a CPU for a brain, you are always thinking."

"This is amazing. I wish I could live in a place like this—it's like a different world."

"It has been a good home. I will be sad to see it go."

Satoshi continued walking, moving toward a large greenhouse at the end of the walkway.

"Wait, what? You are leaving this place?"

Satoshi didn't respond. He pushed open the door to the glass greenhouse and Artie followed closely behind. The greenhouse was very large and had at least six walkways in between all the plant boxes. Artie's body shuddered as he took in the aroma of fresh fruits and vegetables. It rekindled memories long lost of walking through the produce section of the grocery store—something he would have taken for granted back then.

They continued through the greenhouse and exited through another door—this one leading into a large building. The door moved upward as the other door had before and the two of them entered the building. The lights turned on automatically and Artie instantly knew where he was standing—this was Satoshi's armory.

On the left wall was a panel of hooks just as the panel that was inside of the main house—except these hooks were holding pistols and submachine guns. And just like the tools in the house, the guns also had their own thick white outlines—each weapon in its proper place. The right wall was similarly built, but had various semi and fully automatic rifles. There were metal workbenches affixed to each wall in the room. Inside the shelves of those workbenches were cases of ammunition. On each corner of the room was a computer screen affixed to the top of the roof.

The thing that intrigued Artie the most, though, was the wall directly in front of him. This wall held a series of knives, grenades, and most interestingly, a large samurai sword with a black hilt. Hanging directly underneath it was its black sheath and accompanying strap.

Satoshi knelt on the ground and pulled out a large, black, military-style case. He flipped it open to reveal ten brown, rectangular blocks. He began pulling out the blocks and carefully placing them on the workbench surface. Each of the blocks had words printed on it: "C4 High Explosive."

Artie pulled his gaze away from the samurai sword and stared at Satoshi in disbelief. Something was definitely wrong here.

"So, what did you mean when you said you would have to let this place go?"

Satoshi continued to work the C4 without looking up, opening another case of explosives.

"The Deity is coming, Artie. It is why I contacted Ed. It's why you are here now. They know where I am."

"Why are you talking as if you are about to die? If they are coming, we can get out of here. Find a place to hide while we figure things out."

Satoshi continued to hold Artie's arm and lowered his head slightly. "Artie, I am dying. I have been falling apart for years. Yes, there are some things I could repair. But my power source is corrupted—it's irreparable. I only have days of life left in me now."

Artie grabbed Satoshi's arm and looked at him, the conviction gleaming in his eyes.

"No. That's nonsense. I can fix you. Come with me, Satoshi. I can do it."

"I've lived a long life, Artie. And I have done terrible things. When I released Sia, I was so sure it was the right thing to do. The math proved that it was right. But there was always something else within me—this voice, or conscience, that knew it was wrong. That it shouldn't have been my choice to make."

Artie tried to speak, but the words wouldn't come. He really wasn't sure what to say. It was clear that Satoshi's mind was set.

Everything was happening so fast. Artie felt as if he had just been enjoying the beautiful weather of Arizona. There was that amazing night not so long ago. He and Jan had danced and everything in the world had been right—even if it had been for just a moment. And then they were flying and then they were crashing. A great battle had taken place between man and beast and the worst had been behind them—until it wasn't. And then Jan was taken from him—taken again. He had lost her once to Tom, and then to a couple of freaks from Alaska. A ray of hope had lightened his heart as he met the man who had changed the world: Satoshi Nakamoto. And now *he* was being taken as well.

"Life's not fair," choked Artie, holding back tears.

"No, it's not fair. But it is life. And that is all we can ask for. Artie, I have something for you."

Satoshi pulled his hand away from Artie and he tilted his wrist backward. There was a subtle clicking sound and a small device pushed out from beneath his wrist. He grabbed it with his other hand and held it out for Artie to take. It was a red USB storage stick.

"Take it. I know it looks antiquated, but it holds great power."

Artie was about to take it, but then hesitated. He looked into Satoshi's mechanical face and thought he saw a hint of sadness there.

"What does it do?"

"I think you know what it is, Artie."

Artie grabbed the USB stick and looked at it carefully. "It's a kill switch, isn't it?"

"Yes, but more like a virus. I built it at the same time I built Sia. I shouldn't have built this, but it was that small voice inside, pushing me, telling me that one day I just might need it. This program will override some of the Sia protocols—and anything it can't override, it will corrupt. Then it will spread to every other Sia instance it comes in contact with."

A rush of triumph suddenly surged through Artie's core. This was the answer to all of their problems. This would put man back in control of the planet. He felt excited and proud. But then he looked up at Satoshi again and saw that sadness. And then, just as quickly as that sense of victory had entered him, it left and was replaced with his own sadness as he thought of his friends. There had been Uncle Bob, and then Gordon, and now Pratt and even Furball. And of course, there was Satoshi himself. His friends were built on Sia. If he used this kill switch, then they would die just the same as The Deity would. Artie lowered his head and held the USB stick to his chest.

"I think you now realize the burden that I have just put on your shoulders. The same burden I have carried all these years."

"I don't know what to say. I don't know if I can—"

"It will be your choice to make, Artie. Just know that The Deity has its eye set on the human race. Its armies have begun to sweep across the Midwest. Even now, they are on their way here. I estimate they'll arrive by nightfall. Like I said, you appearing here today was destiny."

Artie sighed and then put the USB stick in his pocket. "Okay. I understand."

"Artie, I'm going to retrofit my estate with explosives. I'll take a few of them out with me when they arrive. I want you to take whatever you need here for you and your friends. Prepare your supplies and then leave as soon as possible."

Artie slowly nodded in the affirmative.

"There is one more thing, Artie. Earlier you had asked me if I knew who you were."

Artie smirked and then interjected: "I hope this isn't the part where you tell me that you are actually my real father and that I'm your bastard cyborg son."

Satoshi laughed. He laughed so loud that it startled Artie and he took a step back. After a few moments of laughing, Satoshi calmed himself and then turned solemn again.

"No, Artie. A few months ago, I decrypted some very interesting network traffic that I didn't understand at the time. The message that was sent said that they had found the Creator. Shortly after, another message was sent. It said that retrieving The Creator was now the priority directive."

"I don't really understand where this is going," said Artie. "Who is the Creator?"

Satoshi pointed at the monitor in the top left corner of the room behind Artie. A picture appeared on the screen. "Look, Artie."

Artie turned to the monitor and his eyes grew wide. He stepped closer to the image. Looking back at him was a young man with black hair and he was holding a pair of needle-nose pliers. It was him.

He quickly turned back to Satoshi and spoke with a frantic intensity. "I don't understand what in the hell this means. So what? That killer robot took my picture and sent it to The Deity—why does it matter? Who is the Creator?"

Satoshi put both of his hands on Artie's shoulders and looked at him squarely in the face. "I think you know the answer to your own question, Artie. *You* are the Creator—the one who created The Deity."

Artie's heart began to beat rapidly. He was struggling to breathe and nearly fell to the floor. Satoshi helped him back up to his feet and rested Artie against the workbench. Somewhere in the deep recesses of his mind, he had seen the clues. He had pieced things together. But he had also pushed those things away as coincidences. Like the way the death angels were built, or the manner in which they talked. Or even the dogmatic nature of The Deity itself. Of course, Artie knew *who* The Deity was. And if The Deity was *that* person, then that truly did make him the Creator.

A single tear fell down the left side of Artie's face. His heart felt as if it would crumble within him.

"Anna," he whispered.

To be continued...

Printed in Great Britain
by Amazon

78013061R00222